What if I Fly?

Jayne Conway

I dedicate this book to
the strongest woman I know.
My mother.

BROKEN WINGS

2001

For once you have tasted flight
You will walk the earth with your eyes turned skywards
For there you have been and there you will long to return.
~Leonardo daVinci

Prologue

"Venti iced coffee!" the tattooed barista with the spiky green hair shouts from behind the counter, seemingly oblivious to the small mob of people surrounding her station. In desperate need of a caffeine fix, Will squeezes through the crowd and gratefully grabs his drink, then searches the room for a free seat.

The patrons are taking advantage of the air conditioned space on this steamy day and he waits patiently for a chair to become available, leaning against the newspaper rack stacked with today's issues of the *Providence Journal, Boston Globe* and *New York Times*.

The shop is much more crowded than it's been over the past couple of months. He's gotten used to having his run of the place since the Brown University students made their exodus in May, but now they've begun streaming back into town from their summer breaks, forcing the locals out into Wayland Square in search of alternative shelter. The mildly hostile, but inevitable takeover has begun, the coffee shop overrun with their laptops and stacks of books.

Whatever happened to studying in a library? he wonders.

He feels old. It seems like a hundred years since he walked in their shoes, though it's only been...what? A decade? So much has changed in ten years. *Or, not enough.* Maybe the only thing that has changed is his perspective. What he wouldn't give to go back to those days, he muses, his eyes glazing over.

Mercifully, Will's reverie is interrupted when an elderly gentlemen slowly vacates one of the leather chairs, his favorite place to read. *Perfect.*

He positions himself for a quick turnover before one of the kids in line beats him to the empty seat, then victorious, he settles in, opens the paper to the sports section, and notes with a smile that the Red Sox are coming out of their annual slump and could be headed to the playoffs.

Will attends games as often as possible, though it's not as easy to get away from the office these days. Growing up, he made the two-hour trek north to Fenway Park regularly with his father, a devout fan who was born and bred in Boston. It's his favorite childhood memory.

Reviewing the stats, he takes another sip of his drink and feels a hand on his shoulder, a gentle squeeze. Startled, he looks up from the newspaper and almost spits out his iced coffee. *Julia?* Coughing, he sits up in his chair, his heart hammering against his ribcage. *Is it really her?*

"Hi," she says, softly.

Will rises and takes both of Julia's hands in his, looks into her warm brown eyes and shakes his head in disbelief. It's been almost six years since he last saw her, and hoped, but never believed he'd see her again. Julia's face breaks into a smile and she squeezes his hands.

"How are you, Will?"

"I can't believe you're here," he whispers. "How long have you been in the States?"

"Almost three months now."

Julia has a table in the corner of the room and they sit across from one another in awkward silence. He doesn't know what to say. *I've missed you every day since I last saw you? I can't forget you no matter how hard I try, and I'm not sure I even want to?*

No, he can't say what he's thinking, so he just stares and resists the urge to reach out and touch her. She's more beautiful now than ever.

"How's your father, Will? The last time we spoke his health was improving."

"He's good, in remission," he says, a tremor in his voice. "You remember that?"

"Of course I do. I remember everything about our time together."

"Yeah. Me too."

He remembers their last two days together more vividly than the past six years. Will turns and stares out the window, watching Andy from the bookstore across the street carrying a pile of paperbacks and depositing them in the free bin. Andy raises his hand in greeting and Will nods absently, garnering a worried glance from his friendly acquaintance.

"Will, are you all right?"

He focuses his gaze down into his drink, and away from her knowing eyes. He's never been able to hide his feelings from Julia and God knows he has no right to complain. He made his bed, now he has to lay in it.

"No one's asked me that in a while," he pauses, running his fingers through his hair. "No, Jules… I'm not. I haven't been for a long time."

This is killing him, sitting beside Julia. He's prayed for this moment for so long, to apologize to her if nothing else, but now he wants to run away. Over time, he's trained himself to not feel much of anything, and being around her is stirring up emotions he thought were dead.

I left her sleeping in that bed, alone. I walked away from her. For what? After what he did, he doesn't deserve her kindness or sympathy.

"Talk to me, Will."

"There's nothing to tell. I knew I wouldn't be happy with her," he pauses, "I just never thought it'd be like this..." his voice trails off and he stares into his drink, swirling the green straw in circles.

"Come with me." Julia rises and holds her hand out to him, "Come on. I'm driving your car."

"Where are we going?"

"Does it matter?" she asks.

Will shakes his head and hands her the keys to his Volvo. His wife hates his old station wagon and makes sure they take her Audi convertible whenever they're together in public. He gave up caring what other people think long ago. Only his parents' opinion matters to him, and even that doesn't carry as much weight as it used to.

Julia drives them five minutes down the road to India Point Park at the mouth of Narragansett Bay. The city began a revitalization program last year and is turning this once crime-ridden area into a park with a playground, boat launch and a community center. Other than a few sun worshippers, they're alone.

There's a light breeze coming off the bay, making the heat bearable, and she leads him to the recently built dock, kicks off her sandals, then lies down, arms folded behind her head.

Will has a sense of déjà vu as he lowers himself down beside her, and turns his face to the sky, taking in deep breaths of salty air mixed with car exhaust from the nearby highway. He finds the whoosh of the passing cars above them and the sound of the water lapping below, oddly soothing. For several minutes they lay together in silence watching the clouds pass by, just as they did years ago.

Julia rests her head on his chest and his arm winds around her, naturally, comfortably. Closing his eyes, he imagines they're in their early twenties again, laying on the dock in their hometown making plans for their future, and for the first time in years he feels at peace.

"You have to look for the joy in life, Will," she says. "Sometimes it's the little things that get me through the day."

Will mentally wraps them in an insular world of his own, trying desperately to ward off the inevitable. He knows their time together will soon come to an end and he'll be alone again. It doesn't matter how many people surround him, without Julia, he's alone.

But not now. Right now, he imagines they've spent the past six years building a life together, not apart. Will breathes her in and tries to memorize how her body feels pressed against his side, his arm holding her close, then realizes there's no need...he never forgot. She's a part of him, she always will be.

Their moment lasts for little over an hour, until Julia's phone beeps, forcing him back to reality. She sits up and flips open the offending device to read a text message. *Who is it? A friend? A lover?* He swallows hard, trying not to think of her with another man. Surely, she has a man in her life.

"I have to get going, Will."

Reluctantly, he pulls her to her feet and tucks a stray curl behind her ear, his fingers lingering against her cheek. *Please, don't leave me...* Julia's eyes connect with his for a long moment, filling him with hope, but she sighs and smiles, slowly shaking her head.

His heart sinks...but he understands. Julia deserves more than he can give her. They walk to his car, and for an instant he considers driving them to the nearest airport, but forces himself to continue along Gano Street and take the turn into the parking lot at the coffee shop.

"No goodbyes," she leans in and kisses his cheek, "I'll see you."

And she's gone.

PART I
TAKE OFF

1992-1994

Chapter One

Julia tears through her closet, heaping unwanted clothes in a pile on the floor beside her, several possible dresses spread out on her bed. What does one wear to a blueblood wedding? A few weeks back Will called her at school and asked her to attend a friend's wedding this weekend. *Skip? Chip?* She can't remember his name.

She's home from New York University for the night, heading back to the city tomorrow afternoon, and Will is due to pick her up at her mother's house in twenty minutes. She was so nervous and excited about seeing him again, she didn't give a thought to her wardrobe for this blessed event, until about an hour ago.

Little black dress. Can't go wrong with a little black dress, right? She rifles through the few remaining items in her closet. No! Her little black dresses are back in New York. She closes her eyes, panic rising. *Breathe, Julia. It's just a wedding!*

Then she sees it, tucked away in her closet... the soft ivory, crochet dress she found in a vintage store a couple of years back and never had occasion to wear, before now. She removes it from the hanger, studying the delicate needlework. Her grandmother worked in the lace factory in town, and Julia has a deep appreciation for the skill required to create a dress this intricate. *They don't make them like this anymore.*

She holds the dress against her body, turning side to side, and gazes at her reflection in the mirror mounted behind the closet door. The dress has three-quarter length bell sleeves and rests a few inches above her knee, showing off her legs, one of her best features, or so she's been told.

This will do, she smiles to herself, sighing with relief.

Julia steps gingerly into her dress, careful not to snag the stitching, then studying her reflection in the mirror, she applies a little blush and lip-gloss, sweeps her unruly curls back into a loose chignon, and secures the delicate antique crystal chandelier earrings she found earlier in her old jewelry box. Grabbing a pair of heels from her mother's closet, she's ready to go, with five minutes to spare.

Julia sits on her bed and closes her eyes, remembering the last time she saw Will, the heat spreading from her stomach to her face, her skin flushed with anticipation. It's already the first week of April and she hasn't seen him since his visit to the city two months ago.

She tries to relax and calm the butterflies fluttering in her stomach, taking deep breaths, in and out. She longs for Will while she's away at school…and it pisses her off. She doesn't like that he's always on her mind. Julia, always the master of distraction, keeps as busy as possible and does her best to focus on her studies and enjoy time with friends, but she misses him. Every day.

Earlier this afternoon, her best friend, Gabby, picked Julia up at the train station in Providence. Will offered her a ride, but she needed time alone with her friend for a serious dose of girl talk.

Tonight could change everything between Julia and Will and before she left New York she'd convinced herself she was ready to take this leap into the unknown. However, during the three and a half hour train ride home, her confidence has dissipated with each passing mile, to the point of nonexistence. Gabby is Julia's sounding board, and today she's in desperate need of her friend's wise counsel.

Waiting outside the station, Julia wondered which version of Gabby would make an appearance today. Her friend's a chameleon. Goth, hippie chick, grunge, preppy princess...she's tried them all. She's naturally pretty, but her style changes so quickly, Julia never knows what to expect.

Last year, Gabby swore off getting any more tattoos or piercings. Her body was beginning to resemble an art gallery, so Julia was relieved to hear that! Now it's all about the hairstyle, makeup and clothes. She once asked why Gabby felt the need to constantly change her appearance and her friend shrugged and replied, "Why not?"

"It's so good to see you, Jules!" Gabby cried as Julia approached her friend's bright pink Camaro, overnight bag in hand. Julia smiled to herself, noting the choker studded with spikes, heavy black eyeliner, tight black t-shirt and jeans and high-top Converse sneakers. Punk Rock Gabby has made a reappearance, accompanied by The Violent Femme's blaring from her car speakers.

"You too, Gab. Thanks for picking me up." Julia wrapped her arms around her friend, holding onto her more tightly and a little longer than usual. When they pulled apart, a crease formed between her friend's brows.

"You're as white as a ghost! Jules, look at me. Are you okay?"

"I'm fine," Julia whispered, turning away, but not before she caught a glimpse of Gabby's eyebrow rising, her doubtful expression.

As they pulled away from the curb, she lowered the music and Julia stared out the window, for once oblivious to the changing scenery as they wove through the city, her friend taking the long route to the highway.

She remained silent as they drove by the majestic white marble State House dwarfing them near the station, and the beautiful houses built into the hillside across the river, where Roger Williams first established this colony as a haven for those seeking religious freedom.

Normally, Julia would point out a few historic landmarks, maybe note the preservation of the colonial houses along Benefit Street, or tell a story or two about the infamous Brown brothers, stories Gabby's heard a thousand times by now, but never complains when Julia gets on a roll.

This afternoon, Julia sat quietly, clasping her cold, clammy hands together. They'd been shaking all day and she didn't want Gabby to see how terrified she actually was.

"Jules, you're not fine. You can't bullshit me. I want you to take a deep breath and tell me how you're really feeling."

"You know, Gab, I'm not one of your patients."

Gabby is studying psychology at Brown University and Julia would love to be a fly on the wall during one of her future counseling sessions. She compares her friend to the Magic Mirror in *Snow White*. Stand in front of Gabby long enough and you'll hear the truth, whether you want to or not. Having never visited a therapist herself, Julia doesn't know if that's a good or bad thing, but it would be entertaining.

"Then stop making me probe for answers, Jules! You're obviously nervous about tonight. I've driven you through every historic neighborhood in Providence and you haven't told me one story about HP Lovecraft or the Wampanoag tribe! We passed Prospect Park without you paying homage to your hero, Roger Williams. Hello? Red flag!"

Julia continued to silently stare out the window, not sure where to begin. Her limbs felt weighted down, paralyzed, her mind foggy and unfocused. A rabbit frozen in fear.

"You don't have to do anything you don't want to do tonight, Jules. Just go to the wedding and relax, play things by ear. You're putting too much pressure on yourself. I know this is out of your comfort zone…"

Julia grunted in response. "That would be an understatement…"

What she has planned for tonight is so far out of the realm of her experience she doesn't know what to do with her conflicting feelings. She's not afraid of sex. Julia's had her fair share of experience in the bedroom, but never cared about any of the men she's slept with, having sworn off emotional entanglements long ago.

No, Julia's afraid of what'll happen if she has sex *with Will*. She's terrified of falling in love with him, and has a sneaking suspicion she's already been sucked into the vortex of that tornado, despite her best efforts to keep their relationship platonic.

Julia witnessed first hand the wreckage of a broken heart, and it's an ugly, mangled, pulpy mess, which takes years to scab over, never completely healing. She doesn't ever want to go through that kind of suffering, to be stripped bare and made vulnerable.

Love makes you weak, and I can't afford to be weak.

"Talk to me, Jules."

"I don't know if I can do this, Gabby. I'm afraid he'll destroy me."

"Honey, it wouldn't be love if it didn't."

She gasped in horror. "All the more reason to keep things as they are. We have a perfectly solid friendship. I don't like playing with fire."

"I'm kidding, Julia! Sarcasm! You used to understand my language."

Gabby pulls the car over just before they reach the highway.

"Look, I hate to break it to you sweetie, but *friends* don't have marathon kissing sessions. *Friends* don't feel an uncontrollable urge to touch one another. You're the one forcing *friendship* on a relationship that's meant to be more. Let it go! You're not your mother. You won't fall apart if things don't work out between the two of you. And Will isn't your dad. He's not going anywhere. The man should be nominated for sainthood at this point."

Julia looked down at her hands and noticed the shaking had subsided. Gabby has a way of putting things into perspective for her.

"You're right. It's time to take a chance," Julia swallowed hard, trying to solidify her resolve. "Would you happen to have any valium?" she asked, hopeful. Gabby chuckled and shook her head, no. "What? They won't let you write prescriptions yet?"

"You'll be fine, Jules. Just remember to breathe. That's all you need to remember, deep, deep breaths."

***

Will's face is a picture of concentration as he stares into the mirror above his dresser, struggling to knot his tie. Frustrated, he unwraps the fabric, yanks it off and begins the process all over again. He's trying to make a Windsor knot like his father has shown him a thousand times before, but he's never gotten the hang of it. He hates ties. No matter how loose he makes the knot, he feels like someone's slipped a noose around his neck, strangling him.

"So, my darling brother, you're bringing Julia to Skip's wedding?" his sister Ellie asks, poking her head into his room. She's home visiting from Chicago this weekend and they haven't had a chance to catch up yet. Ellie plops across his bed while he fumbles with his tie.

"Uh huh," he nods, preoccupied.

"I really like Jules," Ellie smiles. "Are things serious between you two?"

He notices the time on the alarm clock beside his bed. *Shit! I'm going to be late.* He can't wait to see Julia and is anxious to get out of the house.

"Hey! Answer my question!"

"Define serious," he says, trying to evade her question.

"Will!" Ellie throws a pillow at him. "What's going on with you guys? You've been seeing her for a while now."

He finishes knotting his tie, and studying his handiwork, shrugs his shoulders. *This will have to do.* Julia won't care about his tie anyways. He sits beside Ellie on his bed and pulls on his shoes.

"I wouldn't exactly say we're seeing each other."

"Will," Ellie frowns. "What the fuck does that mean?"

"That means it's none of your business."

"You're so secretive! I hate that about you! We shared a womb. Surely you can tell me about your relationship with Julia."

Will raises an eyebrow and sits back on his bed.

"Well… it's hard to date someone you only see once every two months. The last time we were together was in February when I had an interview in New York. The distance makes things a bit difficult."

"Yeah, I imagine it would," Ellie pauses. "So, do you have some sort of understanding? You can both date other people while she's away at school?"

He really doesn't want to talk about this with his sister, he hasn't talked about Julia with anyone. Will prefers to keep his private life just that, *private*, but his twin sister is tenacious and she won't give up until she has some answers.

"We've never discussed that. What I mean is we haven't ever... you know."

His cheeks are burning and he reluctantly makes eye contact with his sister. Ellie, for once, is speechless, her face frozen in surprise.

"You've been dating her since last summer and you haven't had sex?" she asks, her voice incredulous, her brows drawn together in confusion.

"That's just it El, we've never defined our relationship. We're... friends. Really, really good friends."

"I'm sorry...what the fuck?" Ellie shakes her head in disbelief. "I've seen you with Julia and you're not just friends. I can cut the sexual energy between you two with a knife, it's that thick!"

Will shrugs his shoulders. She doesn't have to tell him! He can't count the number of times he's tried to get closer to Julia and she's shied away.

"Last summer we didn't even kiss, other than hello and goodbye."

"Seriously?" Ellie's visibly taken aback, and stares at him, mouth open. "I never would have thought...I mean I just assumed you two were sleeping together. You seem so close."

"We are close..." his voice trails off.

When he's not pressed for time, maybe he should have a conversation with Ellie about Julia. This is uncharted territory for him. Most of the women he knows are ready to climb into bed after a couple of dates. He's always been the one to put on the brakes, not wanting to jump into something before he's ready. Maybe his sister can provide some valuable female insight into this situation.

"Julia seemed...I don't know...nervous. Like she's afraid of getting too close. It's not like we haven't done anything." Again, Will feels the color rising in his cheeks.

"What happened when you went to New York?" Ellie asks.

He looks down at his hands with a shy smile. If the circumstances had been different during that visit, who knows what would've happened...

"I see that smile," Ellie nudges him, grinning. "I want details!"

"I'm not sharing details."

"Sometimes I wish you had a vagina," she sighs, disappointed.

"I'll tell you this, then I have to go," Will chuckles, reaching for his jacket. "We went to dinner, then to hear a band at some bar in the Village. I wanted her to come back to our brother's place, but she said no."

"Why?" Ellie asks, frowning.

"She didn't want Peter to hear us," he says, eyebrow raised.

"Oh my god!" his sister bursts out laughing. "She makes that much noise?"

"I wouldn't know, El!" Will runs his fingers through his hair, frustrated, "But I understand her point. I'd rather we were alone too. I don't want to push her, Ellie. Julia's...different. I've never met anyone like her and... I care about her."

"Do you want to be with her?" Ellie takes his hand in hers.

"Yeah," he says, a smile tugging at his lips.

"Do you have the opportunity to be alone tonight?"

"Her mother is sleeping out," he nods, then clears his throat.

"Well then, it is time to man up!" Ellie's face lights up, "Tonight could be the night! But before you go, let me fix that tie."

Will borrowed his parents' car for the ride to Hartford, Connecticut. It's a two-hour drive and he figured they'd be more comfortable in the BMW than his Jeep.

On the drive to Julia's, he can't help but think about the last time they were together, his face breaking into a smile. He had an interview on Wall Street in February and surprised Julia at work, though they'd made plans to meet later that evening. He hadn't seen her since Christmas night and couldn't wait, not while they were in the same zip code.

It was a frigid day, and Will was shivering as he entered the cavernous lobby of the Metropolitan Museum of Art where Julia has a part time job, giving art history tours in the Renaissance wing.

The building is huge but he spotted her almost as soon as he pushed his way through the revolving door. She was standing off to the right near the gift shop, a group of thirty high school students gathered around her, waiting for her tour to begin, and he managed to slip unnoticed into the back of the group while Julia had a conversation with one of the teachers.

A moment later she called the students to attention.

"All eyes on me please." The fidgeting, chatter, and shoving subsided. "Welcome to the Met. Before we begin our tour I have a few rules to share with you." He heard groans from the teenagers. "Hush now," she continued. "Unless you have a gazillion dollars to spare, don't touch the priceless art you're about to see. Hands off the merchandise."

"And rule number two…" Julia raised two fingers into the air, and stopped mid-sentence, her face breaking into a huge smile, her eyes lighting up as they came to rest on him at the rear of the group.

Will covered his mouth to stifle his laughter and Julia looked around the room, as if remembering where she was. "Ummm…rule number two," she continued, "Don't forget rule number one." She took a few steps backwards.

"My name is Julia, if you have any questions during our tour please raise your hand. If I know the answer I'll tell you, if I don't, I'll lie." She winked at him. "Follow me to the right."

The tour lasted an hour and the moment it ended, Julia made a beeline toward him. Without a word, she grabbed the sleeve of his coat, pulling him around the corner into an office and closed the door behind them.

"What are you doing here?" she smiled, lightly punching his arm, "You threw me off my game!"

"I don't know what happened," he laughed. "I was at Peter's place and the next thing I know I'm standing in front of the museum!"

She jumped up and threw her arms around him, and he held her close, pressing her back against the wall… His body tingles, remembering how they looked into each other's eyes, their lips quickly coming together, and the passionate kiss they were in the midst of sharing when her boss walked in on them moments later.

"Umm… Excuse me?"

They froze for an instant, their faces turning various shades of red, then Julia slid down the wall and said, "We were just leaving."

Will smiles as he pulls his parents' car into the driveway of Julia's house. She lives with her mother in a white Cape with dark blue shutters, flowerboxes filled with daffodils and purple crocuses, and boxwoods bordering the front of the house.

Julia's mother, Carol, is outside filling flowerpots with soil. Her mother is a beautiful woman, petite with thick straight brown hair, cut just above her shoulders, high cheekbones and big brown eyes. Julia looks a lot like her, but is taller and curvier, with a gorgeous mass of long dark curly hair.

He has a hard time reconciling the woman Julia's described with the person standing in front of him. When her parents' divorced, her mother had a hard time and started drinking. Apparently she spent the better part of a year drunk in bed, then began going out at night, dressing and acting like a teenager, and bringing home strange men. Before Julia left for college, they had a big blowout, and her mom seems to have gotten her act together over the past few years.

Julia calls her mother a work in progress. He can't imagine what it was like for her, especially as an only child. Divorce is taboo in his family. Once you're married, you stay married, no matter what.

He steps out of the car, smiles and waves.

"Hi Will," Carol rises, brushing the dirt off her jeans and removes her gardening gloves. "Nice to see you again. Go on in. Julia's getting ready."

"Thanks Mrs. Grasso," he says, shaking her hand.

"Please, call me Carol. Mrs. Grasso is my former mother-in-law!"

Will nods and opens the side door to the kitchen.

"Jules?"

"Just a sec! I'll be right there!" she calls from her bedroom.

Someone has been baking. He scans the countertops for cookies, hoping to grab a few for the road, but comes up empty handed. He's always liked her house, it's small, but warm and inviting. The kitchen is painted a cheery yellow, with white cabinets and trim and a colorful collection of Depression-era dishes hang on the wall beside an embroidered map of their hometown made by her grandmother, commemorating Bristol's tri-centennial.

His parents' house has a museum-like quality. Growing up, he was always afraid of breaking one of the many antique lamps, vases, or sculptures scattered around the house. He did his share of damage before coming to the conclusion that the only safe place to play was the finished basement or outdoors.

"Hey there!"

His breath catches as Julia walks down the hallway toward him, a smile on her face.

"You look beautiful, Julia," he says, swallowing hard.

"You like?" She stops and poses for him.

"I like a lot," he says and wraps his arms around her.

Will's heart beats hard against his chest as he gazes with longing into her eyes. *Two months is too long!* He's so relieved her semester comes to an end next month. They'll have the whole summer together before she enters her final year of school.

Julia stands on tiptoe and kisses him on each cheek, her cheeks flushed.

"I've missed you, Will," she grabs his hands, then steps back to study his outfit. "And oh, how I've missed my favorite pants!"

"What? You don't like my clothes?"

He's wearing a white button down shirt, navy blue tie, a madras blazer, and his Nantucket pants. They've debated the actual color in the past, he thinks they're red, she disagrees.

"You look very handsome. You know how I love the pink pants."

"Shut up," he murmurs and pulls her close, feeling the energy flowing between them. He's never experienced anything like it before, a tingling that begins in his fingertips and radiates inward. The closest thing he can compare it to is a runner's high. When he's with Julia he thinks clearer, everything seems brighter and he feels alive, like anything's possible.

He lightly brushes his fingertips along the side of her face, and for the first time, understands what's behind these sensations. *I'm in love with Julia.*

"Are you ready?" he asks, taking a deep breath in.

"Let's do this."

***

An hour into the ride to Hartford, Julia and Will fall into companionable silence. The radio is tuned to the oldies station, playing hits from the Sixties and Seventies, and Julia stares out the window, quietly singing along with The Doors, her head back against the seat. Gabby's words from earlier today are echoing in her head. It's time to take a risk and open her heart.

If Julia didn't care about Will, if what they had was a purely physical connection, she would've slept with him last summer. But she's always known… *this is different.*

They skipped the wedding ceremony at the church and headed straight for the reception, pulling into the country club parking lot a little after six-thirty.

"Jules. Jules." Will lightly shakes her arm and holds her hand to his lips. She turns toward him and smiles. "Were you sleeping?" he laughs.

"No, just thinking…"

"What were you thinking about?"

"Ummm," she pauses. *I was thinking about taking you to my bed later tonight?* "About last summer."

"That was a good summer."

"The best."

Will opens the door and takes her hand, helping her out of the car. She looks around the lot, surveying the landscape, and frowns. *Something isn't right.* It takes her a minute to figure it out. The cars are all the same, an assembly line of BMW's as far as her eyes can see, with a Mercedes thrown in here and there.

She was surprised when Will pulled up in his father's car earlier, and now understands why he did. The Jeep would have been totally out of place in this environment, and she knows deep down, before they've taken one step into this wedding reception, *so am I.*

"What's up?" Will asks. "Everything okay?"

"Yes, yes. I'm fine." She shivers and pulls her coat around her, trying to shake off the uneasy feeling that's settled in the pit of her stomach. Every instinct is screaming for her to get back into Will's car and drive away from this place.

"You ready?"

She nods and forces a smile, the first of many forced smiles she's sure she'll have to plaster across her face this evening.

"What're the names of the happy couple?"

"Skip and Poppy," Will says with a straight face and her eyes grow wide.

"Uh huh... I'm ready." Julia holds her breath for a moment and sighs as they enter the country club.

Chapter Two

The ballroom is an undulating sea of navy blue and pastel. Hundreds of people are milling about, talking, laughing, drinking. *Is there a dress code?* she wonders, then glances down at her outfit, realizing one of her little black dresses would've stood out even more conspicuously than the one she's wearing now.

She pulls the dress down as low as she can without ripping the embroidery, but gives up. There's no way this dress is going to reach her knees. She knows she's in for a long night and braces herself for her first introduction.

"Will, you bastard!" A man in what appears to be the standard uniform of navy blue blazer and khaki pants, greets them. With relief she realizes, Will may be wearing pink pants and a plaid blazer, but at least he's original. He must have known the uniform and chose to wear something different, and she's momentarily comforted by the notion.

We're in this together, two sore thumbs sticking out in the crowd.

"Walker, you son of a bitch!" Will's face lights up, and they firmly shake hands.

"How are you old man? I haven't seen you since the Figawi last May!"

What the hell is a Figawi? she wonders.

"I'm good," Will laughs. "How are you? Is Georgie here?"

"She's floating around somewhere."

Julia watches their exchange, fascinated. Who is this person? Will's chest is puffed out, his back rigid, and his voice a few decibels louder and deeper. *Where is my Will?*

"Walker, this is Julia."

"Enchanted to meet you Julia," Walker takes her hand in his and kisses it. Julia raises an eyebrow, taken aback.

"Charmed," she replies, withdrawing her hand.

"Will, what an exotic creature you have here," Walker proceeds to slowly undress her with his eyes, her own growing wide in disbelief. "Lucky man!" Walker winks at Will. "Save me a dance, Julia."

Not in a million fucking years, she thinks, forcing her second smile of the evening.

A dozen or so Walker clones fawn over her as Will and Julia make their way to their assigned table, and she tries desperately to keep an open mind. Will stops often to introduce her and chat with friends, and she's never felt more uncomfortable in her life.

She's always been able to hold her own in a room full of strangers…before tonight, and she can't help but wonder, *they can't all be this phony…can they?*

Watching the servers maneuvering through the guests, she envies them their anonymity. She wishes she could throw on an apron and carry a tray of hors d'oeuvres. She'd be more comfortable in that role, and she's sure these women would be as well. The men, on the other hand, would prefer she do a striptease and dance around a pole.

Tonight isn't Julia's first foray into this exclusive world. She's spent the past four years on the periphery taking care of the Emerson children, a wealthy family from town. Her eyes wander around the room, remembering the countless hours she's spent with their family and friends, supervising the children at holiday parties and other social gatherings. She didn't realize her position as their nanny protected her from outward hostility.

In the short time she's been here, it's become painfully clear, working a society event is much different from attending one as a guest, or in her case, a plus one.

When Julia thinks of her hometown, she divides it into two tribes. She always felt the term fitting since Bristol was once populated with native Wampanoags.

These days, there's a tiny tribe she calls *The Elite*, primarily white Anglo Saxon Protestants, some of Mayflower lineage, who keep so much to themselves, they're practically invisible to Julia's people. She calls her tribe, *Everyone Else*, mostly Italian, Portuguese and Irish Catholic families, many of them second and third generation Americans.

The Elite live on Poppasquash Neck, a gated community on a small peninsula across the harbor. These families have lived in Bristol for generations, are members of exclusive clubs where they mingle amongst themselves, and send their children to private schools, presumably to keep them away from the rabble.

Most attend the Episcopal Church on Hope Street, though a few families are Catholic and attend St. Margaret's, one of many Catholic churches in town. Will's family has lived on Poppasquash for over two hundred years.

When Julia was young she thought the big houses across the harbor were empty. The older she got, the more she realized that didn't make any sense, but until she landed the babysitting job with the Emersons in high school, she'd never met a single person from that part of town.

The first time she drove down Poppasquash Road was a revelation. She couldn't believe the size of the houses, or how beautifully the grounds were maintained, had never seen such elegance or opulence in person. The Emersons live less than three miles from her home, but it may as well be the opposite side of the globe.

Charles and Claire treat Julia like family and on social occasions she's free to mingle with their guests, but she's always known, she's an outsider. She isn't considered one of the servants, but she is hired help. At these events, after she puts the kids to bed, Julia tries to help clearing glasses and plates, but invariably gets sucked into conversation as she weaves through the crowd.

At the last party she worked, Julia was cornered by an older gentleman who asked her what she thought about the Bush tax cuts. She raised her eyebrows. *He doesn't think I have a clue what he's talking about.* So she set him straight, explaining her thoughts on Bush's economic policy, and after a brief back and forth, he threw his head back and laughed, declaring her, "simply charming."

"Charles, your nanny is a pistol!" he grabbed Mr. Emerson as he walked by. "She has very strong views on the President's economic plan. I thought she was an actress?"

"Our Jules is an historian, Peterson, a brilliant young lady," Charles smiled and winked at Julia. "We're lucky to have her."

She thinks of *The Elite* as voyeurs, trying to get a glimpse into the lives of *Everyone Else*, the other, less fortunate tribe, who exist in a world they'll never know.

Once they have a few drinks in them, *and good Lord those people can drink*, they ask her the most absurd questions. "How many pregnant teens are in your class? Have you ever seen a drug deal in the hallways of your school? What is it like to live over there?"

They'd never ask a cook, maid, server or gardener the sort of questions they ask her. They're invisible. But the nanny doesn't fade into the background, she's part of the action and considered fair game. Julia plays along, sharing surface details, smiling on cue, asking polite questions about their charity work and travels. Everyone has always been pleasant to her, but Julia is under no illusion. To them, she's a curiosity.

At this wedding, she's not just a curiosity, Julia feels like a circus sideshow. The men are ogling her and being disrespectful... she knows that lascivious look well. She can feel their eyes on her, can see the judgment on their faces.

The women she's been introduced to won't make eye contact with her, and turn away to talk to whomever is closest, not bothering to hide their contempt.

Why are they so quick to judge me? They know nothing about me at all!

As soon as they pulled into the parking lot, she knew this would be an experience, but she didn't expect to be treated like an invader or a threat. She wants to shout, *Don't worry ladies! I don't want your men!* Not realizing that, for all intents and purposes, she's already taken one.

She never thought of Will as *one of them*, at least...she didn't.

Will and Julia sit down at a table set for twelve where she meets Carlton and Buffy, Mackenzie and Darcy, Parker and Quinn, Graham and Mimi, and Tucker and Whitney. *Are these their first or last names?* It's a mystery.

Just as the men have their uniform, so do the women. Shoulder-length, straight blond hair of various shades, a pastel suit or dress so dowdy her grandmother wouldn't be caught dead in it, and the obligatory strand of pearls.

They all look the same to me. Julia can't tell them apart except for the color of their dresses.

"How do you know our Will?" the lady in pink asks Julia, her eyes as cold as ice. *Our Will?* Julia fixes her gaze on her and raises an eyebrow. *Buffy, is it?* This woman can't be more than twenty-five and looks forty.

At this point, Julia's had just about enough of their smugness and superiority. She may as well have a little fun while she's here, so she smiles, resting her elbow on the table, her chin in her hand.

"He picked me up at a bar last week." Julia says, fluttering her eyelashes at Buffy, and Will bursts out laughing.

"We've known each other for a year now, right Jules?" He drapes his arm around her shoulder.

"Just about." Her mouth is smiling, her eyes are not. *Forced smile number two hundred and seventy-three of the evening.* Not that she's keeping count.

"We were in a play together this past summer," Will tells the group, sending not-so-subtle shockwaves around the table. The men begin laughing and ribbing Will for doing something "so gay" and the ladies turn to each other in confusion.

Julia sits on her hands and bites her lip, doing her very best to control her anger, while Will turns pink, probably wishing he'd kept that bit of information to himself.

"Whatever were you doing in a play, Will?" Buffy snorts.

All conversation at their table revolves around boats, houses, horses, and parties. His gaffe forgotten with the aid of large quantities of alcohol, Will is talking animatedly with Graham about a trip they took to 'the Vineyard' in high school. To her left, Mimi and Whitney discuss the upcoming 'season' of parties. Julia sits back in her chair, her eyes glazing over while she butters a dinner roll.

They are so boring. How can Will tolerate these people? But he does. What's most disturbing to Julia is this version of Will fits right in.

Her mind wanders back to the Emersons, her only point of reference for people in this social sphere. Julia's never envied them their wealth or status. It didn't take her long to understand that along with immense privilege comes high expectations and an even higher level of conformity.

She would never want to live as they do, more concerned with other peoples perceptions of them than their own happiness. Claire's fixated on remaining a size two and puts a tremendous amount of pressure on herself to throw picture perfect parties. Charles, always trying to impress people with his boats and club memberships. *And the boys!* God, she feels for them.

Every year she receives a Christmas card of the three boys dressed identically, carbon copies of one another, though Julia knows how unique they really are. Carlton, the shy artist, Spencer, the outgoing athlete, and little Edmond who dreams of being a ballerina and loves the color pink. Claire has said more than once they're hoping it's just a phase, "Edmond's only six after all!"

On those occasions, Julia's had to restrain herself from yelling at Claire. *Being different is something to be celebrated, not discouraged!* But not here, not in this world. With dismay, Julia recognizes that one day, her sweet boys will all turn into some version of the men sitting around this table.

The surf and turf is finally served and Julia's thankful to have something to do. She has nothing to contribute to the conversations swirling around her and would love to knock back a few shots of vodka, but she needs to keep her wits about her tonight for several reasons.

One, she doesn't want to get cornered by one of these drunken idiots who may think he can have his way with her. Two, she needs to stay mentally sharp to verbally protect herself from these hostile women. And three, someone has to drive them home tonight and it's not going to be Will.

She limits herself to two drinks, enough to take the edge off, but not enough to loosen her tongue. That could get ugly…quickly. Will, on the other hand, is on his sixth? Seventh?

She's lost count. This is a side of him she's never seen, never imagined existed.

It dawns on her, this is the first time she's met any of Will's friends in almost a year. She's never thought about that before but it seems odd to her now.

Why do we always hang out alone?

Maybe Will instinctively knew she wouldn't fit in? If that's the case, he was absolutely right. And more importantly, she doesn't want to fit in with these automatons. Watching him interact with his friends tonight, she wonders if she's completely misjudged him. *Is this the kind of life he wants?*

The bride and groom dance to Etta James' *At Last* to the applause of three hundred people, while the wait staff circulates, removing the dinner plates. Julia smiles to herself at the song selection. Apparently some things remain the same across social lines, dancing to *At Last* at weddings is one of those things.

Will absently runs his hand along her spine, still deep in mind-numbing conversation. He and his buddies have moved on from sailing to skiing, from the Vineyard to Aspen.

I'm so naïve, she thinks, her stomach turning over. *This is Will's world. This! Right here!* Not the world they've created over the past ten months. Here, among his peers, she sees who he really is for the first time.

She's not completely oblivious. She knows they're from different tribes, but it never seemed to matter. Julia's spent a lot of time with his family and gets along with his sister and parents really well, and Will seemed to adapt to her world without a problem.

But there's no getting around it now, their differences are glaringly obvious tonight, a giant wall between them.

A wave of nausea washes over her and Julia desperately needs to get out of this room, away from this scene and these people. She rises unsteadily to her feet, gripping the back of her chair. The room has started to spin, and if she doesn't get out of here now she's going to be sick. She taps Will's shoulder and excuses herself, searching for the ladies room.

In the safety of the bathroom, she sits in a stall, tears clouding her vision. This isn't how she imagined this evening at all. *Tonight was supposed to be the night...* She thought they'd dance, she'd meet a few of his friends, then they'd go to her house and... *who knows?*

She wanted him. She'd convinced herself Will was worth it. *Now?* She doesn't even know who he is. *Love makes you blind.* She was stupid to allow a chink in the armor. No man is worth the heartache.

Julia grabs a tissue and dabs at her eyes, trying to stem the flow of tears before they begin, and sighs, thinking, *eventually I will have to leave this bathroom.* What an awful thought.

The door to the restroom opens, letting in the sound of the band, and closes behind two women gossiping in hushed voices.

"Did you see her dress? So inappropriate! It's so short and looks like a rag," they laugh.

Are they talking about me? Julia's eyes grow wide and she covers her mouth.

"And her hair! So frizzy!"

They are! I'm the only woman in this place with curly hair. For several minutes she sits in the stall, frozen in embarrassment, while they verbally rip her to shreds. Finally, she peeks through the crack to see the offending women. It's Darcy from her table, and someone she doesn't recognize.

"What can Will possibly see in her? He's so handsome and eligible," the stranger in lavender says dreamily, applying her hideous pink lipstick.

"She looks like a hippie, utterly classless," Darcy adds.

"Well, I guess some guys need to slum it before they settle down."

That is it! Julia's flooded with anger and a slew of other emotions she doesn't fully understand. She pulls herself together, opens the stall and walks deliberately to the sink, slowly washing her hands. They stop talking and glare at her, not one speck of shame between them. Julia shuts off the faucet, grabs a paper towel and turns to face them.

"You want to know why Will is with me?" They raise their eyebrows in response. "He said he's tired of dating boring, uptight girls, like you. He prefers a woman with a pulse."

Their mouths fall open, then Darcy's eyes narrow. Julia's happy to have touched a nerve with that comment, and dries her hands, standing directly in front of them.

"Oh, and I'm the best fuck he's ever had."

She tosses the paper towel in the trashcan and walks out of the bathroom.

Julia is livid and humiliated, her thoughts and feelings a jumble inside her. She actually sees red, and would love to make a scene, maybe grab Will by his collar and drag him out of here, but she'd be giving them exactly what they want. They'd tell stories for years about the screeching greenhorn Will once brought to a wedding.

She has two choices, sit and pout, or put on a show. She'd never give them the satisfaction of watching her shrink into a corner, so she decides now's the time to use a few of the acting skills she's picked up over the years.

Julia spots Will by the bar with a group of men and struts over to him, her hips swaying side to side. *That's right ladies and gentlemen, I have curves.* She grabs Will by the lapel, presses her lips to his ear and whispers, "Dance with me."

Will is obnoxiously drunk. His eyes remain unfocused for a moment, then she watches as they glaze over with lust. He grabs her around the waist and pulls her against him, and her heart begins to pound, the blood rushing to her head. He's aroused, she can feel him against her stomach.

Not a fucking chance, Will!

She wants to push him away, but instead she swallows her anger and sticks to her plan.

She smiles seductively at his friends, who predictably salivate with desire. Julia wants to make sure the ladies see what their men really want. Not their frilly bows, blond bangs, dowdy dresses and sensible pumps. The object of their desire is the sexy Italian chick who's not afraid to show a little leg. She removes the clip from her hair and shakes it out behind her.

"You're mine for the rest of the evening," she says, leading Will to the dance floor. He holds her close and they slow dance to *The Lady in Red.* Julia almost bursts out laughing at the irony. The band is on break and this DJ has a sense of humor. The only red in this room is the blood running through Julia's veins, everyone else's runs blue.

Will's hands wander down her back, one coming to rest on her ass, and she doesn't stop him. She's playing a part for her audience. *Temptress. Sex goddess.* This is her farewell performance. She has no intention of ever seeing any of these people again.

Darcy is standing with a group of women near the dance floor, obviously sharing the story of their recent exchange. Her fiancé, Mackenzie, has been one of Julia's most ardent admirers this evening. If Darcy only knew how easy it would be for Julia to lure Mac into one of the back rooms... it's pathetic how easily men are manipulated when it comes to sex.

Instead, Julia resists the urge to flip Darcy off and rests her head against Will's chest, the sadness settling in. He touches the curve of her neck and tilts her head up, his mouth finding hers, and for the first time she feels...*nothing.* The electricity is gone, which should be a relief, but only manages to make her feel worse.

"Aren't you lucky," she whispers and closes her eyes. "You won't remember any of this in the morning."

Chapter Three

The following afternoon, Ellie drives Will to Julia's to pick up their father's car. He has the worst hangover of his life, and doesn't remember leaving the wedding or the drive home. When he thinks about Julia having to find their way home from Hartford on her own, he's consumed with guilt and shame. He wishes he could remember what happened last night. He vaguely recollects dancing with Julia…but his last clear memory is of the food being served.

Everything else is a blur. Parker and Mac provided him with round after round of drinks from the moment he entered the ballroom. There was vodka, and rum…and tequila involved in his memory loss, that he knows.

When he was in high school, they used to tease him for being a lightweight. "You're Irish, man! Don't be such a pussy." He built a tolerance over time, but since he went to college, he's spent less and less time with his old friends and drinking much less as a result.

Ellie grills him the entire ride across town. His head's splitting open and he wishes she'd shut the hell up!

"Jesus Christ, Will, how much did you drink last night?"

"I don't know, El. A lot."

"She had to drive you home?" Ellie says, gritting her teeth. "Will, you totally blew it!" She whacks him on the side of his head.

"Oww! Stop it!" he cries out, his head throbbing.

"Last night was supposed to be the night. Why would you drink so much?"

Why did I do that? Julia must be so upset with him. He's furious with himself.

"I don't know, El," he stares out the window and shakes his head. "I was hanging out with my friends. That's what we do. Drink."

"You're not in goddamned high school anymore, you idiot." Ellie shakes her head in exasperation, and mumbles all sorts of choice phrases under her breath. *Idiot was the kindest.*

"Well, here we are, you fucking moron. Go face the music."

He struggles to climb out of the car with an awful feeling of foreboding. Julia opens the front door and he makes the journey up the walkway, his head aching.

Ellie's right. I totally blew it.

"Hey," he says softly. Julia silently holds out his keys and he sheepishly apologizes. "I'm so sorry Jules. I shouldn't have had so much to drink. I'm sorry you had to drive us home and I'm sorry I spoiled our night."

"No big deal. Here are your keys," she mutters, still not making eye contact with him.

"You're upset," he says. A statement, not a question.

Julia looks him in the eye for the first time.

"Why did you invite me to that wedding?" she asks, hands on her hips, nostrils flared, then raises her voice, "I want to know. Why?!"

"I asked you because I wanted you there with me." He's never seen Julia angry before. Confused, he pauses, "Why do you think I asked you?"

"I'm not sure!" she yells, throwing her hands in the air. "Were you trying to prove something? That you're living on the wild side? I'm sure you could have found some tall blond stick figure named Kiki or Bunny to tag along! Did you honestly think I'd fit in with those people?"

His mouth drops open, but no words are forthcoming. He's never thought about whether she'd fit in with his friends or not. *Why wouldn't she?* Julia gets along with everyone.

"Jules, I wasn't trying to prove anything to anyone. I just wanted to be with you." He attempts to put his arms around her, but she pushes him away. "Julia?"

Her eyes well up and she fixes her gaze on the ground. He knew she'd be upset but there's more to this than his drinking. *There has to be.*

"Julia, please talk to me. Did something happen?"

"Besides you ignoring me half the night?" she snorts. "Where do I begin?!"

Sitting on her front steps, Julia replays the conversation she overheard in the bathroom. What they said, what she said. He's speechless, can feel the color draining from his face.

"Your friends," Julia pauses, shaking her head. "Those guys treated me like an object, a piece of meat," she chokes back a sob, "and the women...like I'm something they scrape off the bottom of their shoe."

"Julia, I am so sorry." He doesn't know what else to say.

She wraps her arms around her legs, resting her head on her knees.

"Will, you want to know the worst part?" His eyes grow wide, thinking with horror, *It gets worse than what she's already told me?* "The worst part is you didn't even notice," she rubs her hands over her eyes. "I hardly recognized you last night. You turned into someone else, and I didn't like that person at all."

He covers his face with his hands, letting her words sink in, then rubs his fingers over his throbbing temple.

"Did you feel uncomfortable with my family or Gabby?"

"No, of course not."

She nods, contemplative, "Maybe that's because they didn't treat you like shit."

Will's eyes well up. No, her family didn't treat him like shit. He can't say he was totally comfortable around them at first, but they were welcoming. Julia's family isn't anything like his own, but that doesn't bother him. His father didn't come from money, though Will hasn't spent much time with that side of the family. It's almost like his dad doesn't want to be reminded of where he came from.

Julia's extended family is so big, loud and overwhelming, but he's envious of their affection for one another. He knows his family loves him, but except for Ellie, they aren't demonstrative people.

He didn't even know he craved that kind of affection until he met Julia. She's warm and accepting and he royally screwed up last night. What was he thinking? How could his friends treat her like that? He clenches his fists, furious with them, but more upset with himself.

How could I treat her so poorly?

His chin drops to his chest, his shoulders droop, the realization hitting him hard. *I am different around them.* That's the world he was raised in, the world he knows. He understands how to operate in that world, with those people.

He wants to tell Julia the person she saw last night isn't him. *She's* probably the only person who really knows him, but he can't get the words out. He's confused and ashamed and his hangover isn't helping him articulate his feelings.

"I need to take a nap," Julia says, rising. "I didn't get much sleep last night and my train leaves in a few hours."

"Do you need a ride to the station?" he asks, hopeful, and grabs the railing, pulling himself up.

"No. I'm all set." She turns away from him. "Goodbye Will."

Julia disappears into the house, closing the door behind her and he stands immobile, staring at her front door.

Did I just lose her?

He rubs his palm over his chest, his heart heavy and finally walks to the car.

***

From behind the living room curtain, Julia watches Will drive away from her house. The tears are building, threatening to spill over the dam, and she runs to her bedroom, crawls under the covers and hugs her old teddy bear close.

Now she's acting like her mother, crying in bed because of a man... She hasn't called Gabby yet, she's too upset to talk to anyone. Thank god her mother slept out last night. All she wants is to be left alone right now.

Finally, Julia closes her eyes and is flooded with memories of the night she met Will. She wishes she could turn back the clock and take away that night. She wishes she could change a lot of things...

On the first night of rehearsal for *West Side Story*, Will walked into her life, and though she didn't know it at the time, was about to turn her world upside down.

The cast of thirty people had gathered in the recreation room at the Congregational Church for a read through and from what Julia could see, with the exception of the children in the cast, she recognized everyone, having performed with all of them in the past. It was a reunion of small town thespians.

Her eyes were scanning the room when someone unfamiliar walked through the arched doorway, looking a little nervous and very out of place. He was tall, with wavy blond hair, and an athletic build, definitely not one of guys she's performed with for years.

She watched him pick up a script from the table near the door, look uneasily around the room, staying away from the crowd, then turning to read the notices on the bulletin board behind him. His discomfort was palpable.

Who is he? she wondered and moved a little closer to the mysterious stranger.

Julia hesitated for a moment, wondering if she should say hello, then shrugged her shoulders. If she were the new person she'd want someone to welcome her, so she tapped him on the shoulder.

Turning, he smiled, resting his clear blue eyes on her, and she froze for an instant, her eyes wide, momentarily struck dumb by his looks. *He's absolutely gorgeous.* But she was quick to regain her composure and introduced herself.

"Hi. I'm Julia. And…you look a bit lost."

He laughed and took her hand in his, his eyes warm.

"A bit! Hi Julia. I'm Will. Nice to meet you."

"Everyone take a seat!" Sean, the director, called out, indicating the metal folding chairs arranged around the room.

Will sat beside her, his thigh resting lightly against hers, sending shivers up her spine.

"Before we begin, let's introduce ourselves. Most of you know each other, but we have a few new faces in the group. Just the basics, name, role you're playing and any previous acting experience."

Sean began by telling the cast about himself, and then they went around the room.

"Hi, I'm Will Kennedy, and I'm in the chorus. Umm…I can't sing and I have no acting experience whatsoever." He looked down at his hands and smiled while everyone laughed.

"I want to thank Will for stepping up," Sean interrupted. "He volunteered to build sets for the show and I bullied him into helping us out. We needed a few more bodies in the chorus. I promised I wouldn't make him dance!"

Will nodded with a shy smile, his face turning pink, and glanced sideways at Julia. It was her turn to share.

"I'm Julia Grasso, I'm playing Anita, and I was in Cabaret last summer."

They began the read through and she kept losing her place in the script, her whole body tingling with awareness of his proximity. While she was fighting the urge to touch the space on his leg where his shorts ended and his knee began, Will held his script in front of her and pointed to her line.

"Julia…" he whispered.

Startled, she looked up to find the whole cast staring at her, several ladies grinning.

"Your line," Will said, smiling.

"Thank you," she replied, her ears growing hot, and silently reprimanded herself. *Good Lord! He's just a guy!*

Scanning the script, she used her pen to highlight the rest of her lines, and for the remainder of rehearsal, read her part and tried to forget he was there.

When rehearsal finally ended, she excused herself and wove through the crowd to the ladies room. Paula, the choreographer, was washing her hands while Julia leaned over the next sink, taking deep breaths.

"You okay Jules?" Julia nodded, splashed cold water on her face and Paula handed her a few paper towels.

"Thanks. Yeah. I was a bit dizzy but I feel better now," she fanned herself with her hand. "It's warm in there."

"Is that what happened?" Paula giggled. "I thought maybe it was that gorgeous man sitting next to you, getting you all flustered."

"Please, Paula, give me some credit," Julia rolled her eyes.

"Honey, if he was sitting next to me, I'd be doing the same thing," Paula said, tossing the paper towel in the basket.

Julia exited the bathroom, and waved to a few people as she left the rehearsal room, "See you tomorrow night!" She didn't linger like she normally would. The faster she got out of there the better.

Walking out into the fresh night air, she found Will standing near the church, his face breaking into a smile as their eyes met. Julia stopped in her tracks, butterflies fluttering in her stomach. *How does he do that? Why does he make me so nervous?*

Living in New York, she's spent a lot of time around good-looking men, some of them models, but no one had ever thrown her off balance before.

"Hey Julia. What're you up to tonight? Do you want to grab a drink?"

"A drink?" Her eyes darted around the churchyard as people walked to their cars. *He's asking me to hang out with him, alone?*

"Yes, a beverage," Will laughed. "Something to quench your thirst?"

He meant a real drink, not Del's Lemonade. Her instinct was to run, to put as much distance between them as was humanly possible. But she stopped herself, figuring if they were going to be in this play together and spend the following ten weeks in each other's company, she'd better get used to being around him.

So instead of running, she smiled and nervously tucked a curl behind her ear.

"How about some ice cream?" she asked. "Maybe a cone of strawberry or a hot fudge sundae?"

A corner of his mouth turned up, his eyes amused.

"How old are you?" he asked, a smile in his voice.

"Not old enough! I'll be twenty in September. How old are you?"

"I turned twenty-two in January." He gazed at her for another second then nodded his head, "Okay…Ice cream it is."

It was a warm summer evening. The sun set not long before, an invisible artist painting colorful strokes in the night sky. Hints of red, purple, and orange lingered, casting a glow over the town. They wandered through the streets of downtown, neither of them in a hurry.

This section of Bristol is a maze of historical homes, varied architecture, and stunning water views. Julia took this beauty for granted until she moved away to college, but not anymore. She was lucky to grow up in such a picturesque town. Compared to the squalid conditions she witnessed people living in back in New York, Bristol is paradise.

As they made their way to the harbor, Julia shared tidbits of town trivia, more out of nervousness than a desire to give a history lesson. Her hometown has a rich, sometimes troubling history stretching back to pre-colonial days. While the seaports of Providence and Boston became prosperous through the China trade, Bristol gained its wealth from the slave trade and privateering.

"This used to be a holding area for slaves," she pointed to a yellow clapboard house on the corner of State Street. Will stopped and stared at the building, his eyes squinting as he peered into the windows.

"See the bars still on the basement windows?" she continued. "The slave traders would drop anchor in the harbor down there," she indicated the nearby water, "and the slaves that were to be sold to local families were brought here and cleaned up before they were delivered to their owners."

Will turned toward her, his eyes bright with curiosity.

"How do you know all of this?"

"Bristol 101 is a mandatory class," she shrugged, her face serious. "You can't live here without taking it." Will smiled and she continued, "I'm also a history major at NYU, so it goes with the territory."

"I went to Portsmouth Abbey. They didn't offer that class."

The Abbey? He must live across the harbor on Poppasquash, which would explain why she's never seen him before. *What is he doing in a local theater production?* People on Poppasquash hardly ever made their way into town.

Will slowly made his way around the house, looking at it from different angles. She studied him as he investigated, and he seemed genuinely interested.

"Downtown was my classroom. When I was a student at Colt School my teacher used to take us on walking tours of town and give us local history lessons. I think she's the reason I love studying the past. Everything has a story."

What's his story? she wondered.

"How about I buy your ice cream and you tell me more? You have me curious," Will said, extending his hand. Surprised, she nodded and they shook hands to seal the deal.

It wasn't long before they approached the dock where the homemade ice cream shop had opened the previous summer, in her estimation, the best addition to downtown in years. To their right, a large stone warehouse was in the process of being converted into restaurants and shops.

"This building was owned by the DeWolfs, one of the most powerful families in Rhode Island back in the day. They were slave traders. See these stones? They're from Africa, used as ballast on the ships."

She ran her hand along the smooth stone exterior of the building and explained that during the height of the 'Triangular Trade' rum was made in this warehouse from the sugar brought from the West Indies and exchanged for the slaves.

"The shackles used to hold the ships 'cargo' are still attached to the basement walls," she shivered. "It gives me the creeps."

"I had no idea," his voice trailed off as he inspected the building. Will walked in a slow circle, "I've lived here my whole life…" he paused and turned to her, "It's like I'm seeing it for the first time."

"History is everywhere, Will," Julia laughed. "I'm happy to be your guide!"

They walked along Thames Street eating their ice cream, and Will guided her into Rockwell Park, a tiny square on the harbor with a few swings, a slide and a couple of stone benches. It's also home to a dock with several boat slips, all residents anchored for the evening.

The sky was clear and the stars shone bright, a light breeze blowing in from Narragansett Bay. She heard the faint sound of music from the eighties cover band playing at Gulliver's, the local watering hole.

It was a perfect summer night.

Will licked the ice cream dripping down the side of his cone while they sat on the boat launch at the end of the dock. Julia slipped off her sandals, dangled her feet in the water and shivered.

It was early June and the water was still cold, and she wished she'd grabbed her jean jacket out of the car before they walked downtown. She was wearing a sleeveless white cotton sundress, with a thin brown suede belt and the beaded necklace she made the previous year.

Tucking her long hair behind her ears in a futile attempt to tame her unruly curls, she leaned back on her elbows and sighed, looking at the night sky.

Julia glanced sideways at Will. In his khaki shorts, white polo shirt and flip-flops, with his hair blowing in the breeze, he looked like he'd just stepped off a yacht...or the pages of an LL Bean catalogue. Stifling a laugh, she laid back on the dock, her hands behind her head, feet still submerged. *What an odd pair we make*, she thought, *the hippie and the preppie.*

It dawned on her they hadn't said a word to each other since they sat down on the boat launch. *How long has that been? Five? Ten minutes?* Strangely, she didn't feel awkward at all.

They're just two people hanging out, looking at the water and the stars. Will finished his cone and laid down beside her, another few minutes elapsing in silence.

"See there?" he pointed up toward the sky. "That's Perseus."

Her eyes followed the direction of his finger. Julia saw a whole lot of stars, but no distinct pattern.

"Where?"

He scooted over so his body was close to hers.

"I'll show you," Will tilted his head toward her. "Give me your hand. See that cluster of stars?"

He held her hand to the sky, pointing out the outline of the constellation, his touch sending shivers down her spine.

"No," she shook her head.

"See?" He traced her finger along its path a second time.

"Oh, wow! I see it!" she nodded, her eyes lit up. "Out of chaos, there is order!"

Will smiled and placed her hand back down by her side, but kept his hand over hers.

"Perseus was one of the original Twelve Olympians in Greek mythology," his voice was just above a whisper. "He saved Andromeda from the sea monster and they married. See her next to him, right over there?"

Again, Will held her hand and traced the path of the constellation. The light dusting of freckles and blond hair on his hand mesmerized her.

"Yes," she said, softly. "I see it," she turned toward him. "How is it you know so much about astronomy?"

"My father taught us to navigate by the stars, me, my brother and sister. He has a sailboat and we spend a lot of time on it during the summer. It's moored right over there."

Will pointed across the harbor to the yacht club on Poppasquash. Julia placed her free hand over her mouth to suppress a giggle. *Our families are so different.*

"My grandfather had a boat too," she paused. "He used to dock it over there," she pointed to the fishing trawlers parked along the seawall near Thames Street Landing. Will slowly turned his face toward her, the corner of his mouth twitching.

"It smelled so bad on that boat. No one ever wanted to go near it." She scrunched her nose at the memory and they looked at one another, bursting into laughter.

A little while later, Julia glanced at her watch and was surprised to find it was already after midnight. They'd been walking and talking for almost three hours and the time had flown by. She'd never felt such a strong attraction to anyone before, and found these feelings unsettling and confusing.

The setting was perfect for seduction and the night could have easily gone in that direction, but something stopped her. It took her a moment to pinpoint what was different about their interaction.

Energy.

She could feel it running between them, and in that moment she knew she could fall for him. Her throat constricted at the thought and abruptly, she sat up, clearing her throat.

"I'd better get going, it's getting late," she whispered, her voice cracking.

Will rose and pulled Julia to her feet, then touched her arm.

"You okay?" he asked, his eyes narrowing while she straightened her dress and slid her feet into her sandals. She looked away, stretching her arms toward the sky.

"Race you!" she shouted and ran down the dock toward the street, an animal fleeing from danger.

From that first night, Julia was drawn to Will, and she knew the feeling was mutual. They quickly became friends, and she thought that's what they would remain, *should remain*. However, the more time they spent together, the closer they got, and Will made it clear he wanted Julia, *the whole package*, not just sex.

But she doesn't do relationships! And the mere thought of opening herself up to him gave her fits of anxiety. Before Will, she was easily able to stay removed and keep things casual. That night on the dock, Julia knew Will could break through her shield, and it scared the shit out of her...but she couldn't stay away from him.

Now, as she curls up underneath her blanket, she wishes she had.

Chapter Four

Driving away from Julia's house in a daze, Will couldn't possibly feel worse. *I'm such an asshole…* He didn't want to go home so he drove to Rockwell Park and sat on the dock staring across the harbor at his parents' house.

Last night should have been about Julia, but he fell so easily into old routines around his friends. And where did that get him? Hung-over and alone. He closes his eyes, missing her already. *Will she ever forgive me?*

When she shut the door a little while ago, he got the sense she was closing the door on them. *Permanently.* He lays back, pulling his coat around him for warmth and watches the clouds overhead, thinking about the circumstances that brought them together. Not in a million years did he ever think he'd be in a play.

Late last spring, he was home from school, visiting his parents for the weekend and Ellie asked him to grab a cup of coffee with her in town. He spotted a sign near the cash register at the café. The local theater company was looking for volunteers to help build sets for their summer production of *West Side Story.*

Up until then, the only local activities he'd been involved in were sailing related, but he loves to build things and this looked interesting. He lingered in front of the sign and Ellie suggested he call and get involved. "It would be good for you," she said.

He probably wouldn't have done it if not for Ellie's encouragement, and if he hadn't made that call, he never would have met Julia. Now he can't imagine his life without her in it, though after last night, he may have to...

West Side Story finished it's run in early August and they had two weeks before they returned to their respective schools. Will had one more semester at Providence College before he was finally done with college.

He took Julia sailing on his dad's boat a few times, and taught her basic techniques, how to tack and trim the jib. She picked it up pretty quickly, though she said her favorite part about sailing was dropping anchor. Then they'd sit on the bow soaking up the sun, and talk for hours.

Will went to school with the same group of kids from his neighborhood until he went to college, but Julia knows more about him than anyone. He can relax and be himself around her and feels like he's known her forever.

He always sensed something was missing in his life, but could never pinpoint exactly what it was. Now he knows.

Spontaneity.

Before he met Julia, every day was virtually the same as the last, the same people, the same places, the same parties, the same...everything. He was bored, and didn't realize it. His life was black and white with a few shades of grey mixed in.

Then Julia came along, a whirlwind of energy, imagination and warmth. When she's around, he sees life in vivid color.

In the weeks before Julia went back to school in New York, she planned a few adventures for them. She turned a walk through the woods into a scavenger hunt, a trip to Newport into a journey through the Gilded Age.

The day they spent on Block Island was one of the best days of his life. They rode their bikes around the island all day, ate a picnic lunch on the bluffs, and swam in the ocean for hours. It was heaven.

She'd never say where they were going until they were on their way, only what he'd need for the trip. On the first couple of outings, he wanted Julia to tell him where they were going before they left, but she refused, telling him to 'just relax and go with the flow.'

He always thought of himself as laid back, someone who went with the flow. But before he met Julia, he always knew the direction of the flow, and what to expect when he arrived there. Not so anymore. After his initial discomfort, he realized not knowing made life so much more interesting.

By the end of summer, Will didn't know what to make of their relationship. She'd become his best friend and although he didn't want to risk that friendship, he wanted her. He'd never wanted anyone like this before.

He first attempted to kiss her a few nights into rehearsals. He'd walked Julia to her car after they had grabbed a Del's Lemonade in town, and when he leaned into her... the look on her face! Her eyes opened wide and her cheeks turned pink. Julia turned her head and kissed his cheek, laughing nervously, and virtually jumped into her car, waving goodbye. He was mystified as she drove away, had never had that effect on a woman before.

He thought maybe she was still a virgin. She was barely twenty years old when they met and that would've explained her hesitance, but she made a comment alluding to the loss of her virginity.

So what stops her? He was frustrated but also intrigued. There's a part of Julia that's a complete mystery to him.

When she told him she was coming home from New York for Columbus Day weekend, he made a plan.

Will invited Julia to his beach house in Narragansett that Saturday night in October. The first part of his seduction plan involved a romantic dinner. He's not a chef, his repertoire very limited.

He wanted to do something special for Julia so he made the simplest thing he could, fairly confident he couldn't screw up boiling water for spaghetti and heating up a jar of sauce. For good measure he made some garlic bread and a salad. It was by far the nicest meal to ever grace that table.

He heard the wheels of her car crunching loudly on the seashell path as Julia pulled into his driveway, and watched her through the kitchen window, his face breaking into a smile. She parked her blue Chevette and stepped out wearing faded jeans, frayed at the knee, a white shirt, brown ankle boots and her favorite beaded necklace.

She scanned his neighborhood, her hands on her hips, taking deep breaths of salty ocean air, and looking incredibly sexy.

Julia's a beautiful woman. Will doesn't think she has any idea how pretty she is. As far as he can tell, she doesn't have a self-conscious bone in her body, but she doesn't know how to take a compliment. If he makes any reference to her looks, she laughs or blushes and turns away.

A moment later he opened the door and leaned against the doorframe, a big grin on his face.

"Well hello stranger!" she shouted, meeting him on the walkway.

Will lifted Julia off the ground in a warm embrace.

"Aren't you a sight for sore eyes!" he said, firmly planting a kiss on her soft, smiling lips.

They walked into the kitchen, Julia's arm through his.

"What do we have here?" her eyes widened in surprise. "I thought we were going to order pizza!"

"I've got skills," he laughed, and wiped down the counter, a little embarrassed by the mess. He hadn't had a chance to clean the kitchen and the sink was piled high with pots and pans, the stove splattered with tomato sauce.

Will had set the table with mismatched dishes and paper napkins, a wine glass accompanying each setting. In the center of the table sat a jar filled with flowers he'd picked from his neighbor's yard.

"Mr. Kennedy, are you trying to seduce me?"

He turned around, his eyes wide. *Am I that obvious?*

"It's from *The Graduate*, Will," she chuckled. His brow furrowed, confused. "The movie? Dustin Hoffman, Anne Bancroft?" He shook his head, had never heard of the movie. "Will! You are missing out! Do you have a VCR here? We need to rent it tonight! Where's the video store?"

"Not far from here. We can go after dinner and pick it up."

"Perfect!" Julia wandered around the house as he finished cooking. "Three guys live here? Did you clean up for me?"

"A little," he nodded and smiled. "You would've turned around and drove home if you saw it before I cleaned."

"Where are your roommates? I was expecting to see one of them sprawled on a couch playing video games," she said.

"Gone. They went home for the weekend." He could tell by the startled look on her face she was taken off guard.

"Oh, I was hoping to meet them," she said, picking up a few darts from the bookcase and throwing them into the board hanging on the wall.

"I'm afraid you're stuck with me tonight," he shook his head, mystified, and rinsed the pasta in the sink. He hoped she'd be happy they were alone.

"This neighborhood is incredible!" Julia stood in front of the picture window in the living room. It was dark outside but the moon was full and the moonlight was reflecting on the ocean directly in front of his house. "You didn't tell me you live on the beach."

They quickly fell back into their comfortable friend zone and although he was enjoying himself, Will decided to put the next part of his plan into action after dinner.

The actual seduction. He figured, if she pushed him away at least he'd know where he stood.

They discussed the upcoming presidential election while he washed dishes and Julia sat on the counter beside him, drying. She's a die-hard liberal, he's a bit more conservative though neither of them liked the Bush administration.

"The president is a stiff and so deeply entrenched in Washington bullshit. We need someone who's totally removed from the DC political scene. I hope Bill Clinton crushes him next month!"

"Yeah, me too. I think my father would have a stroke if he knew I was voting Democrat in this election."

"It's so strange to me… Your family bears the name of the most powerful dynasty of Democrats in America this century… and you're all friggin' Republicans."

"No," he held up his hand, "I'm an Independent. I vote my conscience. And we are in no way related to those Kennedys!"

He finished washing the last of the dishes, and drying his hands, turned toward Julia. She smiled and handed him the last dish to put away and when he reached behind her to stack it in the cabinet, his chest pressed against hers and the energy between them shifted.

Will positioned his body between Julia's legs, placing his hands on her thighs, a jolt of electricity shooting through him.

She brushed her hair away from her eyes and focused her gaze on something behind him.

"Do you think this a good idea?" she whispered.

Will tucked a stray lock of hair behind her ear and nodded. "Yes," he said, a smile spreading across his face.

Her eyes met his, and he ran his fingertip over her bottom lip, then leaned in and brushed his lips against hers until he felt her gently returning his kiss, her arms winding around his back, pulling him closer to her. He savored the sensation of her arms and legs wrapped around him, pressing their bodies together, every point of contact between them a nerve exposed.

Who knows what would have happened that night if a ghost from his past hadn't interrupted their kiss…

RING! RING!

The house phone cut short their exploration. Startled, Will jumped back, his eyes flying wide open. He was disoriented, the light in the kitchen blinding.

RING! RING!

Julia covered her ears and he winced, the shrill ringing echoing in his head. He sighed and smiled self-consciously, reaching for the phone.

"Hello?" he answered, and paused. "Hello?…" his voice trailed off. He could faintly hear the sound of someone breathing. "Who is this?" he asked, but no one answered.

He glanced at Julia and shrugged and was about to hang up the phone when he heard a familiar voice.

"Hi Will…it's me."

Inhaling sharply, he slammed the phone onto the receiver, his hand covering his mouth and stared at the handset, the color draining from his face.

"Will, are you okay?" Julia jumped off the counter. "Who was that?"

He was silent, his body tense. He could feel a vein throbbing in his temple. *Could it be?* He leaned back against the counter, his hands covering his eyes.

"Sorry," he reached for Julia, hugging her to him, his heart hammering against his chest.

"Will, you're scaring me."

"I'm sorry Jules. I'm… that was…." he stuttered. He didn't want to say it out loud because he didn't want it to be real. "I think that was Avery."

"Avery?" Julia asked, visibly confused.

"Someone I knew a long time ago." He knew she was waiting for him to give her an explanation but he remained silent.

"Do you want to talk about it?" she asked.

"No. No. I'm fine," he whispered into her hair.

He wanted to be fine. *How the hell did she get my number? And why did she have to call me tonight, of all nights?* He held Julia closer to him, all plans of seduction evaporating the moment he heard Avery's voice.

They ended up watching *The Graduate* snuggled up under a blanket on his couch, but he wasn't himself, quiet and distracted, preoccupied with the troubling events of his past. He kept one arm around Julia, the other holding onto her hand for dear life.

Julia knew something was wrong, how could she not? He caught her surreptitiously studying him, her brows drawn together in concern, but to his relief she didn't push him to explain Avery or why he reacted so strongly to her call.

What should I tell her? He wasn't quite ready to discuss Avery with Julia, didn't want to risk what they had by revealing the shame he's carried with him for almost five years, a personal crucifix, his private hell.

During the movie, Julia fell asleep, her head in his lap. He didn't have the heart to wake her, so he sat still for a couple of hours and alternated between watching her sleep and staring out the window at the moonlight dancing on the water, absently running his fingers through her hair while he listened to the waves crashing onto shore.

Eventually, he placed a pillow under Julia's head and covered her with blankets, then kissed her forehead before heading to his bedroom. He felt the need to be alone with his thoughts and lying in his bed, he decided to explain everything to Julia in the morning. He didn't want secrets between them, but when he woke from his fitful sleep she was gone, having left a note on his kitchen counter.

Thanks for dinner. XO Jules.

In the weeks that followed, Julia seemed to be avoiding his phone calls. Normally they spoke two or three times a week. Between Columbus Day and Thanksgiving they spoke a total of six times, each conversation rushed and stilted. She was always on her way somewhere and couldn't talk for long. He realized just how badly he blew it, shutting down the way he did after Avery's call.

Will knew she would be home over the holidays and left a message on her mother's machine the night before Thanksgiving, hoping to see her that weekend, but she hadn't called him back. Discouraged by her silence, he asked his brother and sister to go into town the night after Thanksgiving so he could drink away his sorrows.

They made their way downtown to Gulliver's, a bar for locals. Will purposely chose it because there'd be no chance of running into anyone they know. All of their friends would be at Murphy's Pub, two doors down and Will was not in the mood for socializing. Peter was annoyed when Will insisted on Gulliver's, but came along, claiming he'd bail on them in an hour.

Will loves his brother, but Peter can be a bit of a snob. They're polar opposites, yet have always gotten along despite their differences. His brother's twenty-five, graduated from Yale, and works in banking, and is engaged to a girl from Philadelphia's Main Line. They live together on the Upper East

Side of Manhattan, *in sin*, according to his parents. The wedding is this summer. Peter was always a bit of a player so Will was surprised when he proposed to Sloane.

He's much closer to his sister Ellie. She is as outgoing as he is reserved and is his only confidante. She graduated from Brown last year, and he was upset when she decided to move to Chicago this past summer to work for a non-profit organization. She tries to come home once a month, and they talk on the phone weekly, but he misses having her around. She understands him in a way no one else in the family does.

The bar downstairs was packed so they decided to head upstairs to the loft. It was just as packed as the first floor, but Ellie managed to nab a table by the window and Peter headed straight toward the bar, shoving his way through the crowd to order them a round of drinks.

"Why are you pouting?" Ellie shouted over the din. "You've been in a pissy mood since I flew into town Wednesday night."

"It's nothing. School stuff," he muttered.

"I don't know why you bother lying to me," she countered. "You're the worst liar I've ever met, which is a good thing, but still. I know you, brother o'mine. Spill it."

Peter arrived with a tray of tequila shots and a pitcher of beer, enough to numb the senses, and Will sighed with relief, knocking back two shots in quick succession. His body relaxed as it absorbed the alcohol and he sat back in his chair, grabbing a third shot glass off the tray.

"I may be a bad liar, but I do know how to keep a secret," he replied, staring into his sister's eyes, so like his own.

Ellie raised an eyebrow, "Really? You have secrets? From me?"

Will chuckled and scanned the bar, doing a double take when his eyes came to rest on someone who looked an awful lot like Julia. *But it couldn't be.* She's too young to get into a bar.

He stood up and took a few steps toward her, then stopped, his heart pounding against his chest. *It is Julia!* Gulliver's was the absolute last place he expected to bump into her.

Will squeezed through the crowd and reached her just as she was turning toward the stairs. Emboldened with liquid courage, Will clutched her around the waist and covered her eyes with his other hand and she jumped with a start and grabbed his arm, trying to pry it off of her.

"You left without saying goodbye," he whispered in her ear.

He heard Julia gasp, her body rooted to the spot. A moment later she spun around and he smiled, his eyes searching her face. Before she could stop him, he pulled her close and his lips met hers for a long, slow kiss, the tip of his tongue grazing her teeth. She didn't resist his embrace, but she took a beat before responding, then wrapped her arms around him, returning his kiss.

When Will finally released his hold on her, Julia looked into his eyes, her cheeks flushed.

"Hi Will," she smiled.

He laughed and held her tight, had no intention of letting her escape again.

"Who are you here with?" he asked.

"My friend Gabby. You?"

"My brother and sister," He tilted his head toward the windows, "Come. I want you to meet them."

Her eyes opened wide, and she shook her head in protest, but he grabbed her hand, steering her across the loft and made the introductions. Peter predictably made a visual inspection of Julia and gave Will a thumbs up, prompting Will to roll his eyes in disgust.

"And this is my sister Ellie." His sister rose and shook her hand.

"It is so nice to meet you Julia. I've heard a lot about you."

"I've heard a lot about you too."

An attractive woman with straight light brown hair, wearing jeans, a fitted blue turtleneck sweater, and a scowl approached their table moments later and tapped Julia on the shoulder.

"Oh my god! Gabby, I'm so sorry." Julia cried. "I was on my way back downstairs when I bumped into my friend Will!"

"So you're the famous Will!" Her friend's eyes opened wide, "I was beginning to think you were a figment of Julia's imagination. But here you are, in the flesh!"

"Has Julia been talking about me?" Will asked, rising to shake Gabby's hand.

"Hmmm…you could say that. Or was that some other guy named Will you were talking about, Jules?" Gabby coyly smiled at Julia, batting her eyelashes.

Introductions made, Gabby sat in the empty seat across from Will, beside Ellie.

"So…" Gabby leaned across the table toward him, "Now that I know you're real, let me ask you a question." She crooked her finger, beckoning him to come closer.

He laughed and leaned in, eyebrows raised. "When, dear Will, are you going to ask our fair Juliet out on a proper date? I mean, hanging out on docks, looking at the stars is romantic, sure, but how about dinner at a restaurant? A movie at the Showcase?"

Will opened his mouth to speak, then closed it and turned toward Julia with a smile, while Gabby and Ellie stared at him expectantly. He had every intention of asking Julia out on a 'proper date' but he wasn't going to do it in front of an audience.

Julia's face had turned beet red and she rose to her feet, saying, "I need a drink. Anyone want a drink?" All hands flew into the air. "I'll grab a couple of pitchers," she said and made her way to the bar, Will close behind her.

Five months later, he's sitting at Rockwell Park, kicking himself for being so insensitive to Julia's feelings at the wedding the night before. They'd come so far since Thanksgiving. Every time they were together, they grew a little closer, a bit more intimate. He never pushed her, sensing there was more to her reluctance than modesty, afraid she would disappear if he moved too fast.

Freezing on the dock, Will finally understood how deeply she'd been hurt by her parents' divorce, made the connection between the pain she'd experienced and her need to keep him at arms length.

He closed his eyes and hung his head in shame. He didn't need to have a talk with Ellie about his relationship with Julia. He finally gets it.

Julia's afraid of being abandoned.

And that's exactly what he did last night at the wedding. He left her to fend for herself and unintentionally fed her to the wolves.

Chapter Five

Julia has no desire to see Will. It's almost Memorial Day, her semester is just about over and she'd prefer to stay in New York this summer. She's been kicking herself over the past six weeks for being so stupid, for letting herself fall in love with Will. She knows better!

Since the wedding, Will's called her and left a few messages on her machine. She spoke to him once, an incredibly awkward conversation. He apologized, she made small talk. He's trying to make things better, but she doesn't see how that's possible. *I don't even know who he is!* And Julia doesn't want any part of the world Will introduced her to that night. If that's the sphere he operates in, he can do it without her.

She was offered a job as a live-in nanny in the Hamptons for the summer and had accepted it, but was forced to back out when her father called the night before her last final. Her grandmother had a heart attack and wasn't doing well. In a panic, Julia rented a U-Haul, loaded it, and was on the road the second she finished her exam the next day.

The first time Julia visited the hospital, she was afraid to approach the bed. Her grandmother was hooked to all kinds of machines with lights blinking on and off, an IV taped to her arm. Gram looked so tiny, so fragile. She's always been small, but she seemed to shrink considerably since Julia's last visit home.

Hospitals have always made her uncomfortable, and she avoids them if at all possible. When her other grandmother was dying, Julia hardly visited her and still regrets it. She won't do that again, she couldn't live with herself if she wasn't there for Gram. Julia tiptoed across the room and sat in the chair beside her bed, holding and kissing her grandmother's hand.

A few minutes later, Gram woke up and her face lit up when she saw Julia sitting by her side.

"Julietta! My angel." Julia burst into tears. "No, no. Don't cry."

"Gram, don't ever do this again!" she cried, scolding, then kissed her sweet face.

"My Juliet, we all have to go sometime." Gram laughed, "But don't you worry, my time isn't up yet."

Her grandmother has been upbeat with her many visitors, and the nurses adore her. Gram spends her days watching her soaps and gossiping with family and friends, much like she does when she's holding court at home.

Every day over the past two weeks, Julia has driven to Newport Hospital to visit her. The family takes shifts throughout the day and Julia is due at the hospital for the six to nine o'clock evening shift.

Today, she made it to the hospital in record time. Summer traffic in Newport sucks. It can be a nightmare with the influx of thousands of summer vacationers congesting the roads.

She pushed opened the door, her eyes scratchy with fatigue. Whenever she comes home to Rhode Island from the city she has a hard time sleeping. It's the silence. She's become accustomed to city noise around the clock, sirens, horns blaring, people yelling, and music booming through the walls of her dorm room. The first few weeks she spends in the absolute quiet of her hometown, the ringing in her ears seems louder than the noise she left behind.

"She's doing really good today Jules." Her aunt and uncle greet her as she walks into the room. She kisses them both on each cheek. "Looks like they're going to spring her Friday."

Oh thank god! They fill her in on today's doctor's visits, her vitals, medications, and meals.

"She doesn't like the chicken salad," Auntie Linda whispers.

"That isn't food!" her grandmother chimes in, "Who cooks this shit?"

Julia bites her lip. *Gram's back!*

"So fill me in," Julia settles into the chair beside the hospital bed, "Who's running around behind whose back today?"

Her grandmother is obsessed with *One Life to Live*. Julia doesn't watch soap operas, but Gram loves to share their evil doings.

"I know you don't like the soaps Julietta."

"Oh, but I love listening to you tell me about them!"

"Not today my sweetheart. I want to talk to you."

"What's wrong Gram?" She leans forward and stares at her grandmother's face.

"With me? Not a thing. With you? A whole lotta something."

"I'm fine Gram. Really. Just tired." She takes a deep breath, holding her grandmother's hand.

"Don't bullshit me Julia."

She frowns. *Gram never calls me Julia, only Julietta.*

"It's boy trouble, yes?" Reluctantly, Julia nods. "Is it that boy you brought to the house?"

Again she nods. Julia brought Will to her grandmother's house over Thanksgiving weekend. Every Sunday morning, dozens of relatives and friends cram into her grandmother's tiny apartment to partake of her legendary meatballs, and before Will dropped Julia off at the train station that Sunday, they made a pit stop. Will wanted to see for himself what the fuss was about. He wasn't disappointed.

"Tell me what happened," Gram said, squeezing her hand.

Gram listened to her talk for close to an hour, patting her hand sympathetically, and wiping away Julia's tears.

"I thought I loved him, Gram," she sighs, "I'm so confused. He's two different people."

"Who is he when he's with you, my Juliet? That's what's important, the person he is with you. He was raised in a different world, but it sounds like he wants something different from what he knows. He wouldn't be with you if he wanted more of the same."

"Even if that's true, Gram, it could never work."

"Julietta, mi amore. Says who? Some nincompoops who don't know you? Forget about them. There are only two people who matter. You and your Romeo. Follow your heart my angel. It's not every day you meet someone who feeds your soul."

If only it were that simple! Julia rested her head on the hospital bed, her grandmother gently stroking her hair.

"I love you my little angel."

"I love you too, Gram."

A little after nine, her grandmother sound asleep, Julia fixes her blanket and kisses her on the forehead before making the journey home.

It took Julia hours to fall asleep once she left the hospital, her grandmother's words echoing in her head. *Only two people matter...me and Will.* Those are the last words she remembers before drifting off.

"Follow your heart..." her grandmother says, floating above her. Confused, Julia tries to hold her, pull her down onto her bed, but Gram's just out of her reach. "Goodbye my Julietta," she whispers, then kisses her cheek and disappears.

Julia wakes with a start, her heart racing, her nightgown clinging to her, damp with sweat. *Gram!* It's still dark outside, the middle of the night and she grabs the clock off of her nightstand. *Three forty-five.* She sits back against her pillows. *I had a dream.* At least, she thinks it was a dream…but it felt so real. It couldn't be real, could it?

She's gone. I feel it. Tears fall down her face. *No! Gram! Don't leave me!* Her grandmother has been the one constant adult presence in her life and now she's gone.

Julia sobs into her pillow until there aren't any tears left, then stares at her bedroom ceiling, waiting for the phone call she knows is coming. At six o'clock the phone finally rings and she reaches for it on her nightstand, her arms leaden.

"Hi Dad."

"Julia, she's gone. Gram died about two hours ago."

"I know," she whispers and places the handset on the receiver.

***

The Fourth of July is just two weeks away and the whole town is gearing up for the celebration. Normally Will enjoys the festivities, but this year he's not in the mood. He has a lot on his mind as he mows his parents' sizeable lawn. They have a gardener for the flowerbeds and to prune the trees and shrubs, but he and his siblings have always had household responsibilities and pitch in where needed. Mowing the lawn is his job and he doesn't mind doing it.

He loves his parents' property, its proximity to the water and the view of town across the harbor. Will's family has strong roots in Bristol. His mother, Ruth, was brought up on Poppasquash Neck and is the descendant of one of the town's first families.

Her family is old money, civic-minded philanthropists. Will never asked how the family came into their money, though he suspects it had something to do with the 'Triangular Trade' Julia told him about. He and his siblings have sizeable trust funds, but he can't touch the money until he's twenty-five. He doesn't want to, would prefer to make his own way in the world and save the money for his own children.

Will's father, Mitchell, comes from a very different background. He was raised in South Boston and has worked hard for his success. His grandparents emigrated from Ireland and didn't have 'two nickels to rub together' but they made sure his father was educated.

His father is a brilliant man with an analytical mind, a respected leader in the business community, and Will admires him tremendously. He attended Boston Latin, and worked his way through Harvard, winning the heart of Ruth Ellery in the process.

His mother attended Wellesley College and met his father there at a dance. Her family wasn't thrilled that she married outside of her faith and converted to Catholicism, but they grew to respect his father for his values, work ethic and determination.

It's warm out today and the sun is beating down on Will as he contemplates his next moves. He has an interview in Washington, DC next week and for once he's interested in the position. It's an entry-level government job with the Treasury Department.

Since spring, he's been working at Petersons Yachts, learning to build boats from the ground up and he loves it. He gets satisfaction working with his hands, building something that'll bring pleasure to other people. He's making pretty good money, but his father doesn't consider it a suitable career.

"I didn't pay for your education to watch you become a laborer. You'd be taking our family backwards, not forward.

Do you want to live like my father, slaving outdoors all day, scrimping pennies? I've worked hard to give you every opportunity in this world. I expect you to take advantage of your good fortune."

Except for leaving Princeton, Will's done everything expected of him, by his parents, and by his friends. Blindly, he's followed the path set out for him since birth and it doesn't feel right anymore. But he's tired of arguing with his father. They've always had an easy relationship and it's been strained since he finished his degree in December.

His father says he wants what's best for him. How can he possibly know what makes Will happy? He's never asked him what he wants. *Hell, I don't even know what I want!* He feels like he's just starting to figure things out for himself.

Last night, his mother came to his room to have 'a talk'.

"Will, what's going on with you? Why don't you take one of the jobs you've already been offered?" He sat on his bed and sighed. "What is it sweetheart?"

"Mom, my heart just isn't in finance. I don't know what to do."

"Well, dear, you could've changed your major at any time, but you didn't." She patted his knee, "No one told you to go into Daddy's field."

He thought about going into engineering when he transferred to PC, but he didn't. He wanted to make his father proud, so he chose to follow in his footsteps. It's his own fault, he put himself in this situation. The last thing Will wants to do is disappoint his parents again, and after his mother left his room last night he realized he has to learn to live with his choice.

This position in Washington is a compromise in his eyes. His father wants him to get a job in the private sector, but at the very least Will needs to find greater meaning in his work, even if he is a small cog in a giant machine. He'd rather contribute to the greater good than work for an equity firm making a few rich people, richer. It's not in his nature to make waves, and it's time to make peace with his father.

Since the wedding, he's stayed away from the yacht club except to go sailing on his dad's boat, and has for the most part avoided his old circle of friends. The few times he's been in their company he felt awkward. They're strangers to him now.

Something shifted in him, he's looking at everything through a new set of lenses and he doesn't like what he sees. He was struck by how much his friends value appearance over substance and couldn't believe he never noticed that before. There's a total disconnect between the life Will was living and these new feelings of dissatisfaction. Even when he was hanging out with his friends he felt lonely and that is an unfamiliar, uncomfortable feeling. Moving away from Rhode Island would be a good thing…a new beginning.

He misses Julia so much. He's replayed the night of the wedding a thousand times in his head, what he can remember of it. The guys did leer at her. They made comments to him about how sexy she was, and how lucky he was to have a 'hot little number' like her. He didn't stop them. He was proud to have Julia with him and objectified her as much as they did.

Julia is beautiful. She is sexy.

But the difference is he loves her. If he thinks those things, he should tell Julia, not some jerks. When he told Ellie what Julia shared about her experience at the wedding, his sister stared at him, wide-eyed, mouth hung open. Finally, she shook her head and walked out of his room, saying, "I've got nothing."

Neither do I.

Julia doesn't want to talk to him, she's made that very clear. He's left four messages on her mother's machine since her semester ended and she hasn't called him back. He wants the opportunity to make things right but isn't sure how to get her to listen to him, to understand just how sorry he is, to prove he's not like her father. He'll never abandon her again.

Covered in sweat, dirt and grass, Will finishes mowing the lawn, puts away the mower then heads to the front yard to pick up the shirt he left there earlier. Walking around the house, he turns the corner and stops in his tracks.

"Julia."

She's standing at the foot of his parents' driveway, kicking a rock back and forth with her feet. They stare at each other for a long moment, then she runs to him, throwing her arms around his neck. He's speechless, a rush of warmth spreading through his body. *She's here.* He can feel her body shaking while he holds her.

"Gram died last night," she whispers into his neck.

"Oh Julia, I am so sorry," he breathes into her hair, stroking her back.

They embrace in his driveway for several minutes and he tries to quiet the thoughts flying around in his head. He could try to analyze what this means, her being here, but all he wants to do is hold her. Eventually, he kisses the top of her head and leans back so he can see her face, his arms still around her, afraid to let go.

"You're all sweaty," she grimaces, wrinkling her nose.

"Come in. Give me five minutes to rinse off and let's get out of here."

She smiles weakly, "Okay."

***

After Will showers, they climb into his Jeep and head downtown. Neither of them has eaten breakfast and Julia suggests Hope Diner, thinking a little comfort food is in order.

She hasn't been there in months, not since she brought Will there last November. The diner is a local institution, her father used to take her there every Saturday morning, and to her surprise, Will had never been before.

On the drive across town she stares out the car window and rests her hand on Will's thigh. The moment she wrapped her arms around him in his parents' driveway she felt the pain draining from her body and was comforted by his presence.

Gram's gone... she can't wrap her head around it. She wants Will to drive to her grandmother's house, to open the kitchen door and find Gram behind the stove, cooking up a batch of meatballs.

My Julietta... She can actually feel her grandmother's fingers pinching her cheeks and her eyes fill with tears as Will pulls into the lot at Hope Diner. Nothing ever changes here. Julia finds comfort in that.

"Will! How are ya fella?" Maria greets them as they enter. "And Jules! Come here darlin', it's been too long!"

Maria remembers his name from Thanksgiving?

"Hey Will, Sox lost last night." Tommy pokes his head around the corner, "You owe me a dolla."

"I know, I know," Will walks over to Tommy, hands him the money, and they shake hands, "Best out of five?"

"Nah, the Cahds will sweep this. Did ya see how they played last night? Makes me wanna be a Yankee fan."

Will cringes and holds up his hand, "Blasphemy!"

"Ah, Jules!" Tommy notices her standing beside Maria, mouth agape. "Welcome back, kid!"

She walks over to the grill, dazed, and kisses him on the cheek.

"What's going on here?" she asks.

"Whaddya mean?"

She raises her eyebrows and waves her arm around indicating Will, Tommy, Maria.

"Oh, Will comes in here all the time now, don't ya handsome?" Maria says flirtatiously, a twinkle in her eye. Will leans down and kisses Maria on the cheek, making the portly fifty-year-old waitress blush.

Julia opens her mouth to speak, but nothing comes out. She's absolutely stunned by this turn of events, and begins to laugh. Nothing could've surprised her more!

"What?" Will grins.

"How long have you been coming here?"

"Oh, a few months now. I work at the boatyard and usually stop here for breakfast."

The boatyard?

"When did you start working there?"

"In April," he says, the corners of his mouth turning down a fraction of an inch.

"Oh."

"What will you two loves have today?" Maria seats them by the window, "The usual?" They both nod. "Got it."

"Jules, I really am so sorry for your loss. I only met her that one time…I'm glad I did. She must've been very special."

Her eyes fill with tears remembering how her tiny grandmother pointed her finger at Will when she brought him to the house, telling him to treat Julia right, then reached up, pinched his cheeks and winked before shoving a bowl of meatballs into his hands.

"Thanks, Will," she pauses, "You know, my conversation with her, last night…" her voice trails off…*was it really last night?* She turns away from him, her eyes unfocused. "Our last conversation was about you."

Will takes her hand in his and raises his eyebrows, expectantly. She hesitates, then smiles and shakes her head, wrinkling her nose. She doesn't want to share what Gram said with him yet, and resting her head in her free hand, looks out the window at the boats bobbing in the harbor.

***

The funeral home is overflowing. Julia's grandmother was a beloved woman in the community and the line of mourners extends out the door and around the corner.

Will still doesn't know what her grandmother said to Julia, but it brought her back to him and he'll always be grateful.

Thank you, Gram.

Beside the coffin are pictures of her family, the photos her grandmother had hanging in her tiny parlor. Will smiles when he notices the photograph of Gram and Joe Montana displayed prominently by her side.

When he went to her grandmother's for meatballs, Will saw the picture and questioned Julia. Someone had pasted her grandmother's face on a much younger woman's body in the picture. Julia said her uncle made it and explained her eighty-five year old grandmother was desperately in love with the thirty-year-old pro quarterback. He burst out laughing and Julia said, "Hey! Joe could return the feelings. You never know!"

Tonight, Julia is standing beside her cousins in the receiving line, wearing a plain black dress, hair pulled back in a ponytail, her face pale. She's anxious about spending time with her father and stepmother tonight and asked him to stay until the end of the wake. Except for once at the hospital, this is the first time she's been in their company since before their falling out last Christmas.

Will still can't believe her father, *any father for that matter*, would call his daughter and tell her to not come to Christmas dinner, explaining that it would make his new wife uncomfortable. He's been watching the interaction between Julia and her dad all night. There's no warmth there, even in this time of sorrow.

He wants to punch her father in the face and make him feel real pain, then wrap his arms around Julia and protect her from his cruel indifference. She once said she'd never forgive him for leaving her mother or for siding with her stepmother, but he can see the hurt in her eyes. If her father showed remorse and tried to make things right, Julia would forgive him. She's stubborn, and can hold a grudge, but she's also forgiving. The fact that he's here is proof.

"You know, you really hurt her." Gabby takes a seat beside him in the back of the funeral parlor.

"I know," Will says and cringes, waiting for the verbal onslaught. He's always appreciated Gabby's candor, she reminds him of Ellie that way, but tonight he steels himself for her wrath. She must hate him after what he did to Julia. He deserves whatever she throws his way.

"How do I put this delicately?" she pauses, contemplative. "Sorry, not possible. Your friends are assholes."

"I know." He nods his head, contrite.

They sit in silence for a minute.

"I don't think you're an asshole," she says, elbowing him.

"Thanks Gabby," he smiles, taken aback. *That's a good sign.*

"Don't get me wrong, Will, I think you're an asshole around those people you call friends, but not deep down. You know what I'd do if I were you? Cut the cord. Those people are only going to drag you down to their level."

Will looks at his hands, and nods. He's been thinking the same thing and wants to put as much distance as possible between himself and Poppasquash.

"You want to know what I think?"

His eyes grow wide, he's not sure he wants to know, but Gabby continues.

"I think she makes you a better person. And I think you know that."

"Yeah. She does." He bobs his head in agreement. *What's Julia's nickname for Gabby again? Buddha?*

"Everyone is entitled to make a mistake. That wedding was yours. You don't get to make another one of that magnitude." Gabby pauses, "Look…I know this is none of my business, but I love Julia and she cares about you. In all the years I've known her, Julia has never let her guard down for any man. Only you."

"Is that true?" Tears prick the back of his eyes and he quickly looks down.

"I've never seen her as happy. Or as sad," she says, solemnly.

He rests his head in his hands, and discreetly wipes a tear away.

"You made a huge mistake at that wedding, Will. She was finally ready to open up to you that night. Did you know that?"

Will closes his eyes, takes a deep breath, and shakes his head. He felt it, but he didn't know for sure.

"Do you have any clue how hard that was for her? As I'm sure you've noticed by now, trust doesn't come easily for Julia. She thought she knew you, but after the wedding she felt like she didn't know you at all. She doesn't trust herself or her judgment, which is really sad."

They sit together in silence while Will rubs his throbbing temples.

I hurt her. Julia doesn't trust me.

Gabby isn't saying anything he doesn't already know. But hearing it from someone else, her best friend, is painful.

"So, Will…what's your plan? I'm trying to help you, but…I don't know…" she hesitates, "It might be too late."

"Why do you say that?" he asks, startled. *Too late?*

"She started dating someone when she went back to New York."

Will gasps, his eyes wide. Gabby knocked the wind right out of him.

"She's seeing someone?" he whispers.

"Oh, Will…" she smiles and pats his knee, "Did you think she'd always be available? Julia's the real deal, but you already know that. I think you two could have something special." Gabby looks directly into his eyes, "Don't fuck it up."

She stands abruptly and walks away.

She's dating someone… Of course he knew it was a possibility. Lots of men have probably asked her out, but she never talks about that part of her life, and he doesn't like to think about the men she meets in New York.

He's been in denial.

He's had the opportunity to date other women over the past year, but hasn't wanted to, *especially* since April. Julia's been on his mind constantly, and the few women he's met don't interest him at all.

He wants to know about the guy she's seeing. *Is it serious?* He can't ask her, but the question is gnawing at his stomach. He can't stand the thought of another man touching her. His heart aches knowing he's responsible for this, he pushed her into someone else's arms.

Gabby seems to think he still has a chance with Julia. That's promising, but if he has to settle for friendship, he has only himself to blame.

Ellie's home for the holiday weekend and Will pulled her aside almost the second she walked through the door, and lead her down to the dock near their parents' house. This has always been their spot, where they share confidences and dispense advice to one another.

He needs to come up with a plan to gain Julia's trust. Since the wake, he's spent a lot of time with Julia, but she's kept him at arm's length.

"What should I do, El?"

"I'm not sure what you're asking, Will. She's forgiven you, which makes her a better person than me! Or is it 'than I?' I can never remember…"

"Nice Eleanor. Way to make a guy feel good."

"William, it's going to take time for her to trust you again. If she didn't care about you she wouldn't have shown up at the house the morning her grandmother died. She wouldn't have asked you to stay with her after the wake. She wouldn't take the time to see you at all after that nightmare wedding you took her to. Time. Just keep doing what you're doing!"

"I'm moving to DC next week," he sighs, lying down on the dock, "That doesn't give me much time."

"Did you think you were going to win her heart in a week?" she laughs, "And then what? Disappear for weeks at a time?" Ellie lies down beside him, her arms behind her head, "The situation is different now."

"How so?"

"You two had a fire raging and you doused it pretty good. Is the spark still there?"

"For me, yes. I'm not sure about Julia. We get close, then she pulls away."

"Sorry, brother, I don't have any words of wisdom for you. If it's meant to be, it'll be. You can't force this to happen. You can't make her trust you."

He sits up and grabs a rock, throwing it forcefully into the water. That's not what he wanted to hear. He thought Ellie would be able to help him.

"I'm curious, why are you so anxious to turn this into a relationship now?" she asks. "You weren't in any hurry over the past year. Why now?"

He pauses, considering whether he should tell her, then sighs.

"She's seeing someone in New York. At least, she was. I'm pretty sure she hasn't seen him since May."

"How do you know this?" Ellie sits up, her eyes narrowing, "Did Julia tell you?"

"No, she hasn't mentioned him at all. Her friend Gabby told me at her grandmother's wake."

"And now you're desperate to declare your feelings to her?" Ellie lifts an eyebrow, "Because you're afraid she's going to run off with another guy?"

He stares at his sister, his brows drawn together and Ellie rises, shaking her head.

"Fucking men!" she hisses, and walks back to the house.

***

Julia's floating on a raft in her pool beside Gabby and looks at the sky, watching the clouds transform as they drift by. She studies the billowing white shapes above her. *I see a mermaid...I see a horse.* She spent hours playing this game when she was little. *There goes a shark and a monkey...*

It's been a month since her grandmother's funeral and she's seen Will almost daily since then, but she doesn't want to think about him right now. All she wants is to relax, but Gabby is making it impossible.

"Jules, Will is crazy about you. What do you want to do?"

"Right now? I want you to close your mouth and leave me alone. Let me float in peace in my sea of tranquility."

"Sea of tranquility?" Gabby jumps up and down in the pool, making waves, and splashing Julia, "How's that for tranquility?"

"Okay, okay! Stop!" Julia shouts. With resignation, she realizes there will be no peace today, at least not until Gabby gets some answers. "I don't know what I want. I enjoy his company. How's that?"

"An unacceptable response." Gabby's lips are pursed, a furrow forming between her brows, "Julia, your grandmother's last words, *Follow your heart!* What does your heart tell you?"

Julia raises an eyebrow. She doesn't trust her heart. She let down her guard, and opened herself up to Will, only to have him prove she may have been right about love all along.

"My heart says it's confused and to leave it alone. Why is that so hard for you to understand?"

"Are we back there? Really, Julia? Sweetie, you're gonna have to open your heart to someone, sometime," Gabby sighs, "Why not Will?"

"Because of the Montagues and the Capulets."

"Who?"

"From *Romeo and Juliet.* We're star-crossed lovers, from different worlds, just like in *Romeo and Juliet,* and look how that turned out!"

"Oh my god. You're comparing your situation to *Romeo and Juliet?* Your families are not at war! Julia, please take this seriously," Gabby begs. "Please? For just one minute?"

"Why does this matter so much to you? We're talking about my love life here, not yours! Ever since Gram's funeral you've been pushing Will on me. Why? You hardly know him!"

"I want you to take a risk for once! Tear down the goddamned wall you've built, like they did in Berlin, one cement block at a time."

"Nice touch, Gab. Trying to lure me in with a history reference. Can't you see that I don't need a man to be happy? I'm quite content on my own, thank you."

"Exactly, which is how I know you're ready for this. If Will came into your life two, three years ago, no way. You weren't ready to be in a relationship back then, but now? You're ready, Jules. Don't squander this chance with Will. You love him, I know you do. And, Jules, he loves you, it's written all over his face."

Julia sighs, resting her arms on the raft.

"Gabby, you're right, I've never felt anything like this, and a few months ago I was willing to take that chance, but after that wedding...Love isn't always enough. You have to be able to live together, co-exist on the same playing field. Our lives are too different."

"How can you say that? You grew up in the same town. You were both raised Catholic. So his parents live in a fancy house, he attended private school, and has a trust fund? Who cares? You aren't from different freakin' planets! His family likes you. Does it really matter if the people he grew up with are narrow-minded assholes? They don't mean anything."

"That's where you're wrong, Gabby. You weren't at that wedding. You didn't see what I saw or feel what I felt. I am not welcome there, Gab, not unless I'm in a maid's uniform. Will can't stay away from that life forever. Right now he's angry with them, but it'll pass, and he'll be right back at the yacht club, acting like someone stuck a pole up his butt. Talking about Figawis and trips to Aspen."

"You're too young to be this cynical, Jules."

"I don't think I'm cynical, Gab, I'm trying to be realistic! Fine. Let's take his friends out of the equation. Will just got a job in Washington, DC! He's moving there next week. Logistics! I'll be in New York, he'll be in DC. That's over three hours away. How can that work? I still have another year of school. We'd hardly ever see each other. Why bother starting something that doesn't have a chance of getting off the ground? It just doesn't make sense."

"See!" Gabby throws her hands up in frustration. "That's your problem right there! Love doesn't make sense. You just have to be willing to take a chance."

"Well, I'm not willing. Not now."

"Really? Then answer this question and I'll leave you alone. If you're not willing, as you say…why do you spend every night with him?"

Julia reclines on the raft and folds her arms across her chest, clenching her jaw tight to keep from saying the words that instantly came to mind… *because I can't stay away from him…*

"Can't answer that one, huh?" Gabby snorts. "Fine. I'll keep my mouth shut."

Chapter Six

Summer will soon turn to fall, the evenings already have a chill in the air as Julia prepares to begin her final year of college. After this year she's officially on her own, and it's a liberating, albeit scary thought. As horrible as things are with her father, he still pays her tuition and her rent. They've never discussed it, but Julia assumes her dad will end her support as soon as she graduates. She's always had safety nets, and come June, they're gone.

She's moving into her first real apartment this weekend and has been packing for days, going through boxes of her grandmother's dishes, silverware, pots and pans before everything is sent to Goodwill. She doesn't want to use her savings if she doesn't have to.

Julia and her friend Rhonda found an off-campus apartment in Brooklyn Heights, a relatively short subway ride from her university. It's small, with two bedrooms, an eat-in kitchen, and a decent sized living room with an incredible view of the Manhattan skyline and the Brooklyn Bridge.

Will has called her often since his move to Washington last month, but he hasn't shared much about his new life. He seems to like his job, has gone out for drinks with people from the office a few times, and been to a couple of Red Sox-Orioles games in Baltimore, but other than that... nothing. She's tried to pry details from him, but he hasn't been very specific.

She hopes he's making new friends in Washington. If he had Ellie's huge, outgoing personality she wouldn't worry, but his shyness can be misconstrued as aloofness, and that could be a problem. She doesn't want him to be lonely. On the flipside, maybe his reluctance has to do with a woman. He could be dating someone and doesn't want to tell her. How would she feel if he was dating another woman? Her stomach twists into knots at the thought.

Before he moved Will made it pretty clear he wanted to pick up where they left off before the wedding, but she chose to keep the status quo. It wasn't easy. All of their late night swims, bonfires on the beach, walks through the woods, talking until dawn. Time passes so quickly when they're together.

By the time he left for Washington, DC she was thoroughly confused. Admittedly, she loves him, she wants him, but she doesn't *trust him*. Not completely. He says he's through with the people he grew up with and that world of pretense and privilege. *Is he really?* She doesn't know. If she had the answer to that question, their relationship would be easy to decipher.

Old life? Friends. New life? Love. Simple!

There's one thing she's come to understand. It isn't a matter of whether he can operate in her world or she in his. The question is can they create a world of their own? That's the only way it'll ever work between them.

Right now he wants her, but until he figures out the direction he wants his life to take and has the conviction to stand by his choices, she can't risk getting involved with him.

Of course this wasn't obvious to her when she was around him every day, but since he's been gone, she's gained perspective. She can't lose sight of that, no matter what her heart desires.

"Are your parents helping you with the move?" Will asks during their now daily phone call. Lying across her bed with the cord wrapped around her hand, she stares at the boxes stacked around her bedroom.

"No. I've rented a U-Haul and I'll be okay. I don't have that much stuff." Actually, she does, but she doesn't want Will to feel sorry for her.

"Who is helping you then?"

"No one. I am moving myself into my apartment. Well, the bed and big stuff is being delivered earlier this week, but my clothes, books, and boxes, yes. I'm strong Will, I can handle it!"

"I'm going to meet you there," he says without hesitation.

"What? No, you don't have to do that…I'll be fine." She's startled by his generous offer.

"Julia, I'll drive up and help you. It's no big deal. I don't have any plans this weekend."

She pauses, wondering if this is a good idea. Spending the weekend alone in her apartment with Will? That could be a disaster. She had a hard enough time limiting their touching to hugs, holding hands, innocent kisses, and a bit of snuggling in the weeks leading up to his move.

But over the past month her resolve returned. She thinks she could handle spending a day or two with him without getting intimate.

"Thanks Will. That'd be great. I think a friend of mine is having a party Saturday night. Would you like to come with me? Or do you want to go see your brother?"

"I'd love to go with you. Let me get a pen. I need your address."

There's a reason people with money leave New York City in the summer… it's a hot mess. The sun beats down relentlessly on the city streets and sidewalks, steam rising, the air thick with humidity and the foul stench of millions of bodies confined to close quarters.

It's slightly more bearable in Brooklyn, the trees lining the streets giving the impression of fresh air and more open spaces.

They planned their travels so they'd arrive in Brooklyn at approximately the same time. A little after ten Saturday morning, Julia pulls the rented truck up to her new apartment building and spots Will's Jeep parked in front. He's leaning against his car with a big grin, looking impossibly handsome in his khaki shorts and light blue t-shirt.

Her heart skips a beat at the sight of him, and she closes her eyes, takes a deep breath, and remembers the promise she made to herself before she pulled out of the driveway this morning.

Perspective! Do not let your heart take over rational thought.

"How long have you been here?" she smiles, stepping down from the cab of the truck.

"Just a few minutes. Good timing!" Will picks her up and swings her around. "It's so good to see you Jules!"

"You too, Will," she sighs, her resolve melting as his arms tighten around her. This is going to be much harder than she thought…

It takes them almost an hour to carry in all of her boxes. Her apartment is in an old brownstone and there's no elevator, so they've had to carry everything up two flights of stairs with every trip.

Thank god Will's here, is the only thought running through Julia's head by the time they finish. She thought she was going to pass out about half way through, though Will's done the majority of the heavy lifting, carrying three boxes for every one of hers.

She still can't believe he drove three hours to help her move in. She's so used to doing things for herself, it never occurred to her to ask anyone for help with this move. Having been the de facto adult in her life for so long… it's nice to lean on someone for a change.

Once everything is in the apartment and her boxes are stacked in the appropriate rooms, Will opens his tool chest and goes straight to work, hanging curtain rods and shades, and putting her bookshelves together.

Watching him from the corner of her eye, Julia unpacks her clothes and books, then makes her bed, increasingly surprised by how organized and efficient Will is, qualities she's never had occasion to witness before now.

"Do you need something?" Will asks, interrupting her musings.

"Huh? What?" she sputters, dropping a pillow.

"Julia, you're standing there staring at me," Will laughs. "I thought maybe you needed my help."

She shakes her head, trying to snap herself out of her fog.

"No…no. Just tired."

Will rises and massages her shoulders, and it feels so good, she tilts her head back and leans against him, a groan escaping from her lips.

"Do you want to take a break?" Will whispers in her ear, sending waves of desire through her body, her knees almost buckling beneath her.

Julia turns around and studies his face, can see the longing in his eyes, a reflection of her own. She's bites her lip, the heat rising to her cheeks, and takes a step back. *This isn't supposed to happen*, she reminds herself, and folds her arms across her chest, a barrier between them.

"Sure," she forces herself to adopt a cheery tone, and turns away from him. "We've been at this forever." Julia walks toward the door and straightens out her ponytail. "I'm starving. Let's grab something at the deli around the corner. My treat."

Will remains in the spot she left him, his eyes narrowing.

"I'll go," he says. "You get some rest."

While Will's out, Julia grabs a blanket, lays it across her bed and collapses with a sigh. That was a close call...way too close for comfort. And he seemed upset before he left. What is she supposed to do? They've only spent four hours together and she's ready to cave. How is she going to make it through the next thirty-six hours?

They need distraction. There's the party tonight...and she can take him sightseeing in the city tomorrow before work. *But what about the sleeping arrangements?* She never thought about where Will would sleep this weekend. Her roommate's bed hasn't been delivered yet. *This is bad.* She set herself up for failure.

Julia closes her eyes, desperately trying to drown out her own thoughts, and was about to drift off to sleep when Will returns with their sandwiches.

"Jules?" he calls out as he enters the apartment, then sits on the edge of the bed, his hand on her arm and whispers, "Are you hungry?"

Mmm hmm," she murmurs, her eyes closed.

Will rifles through the kitchen cupboards in search of glasses and plates. *I really should go into the kitchen and help him, he must be exhausted too.* But it feels so nice to be taken care of.

Will takes care of me.

The thought drifts into her consciousness and wakes her from her sleepy state. He's been taking care of her since Gram died, from the moment she ran into his arms in his parents' driveway. Even after he moved to Washington, he's called her regularly, checking in.

How did I not see this before now? And what does it mean? Does he think she's fragile? That she needs looking after? Or is it because of what happened at the wedding? That's the most likely answer. Guilt is a big theme in Will's life. She doesn't want him to feel like he has to 'make things right' with her.

Will returns to the bedroom and sets their sandwiches down on the nightstand then hands her a glass of ice water and sits back on the bed while she studies him.

"Julia, you're doing it again," he raises an eyebrow and takes a bite of his sandwich.

"Will, you know you don't owe me anything, right?"

"Where did that come from?"

"You've been so good to me..." she shrugs, "I know you feel bad about what happened at the wedding...We had a bad day. I don't want you to do things for me out of guilt or a sense of obligation."

Will sets down his plate and turns toward her, sliding his fingers through hers.

"Jules, I want to do things for you, help you if I can... because I care about you. No other reason."

Her lips part and her heart pounds against her ribcage. Will leans in and kisses her softly, his hands cupping her face.

"Julia...I..."

Her eyes open wide. She knows what he's going to say and she's not ready for this. She covers his mouth, interrupting him.

"No... don't say it."

Will removes her hand, his forehead resting against hers.

"Why?" he asks, his eyes sad and hurt.

"Because it's a four-letter word. Because once you say it you can't take it back."

She closes her eyes and he squeezes her hand.

"Julia, I won't ever hurt you again."

"Will..." she pauses, "No one can make that promise."

The party is in full gear by the time they make their arrival. Earlier this afternoon, after the big talk, they took showers and napped for a few hours, then got a bite to eat before the party. They didn't discuss the four-letter word again.

Will drove them over the Brooklyn Bridge and followed her directions to her friend Anna's brownstone in Greenwich Village. The place is packed, people are sitting on the front steps and dozens more are crammed into the first floor of the building. Julia greets several friends as they make their way to the overcrowded backyard.

The yard is small, more like a patch of grass with brick walls enclosing the space, a mini fortress. Grass is a luxury in Manhattan and people pay a fortune for a bit of green. Fairy lights are strung up and a fire pit is roaring toward the back of the courtyard.

Julia grabs a couple of beers from the cooler near the door, hands one to Will, and leads him to the side of the patio where several of her friends are gathered. Will is soon engaged in a conversation with a couple of her classmates and Anna leads Julia across the courtyard.

"Hey gorgeous."

"Brad!" Her heart stops beating and she holds her breath. "What are you doing here?"

She dated Brad briefly before she came home this summer. The match surprised a few of her friends. They said he wasn't really her type, which translated, meant, he's not an intellectual. But that's the beauty of not getting emotionally involved! You don't have a type.

Brad's in his late twenties, tall and very muscular, a bit rough around the edges, with a strong New York accent. They had a great time together, but she hasn't given him a thought since she left in May.

Gabby strongly disapproved of her tryst, accusing Julia of using Brad to get over Will. Well, yes, that's exactly what she was doing, and Julia wasn't ashamed to admit it. Brad used her for sex and she used him as a diversionary tactic. *He's very good at diversion.*

Worldly and wise in so many ways, Gabby is a romantic at heart and doesn't believe in casual sex. "How can something so intimate be casual?" she asked, not for the first time. "Easily," Julia responded. "Remove emotion, insert fun."

It's not very complicated.

Brad leans in for a kiss and connects with her cheek. *Dear God, not in front of Will!* She scans the crowd and watches him crossing the courtyard, in search of her.

"Come here, Jules…" Brad slips his arm around her waist and pulls her away from the fire pit, "I've got something to show you," he whispers seductively, kissing her neck.

"Whoa! Hold on there!" she says, disentangling herself from his grasp, then holding her arms out to ward off further contact.

"What's the problem, Julia?" he asks, annoyed.

"The problem, Brad…" Julia catches Will's eye. He's staring at them from the middle of the courtyard, apparently in a state of shock. "The problem is I'm not here alone," she smiles stiffly.

Brad stares at her vacantly for a moment, the light of understanding slowly flickering on. *It's true*, she silently concedes, *he's gorgeous, but not very bright*. That's what she liked most about him, she didn't have to think when they were together.

Seconds later, Will is standing beside her. He isn't smiling as he extends his hand toward Brad.

"Hi, I'm Will."

"Oh!" She freezes, flustered, and says, "Will, this is Brad. Brad, this is my… boyfriend Will," she winces as soon as the words tumble from her lips. *Why did I say that?*

"Nice to meet you, Brad." Julia watches the two men squaring off, warily shaking hands.

"Yeah, you too." Brad flexes the muscles in his chest and chuckles dismissively, "Will, is it?"

"Yes, I'm Will. Julia's boyfriend."

Brad nods, backing away, and extends his thumb and pinky, an imaginary phone. He places it near his face, and mouths, *call me*, as he turns away. *Shit!* Julia closes her eyes wondering how she's going to explain this one.

Will grabs her hand and leads her to a bench in the corner of the yard. It's still loud and crowded, but they have a modicum of privacy.

There, they sit in silence for a minute. *Two minutes.*

She has no idea what to say, can't begin to imagine what he's thinking. How would she feel if some girl wrapped her arms around him and kissed him in front of her? *Like shit.*

Finally, Will holds her hand to his mouth and kisses her palm, then takes a deep breath in before he speaks.

"I have no right to ask you this, but I want to know. Are you seeing Brad?"

"I was," she mumbles, and stares into the fire pit a few feet from where they're sitting, "Before I came home this summer."

"Are you still seeing him?"

"We didn't end things before I left," she shrugs and squeezes his hand, "Things change, Will. Things have changed."

He nods and they continue to sit in silence for a few more minutes.

"How did you meet him?"

"He works with the film studies department at NYU. He does the lighting and rigging for student projects."

Again, he nods, pensive.

"You take film classes?"

"No. I was in a student film last spring. One of my friends wrote the script and asked me to be in it."

"Was it serious?" he asks, the muscles in his jaw visibly tightening.

"No, it was a lighthearted comedy," she says, and Will raises an eyebrow. She giggles nervously, perfectly aware he wasn't asking about the film. "No. Not serious. At all."

Will takes a deep breath in and out, a semblance of a smile settling on his face.

"Want to play Truth or Dare?" he asks, wrapping an arm around her shoulder.

"What?" she chuckles, "Why?"

"I just realized I don't know a lot about your life outside of Rhode Island. You major in History and Museum Studies, that's what I know. But, acting in movies? Dating older men? What else don't I know? Why don't you ever tell me about your life in New York?"

"You haven't asked."

By the time they return to Julia's apartment, it's almost one o'clock in the morning. After their talk, they were able to relax and enjoy the party. Thankfully, Brad took off. *Out of sight, out of mind!* Her friends from school were only too eager to share stories about Julia's life in the Big Apple with Will. She can't imagine he'd have many more questions after tonight!

Should she have told Will about Brad? Maybe, but she didn't see the point. Brad was a fling, their month together about sex, nothing more. And in her defense, if one was needed, Will was out of the picture as far as she was concerned. He made her heart ache and she didn't like it.

"Is this okay?" she asks, carrying two glasses of ice and a bottle of vodka into her bedroom, offering one to Will. He nods and sits back on her bed.

"I can't thank you enough for all of your help today, Will. Really. You went above and beyond." She pours vodka into their glasses, then turns on her stereo.

"No problem, Jules. I'm glad I could help. Salute," he says, clinking his glass against hers.

"Cheers," Julia smiles.

They recline against the pillows on her bed, listening to music, and sip their drinks. The sexual tension in the room is palpable. She can touch it, can feel the energy swirling around their bodies, drawing them closer together. It's a powerful force, and Julia's resistance is dangerously low.

Will takes her hand in his and she closes her eyes, singing along to *Believe* by Lenny Kravitz. She's never really paid attention to the lyrics before. *I can have what I want if I believe in myself?* She frowns, mulling that over. *We want to be loved...*

That is all people want, isn't it? Can she do that? Love someone and be loved?

Feeling Will's body beside hers, she forgets why she shouldn't get involved with him. Could be the alcohol, but she knows she came up with very good, grown up reasons not to. Now, her mind is drawing a blank. All she knows is she wants to touch him...to feel his skin against hers...

Will brushes the hair away from her face, his fingertips tracing her cheekbones, then her lips and she's dizzy with longing. He caresses the slope of her neck, grazes her collarbone and rests his hand between her breasts. Her eyes are still closed and she can hardly breathe, but she doesn't want him to stop, will actually cry if he does stop.

He continues exploring the contours of her body, running his hands along its peaks and valleys, and she turns to him, slowly opening her eyes. Will searches her face. *He's waiting for a signal from me. He wants my permission to continue.*

"Will...I'm scared," she says, burying her face in his neck.

"Jules, it's me. Don't be nervous...I won't do anything you don't want me to do," he says, his voice so tender.

"Did you mean what you said earlier today?" she asks.

"The four letter word?"

"That, and the other thing."

Will places his finger under her chin and tilts her head. He nods, "I will never hurt you again Julia."

She rolls onto her back, biting her bottom lip, and stares at the ceiling. She wants to believe him. *You've just got to believe…in yourself.* She does want it. She loves Will and she wants to be loved by him. And if it turns out to be a huge mistake, she has Lenny Kravitz to blame.

Julia rolls back onto her side, facing him.

"I believe you."

Will exhales and smiles.

She touches his face and kisses him, tentatively at first, her desire, a slow burning fire spreading from her core to her outer limbs, the intensity of the heat growing, his hands and lips fueling the flames.

"Julia…I've wanted to do this since the day we met," he says, his hands sliding beneath her shirt. She aches to feel his skin against hers, to feel him inside of her. Will impatiently pulls off his shirt, then removes hers, his lips tracing a path from her stomach to her mouth.

The exploration has begun, their bodies humming with excitement. Will unhooks her bra, freeing her breasts and his tongue circles the hard peaks, his hands roaming her body.

Slowly they touch and taste, the pressure building, threatening to consume her. She's never felt this before, has never wanted someone so much, it physically hurts not to have him.

Julia slides off his boxers, and wraps her fingers around his length, stroking him, inviting him in. Will gasps and looks into her eyes.

"Yes," she nods, smiling.

His mouth comes down hard on hers while he removes her panties, then sinks his fingers into her. Julia arches her back and moans. *Please!* She's ready, her body writhing with anticipation. She feels the weight of him on her and sighs.

"Do you have something?" she whispers.

Will stops cold, his free hand covering his mouth.

"Oh my god," he murmurs, reaching for his wallet. "Please God, let me have one..." he mutters under his breath.

Will exhales, then shakes his head and she registers his disappointment.

"No, no, no, no, no!" she cries. *Are you frigging kidding me?!*

"This can't be happening," he groans, lying down beside her. "I don't suppose you keep a box around the house?"

"No...oh my god! No," she covers her face with her hands. "I need a cold shower," she mumbles.

"Well, then, I guess we're going to have to get creative," he says sliding down the bed, his lips between her thighs.

"Creativity is good," she whispers, her breathing uneven.

Julia is the first to wake later that morning and she is still, watching him sleep for a few minutes, a smile on her face. She slept soundly, their bodies molded together, his arms wrapped around her. Usually she likes her space in bed, but she feels well rested this morning.

Visions of last night flash through her head, his body, his taste, his touch and she's instantly turned on. They were uninhibited, passionate... Julia kisses Will's neck, his shoulder and he slowly stirs.

"Good morning," he smiles.

"Good morning," she says, raising an eyebrow. "We're naked..."

He stretches his arms and legs, and turns toward her, already hard.

"Yes, we are," Will murmurs, running his hand over her breasts, down her stomach, between her legs, and kisses her gently. His fingers find the spot he discovered last night, the one that makes her moan. She inhales sharply, her back arching.

"You didn't happen to stop by a drugstore while I was sleeping, did you?"

Julia shakes her head, and Will positions himself above her. She wraps her legs around him, ready to throw caution to the wind, but she knows he wouldn't dare. Will learned that lesson the hard way. She slowly kisses a path down his torso and takes him in her mouth.

"This will have to do for now."

He closes his eyes and sighs.

Chapter Seven

For Julia's twenty-first birthday, Will's planning something special. He has to attend a conference near Gettysburg, Pennsylvania for a few days and she's taking the train from New York to meet him there on Wednesday.

Some girls love champagne and roses, Julia would rather scour a battlefield or spend the day in a museum. And he knew that without her having to say a word. Thursday evening they're driving down to Will's place in Georgetown for the remainder of the weekend.

Being a European history major hasn't diminished her love of American history in the least. She's never been to Gettysburg and is excited to see for herself where this pivotal Civil War battle took place, and the graveyard where Lincoln delivered his famous address.

As soon as she got off the phone with Will, she ran to the library and checked out a few books on the siege, studying the maps and troop movements during the three-day battle.

"You know, most girls wouldn't find exploring a Civil War battlefield exciting," Will chuckled.

"This is my version of Disneyworld," she laughed over the phone, "Between Gettysburg and Washington, DC, I'll be in history heaven!"

"I had a feeling you'd like it…"

She hasn't laid eyes on Will in over two weeks, not since the weekend he helped move her into the apartment. Their

JAYNE CONWAY

time together was too brief and once she allowed herself to indulge in their passion, she found it almost impossible to tear herself away, a child with a bright, new, shiny toy she couldn't put down. And her 'toy' had a mind of his own, discovering all types of new ways to stimulate her.

Later that afternoon, she had to work at the museum and they frolicked in bed until the last possible second, quickly showered, and grabbed a bagel before Will dropped her off at the Met on his way back to DC. They talk on the phone most days but it's not the same.

As the train pulls into the station, she searches the platform for him. She's breathless with excitement, her skin tingling, anticipating his touch. When the train screeches to a halt, she grabs her bag from the overhead bin, and peeks out the window again. *Where is he?*

Before she descends the final step onto the platform, he's standing in front of her, smiling ear to ear. Julia freezes for a moment, her heart swelling in her chest, and leaps into his arms. Will holds her close and she breathes him in. She's always loved the way he smells, it's intoxicating. Her mouth finds his and they embrace, their kisses filled with longing.

"Where's your car?" she asks, anxiously. She can't wait any longer, and just in case he forgot, she brought her own box.

The drive to his hotel took twenty minutes, and as soon as Will shifts the car into park, they make a run for the lobby doors and reach his room half dressed, her arms wrapped around his chest. Will fumbles with the room key while she slides her hands down to unzip his pants.

"Jules, you keep doing that and I'll never get this door open."

They enter the dark room, removing what remains of their clothing, leaving a pile near the door.

"Miss Grasso…" he says with a wicked grin, "The things I'm going to do to you…" Will scoops her up over his shoulder and she squeals with pleasure as he carries her to the bed.

They spend the next few hours eagerly exploring each other's bodies, a blur of mouths, tongues, fingers, legs, skin, and exquisite release, after which they collapse in exhaustion, their limbs entwined.

"That was definitely worth the wait," she says, holding her hand to her chest, trying to catch her breath.

Will rolls on top of her, pinning her arms above her head, and covers her mouth with his hand.

"You're not going to stop me this time, Julia…I love you." Will releases her arms and removes his hand.

"Why?" she whispers, blinking back tears.

"Jules, when I'm with you, I feel… alive. Like we can take on the world together." He wipes away her tears, his lips meeting hers, "Remember my promise."

"Will…I'm so in love with you."

The following morning, Will and Julia drive to the battlefields of Gettysburg, investigating until the park closes, and then drive south, arriving at his place in Georgetown close to eleven that evening.

"Didn't JFK and Jackie own a place near here?" she asks when they pull up to his townhouse, "I remember reading that they lived on one of the alphabet streets. K? L? I don't remember…"

"You're close, they lived on N Street, not too far from here. I think that's why my father wanted to buy this place. Even though he's a Republican, he's a huge admirer of JFK."

On the first floor, Will walks her through the kitchen, a dining room with a table and chairs his parents gave him, an empty library with a stereo, and a living room with a fireplace. No couch, no end tables, nothing.

They walk up the stairs to the second floor, which includes Will's bedroom, bathroom, and walk-in closet. There's also a second, unfurnished bedroom and bath, and a den with a couch, television and built-in bookshelves. On the third floor is a third bedroom and bathroom, as empty as the rest of the house.

"Will, this place is huge! Where's your furniture?" she laughs.

"I haven't gotten that far yet," he buries his face in her neck, his hands wandering beneath her shirt. Will unhooks her bra with one hand, his other cupping her breast and kneels down, unbuttoning her jeans.

"Maybe we should eat something?" she suggests, her voice just above a whisper.

"Are you hungry?" he murmurs, pulling her pants over her hips to the floor. She reaches down and tugs off his shirt, running her fingers over his bare chest.

"Yes. Yes I am." She raises her arms and Will removes her shirt and bra, then lifts her off the ground, and carries her to his bedroom.

Julia wakes with a start, and reaches for Will, but the bed is empty and cold. "Will?" she calls out, her brow furrowed. It takes her a moment, but then she remembers, he's at work today and she's on her own. The alarm clock beside his bed says it's almost nine. He must have left two hours ago. On the nightstand beside the bed is a piece of paper, folded in half with her name written across it. She picks it up and reads…

I didn't want to wake you. See you tonight. I love you. W

She holds the note to her chest, smiling. *He loves me…* She lies in bed for a bit, looking around the room. The walls are bare. She doesn't see any photographs of his family. Just his bed, a nightstand, an old bureau and several stacks of books.

She climbs out of bed and finds a clipping from their hometown newspaper on his bureau, a grainy picture of her that was published last summer when they did *West Side Story*. She can't believe he kept it!

Last night, she didn't get a good look at his place. It was dark and some of the rooms don't have overhead lighting. Will has yet to buy any lamps. She pulls on a pair of leggings and one of his sweatshirts, and pads down the carpeted stairs. There's nothing homey about this place, nothing that indicates Will lives here. It's strange, cold and impersonal.

She looks through his kitchen cupboards, makes herself some tea and an English muffin, and tops it with peanut butter. There are a few spotty brown bananas on the counter, but she's too hungry to care.

Through the French doors leading to the backyard, she notices a lovely garden and heads to the patio carrying her breakfast. Whoever lived here before Will had a green thumb. Even in late September the garden is full of color, and Will seems to be maintaining it, or hired someone to do it.

On the flagstone patio is a lounge chair, and a small wrought-iron table with four chairs and a striped umbrella. She eats her breakfast and sips her tea, wondering what she should do next.

It's much quieter here in Georgetown than in New York. She's never liked silence, it invites unwelcome thoughts. She sits back and watches a bird splashing in the small bath next to the azaleas.

Since the weekend Will helped her move to Brooklyn, he's been on her mind, but she's kept herself busy with school and work. Her friends have been teasing her, saying she's been floating on a love-filled cloud for the past few weeks, a constant smile on her lips and a twinkle in her eye.

Sitting in the relative silence of Will's backyard, she frowns, unpleasant thoughts beginning to swirl in her head. Except for a lengthy phone call to share the news with Gabby, Julia hasn't had time to genuinely reflect upon their circumstances. When it's just the two of them it's so easy to forget the outside world, to overlook the differences that kept them apart.

Spending time with Will clouds her thinking. When they're together, she doesn't believe he'll ever come to resent her for keeping him from the world he knows. *But he might one day...* She'd give anything for the sound of sirens screaming and taxis blaring their horns right now!

We're in love! Julia's heart stops at the thought. *Love!* Her throat closes and she begins to hyperventilate, then leans over and rests her head between her legs, reminding herself to take deep breaths.

What does it even mean to be in love? To want to be with that person more than anyone? To give your heart away and trust he won't break it into a million pieces? Will promised he'd never hurt her again. She believes he'd never intentionally hurt her, but that doesn't mean he won't hurt her. There are no guarantees.

Julia runs into the kitchen, picks up the phone and dials Gabby's number. Her friend will have some advice, some soothing words of wisdom. After five rings the call goes to her answering machine. *Goddammit!* Julia slams the phone onto the receiver and slides to the floor. This isn't good.

Immersing herself in the past has always been a perfect distraction from the present, so she picks up her copy of *The Killer Angels* and attempts to read about the battle of Gettysburg, hoping to take her mind off these paralyzing thoughts. But she re-reads the same paragraph a dozen times, and finally gives up. Too many confusing thoughts are crowding her head, too many scary scenarios.

She feels the desperate need to escape Will's home, to run from these feelings, so she heads upstairs, jumps in the shower and takes the Metro across town to explore the sights.

Julia visits the Lincoln and Jefferson memorials, then takes a long walk along the National Mall. She's been sightseeing for hours and knows it's time to head back to Will's house, but she doesn't feel quite ready to go.

What is she going to do? Listen to her heart or her head?

She finds an empty bench and kills some time people watching. Old couples and young couples walk by hand in hand, along with harried families trying to navigate the city with small children in tow, and men and women in suits carrying briefcases, looking official and important.

Maybe love isn't the destructive force she thought it was. Her mother's face flashes before her. Carol's doing really well these days. She went back to school a couple of years ago and stopped drinking for the most part, limiting herself to a glass of wine occasionally. Last year she got a great job as an executive assistant to the president of the local university and she loves it. Her mother even started dating a nice man this past summer, someone Julia approves of. Carol's in a good place now, but Julia can't help it…she keeps waiting for the bottom to drop out from under her.

She's lost in thought when an old homeless woman approaches her. She's so familiar, her face kind and gentle. The lady reminds Julia of Gram, and her eyes begin to water as she searches through her bag for money. *Gram, I wish you were here. I could really use your advice right now.* She finds a few dollars and hands them to the elderly woman, who holds Julia's hand for a moment and nods, shuffling toward the Reflecting Pool.

She closes her eyes, remembering her conversation with Gram the night she died, and can hear her grandmother's voice in her head. *Follow your heart my angel, it's not every day you meet someone who feeds your soul.*

She smiles and takes a deep breath in. She knows the answer, she's known it all along. It's time to go home to her Romeo and take a chance on love.

***

Julia's birthday falls on a beautiful, early-Autumn day, crisp and comfortable. After spending most of the morning in bed, they enjoyed brunch at a bistro near his place, then drove to Mount Vernon, where the Fall Wine Festival is being held this weekend. Will saw the advertisement in the newspaper earlier this week, and Julia jumped at the chance to see George Washington's home in person. Neither of them is particularly interested in wine, but he knows Julia's fascinated by the lives of the Founding Fathers.

At the end of the house tour Julia spends several minutes staring intently at a portrait of the President.

"This is an original by Gilbert Stuart."

He scratches his chin, pensive. *I know that name...* Julia's eyes open wide.

"Will, please, you're from Rhode Island! Have you no state pride? Don't tell me your fancy private school never took you to Gilbert Stuart's homestead? I'm starting to think you didn't get your moneys worth!"

"No, they did, in maybe the third grade! And I remember seeing the signs for his birthplace on the way to the beach house."

"How about Slater Mill in Pawtucket? Did they take you there? The birthplace of the Industrial Revolution in America?" she asks, hands on hips, eyebrow raised.

"Okay, Miss Grasso. You're head's getting too big to fit in here."

Will grabs Julia's hand, pulling her out of the house, onto the veranda where 'George and Martha Washington' are greeting guests, answering questions about 'their' lives.

"We need to find an outhouse or a barn," he says, eyeing the outbuildings and fields.

"What for? They have bathrooms in the visitor's center."

"I think you need a good spanking," he says, wrapping his arms around her.

"Really?" Julia laughs, "And who's gonna give it to me?"

"Not George Washington." He leans in and whispers in her ear, "I want you right now."

"You're serious?" Julia blushes, her eyes wide, questioning.

He nods his head, tightening his hold on her so she can feel just how serious he is. Julia begins to laugh, then takes his hand, leading him off the porch.

"Thank god I'm wearing a skirt."

They walk through the rolling fields of Mount Vernon in search of privacy and find a spot behind one of the barns. After waiting a few minutes to see if anyone passes, Will presses Julia against the exterior wall of the building, his hands reaching beneath her skirt, pulling down her panties.

Julia unzips his pants and he lifts her, his mouth against hers and thrusts himself inside her, over and over again. Her nails bite into his flesh, and she wraps her legs around him tightly. He can tell she's about to climax, and he can't control himself anymore. Julia throws her head back, biting her lip to keep from crying out, and he feels her body pulsing around him as he comes.

They collapse on a pile of hay, kissing and catching their breath before hastily adjusting their clothes. That was definitely the most reckless thing he's ever done, sex in a public place, in broad daylight! But he had to have her just then...

Will zips his pants, and his heart stops. He leans back against the barn wall, and feels the blood draining from his face.

"Julia."

"Will, what wrong?"

"We didn't use anything."

"Oh, fuck!" She slaps her hand over her mouth.

Jesus Christ, what did I do? He holds his head in his hands for a moment, then takes a deep breath in and turns to Julia. She looks petrified. The last thing he should do is panic.

"Hey, look at me," he says, and she turns warily toward him. He runs his finger over her lips, smiling. "No matter what. I love you."

"You'd love me fat and pregnant?" Julia raises an eyebrow.

"Yes," he says, taking her hand in his.

"Will, I'm twenty-one, you're not even twenty-four…" she frowns, her voice trailing off. "Well…I doubt I'm pregnant, I'm due in a day or two." Julia shrugs, "I don't want to think about that now. Let's go visit with George and Martha on the veranda."

As the sun sets over Mount Vernon, Will and Julia relax on a blanket listening to a live blues band playing near the mansion. The tickets to the festival included a bottle of wine, and cheese and crackers. Julia's lying across the blanket, her head in his lap, both of them enjoying the music and the moment.

"Will? Do you think a person's heart can burst from being too happy?"

"I don't think so." He leans over and kisses her softly. He's wondered the same thing himself.

"I hope not, because mine feels like it could." She eats a couple of crackers. "Will?"

"Yes, Jules?" He smiles, twirling one of her long curls around his finger.

"Does it seem odd to you that a blues band is playing at George and Martha's house? 'Cause I'm pretty sure blues music wasn't around in the 1700's."

Upon their return from Mount Vernon, they head straight upstairs to Will's bedroom, and he sits on his bed and watches, mesmerized, as Julia washes her face, takes off her earrings and pulls her hair back into a ponytail. *I love her so much…*his life felt empty without her in it.

Those three months after the wedding, when she wouldn't talk to him were terrible, he felt so ashamed and lonely. *What if she never came back to me?* The thought physically pains him. She gave him a second chance when her grandmother died. He did nothing to deserve that chance, but he won't squander it.

"Jules, what are you planning to do after you graduate? Are you thinking of staying in New York? Or would you consider moving…I don't know… maybe here?"

"Well…I've been thinking DC would be a natural fit for me."

"Really?" he sighs with relief. If she said no, he'd seriously consider relocating wherever she plans to live.

"Uh huh," Julia nods and walks toward him, removing her shirt. "Yes, there are so many possibilities down here." She pushes him back on his bed, reaching for his belt, "I could find a job at one of the museums, I've always wanted to work at the Smithsonian…"

Julia takes off her skirt, and removes his pants.

"I am so relieved to hear you say that!" He slides her underwear to the floor, "The next eight months are going to be tough…" he kisses her soft neck, her breasts, "…with all the commuting back and forth."

Julia nods her head, inhaling sharply as he slides a finger inside her, "But knowing there's a light at the end of the tunnel makes it bearable," he whispers.

"Yes, bearable…" she says, pulling off his boxers, and climbs onto the bed.

"I have this big place." Will positions her above him.

"Yes…" Julia slides her hips down, slowly taking him in, an inch at a time.

"So, I was thinking…" he grabs her hips, his breathing labored, "Maybe, you could live with me?"

"What?" Julia freezes.

"I want you to live with me." He sits up and wraps his arms around her waist, looking into her eyes.

"Give me five minutes, then we'll talk."

Julia pushes him back against the bed, tightens her hold on him and closes her eyes, her back arching, as he cries out her name.

Breathless, Julia collapses beside him, and remains silent for a few minutes, staring at the ceiling. He turns on his side and watches the conflicting emotions flash across her face, and holds his breath, praying he didn't scare her away.

"Jules, I know this is a huge step and we haven't been together very long…" he rolls on top of her, kissing her gently. Julia's brow furrows, and he runs his finger over the creases on her forehead, "Actually, we have…just not in the biblical sense."

She giggles and turns to him, "The biblical sense?" she laughs again. "Will, my instinct is to say yes. But let me think about it while I'm in New York. I need a clear head to make that kind of decision and my head is definitely not clear when I'm around you!"

"Fair enough."

Chapter Eight

A woman cannot survive on sex alone, her grumbling stomach reminds her. She's not complaining, but honestly can't remember the last time she ate a real meal. They've been subsisting on whatever food they can scavenge from his nearly empty cupboards.

This morning she combed through his kitchen and managed to find what she needs to make pancakes while Will's out for a run. *Flour, sugar, milk, butter, eggs*….she pours each ingredient into the bowl, her head in the clouds.

She's never been happier in her life. Love is a magical feeling. *Will's magical*. She can't believe she denied herself this pleasure all this time. *What was I thinking?* She knows what stopped her, but fear has gotten in the way of her happiness for too long, she has to have a little faith.

The thought of going back to New York later this afternoon is making her nauseous. She doesn't want to leave him, but she doesn't have a choice. In three months she'll be on winter break, and her internship begins in late-January. Will said he'll come to New York every possible weekend and she'll come down to DC when she can.

It won't be that bad. She closes her eyes, taking slow breaths, in and out. *Who am I kidding? It'll be hell.* She wants this year to be over so they can be together.

UB40's reggae version of *Can't Help Falling in Love with You* comes on the radio and she turns up the volume, dancing around the kitchen while she mixes the batter. Using the wooden spoon as a microphone, she twirls around, then screams.

"Oh my god, you scared me!" she cries, her cheeks burning with embarrassment. She didn't hear Will come in through the front door.

He's standing in the doorway to the kitchen, his t-shirt soaked with sweat, wearing a Red Sox cap and a huge grin.

"Are you laughing at me?"

"Never. You're adorable." Will gives her a sweaty hug and kiss.

"Go clean up, breakfast is almost ready."

"Why don't you come upstairs and join me?" Will asks as he runs up the stairs, stripping out of his sweaty clothes as he climbs.

Tempting, very tempting. Her stomach begins to burn with a different kind of hunger, so she turns off the stove and follows him upstairs. *What's another twenty minutes?*

Running back downstairs to finish making breakfast, the doorbell rings, startling her. Will's still in the shower and she's wearing one of his t-shirts, her wet hair pulled back into a ponytail.

Should I answer it?

She hesitates, making sure the shirt covers all necessary body parts, then opens the door to find a woman standing on the stoop. She has long blond hair, blue eyes and very sharp features, and is dressed conservatively in black pants, a pink cardigan set, carrying a Chanel purse.

Is she a wealthy Jehovah's Witness?

"Can I help you?" Julia asks, politely.

"I'm looking for William Kennedy?"

The woman checks the number on the house again, and Julia feels a knot growing in her stomach. *Who is this woman?*

116

"He's indisposed. Is he expecting you?" She pulls the t-shirt down, praying her underwear isn't showing. This woman's giving her the creeps, the way she's inspecting her.

"Are you Julia?"

She knows my name?

"I'm sorry, have we met?"

"No. I'm Avery Smith. An old friend of Wills."

Avery? Ex-girlfriend Avery? Julia raises her hand to her mouth.

"Babe, can you bring breakfast up here?" Will shouts from the top of the stairs, "We have a few more hours of celebrating before you go!"

She cringes, turning toward the sound of his voice and willing him to stop talking. Julia holds her breath, her cheeks hot with embarrassment, and Avery's eyes have narrowed into slits, her mouth pinched into a tight, straight line.

"Julia!" Will shouts again, descending the stairs in a towel, his hair dripping wet. "Are you okay? Who is it?" he asks, pulling his towel around him tightly.

"You have a visitor," she says, eyebrows raised.

Will shakes his head, confused, then takes a few more steps down and freezes, his mouth dropping open.

"William! So good to see you!"

"Avery?" he whispers. "What are you doing here?"

"That's how you greet an old friend?" Avery pouts.

"Sorry….no…of course not." He shakes his head and stutters, "Uh…you caught me off guard. I'll…I'll be right back, let me put on some clothes."

Facing off with this polished, elegant woman, Julia feels exposed. She may as well be standing in the doorway naked as a jaybird.

"Please, come in, Avery," she says with as much dignity as she can muster, "Have a seat in here." She waves her arm to the right, indicating the dining room. "Excuse me," she mutters and runs upstairs to the bedroom.

"Will, what the hell is she doing here!?"

He's thrown on a pair of shorts and a polo shirt, and wraps his arms around her, trembling.

"I don't know Jules. I don't know how she even found me."

"What're you going to do?" She grabs clothes from her duffle bag, and pulls on leggings and a sweater.

"I have no idea. Come with me."

Avery holds her arms out for a hug as they enter the dining room and Will walks zombie-like into her embrace.

"It's been too long Will. Five? Six years?"

"Something like that." Will nods slowly, "Avery, this is my girlfriend, Julia."

"So you're Julia. I've heard so much about you!" Avery rests her icy blue eyes on her, planting a fake smile across her face.

"Really? From whom?" Julia's stomach's in knots, but she puts on a brave face and looks Avery in the eye.

"Oh, here and there!" Avery throws her head back and laughs, "Rhode Island is such a small place."

Julia knows exactly who told Avery about her. It had to be those horrible women from the wedding.

"Avery, how did you find me?" Will grabs Julia's hand, his fingers clasping hers tightly.

"Were you hiding, Will?" she laughs, "I bumped into Joe Butler from your old neighborhood. He told me you were living down here and gave me your address."

"Joe Butler gave you my address?" Will asks, skeptically, "I haven't spoken to Joe since we went skiing after Christmas last year."

"Well, when he told me you were living here I asked him to get it from your parents."

Something is not right with this woman, Julia thinks, studying Avery, brow furrowed. She squeezes Wills hand, trying to transmit some chutzpah his way, but he's crumbling before her eyes. *Come on Will, get it together!* She wants Avery out of the house, her mere presence is sucking the oxygen from the room.

"Why don't you two go out back. Avery, would you like some water or tea?"

"No. Thank you," Avery answers without a glance her way, and slides her arm through Will's as they walk toward the patio.

Julia spies on them from the kitchen window. Will seems desperately uncomfortable, sitting in a wrought iron chair, his back rigid, and staring straight through Avery. *What on earth is she doing here?* Her body language is delivering a pretty clear message. She touches Will's arm and thigh repeatedly as she talks, leaning toward him the entire time. Her behavior is blatantly flirtatious.

If Avery leans in to kiss him, I'll have no problem throwing the first punch.

Her stomach sinking, she walks into the pantry and slides to the floor. There's nothing coincidental about this. Call it woman's intuition, but she feels it in her bones. Coming to Washington was a calculated move on Avery's part. That woman's trying to worm her way back into Will's life. *Why now?*

Julia rests her head in her hands and sighs, remembering what Will shared with her last Christmas. An innocent game of Truth or Dare turned into a confessional and he finally revealed to her what happened with the mysterious Avery.

After Christmas dinner with Will's family, they went sledding at Burr's Hill Park, navigating the hills for over an hour, and getting soaked in the process. They headed to her house and changed out of their wet clothes, then arranged the blankets and pillows in front of the fireplace, drinking hot chocolate, then vodka.

119

"Want to play Truth or Dare?" Julia asked on a whim. She had no idea she was taking the lid off of Pandora's box.

"How old are you again?" Will shook his head and laughed, "Twelve?"

"So you don't accept the challenge?" She raised an eyebrow and waited.

"Really, Jules? Fine, I'm game. I've never played it before."

"You've never played truth or dare? Okay then, me first. What'll it be?"

"Truth," Will said after a moment.

Good. Julia wanted to get to the bottom of the Avery situation.

"Let's see. I'll start with a standard question, to ease you into the spirit of the game," she paused. *Oh, to hell with it! May as well get straight to the point!* "Who's Avery?"

"That's a standard question?" he sputtered, then stared into the fire for a moment before answering. "Someone I dated in high school. We broke up before I left for college,"

Julia sensed there was much more to the story, but didn't push him. Yet.

"My turn, Jules," he cleared his throat, clasping his hands together. "Truth or dare?"

"Dare." She didn't want him poking around in her head!

"I should've known," Will chuckled, "Are there any guidelines or restrictions I should know about?"

"Hmm…" she tapped her finger against her temple, in faux thought, "Well, the last time I played this in middle school there weren't."

"Excellent," Will smiled, "I dare you to climb the tree in your backyard. Naked." She choked on his last word, then coughed, holding her hand in the air.

"Okay. I just made a rule. No nudity."

"Julia…" Will's shoulders sagged, "You just took all the fun out of this for me."

They went back and forth a few rounds, and she took it easy on him, laid off the Avery topic for a little bit. But she was determined to get to the bottom of that situation! So, after a particularly ridiculous dare, she decided to dive back in.

"You're not getting off easy after that one!" she laughed, "Get ready, Will."

"I'm ready," he smiled, taking a deep breath in. "I pick dare."

"I dare you to tell me the real reason you and Avery broke up."

His eyes grew wide, then he took a sip of vodka, paused and sighed.

"Do you really want to hear this?" he asked, turning to her.

"I really do," she nodded, "Take another sip, it'll loosen your tongue."

"We dated for about a year," he sat up and stared into the flames. "She was the first girl I ever slept with." Another swig of vodka. "It was high school, Julia. She was pretty and we had the same group of friends, but...I don't know...something was missing. We didn't have a lot to talk about when we were alone. I did break up with her before I went to college, that's the truth. It wasn't a complicated split."

She remained silent, waiting for him to continue. She could see the pain in his eyes. *What happened between those two?*

"You can tell me, Will," she whispered. "I won't judge."

"I came back from school over Thanksgiving and saw her at a party. We were both drunk and ended up having sex." Will turned to her, his eyes clouded with tears. "It was just sex. I didn't want to get back together with her. A month later, I came home for winter break and she called me, crying. She said she was pregnant and the baby was mine."

Oh. My. God.

"I didn't know what to do." Will laid back against the pillows. "She was a senior in high school. I'd just started college.

My parents would've killed me. I thought about asking her to marry me. That's what people do, right?"

"Not necessarily, Will... this isn't 1955!" She brushed the hair away from his face, and noticed a tear seep from the corner of his eye. "So, what happened?"

"She had an abortion," he said, his face crumpling, "I'm Catholic, Julia. Abortion is wrong and I did nothing to stop her."

Wow. She could see how that'd mess with the head of a good Catholic boy.

She was raised Catholic too, but fundamentally disagrees with key church policies, that one included. But, it didn't feel like the time to make an argument for a woman's right to choose. She lay down beside him, and held his hand.

"Did your parents find out?"

"No. I've never told anyone. Not even Ellie."

"So, that was five years ago? Have you seen Avery since then?"

"No. She had a nervous breakdown that same year and spent some time in a hospital," he said, his face pained and etched with guilt. "She sends me letters once in a while, and I'm pretty sure that was her on the phone Columbus Day weekend, which is a first. I've never written back. What would I say? *So sorry I ruined your life?*"

"Will, it's not your fault," she sighed.

He turned sharply, and looked directly into her eyes.

"Of course it is."

"No, Will, these things happen. It was a mistake. You can't blame yourself."

He closed his eyes and held onto her, letting the tears fall. She ran her fingers through his hair, trying to soothe him. *Aren't we a pair?* Everyone's damaged in some way. Some people bottle it up, others wear their pain on their sleeves for the world to see.

Avery, the source of Will's shame, his guilt, is sitting beside him in the garden. *And she wants him back.* Julia felt sympathy for Avery when Will shared their story, but having met her in the flesh? *Not anymore.*

She stands in the middle of the kitchen, paralyzed with indecision. Should she stay here and give them privacy, or go outside and join them? Julia peeks through the window again and makes an executive decision. That woman will devour him, she can't leave him alone with Avery.

So, she takes a deep breath, walks outside and sits beside Will, wrapping her fingers around his cold, clammy hands. He turns to her, his eyes filled with...*Fear? Anxiety? Guilt?* It's hard to know which of these emotions have taken over.

How long can this go on? Will's being polite, mechanically answering her questions about his life, but Avery doesn't have an off switch. She could jabber away all afternoon without anyone's input!

"Avery, why are you in DC?" Will asks, the light bulb finally switching on.

"I'm living in Washington now too! Just ten minutes from here. Isn't that a lucky coincidence? I'm attending the Art Institute of Washington. I've always loved painting and it's a great school, so I thought I'd get my degree, at last!"

"Umm...Wow, really?" Will sputters, "You live here?"

"You had the best art and design school in the country right there in Providence. Did you apply to RISD?" Julia asks. She isn't so easily fooled. *A great school?*

"No, I was looking to move to warmer climes," Avery answers, her eyes narrowing.

I'm sure you were. Julia smirks, returning her glare.

Avery scoots closer to Will, a dog staking its territory. *Next, she'll pee in a circle around Will to ward off intruders,* Julia thinks, covering her mouth to stifle a giggle. Could Avery be any more obvious?

Over the next thirty minutes, Avery hardly pauses for breath, excluding Julia from conversation by focusing on their shared past and discussing the lives of mutual friends. The same friends Will has rarely seen since April and said he has no desire to see again. *Doesn't she see how uncomfortable we are? That she's not wanted here?*

"I'm sorry," Will interrupts Avery, "Please excuse me for just a moment." He stands abruptly and walks into the house.

Julia's jaw almost drops. *He's leaving me alone with her?* What are her choices? Follow him like a puppy or stay and deal with the situation? And Avery is definitely a *situation*.

She won't allow Avery to make her uncomfortable in Will's home, so she takes a deep breath, leaning back against her chair, and fixes her eyes on the woman who has chosen to be her adversary. For over a minute they stare each other down, until Avery leans in toward Julia, her eyes narrowing.

"There is no way he ends up with you," Avery whispers.

"Is that a challenge or a threat?" Julia asks, eyebrow raised.

"Take your pick," Avery smiles and flicks her hand into the air, dismissive.

"I guess time will tell."

Just then, Will re-enters the garden and stops in his tracks, his eyes darting between the two women. The tension between Julia and Avery is thick, a solid mass making it difficult to breathe the air around them. It's enough to spur Will into action.

"Avery it's good to see you. I'm glad you're doing well. But I'm afraid Julia and I have plans and we need to get ready."

"Are you kicking me out, Will?" Avery pouts.

Julia rolls her eyes, and looks at the sky. *We are dealing with a master manipulator here!* Avery knows exactly how to play the guilt card with Will.

"Umm…" he stutters, "No…it's just…uh…we have to go…" his voice trails off and he reaches for Julia's hand.

Jesus H. Christ! He's disintegrating!

"So nice to meet you." Julia stands, and extends her hand toward Avery. "And good luck… with school."

"I don't need luck." Avery smirks and rises, grasping Julia's hand more tightly than necessary.

Together, they escort Avery to the front door. Julia would love to kick her to the curb.

"I'm so glad we're living close to each other again," she says, hugging Will to her, "I'll see you soon." Then, blowing him a kiss, Avery slides into her Mercedes and pulls away from the house.

Filled with disgust, Julia closes the door and walks back to the garden, arms folded across her chest. She doesn't know if she's angry with Avery or Will. Maybe both! *What spell did that witch cast over him, rendering him completely helpless?*

A few seconds later, Will shuffles into the backyard, his eyes glazed over, and her heart melts a little when he kneels at her feet, wraps his arms around her, and rests his head in her lap.

So, that was Avery. That horrible woman is the object of Will's guilt and self-loathing? She takes several deep breaths, struggling with perspective as she watches the clouds drift by on this otherwise beautiful day.

An hour ago she and Will were in the shower. *Now?* That vampire has sucked the energy out of them both. This is far from over. Avery's a ticking bomb.

Will hasn't moved a muscle since he laid his head in her lap several minutes ago. She knows how difficult this must've been for him, given their history, but seeing how ineffectually he dealt with Avery left a bad taste in her mouth. *Why didn't he just tell her to leave?*

A few more minutes elapse in silence.

"Are you okay?" she whispers.

"Jules. I don't know what to say," he shakes his head, sitting back on his heels. "I can't believe she was here. That was surreal," he pauses, "I'm so sorry she ruined your day."

"Will, please, she hasn't ruined anything for me, but we need to talk about her. That woman's not going anywhere."

"What do you mean?" he sighs and pulls his chair close to hers.

"You said she writes to you. What did her last letter say?"

"I have no idea."

"What do you mean? When did she last write to you?"

"My mother forwarded a letter to me a few weeks ago, but I didn't read it. I haven't read any since the first one she sent."

"So, Avery's been writing to you for over five years and you've never read a single one?" she asks, incredulous.

"No. I just stick them in a box in my closet," he mutters.

"Are you serious?"

So…Will has no idea what Avery's life has been like since the abortion. In his head, she's still suffering from whatever caused her breakdown years ago. The woman who sat across from her in the garden, challenging her, is not on the verge of a nervous breakdown. She may be fixated on Will, but she's in control of her faculties.

"Will, listen to me. Avery wants to get back together with you."

"Julia, that's ridiculous." Will scoffs, shaking his head.

"Avery said to me, and I quote, *There is no way he ends up with you.*"

"What are you talking about? When?" he asks.

"When you left us alone for five minutes," she says, irritation creeping into her voice.

"This is crazy! I'm so sorry I left you alone with her. I couldn't think. I just needed a minute."

"I can take care of myself. My question is…can you?" She looks into his eyes, "Will, she lives nearby. How will you handle her dropping by unannounced in the future?"

"In the future?" Will shakes his head, "We made it clear to her we're together. I don't think she'll come back. And even if she does, I love you, not her."

"So, you'll tell her to go away *when* she comes back? Because, I'm telling you, it's *when* she comes back, not *if*."

Will leans back in his chair, and looks at the sky for a moment, saying nothing.

"Will? You'll turn her away when she comes back. Right?" Her voice is loud, firm.

"Jules, how can I turn her away? Avery's been through a lot because of me. Because of what I did to her. What if she goes off the deep end again? I couldn't live with myself."

"Will!" She stares at him in disbelief. "She's not your problem! She's not your responsibility. It's not up to you to take care of her. I know it was a difficult time, but there are millions of women who terminate pregnancies and move on with their lives! She has other issues going on that have nothing to do with you or what happened between the two of you."

Will looks down at his feet and she gapes at him, stunned. *He still blames himself.* He still believes it's his fault Avery had a nervous breakdown. It's a burden he's carried with him for years and for some reason, he isn't ready to put down the cross. *Why?* It doesn't make any sense, but she realizes there's nothing she can do about it, and that makes her furious!

"Jesus, Will!" She jumps up and shouts, "This is absurd! Who does that? Who drops by their ex-boyfriend's house unannounced after six years? Who moves hundreds of miles away from home to live ten minutes away from their high school sweetheart?"

Tears of frustration cloud her vision. *Doesn't he see how ridiculous this is?*

Will remains silent, holding his head in his hands, visibly shaken. Julia throws her hands up in disbelief and walks into the house, slamming the French door behind her.

Goddamn that manipulative witch! Goddamn Will and his unrelenting guilt!

She runs up the stairs to Will's room, lies on his bed and closes her eyes, a feeling of dread washing over her. But then she remembers, *the letters!* Julia flies across the room to his closet, and there, shoved into the back corner on the top shelf, sits a box. Her heart racing, she grabs the step stool and climbs it, then reaches for the box and carries it to his bed.

What will I find inside?

Biting her lip, she turns the box upside down and dozens of letters fall out, unopened, just as Will said. Julia swallows hard, her eyes growing wide, as she spreads them out on the bed. There are almost a hundred letters here! Avery has written Will at least one letter every month for almost six years!

This is not normal behavior! No, this is scary. That woman's obsessed. Even if he never opened a single one of these envelopes, he'd have to be blind not to realize her intentions. *Is Will blind?* No, he just doesn't want to see.

It's not her place, but she's dying to open them, wants to get some insight into Avery's head. Holding one up to the window, she tries to make out the words, then tosses it back into the pile. She can't read these, as much as she'd like to. It's up to Will to open them. Besides, the sheer quantity speaks volumes.

Julia knows Will isn't strong enough to send that witch away, and Avery is so manipulative she'll work him over until she gets what she wants. Shoving all of the letters back into the box, she puts it back where she found it, then cries into his pillow until she falls asleep.

***

Will doesn't have a coherent thought in his head. *What the hell happened here today?* He needs time to process… everything.

Avery!

Why would she come here? He almost passed out when he saw her standing in his doorway, with Julia. Yes, she's sent him regular letters, but did she really think he'd want to get back together with her? It's been years since they dated! Their circle of friends in Rhode Island overlaps, but she lives in Newport, and he's managed to avoid her by staying off the island.

He thought his silence sent a pretty clear message, but, in retrospect, the fact she still writes means his message wasn't received. He doesn't want to deal with Avery, so every time he receives a letter he shoves it in the box, and tries to push all memories of her out of his mind. That's a part of his life he doesn't want to remember.

He was equal parts devastated and relieved when he found out Avery aborted their child. He didn't want to have a family with her, but he didn't want her to terminate her pregnancy either. When he heard she had a nervous breakdown shortly afterwards, Will sank into a depression. He couldn't focus on school, and dropped out of Princeton after his first year.

His parents knew something had happened, could see the change in him, but they didn't press him for details, maybe sensing they wouldn't like what he had to say. They agreed to him taking time off to travel, and he spent the better part of a year sailing in Australia, New Zealand and Hawaii.

What would he do if Avery showed up at his door again and Julia wasn't here? *I would talk to her.* He couldn't lie and say he'd slam the door in her face. That's what Julia wants him to do, but he couldn't. Now that he's seen her, he needs to know

Avery's going to be all right. It would free him to know he didn't leave her with a permanent scar.

Julia's upset. He knows how difficult it is for her to trust people, and she sees Avery as a threat to their relationship. But he knows how he feels about her. Avery couldn't change that even if she wanted to. Now he needs to convince Julia.

He finds her fast asleep on his bed, her face blotchy from crying and feels guilty for leaving her alone all this time. He climbs into bed, wrapping his arm around her waist, and holds her close to him. Julia nestles her body into his but he can tell by her breathing she's still asleep. Today took a lot out of them both. He closes his eyes and runs his fingers through her curls, and a few minutes later she begins to stir.

"I love you Julia," he whispers.

She rolls toward him, her big brown eyes meeting his.

"Did that really happen? Was she really here?"

"Yes." He nods his head and she begins to turn away, but he stops her. "Julia, if Avery shows up at my door again, I'll set her straight. She won't have any doubt about my feelings for you. It doesn't matter if she wants to get back together with me Jules, because I love you. Nothing is going to change that. She can never, ever change that."

She wraps her arms around him, resting her head against his chest, and sighs.

"Will, I found the box. I didn't open any of the letters, but I think you should. You need to understand who you're dealing with."

He doesn't want to read them, only kept them because he thought it would somehow be wrong to throw away her thoughts. But that's ridiculous, it's not like Avery knows he was trying to be respectful of her in this one small way. No, what he plans to do is throw them in the garbage, and if she shows up again, he's going to tell her not to send him anymore.

"Look, Will, you know how I feel about this situation…I trust you to handle it."

"Julia, I promise you, I'll take care of Avery."

Chapter Nine

The past six weeks have been a flurry of activity. Julia's schedule has been jam-packed between school and work and she hasn't had the opportunity to go to DC since her birthday in September. Every weekend, Will drives up to New York, arriving late Friday evening and leaving by eight o'clock Sunday night. *Forty-five hours of pure bliss...*

Just as Julia suspected she would, Avery stopped by Will's unannounced later that week. According to him, they sat outside and had a long talk. He feels better knowing Avery is doing well, that she likes school and is making friends.

Will said he made it clear to her he's in a relationship and he believes she understands his boundaries. Julia doubts it, but he hasn't mentioned her since. She doesn't trust Avery, not for one second, but for the time being she seems to have disappeared from the picture.

Most weekends they have her apartment in Brooklyn to themselves. Her roommate, Rhonda, found herself a boyfriend with his own place uptown and that's worked out perfectly. Their time together is precious and goes by far too quickly. The four days in between seem to drag on interminably, despite the demands on her time.

She doesn't want to become one of those women who lives and breathes for the man in her life, but when she's with Will, everything else becomes background noise.

They have voracious appetites for one another and spend most of the time they're together in bed, making up for those four days spent apart. Julia had several lovers before Will, more than she'd care to admit, but none of her previous experiences come close to what she shares with him.

Love was the missing ingredient.

"We've been invited to dinner Saturday night." Will says over the phone Tuesday evening, the week before Thanksgiving. "Ellie's coming to New York with her boyfriend this weekend. What do you think?"

"What do I think? Of course we'll go! That'll be so much fun. I can't wait to meet Kevin!"

"Sloane and Pete are going too. Ellie and Kevin are staying with them. It'll be a good time."

She's silent for a moment. Julia has never warmed to Peter. He and his wife, Sloane are so much like the snobs she met at that wedding.

"Where are we meeting them?" she asks, her excitement dimmed considerably.

"Well, we're going to Pete's place for drinks, then they want to go to dinner at Le Cirque."

"Let me guess, Sloane suggested Le Cirque."

"I don't know. Come on babe, it'll be fun."

"Fine," Julia sighs. "All I have to do is find a pastel boucle granny dress, pearls and some sensible pumps and I'm all set."

"Jules, dress like you. Wear a tie-dyed t-shirt dress and cowboy boots, I don't care. Just be yourself."

"Are you wearing the pink pants?" she asks.

"Julia, they're red."

Her fingers fly over the typewriter keyboard as she sits at the kitchen table, surrounded by stacks of books. Julia has a paper due on Monday and is starting to panic. Will should be arriving in a couple of hours and she's cutting it close to the wire. With Ellie in town, they have such a busy weekend planned and she won't be able to relax with this paper looming over her head.

A little after seven o'clock, the key turns in the lock. *Rhonda?* Julia cranes her neck to peek at the door.

"Hey!" She runs into the living room and throws her arms around Will. "You're early!"

He drops his bag near the door and scoops her up in a bear hug. "I thought I'd surprise you," he murmurs into her hair.

"I'm so happy to see you. I hate when you're away." She buries her head in his chest, her heart swelling.

"Then we're even, 'cause I hate being away from you."

They hold each other close, until Julia reluctantly releases her hold on him. Will removes his coat, tossing it over the back of the chair, and she sighs and smiles. He's looking exceptionally gorgeous tonight, wearing jeans and an argyle sweater that brings out the blue in his eyes.

She's shabby in comparison in old sweatpants and a ratty t-shirt, wearing dorky glasses, and her hair piled on top of her head with a scrunchie. Will's seen her in this exact ensemble dozens of times, but still...she should probably make more of an effort.

"If I knew you were coming early I would have dressed for the occasion."

Will sits on the couch and pulls her onto his lap, then removes her glasses and carefully places them on the coffee table.

"You look beautiful," he says and kisses her deeply, causing her whole body to tingle.

"Come with me," she says, a slow seductive smile spreading, and leads him into her bedroom.

The paper can wait, Julia can't.

She's given her dinner attire some serious thought. Julia wants to be herself, but she doesn't want to feel completely out of place at the old fart restaurant they're going to this evening. *Why would a twenty-five year old woman purposely pick the most uptight restaurant in the city?* Then again, it's Sloane, so nothing should surprise her.

She's narrowed it down to three little black dresses, all vintage scores from a shop in the Village. They're in New York City now, not some stuffy Connecticut country club. Everyone wears black here, even on the Upper East Side.

Julia tries on the first selection, inspecting herself in the mirror from various angles. Each dress falls just below the knee, she wouldn't want to make the mistake of showing off too much leg again, but the styles are very different.

This particular dress reminds her of Audrey Hepburn in Breakfast at Tiffany's. It's sleeveless with a boat neckline, cinched waist and a straight skirt. Classic style, simple. The dress isn't tight, but it emphasizes her curves. She studies her reflection in the mirror. Her figure is more Sophia Loren than Audrey.

In her experience, blue bloods don't have much in the way of curves. *Why is that?* Even Ellie is slender with narrow hips, long legs and smaller breasts. *Do they breed them that way?* Is there something in their genetic makeup that causes women to have boyish bodies?

Julia's never going to blend in with them in that department! She steps out of her dress and studies herself in the mirror, appreciating the fullness of her breasts, her narrow waist and 'child-bearing' hips, as her grandmother used to say.

She's comfortable in her own skin, how many women can say that? *Not many.* She'll be damned if she tries to fit into someone else's mold.

The most modest of the three dresses has three-quarter length sleeves, a scooped neckline with a fuller A-line skirt, and the third dress has spaghetti straps, a low neckline and a fitted bodice and skirt. In order to zip up the last couple of inches, Julia takes a deep breath in, then laughs at the results.

The dress pushes up her breasts and she has an impressive amount of cleavage. There is no way she can wear this dress tonight, though she suspects Will would enjoy the view. He's never seen her dressed like this before. Her style's more casual and designed for comfort.

"Will, can you come in here please?" She slips on the heels she plans to wear with whichever dress she selects.

"What's up?" he asks, walking into the room and halts in his tracks. "Holy shit!"

She spins around to face him, forcing herself to keep a straight face. His eyes are practically popping out of his head.

"Oh my god, Julia. Is that what you're wearing tonight?"

"Do you like this one?" she asks with a smile.

"You look amazing," he pauses. "However, if you wear that I won't be able to keep my hands off you all night."

"That's probably not a good thing with your siblings there," she laughs. "Let me try the other two on for you. Unzip me please."

Will walks up behind her and pulls the zipper down, slides his hands inside her dress, running his fingers against her skin, then slips the straps off her shoulders and watches as it falls to the floor.

Julia raises an eyebrow, then steps out of the pile of fabric and faces him in nothing but her only pair of sexy underwear, and three-inch heels. Will pulls the clip from her hair, sending it cascading down her back.

"You're the sexiest woman I've ever seen." He runs his hands down her back, transfixed.

"Will…I look like a stripper."

He shakes his head and slides her panties to the floor. "Will... focus. I need your help picking out a dress," she protests, unconvincingly.

"Oh, I'm focused." He takes off his shirt and kneels down, his mouth and hands on her breasts, "Very focused."

She closes her eyes, running her fingers through his hair. *Yes, you are.*

Julia's been dreading this evening from the moment she discovered Peter and Sloane would be joining them. She's often wondered how children raised by the same parents, in the same environment, could turn out so differently.

How is it Peter fell victim to the world of pretense they were all raised in, while Will and Ellie turned their backs from it? Julia can't say she dislikes Peter, she hardly knows him, but she's uncomfortable in his presence, which is a blessedly rare occurrence.

On the other hand, she's been looking forward to seeing Ellie and meeting this new boyfriend she's been gushing about over the past couple of months.

Will and Ellie talk on the phone at least once a week, usually on Saturdays while Will's at her place. She's grown close to his sister during these calls. From the start, Ellie has included Julia in their conversations, and after a while, Will decided to hand over the phone so they could talk without using him as an intermediary. She was worried he'd feel left out, but he's happy she gets along so well with his sister.

When they arrive at Peter's place later that evening, Ellie greets them at the door with a radiant smile, and pulls them into the apartment.

"I'm so happy to see you both!" Ellie hugs Will and Julia, then whispers, "Sloane's in a mood!"

Julia rolls her eyes heavenward. *Here we go!*

"Why?" Will frowns. "What's going on?"

"Who knows!" Ellie shrugs, "Maybe because we were late? We didn't get here until six because our flight was delayed."

"Where is everyone?" Will asks.

"Kevin will be right out." Ellie grins, "I can't wait for you to meet him." Then she points to the kitchen, "And the happy couple is in there."

A moment later Kevin joins them in the living room, and introduces himself with a warm, friendly smile.

"I finally meet your twin!" Kevin shakes Will's hand, "You two do look a lot alike!"

"You think?" Will squints and inspects Ellie, "I've never seen the resemblance."

"That's because I'm so much more attractive than you," Ellie teases.

Kevin's a handsome man, a little taller than Will, with beautiful green eyes, close-cropped dark curly hair and light brown skin. Ellie's told Julia a lot about Kevin before tonight, he's a sports agent, has a law degree, and is from Chicago.

Ellie didn't mention that Kevin's black, and she has to admit to being a bit surprised when he entered the room. Not that it matters to her…or Will from what she can see, but she can just imagine what Sloane and Peter are discussing in the kitchen. Last Christmas, Sloane made it very clear how she feels about Julia's ethnic background. Ellie dating a black man must have sent her over the edge.

The two couples sit down on the couches facing each other and she studies their body language while they talk. She notes how closely they're sitting, Kevin's arm around Ellie's shoulders, her hand on his knee. They light up every time their eyes meet. They're in love and she couldn't be happier for Ellie. After a few minutes of small talk, Will asks Kevin how they met.

"Ooh, let me," Ellie says. "I'll give you the abridged version. I was organizing a fundraiser for the Foundation, trying to get some star athletes to attend. Apparently Michael Jordan and other celebrity athletes aren't listed in the phone book, so I had to call around and go through their agents. We met for lunch to discuss his client and the benefit…"

Ellie smiles at Kevin and he continues the story.

"We were half way through lunch and Ellie asked me out on a date. She was a shameless flirt, but I was still a bit surprised. I'm not used to women being so forward," he teases her. "But I said yes anyways."

"And that was that!" Ellie sighs. "We've been together since."

Just then Peter joins the group, his face pale, his body tense. It's obvious Sloane's going to cause problems tonight.

"Hello everyone," he says, gripping the back of an armchair. "Oh, Julia. Nice to see you again. I understand it's because of you I get to see so much of my little brother."

"Guilty as charged," she says. When she has to work at the museum for a few hours every other weekend, Will usually hangs out with Peter.

"Sloane will be out shortly. She had to make a call." Peter says, and fidgets behind the chair, painfully uncomfortable. Whether his discomfort is due to Kevin or Sloane, Julia doesn't know, but she hopes it's the latter. She'd hate to think Will's brother is racist.

There's an awkward silence and she begins to sympathize with Peter, sensing he's caught in the middle of a difficult situation. Neither of his choices are appealing. *Piss off his wife? Or piss off Ellie?* She wouldn't want to be in his shoes.

"Well, I'm starving," Ellie declares. "If we're going to make our reservation we'd better get going. Jules, come with me, let's get Sloane."

She follows Ellie through the swinging door into the kitchen but it's empty. Then Julia notices the phone cord stretching into the pantry, the door cracked open an inch.

Ellie raises her hand to knock on the pantry door when they overhear Sloane saying in a hushed voice, "What am I supposed to do? My sister-in-law is dating a black man! They're staying at my apartment for four days! We can't go to Le Cirque now. Everyone will see us."

Julia's jaw drops and Ellie opens the door, her face red with rage, grabs the phone out of Sloane's hand, and slams it on the receiver.

"You fucking bitch. How dare you? It's 1993, you racist piece of shit."

"Ellie, I…" Sloane cowers in the corner of the pantry.

"Don't say another fucking word," Ellie points her finger inches from Sloane's face. "Not one word."

Julia froze during their exchange, her eyes wide with shock, but mobilizes into action before Ellie has the opportunity to attack Sloane. She crosses the kitchen and grabs Ellie's arm, yanking her away from her sister-in-law, and Ellie forcefully pushes the swinging door open into the living room.

"You'd better go straighten out that wife of yours," Ellie glares at Peter.

Peter's shoulders sag in resignation and he mumbles an apology before setting his jaw and returning to the kitchen. When he's gone, Ellie begins to tremble and Kevin rushes to her side.

"We aren't staying here." Ellie shakes her head, "No. We're leaving now. Will, can you drive us to the Plaza?"

"Of course, El…" Will whispers, his eyes sad.

"Let's get our bags," Kevin says and they disappear into the guest bedroom together.

Kevin and Ellie check into the Plaza and invite Julia and Will upstairs for a drink. When they enter the suite, Julia follows Ellie into the bedroom, and Will's sister dissolves into tears the moment the bedroom door closes behind them. Julia holds her as she cries and when the tears subside, she hands Ellie a tissue.

"How could anyone be so awful?" Ellie cries, "I was going to tell Peter about Kevin before we arrived, but it seemed so silly. I mean, what difference does it make if he's black, white or purple? I wouldn't feel the need to tell him I'm dating a guy with brown eyes! Or blond hair! It's the same thing for Christ's sake!"

"Ellie, there are some ignorant people in this world. Sloane is one of them. You can't let those people drag you down or take you away from what you want." Julia squeezes Ellie's hand. "If you mean that much to each other, and I can tell you do, don't let anyone who doesn't respect what you have into your world."

"Thank you, Jules. You're absolutely right." Ellie nods, wiping away her tears.

Julia grabs a tissue off the nightstand and wipes away the mascara running down Ellie's cheek.

"Now, let's freshen up. We're going out tonight, and not to some stuffy joint like Le Cirque. We're going to have fun!"

Chapter Ten

Julia's been staying with Will for over a week, since finals ended in mid-December. She hadn't been to Washington in almost three months, not since her birthday, and was shocked to discover Will had gone furniture shopping. His house isn't the echo chamber it once was.

How strange he never mentioned it to me.

That's a pretty big thing to leave out of their nightly phone conversations. Maybe he meant it to be a surprise? The living room is now fully furnished in various shades of blue and white with a natural chunky wool and jute rug. The theme is nautical and preppy and it reminds her of his parents' house.

Will went all out and purchased two white couches with thin blue stripes, a couple of marine-blue armchairs, end tables, a coffee table, multiple lamps, and a sofa table with a small replica of a wooden sailboat and a couple of photos of his family in silver frames.

Over the fireplace he hung a large black and white photograph of a sailboat. He even has tchotchkes on the fireplace mantle. *Is that a fake Faberge egg?*

"Wow, Will! This is all very grown up. You have matching throw pillows...and andirons!" she exclaimed upon arrival. "Did you hire a decorator?"

"No, of course not," he wrapped his arms around her waist and changed the subject. "You know what I realized?"

"What's that?"

"I don't have a single photograph of you. Not one."

"Is it hard to remember me when I'm gone?"

"No," he shakes his head and smiles. "When I close my eyes I can picture every inch of you. But I still want one…"

"I think we can manage that," she says, picking up a photo of his family. "Do I get a silver frame and everything? Or are you going to stick me in the drawer of your nightstand and take me out at night to perform unspeakable acts?"

"Can't I do both?" he laughs and winks.

Tomorrow, Julia and Will are making the eight-hour drive to Rhode Island for the holiday. They're both dreading this visit and would prefer to stay in Washington, but Will doesn't want to disappoint his parents. She really likes his parents, but dear God! *He's a grown man! When will he outgrow the 'Mommy and Daddy' approval stage?*

This is one of the few times she's grateful she comes from a broken home. Her parents have been too busy managing their own lives to get involved in hers. The only person she needs to prove anything to is herself.

They're only staying three nights, but it'll feel like a week. She's so used to sleeping in Will's arms and they won't be able to once they're at their respective parents houses. While they're packing their bags for the trip, Julia can't stop herself from whining.

"This isn't right! We're being punished for visiting our families!" she cries. "Three long nights…"

"But when we come back home, we'll have an entire week together. Eight days…all day and all night." Will arranged to take his vacation between Christmas and the New Year.

"Now that sounds heavenly," she sighs, and resigns herself to the unavoidable.

Will wraps his arms around her, and Julia rests her head against his chest and listens to his heartbeat, thanking whatever force brought them together. She never imagined she could be this happy. *To love someone and be loved by them?* It's a rare gift. Which reminds her...

"I want to give you your Christmas present before we leave," Julia says, reaching for her duffle bag. She pulls out a wrapped gift and hands it to Will.

"You don't want to wait until Christmas to exchange gifts?" he smiles.

"Trust me...you don't want to open this in front of your parents."

Will sits on the bed, pulling her down beside him. He holds the package to his ear and shakes it, then unwraps it and throws his head back laughing. It's a leather bound copy of the *Kama Sutra*.

"Okay... It's really a gift for both of us. I saw it in a bookstore and felt compelled to buy it."

Will flips through the pages, "We've done that one... and that one... and that one..." he pauses. "What're they doing here?"

"I'm not sure," she studies the page, tilting her head, "How can she bend her leg like that?"

Will shakes his head, puzzled. "Don't know, but we can try! Thank you, Jules."

"I have another present for you," she smiles seductively. "It's a companion to the book...I think you're going to like it." Julia unbuttons her jeans and pulls them over her hips, letting them fall to the floor, then reaches down and pulls her sweater over her head. Will watches her shed the remainder of her clothes, his eyes never leaving hers, and she takes a step closer to the bed and his waiting arms.

"You give the best gifts," Will murmurs, his mouth finding hers.

The following morning they make their final preparations for the journey up North. The forecast is calling for snow all along the eastern seaboard and they're trying to stay ahead of the storm.

"You know," Will zips both of their bags and places them near the bedroom door, "You've never given me an answer about moving in after graduation."

"I haven't, have I?" she says, picking up the room and putting their extra clothes back in the drawers. "Well… that's a really big decision."

"Yes, it is."

"I've given it a lot of thought…" Julia pauses and looks down at her hands.

"And?"

"Of course I'll move in with you!" she exclaims.

"You will?" His face lights up and he swings her around.

"I can't wait," she laughs, "We just need to get through the next few months!"

While Will is outside putting their bags in his Jeep, Julia steps into the living room, eyeing the many changes he's made. It's very tasteful, but not at all her style. The library has a new rug, similar to the one in the living room, with a loveseat and two dark brown leather chairs. With a few adjustments they can make this 'their place.'

"What're you thinking about?" Will asks, walking up behind her.

"I was thinking since I'm going to be moving in here…" She turns and wraps her arms around him, "Maybe we should make future decorating decisions together? Add some color?"

"Do you hate the furniture?" He looks around the room, his brow furrowed.

"No, I just want it to be our home, a reflection of both our styles. Am I being too pushy?"

"No, not at all." Will kisses her forehead, "We'll do this together. I like the sound of that. Our home."

***

Will's a little nervous about meeting this side of Julia's family tonight. If he's completely honest with himself, he's more than a little nervous. *Petrified is more like it.* Julia has fourteen first cousins on her mother's side of the family, all between the ages of eighteen and twenty-eight…and every one of them will be at Christmas Eve dinner.

Normally he wouldn't be this anxious, but they're the brothers and sisters Julia never had, and Will wants them to like him. What if they don't? What if they never give him a chance and assume he's some snob from Poppasquash?

Before Ellie met Julia, his sister half-joked about Julia being a townie with hopes of snatching a wealthy husband. Ellie ate her words once she met Julia, but his brother was awful. The night Peter met Julia at Gulliver's, he had plenty to say in his drunken state. He called Julia 'a hot townie' he should use for sex until something better comes along. His brother is an idiot sometimes.

Did their opinions influence the way Will feels about Julia? Not one bit, though if Ellie hadn't liked Julia once they'd met, he would've had cause for concern.

There's nothing Will can do about where or how he grew up. The class divide in Bristol is pretty wide and fueled by mutual distrust. Will never gave any thought to the division in town until he took Julia to that wedding. Her experience shined a light on the problem and he hopes her family gives him a chance.

Julia's aunt lives in one of the newer developments in town. Will pulls his Jeep onto Adams Drive and notes that all of the houses are colonial-style, carbon copies of one another. *The developer was either lazy or lacked imagination.*

Though the houses are the same model, each exterior is uniquely decorated with lights and lawn ornaments, some garish, others more subdued. Some remind him of the Griswold's in the movie *Christmas Vacation*, with lights attached to every square inch of the house.

Blinking colored lights, blinking white lights, a train set up around one house, inflatable Santa's and snowmen. He's getting a headache looking at the displays. Her aunt's house isn't one of the Griswold houses, which is somehow reassuring. Only a few white lights on the bushes out front, and a couple of wreathes.

Walking up the path to the front door with Julia, he can make out the shapes of dozens of people inside the house, even through the misty windows. *Dear God, there are a lot of people in there!* Before they left her house, Will shared his fears with Julia and she assured him her family wouldn't pre-judge, said to just relax and be himself.

Be himself? This is one of those occasions Will wishes he had Ellie's outgoing personality. His sister wouldn't flinch walking into this gathering, would probably have them eating out of the palm of her hand in minutes.

"You made it!" Julia's aunt, an attractive woman in her early forties, greets them. "We were starting to worry about you." They embrace and kiss each other's cheeks.

"Hi. Sorry we're late. This is my boyfriend Will," Julia squeezes his hand. "Will, this is my Aunt Debra, my mom's sister." He extends his hand to shake hers, but she swats it away and gives him a hug.

"Welcome Will. Hope you're hungry!"

"Starving, actually." He smiles, feeling better already, and her aunt takes their coats.

"Well, there are appetizers in here and you two can take the next shift."

The living room is crowded with her cousins and aunts and uncles and Will's reminded of the time he went with Julia to her grandmother's house for meatballs. Gram lived on the first floor of a two-family house in the Italian section of town, her kitchen no more than twelve by twelve feet in size, the living room even smaller. There had to be twenty people squeezed into her tiny apartment that day. Her aunt's house isn't nearly as small, but it's equally packed.

"Julia!"

"Buon Natale! So good to see you all! This is Will."

"Merry Christmas," he says, trying to smile naturally, "Nice to meet you all."

Her aunts and uncles seem friendly enough, their demeanors inviting, but he's on the receiving end of some not-so-welcoming glares from her cousins, specifically the males. Their arms are folded across their puffed up chests, their eyes distrustful.

Is this how Julia felt when she walked into the ballroom that night? Totally exposed and on display? How would he feel right now if she were as oblivious to his feelings, as he was of hers at the wedding? He shudders at the thought. This could be a very long night.

Julia leads him into the dining room where 'first shift' is eating. The table seats ten people so there are at least two more shifts to go.

Carol's standing over the sink straining the pasta for second shift when they enter the kitchen to get a desperately needed drink.

"Ah, glad you two made it. There's wine in the fridge, vodka in the freezer and spiked eggnog on the counter. Help yourself."

"Ma, do you need any help?" Julia kisses her mother's cheek.

"No, no, Debra will be right back. I'm fine. Go relax, enjoy yourselves."

"Is Ron here?" Julia asks. Ron's her mother's boyfriend. They've been dating since last summer and Julia said she's never seen her mother happier or healthier.

"Not yet, sweetie. He's visiting with his family but he'll be here later," her mother smiles. "Now, go! Have fun! Your cousins are waiting for you."

Moments later, second shift is called and Will swallows hard as they make their way to the table. This is where the interrogation will begin. Julia squeezes his hand reassuringly and they're the first to take their seats at the far end of the table.

Soon, he's surrounded, or should he say dwarfed, by her male cousins, all as big as linebackers. They're trying to intimidate him, he's sure of it. Will breaks into a cold sweat and seriously considers excusing himself and hiding in a bathroom. Instead, he takes a deep breath and introduces himself to her brawny cousins, one by one, making sure to look them in the eye. *Show no fear!*

Two large bowls of pasta are placed on the table. There are also a few gravy boats filled with extra tomato sauce, bowls of parmesan cheese, a large antipasto salad and garlic bread.

"This is our special pasta. We only eat it on Christmas Eve," Julia whispers.

"Why is it special?" He peers into the bowl. It looks like regular spaghetti with red sauce and black olives.

"I'll tell you after you try it."

"Okay," he frowns, "Now you're just scaring me."

Julia laughs, as do her cousins seated around them.

"No worries, Will," Dave pats him on the back, "Nothing that'll kill ya."

Will stares at the pasta with some trepidation.

"Just try it. It's good," Julia assures him.

He twirls a bit on his fork and takes a bite, trying to figure out what makes it special. It's very good, a little salty, but tasty. He takes another bite. The linebackers are watching him eat, waiting for his reaction.

"Okay, I like it, now tell me the secret ingredient."

Again, the room echoes with their laughter.

"Do you like fish, Will?" Michael asks, a smile on his face.

"Yes…" Will stares at his plate. There isn't any fish that he can see.

"Anchovies," Julia tells him. "We put anchovies in the sauce on Christmas Eve." He's confused. He doesn't see anything resembling an anchovy. "It disintegrates into the sauce when it cooks."

Will puts his fork down and makes a face.

"Why do you put anchovies in the sauce?"

"It's an old family custom started by my great-grandparents. On Christmas Eve, Italian families traditionally serve seven courses of fish. My great-grandparents had twelve children and were too poor to buy the fish. But they could afford the anchovies, so they put it in the sauce and that's how our family has done it for over a hundred years."

Will nods and contemplates his next move. Her cousins are eating and keeping one eye on him, waiting to see if he'll eat anymore. If he doesn't eat the pasta, they're going to bust his chops all night, he can feel it.

"I like it." Will picks up his fork and takes another bite.

"Ah! Thank you, Will! You just won me twenty bucks!" Dave claps him on the back again, his eyes narrowing as he says, "I knew you'd eat it. You look like the kind of guy who likes to try new things."

Will raises an eyebrow. Is Dave suggesting Julia's something he's trying out?

"True Dave, and when I find something I like, I stick with it."

"Good to know, Will," Dave nods and smiles, "Good to know."

Julia wasn't exaggerating. She does have fourteen 'brothers and sisters' and her eight very large brothers are extremely protective of her.

The rest of the night went smoothly, and Will was eventually able to relax and enjoy himself. Dave must've signaled to the others to lay off the intimidation tactics, because over the course of the evening they included Will in conversation, which, amongst the men, completely revolved around sports.

No politics, no religion, nothing polarizing. Julia's cousins are rabidly devoted to every New England team, and this is where Will found common ground.

A little after eleven o'clock, Will and Julia prepare to leave. They're joining his family for midnight mass. Will helps Julia with her coat, then pulls on his own, and holds up the Yankee Swap gift he ended up with. Gifts ranged from perverse to ridiculous. He's now the proud owner of a set of ceramic coasters, each with a different dirty limerick. *There once was a man from Nantucket...*

"Will, it was nice to meet you. Hope we see you over Easter." Dave shakes his hand and Will and Julia bid farewell to the rest of her family.

Once outside, Will wraps his arms around Julia, and sighs. He made it through the evening intact. Thank god they didn't treat him like an alien being from planet Poppasquash.

"Everyone really liked you," Julia says once they're in his Jeep. "I know they gave you some shit at first, but thanks for being such a good sport."

"I really liked them too," he says with genuine relief.

***

Christmas dinner with Will's family is as uncomfortable as Julia suspected it would be. The tension in the room is palpable. This is the first time everyone has been in the same room since the evening they went to dinner before Thanksgiving, while Ellie and her boyfriend Kevin were in New York. Julia can't believe Sloane had the nerve to come to Christmas dinner after that fiasco.

Peter's apologized to Ellie for his wife's behavior more than once, but Sloane hasn't and that's a problem. Ellie wants to watch Sloane squirm, but she's making everyone else uncomfortable in the process.

Halfway through dinner, Will's father puts down his fork and asks the question everyone out of the know is thinking.

"What the hell is going on here?"

Everyone at the table freezes and Ellie smiles.

"Why don't you ask Sloane?"

Sloane turns pink and promptly leaves the table, dropping her dirty fork and knife on Mrs. Kennedy's expensive oriental rug. Will and Peter grab Ellie and hurriedly escort her out of the dining room while Julia sits, trapped at the table with Will's parents, aunts, uncles and cousins, holding her breath and wondering who will be the first to speak.

No one says a word for several minutes, then Mrs. Kennedy begins to clear the dishes from the table. Those left seated, quietly excuse themselves and retreat into the living room, heading straight for the liquor cabinet.

Julia pours herself a large glass of wine and takes a seat on the couch near the fireplace in the living room, wishing she and Will could go back to her mother's house. Carol and Ron left for Jamaica early this morning and they'll have the house to themselves tonight before they drive back to DC in the morning. After the tension of today, her mom's place would be paradise. *Spending time with family over the holidays is highly overrated.*

A half hour later, Ellie, Peter and Will are still in their father's study, and Julia notes Mr. and Mrs. Kennedy seem to have successfully brushed the situation under the rug. Will's dad is enjoying his second scotch on the rocks, laughing with relatives, while his mother sits at the piano playing Christmas carols. If his parents want to pretend everything is fine, Julia figures that's their prerogative. She admires their ability to make the best of a bad situation.

Ellie could've handled this better. It's one thing to hold a well deserved grudge, quite another to drag everyone else into it.

She's lost in thought when Sloane takes a seat in the armchair beside her. Julia eyes her warily as Sloane straightens the fabric of her cream colored skirt and crosses her legs, settling in for a chat.

She can't imagine why Sloane would want to have a conversation with her now. What could they possibly talk about? On the three occasions Julia's been in her company, Sloane has treated her with nothing but disdain. And Julia hasn't bothered to disguise her dislike of Will's sister-in-law.

"Julia, I understand you've met Avery."

"Yes, I have," she replies, startled. "I wasn't aware you know Avery."

"Oh yes, we go way back!" Sloane smiles, "We went to boarding school together."

Julia nods and smiles stiffly. *Well, that explains a lot!* If Sloane and Avery are friends, and Avery wants to get back together with Will, then Julia is an unwelcome obstacle.

"Peter and I saw her at the Nantucket Christmas Stroll a couple of weeks ago. She said she's been spending a lot of time with Will since she moved to Washington."

"Really?" Julia's heart stops, and she swallows hard, but manages to keep her smile in place, "She said that?"

"Yes, she's been helping him decorate his place." Sloane picks up her glass of wine, taking a sip.

Julia's mouth falls opens in disbelief. She doesn't want Sloane to see how badly she's rattled, but she's sick inside.

"Well, she's doing one hell of a job." Julia forces a smile and scans the room, searching for Will.

She doesn't want to jump to conclusions, but she remembers the look on his face whenever she mentioned the new décor. She has a bad feeling about this but no doubt Sloane will report this conversation to Avery and she's not going to provide any additional material.

Will and Peter enter the living room and Will takes a seat beside Julia on the couch, holding her hand in his. She smiles, her eyes searching his for deception, but all she senses is his exhaustion. His body is slack, his eyes glazed over. Peter asks Sloane for a moment and they leave the room.

"Where's Ellie?" Julia asks.

"She's still in the study. Pete's going to try and convince Sloane to apologize to her. You know what really pisses me off? Sloane knows she was inappropriate, but she's angry with Ellie for putting her in that position!" He leans back against the couch and runs his hands through his hair. "I feel awful. I don't want this to ruin the holiday for my parents."

"They seem fine now. Will, this has nothing to do with you. This is between Sloane and Ellie. Maybe you should stay out of it, let them figure it out."

"I was trying to persuade Ellie to at least pretend everything is fine between them. To stop staring Sloane down every opportunity she gets, but she said she wouldn't."

She leans against Will, resting her head on his shoulder and considers mentioning what Sloane said just then, but there's enough drama at the moment. Will wraps his arm around her and Julia overhears Peter explain to his parents that they have to leave. Sloane 'promised' a friend of hers they'd stop by for dessert.

"Well, Sloane has refused to budge. Great."

"Is Ellie waiting for her in the study?" Julia asks. Will nods and begins to rise, but Julia stops him. She wants to talk to Ellie herself. "I'll go. You just relax."

Julia opens the door to the study and finds Ellie sitting behind her father's desk, feet up, hands behind her head.

"That's a serious 'don't fuck with me posture' you have going on there." Julia says, closing the door behind her.

"I thought you were Sloane." Ellie relaxes and smiles, "She's not coming to apologize, is she?"

"No." Julia slowly shakes her head. "You too may be the most stubborn women on the planet. They just left. Peter made up some excuse to your parents and they took off."

"Well, at least now I can relax and have some fun."

Julia takes a seat across from Ellie and looks down at her hands.

"What's the matter, Jules?"

"I need your advice," she pauses, wondering if she should discuss this with Will's sister. They've become good friends, but Ellie's allegiance lies with her brother. After a moments consideration she decides to confide in Ellie. "Sloane said something to me when we were in the living room a little while ago..."

"What did she do now?" Ellie throws her hands up, "Jesus H. Christ does that woman ever give it a rest?"

"She told me Avery's been visiting Will. A lot. And helping him decorate his place. Or should I say our place now that I've agreed to move in with him."

"Okay, one," Ellie's eyes open wide. "When did you guys decide to move in together? Oh my god, that's wonderful!"

"Right before we came home."

Ellie claps and sits back in her chair, smiling.

"Ellie, did you hear the first part?"

"Oh, right," she blinks, "Avery visiting. She's totally lying! Will wouldn't keep something like that to himself."

Julia's not convinced.

"Have you been to Will's new place?" Ellie shakes her head, frowning, and Julia continues, "I hadn't been there since September. He always comes to New York to visit me. In the three months I was away he fully furnished the first floor. I'm talking decorative pillows, color coordinated everything. Does that sound like Will to you?"

"No." Ellie frowns, "My brother couldn't match socks never mind decorate a house. Maybe he hired a professional?"

"I asked him. He said no and changed the subject."

"I'm going to get him right now," Ellie rises. "Ask him Julia. Will doesn't know how to lie. Just ask him and see what he says."

"Okay."

***

"Hey babe, what's up?" Will sits beside Julia on the leather sofa in his father's study and takes her hand.

Thank God she's here today! This Christmas has been so tense and Julia is the calm in the center of this storm. Maybe it's time to make their escape and head to her mother's house. They'll have the house to themselves…

"I have to ask you something and I need you to tell me the truth."

"Of course." His brow furrows, "What is it?"

"Have you seen Avery since you had that talk with her after my birthday?" Julia asks, looking directly into his eyes.

Oh dear God. He looks down, feels the color rising from his neck to his face, then returns her gaze. He's not going to lie to her.

"Yes."

Julia's face turns white.

"Avery told Sloane she sees you often, and has been helping you decorate your place."

He closes his eyes and nods his head. *Sloane!* It never occurred to him that Avery and Sloane are still friends. Avery never mentions his sister-in-law when she visits.

"How often Will? How often do you see Avery?"

"She stops by every once in a while," he mumbles, rubbing his fingers over his temple. He can't blame Sloane for opening the bag on this one. *I should have told Julia months ago...* He meant to, but the timing never felt right.

"How often is that?" Julia's voice rises, "Once a month? Once a week?"

"Maybe once a week," he sighs.

Julia stands abruptly and paces around the room.

"Jules, listen. We're just friends. She understands we're in a relationship. I was going to tell you but...I don't know...I didn't want to upset you for nothing."

She stops and glares at him.

"It's not nothing," she whispers angrily and leaves the study.

His sister appears moments later and closes the door behind her.

"William, what the fuck did you do?"

"Please Ellie," he holds up his hand, "not now."

"I'm not going anywhere until you tell me what happened," she stands over him, jaw clenched. The last thing he needs is his sister's wrath right now.

"I need to talk to Julia."

"Good luck with that! Julia's gone. She left."

"What?" He sits up with a start, then lies back on the couch, resting his arm over his eyes, his stomach churning.

"Please tell me you didn't let Avery decorate your house. Please, Will. While I still have some faith in you."

He's silent, his thoughts racing. *How can I make this right?* It took Julia so long to trust him…she'll see this as a betrayal of that trust. Ellie grabs a chair and pulls it over to the couch.

"Will…I'm trying very hard to understand what's happening here. Are you saying that you let your ex-girlfriend from a thousand years ago weasel her way back into your life… and furnish your home?" His head is pounding. "The home you asked Julia to share with you?"

He nods his head. *What the hell did I do?*

"Will, are you insane?!" Ellie shouts, grabbing a pillow and hitting him, "What the fuck is wrong with you?!"

"Ellie stop, okay?" He holds his arms up to shield himself, "Just stop. This is bad enough as it is."

"Please explain this to me, like I'm a child." She sits back in the chair, dropping the pillow to the floor, "Because this makes absolutely no sense. None, at all."

"Do you remember when I told you Avery stopped by the day after Julia's birthday?" Ellie nods. "Well, she stopped by unannounced later that week and I explained the situation to her. That she can't just stop by anytime she feels like it."

"Wait a second," Ellie holds up her hand, "You told her not to stop by unannounced? You didn't tell her to stop coming by entirely?"

"El, how could I do that? She just needs a friend to talk to. Avery's harmless." Ellie's eyes are wide, disbelieving. "What! Why are you staring at me like that?"

"Can you possibly be this clueless?" She bites her lip and takes his hand in hers, "William. If she's so harmless, why is

Julia gone? Why didn't you just tell her from the start that Avery's been stopping by? Why did you feel the need to keep it a secret?"

He opens his mouth to speak but Ellie stops him, "Will, don't bother. You kept it a secret because you knew Julia would tell you to make her stop. And you hate confrontation. It's one of your weaknesses."

He sits back and rubs his hands over his eyes. His sister's right. He didn't want to hurt Avery, and he didn't want to upset Julia. So he did nothing.

"Avery's so manipulative Will, can't you see that? You have to put a stop to this or she'll destroy the best thing that's ever happened to you. God brought you and Julia together. You can't let Avery come between you!"

He nods his head. He knows that's what he needs to do, but how can he tell Avery to go away? Ellie doesn't understand because she doesn't have all of the facts.

"Go get Julia, Will." His sister stands up, hands on her hips, "Put a stop to this bullshit with Avery and make things right."

***

Julia didn't go straight home. Whenever she's having a tough time she gravitates to the water. Even in New York City. *Tough day?* Take the subway to South Street Seaport. *Really bad day?* Hop on the Staten Island Ferry. The water has a soothing effect on her, calms her nerves, and helps her think clearly.

From his parents' house, she took a drive through Colt Park, parked near the boat launch and decided to take a walk along the water. It's freezing out and the wind is whipping off the bay, but she doesn't care.

She hasn't felt anything since she left Will's house. Nothing. She hasn't cried, gotten sick. She feels empty. She should've known this was too good to be true. He's too good to be true. People don't get everything they want in life, why should she? Love makes you blind. Julia knew something wasn't right when she mentioned the living room décor. She felt it and ignored her gut.

Lesson learned. The gut is fool proof.

Slowly, Julia makes her way back to his car, and sits behind the wheel. Closing her eyes she takes a deep breath in. *I can smell him.* She loves how Will smells, no cologne, just his skin. She rests her head on the wheel and the tears start to fall.

Gabby doesn't know what the hell she's talking about. Julia wants to take her frigging cupid's bow and arrow and torch it.

A half hour later she drives to her mother's house, all cried out. She's not surprised to find Will waiting for her when she pulls into the driveway. She doesn't look at him or speak but doesn't stop him from entering the house. She walks to her bedroom and closes the door behind her and thankfully Will has the sense not to follow.

Lying across her bed, she reaches for the phone to call Gabby, but replaces the handset before she dials. *This, I have to handle alone.* It's time to follow her own instincts, not the directives of her well-meaning friend.

Finally Julia enters the living room in her pajamas and sits beside Will, her blanket, a cocoon protecting her. He lit a fire while she was in her room and she stares into the flames.

"Julia. I'm sorry I didn't tell you she's been stopping by. It was wrong."

She nods and continues watching the fire. She feels nothing again.

"I promise you we just talk. Julia, please look at me."

She turns her eyes toward him, but stares right through him.

"Please Julia…" he takes her hand and she quickly withdraws it. She doesn't want him to touch her.

"I opened my heart to you," her voice is soft, calm. "I put it all out there and you lied to me."

"I didn't lie to you, Jules," he says, a twinge of desperation in his voice.

"Yes you did," she nods her head, her voice steady, "You lied by omission."

"I didn't want to upset you. I was wrong."

"You didn't want to upset me?" She glares at him. "No, finding out from your sister-in-law was much less upsetting than you telling me yourself. Or, even better, I could've waited for Avery to tell me herself when she pops by to say hello sometime over the next few weeks. That wouldn't have upset me at all."

"I told her not to come while you're there."

"Why is that, Will?" Those words snap Julia out of her anesthetized state. Anger flashes across her face and she yells, "If you're doing nothing wrong, why tell her to stay away? You're not only lying to me, you're lying to yourself! You knew this was wrong. And you did it anyway. Why? Because you're afraid of hurting her?"

Will nods, his head bowed. Her eyes open wide, stunned. His words are an arrow straight through her heart.

"What about me, Will? What about my heart? What about hurting me?" Tears spring into her eyes, and she rests her head on her knees.

He leans in to hug her and she jumps at his touch, pushing him away. Julia closes her eyes, trying to figure out what to do. *I love him*, her heart reminds her. Does she want to throw what they have away?

She believes Will when he says nothing happened between them, despite Avery's best efforts she's sure. He can be so completely oblivious sometimes. He wants to believe the best in people and thinks he can help Avery.

Julia knew this wasn't over. *She knew it!* The way she sees it, she has two choices, sit back and let Avery destroy them, or confront the viper, face to face. Maybe it's time to find out what Avery's thinking for herself.

"I want you to invite her over for drinks. This week. And I want you gone. Just me and Avery."

"Alone?" Will blinks in astonishment, "I don't think that's a very good idea."

"I want to talk to her myself," Julia rises, standing over him. "And I'm telling you now Will, if you don't agree to this I don't want to see you again. Do you understand that? You lied to me."

"I don't want to lose you, Julia." His face is pained and her chin begins to tremble.

"You've put her feelings ahead of mine for the past three months. Now it's time for you to put mine ahead of hers."

"Okay. I'll do it. Anything."

Chapter Eleven

Julia watches from the library window, as Avery pulls up to Will's house in her black Mercedes. *Black. The color of her soul.* Avery exits her car, tossing her blond hair over her shoulder and pulls her fur coat tightly around her. She's wearing a dress or skirt, hard to tell yet, and heels. *Where does she think she's going? A gala?*

Julia's wearing a soft, fitted cream cashmere sweater she found at a consignment store, worn bootleg jeans and her bitch kicking ankle boots. She figures she's going to need them.

"Are you sure about this?" Will walks up behind her, "You want me to leave you here alone with her?"

She turns to him and nods, wraps her arms around his waist and holds him tightly. She has to do this. Avery needs to be put in her place.

They've been back in Washington for two days. Since Christmas, they've come to a détente of sorts. She conditionally forgives Will for keeping this from her but he has to tell Avery to stay away and she knows he's dreading it.

"Julia it's so good to see you again. I'm sorry if there was some misunderstanding the last time we saw each other."

"Yes, well that's all water under the bridge now, isn't it Avery?" Julia smiles. This is all a show for Will. He won't leave if he thinks she's upset.

"I've been looking forward to getting to know you. Will's said so many wonderful things about you."

"Has he?" Julia kisses Will's cheek, "Thanks babe. I think it's time for you to go. See you in an hour."

"Okay, I'll see you soon." Will pulls on his coat, stands between them, and hesitates. Kissing Julia, he whispers, "You're sure?"

She nods her head and he reluctantly leaves them alone.

"How do you like how his place is coming along?" Avery asks the moment Will closes the door behind him. "We found this couch at Sabun House here in Georgetown. And this rug, I love this rug. I saw it at Cady's Alley and fell in love with it. I called Will and told him to meet me right away. I was so excited when he bought it. Doesn't it look perfect with the other furniture we've picked out together?"

The bitch didn't waste any time! Julia won't give Avery the satisfaction of showing any emotion.

"Let's cut through the bullshit, Avery. What are you hoping to accomplish here?"

Avery stops at the sofa table where Julia has a bottle of wine and three glasses waiting.

"May I?" Julia nods curtly and Avery pours herself a glass of wine. "We found these glasses at Cartier. Love them." She holds one up to the light, then looks at Julia, "I thought I made myself clear the first time we met."

"I see. So you're just waiting for an opportunity to pounce," Julia pours herself a glass of wine. "Is that it?"

"Julia, he'll realize you two aren't suited for each other on his own." Avery picks up a photograph of his family, "I don't need to do a thing. You can't share a life with him. You don't fit into his life. And you know you don't."

"Wow, Avery. You certainly are confident...or delusional. It's hard to tell the difference, they look so similar," Julia takes another sip of wine...*God, I hate this woman!* "Will and I have created our own life. Together."

"You only think you have," Avery chuckles, "You're Will's last fling before he's ready to settle down. He's experimenting. I've seen it happen with every guy I know. You'll see. Women like you don't end up with men like Will." She turns to face Julia, "You know I'm right."

Avery takes a seat on the blue armchair, runs her hand over the fabric, smiling to herself. Julia's lightheaded, and feels the heat rising from her neck to her cheeks.

"Think about it Julia, what could you possibly offer him? Men like Will need someone who can help them advance their position. You would only hold him back."

She knows Avery's trying to get under her skin... *and it's working*.

"Avery...I can offer him something you never will."

"And what's that Julia?" Avery raises an eyebrow, sardonically.

"Love."

"And what makes you think you have the monopoly on that?" Avery's face turns pink, "You think I don't love him? Why do you think I'm here? I've always loved him. I've loved him enough to give him his space when he needed it, and I love him enough to save him from his own folly."

"That's so sad, Avery. To love someone all of these years, who doesn't love you back." Julia's face reflects pity but her throat is closing, threatening to choke her. "No. What you feel isn't love, it's entitlement. You want something you can't have, but think you deserve. That's not the way it works. Right now Will feels sorry for you, but he'll see through you. Eventually, he'll see right through you're little act. And I'll give it to you, you're a hell of an actress."

"Oh, Jules, call it whatever you like, but my little act, will take me right to the altar. I hear wedding bells in our future."

"If that happens *Ave*," Julia stands toe to toe with her nemesis, "You two deserve each other."

***

This has been one of the longest and most stressful hours of Will's life. He's driven around town aimlessly, praying they're able to resolve their differences so he won't need to have that discussion with Avery.

Julia's been distant with him over the past few days, not that he blames her. She said she understands his intentions were good, and reminded him "the road to hell is paved with good intentions." He heard that expression a lot growing up.

Ellie called him this afternoon and was more direct. She told him to "grow a pair."

If it comes down to it, if he has to choose, the choice is clear. If the only way to keep Julia is to stay away from Avery then it's done…as much as he's dreading that conversation.

Exactly one hour later, he turns the corner onto his street and Avery's car is gone. *This can't be good.* He just assumed Avery would be here when he got back. They didn't make a plan. Julia was going to talk to her… *then what?* Will parks his car in the garage and comes in through the back door.

"Julia?"

He finds her standing near the couch, drinking a glass of wine, her face strained.

"Babe, what happened?"

Julia refills her glass and pours one for him, stands near the fireplace and takes a huge gulp.

"Oh, me and *Ave*, that's my nickname for my new best friend, we had a good talk." Julia takes another big gulp of wine.

Shit. This is worse than he thought. He knew he shouldn't have left them alone.

"Let's see if I can summarize. Basically she thinks we'll self-destruct, so she doesn't need to do anything but wait.

Eventually, you'll be rid of me and run straight into her arms because I'm not good enough for you. That's it in a nutshell." Julia drinks the rest of her wine in one swig.

"So there you go! Invite her over for dinner and a movie, because fuck it! I'll be gone sooner or later. You two can be best buddies in the meantime."

"Julia, that's ridiculous. Honey, come sit down."

"You know what?" Julia stares at the couch, "I think we should fuck right here on the couch the two of you picked out together." He winces at her words. "Or on the rug she bought with you. That's all I'm good for, right? A good fuck? Guys like you always go back to their own kind." She opens another bottle of wine.

"Julia. You're talking crazy. Please."

He's paralyzed. He's never seen Julia like this.

"No, Will, I want another drink in the fucking wine glasses Avery picked out!" Julia hurls the glass into the fireplace, obliterating it. "Did you two register somewhere? Let's save everyone the time and go buy the shit right now!"

Julia lies on the floor in front of the fire and stares at the ceiling.

"Oh, God, the room's spinning." She closes her eyes, pressing her hands against the floor. "Are you just wasting time until something better comes along?" Julia whispers, "Is that what this is, Will?" She curls her body into a ball, tears streaming down her face.

"Julia, she's wrong." He sits on the floor beside her, afraid to touch her. Her pain is tangible, and he wants to make it better, but doesn't know how. "I love you, Jules. Please, never doubt that. I want us to be together, always."

Watching her suffer, he's filled with rage. *What the hell did Avery say to her?* Every time she stopped by she seemed genuinely respectful of his relationship with Julia. She may have flirted a little, but she never made any moves on him. He

169

thought she understood the situation, but apparently he was wrong.

He'll deal with Avery tomorrow. Right now Julia needs him.

"Jules, I'm going to pick you up and get you away from all of this broken glass, okay?" She remains silent. "I'll take that as a yes."

He brushes the glass away from her with a throw pillow, lifts her into his arms and looks around the living room.

Avery did pick out everything in here. Why did I let her do that?

It seemed harmless enough at the time. He needed furniture and it gave them something to talk about and seemed to make her happy. But this isn't Avery's home. It's his home, and Julia's home. His stomach turns thinking about the mess he's made of everything.

He can't stay in this room. Will carries Julia up to their bedroom, the only room Avery hasn't touched.

"That vulture...she's swooping in..." Julia mumbles, "Too weak...you can't stop her..."

"Shhh, Jules. Don't do this."

Julia passes out and he gently lays her down on the bed, covering her with a blanket. *What have I done to her?* Will lies down beside her, brushing her hair away from her face.

"Julia, I'm so sorry..." he whispers.

***

Oh my god. Julia winces, her head throbbing. She can't focus her eyes and a wave of nausea washes over her. Pushing away the comforter, she runs to the bathroom and grips the toilet, emptying her stomach. Will sits beside her, rubbing her back.

"That's right, get it all out."

She retches until there's nothing left, and collapses on the cool tile floor. Will carries her back to bed, propping her up against him and lays a cold washcloth on her forehead, then helps her take a sip of water.

Julia can't think. *What happened?* She looks around the room, confused, then turns to Will and is flooded with memories of Avery and the horrible things she said the night before.

Women like you don't end up with men like Will...

"Leave me alone." She slumps down on the bed and turns away from Will.

"No, Julia. I won't leave you alone. If you don't want me to touch you, I won't. But I'm not leaving you," Will says holding back tears, "I love you, Jules. Tell me what to do, please."

She hears him, but can't speak. The pain is unbearable. *Is this what my mother endured for a full year?* No wonder she wanted to drink away the pain. Her father ripped her heart out and she was in agony.

But Will isn't gone. He's right here holding her, trying to soothe her. *Will is not my father.* She's not alone in this bed. Julia turns toward him and wraps her arms around his chest.

"Make her go away. Please..." she whispers, tears streaming down her cheeks.

"I'll tell her to go away. I promise."

Chapter Twelve

The past four months have been grueling for Julia. Her internship at The Cloisters Museum was amazing, challenging, and exhausting, but worth it. They've offered her a job as an Associate Curator and as much as she loves it there, she's declined.

Julia wants to move to DC to be with Will and she has an interview at the Smithsonian the week following graduation. *The Smithsonian!* Working there would be a dream come true.

Only three more weeks to go.

After that horrible night with Avery, Will kept his word and told that woman to stay away. He asked her back the following evening and Julia listened from the next room. Will was surprisingly direct. He said he felt bad about her troubles, but he never wanted to see or hear from her again.

Avery left without a word, however, within a month she was back at it, calling and dropping by his place regularly. Will's forced to screen his phone calls and check who's at the door before he answers. She thinks he should get a restraining order…there's something wrong with that woman.

Julia's tried to forget what Avery said that night, but it lingers in the back of her mind. She wasn't entirely wrong. Julia doesn't fit into the life Will once had, but that's not the life he's living now. It's not the life he wants to ever live again, or so he says.

Avery definitely touched on a nerve, sparking intense feelings of insecurity, an emotion she's tried to quell since. Is she holding Will back because of her tribe? Would he be better off with one of his own kind? Someone with powerful connections? She's pretty sure her Uncle Vinny's mafia ties don't qualify. What if Will comes to resent her?

Julia's spent a lot of time mulling this over, and has talked to Will about his hopes for the future. It's so important they both understand what they're getting into. *We'll be living together!* They're basically agreeing to share their lives...without official documentation.

He doesn't have great career aspirations, other than to make his father proud. She's far more ambitious than Will, maybe because she's always known she'd have to work hard for what she wants in life. He's had everything handed to him on a silver platter. His trust fund ensures his financial future, whether he works or not. Julia doesn't have that luxury.

So her question is... *What would make Mr. Kennedy proud?*

Unlike so many of his peers, Will's parents don't see marriage as a financial or power merger, probably because his dad comes from a background similar to her own parents. She doesn't see them as an obstacle, they've embraced her from the beginning.

She doesn't know what to do with these feelings of insecurity. Every once in a while she has a panic attack, convinced he'll leave her for one of his people. She doesn't doubt Will's feelings for her... but can those feelings be sustained, long term, in the real world?

He's been coming to New York almost every weekend, and with her workload, it's been difficult on them both. This was an important semester and she's given her internship and her course work her full attention.

All weekend, she writes papers, or studies and Will spends a lot of time alone, either reading on the couch or walking around the city. They knew it would be hard but actually living through it has been much more difficult than either of them expected.

Julia's supposed to go to Washington this weekend, her first visit since January, and she's dreading it. She doesn't want to spend time at the townhouse, even if Will's in it. She told him she couldn't live there, that she wants them to find a place of their own, and he's agreed. They'll look for a new place when she moves down to Washington after graduation.

On the last day of her internship, several of her co-workers from The Cloisters ask to take her out for drinks to celebrate, and to try and convince her to take the position she was offered.

Julia's torn. Last weekend Will was visiting his parents and she didn't see him. If she doesn't go to Washington it'll be the longest they've been apart since last summer. Her train leaves in three hours so she agrees to a drink, but insists they pick a bar near Penn Station.

A half-hour before the train leaves, and several cocktails later, she calls Will.

"Baby, I'm not going to make it tonight. I've been celebrating with my friends and I'm a little drunk. I don't think I should travel. And I really need to work on a paper this weekend. Can you drive to New York tomorrow morning? Until finals are done it's going to be tough to get out of town."

"Sure, I'll see you tomorrow around noon," he sighs, "I love you."

"Always."

***

Will hangs up the phone, depressed. The past few months have been really hard. Julia's pulled away from him. He's not sure if it's the amount of pressure she's under from school and the internship or because of what happened with Avery. She's preoccupied and when they have sex, the way she looks at him sometimes... like she doesn't know who he is.

He knows Julia doesn't trust him completely and he wanted to talk to her about it tonight, but now that'll have to wait. He doesn't mind driving to New York tomorrow, what upsets him is she didn't want to see him tonight, after two weeks apart. *Why didn't she ask me to drive up tonight?* He loves her and not knowing how she feels is eating away at him.

The Sox are playing the Yankees, so he goes up to the den and pours himself a drink, the first of many. A few hours and a half bottle later, the doorbell rings and his heart leaps in his chest. *Julia changed her mind and took the train after all!*

He runs down the stairs, flings the door open and finds Avery standing on his steps with a big grin. He hasn't spoken to her since January when he told her to stay away. After what she did to Julia it was easier to do than he thought it'd be.

"Avery. You need to go." His speech is slurred and he tries to close the door, but she slips in and walks into the front foyer.

"Will, are you drunk?"

"Avery you have to go. Now."

"Let me help you." She puts her arm around his waist and walks him into the living room. "What are you drinking?"

Will wakes up with a splitting headache, his vision blurred and his mouth bone dry. He reaches for the water bottle he usually keeps on his nightstand, but it's not there. *Shit. I shouldn't have had that much to drink.*

It's still dark out but the glow of the streetlight outside his window is making his head pound. He grabs his pillow and pulls it over his head, groaning, then turns onto his side and feels someone beside him.

Julia!

He wraps his arm around her and nuzzles her neck, then freezes. *This isn't Julia.* He turns on the light and his stomach lurches. *What did I do?*

Avery is asleep beside him, naked. *And so am I.* His head is spinning and he runs to the bathroom and vomits. *What happened last night?* He vaguely remembers the doorbell, and telling Avery to leave... and that's it. He has no memory of the rest of the night.

He sits on the cold tile, his head resting on the porcelain seat. *What am I going to do?*

As the sun comes up, Will walks into his bedroom, pulls on his boxers and stares at Avery, his eyes filling with tears. *This is it.* Julia will never forgive him. He'll never forgive himself.

"Avery," he shakes her, "Avery!"

She turns onto her back, stretches and smiles.

"Well good morning..." she reaches up to kiss him and he turns away.

"Avery, stop it."

"Will, what's wrong?" She looks wounded by his words.

"I want you to leave." He rests his head in his hands. "Please," he whispers.

"You didn't want me to leave last night." She runs her hand along his back and kisses his shoulder. He flinches, pushing her away.

"I don't know how this happened..."

"Oh, Will," Avery bursts into tears. "You said you wanted me. Last night you begged me to stay."

"I don't remember anything."

"I never would've stayed if I thought you'd regret it," Avery sobs.

"I'm sorry but I need you to go. I have a lot to think about."

"I'll go," Avery wipes away her tears and scoots off his bed. "But please call me. I'm so confused."

He nods his head. Anything to get her to leave.

Once she's gone, Will stands over his bed, and stares at the imprint of Avery's head on Julia's pillow. Filled with anger, he pounds his fist into the pillow, then strips the bed and throws the sheets in the garbage.

He turns on the shower, and makes sure the water's scalding hot before he steps in, then takes a facecloth and scrubs his skin, trying to wash his sin away. *It's hopeless*, he slides to the bottom of the tub, holds his head in his hands and cries.

He's supposed to drive to New York this morning but he can't do it. If he goes to see Julia, it's over. *Today.* But if he stays home, he can pretend they're together for another week.

Around noon, he crawls under his comforter, picks up the phone and calls Julia, his heart heavy.

"Hey! Where are you? I thought you'd be here by now!" her voice is cheerful, affectionate. He swallows hard, holding back his tears.

"I'm sorry, Jules. I'm sick. A stomach thing. I can't drive."

"Oh, no! I'll get on the next train and come take care of you. Bring you some chicken soup and a lot of TLC."

"No, sweetie, I don't want you to catch this. The last thing you need in the final stretch is to get sick."

"I don't care about that, I miss you so much! Will...I was dreading staying at your house, that's why I didn't come down last night. I was a bit drunk, and I do have a paper to work on, but I'm such a jerk, I should've just told you. I was afraid all I'd think about was Avery and those things she said. I love you so much and I can't let her words come between us. I have to let it go. I'm so sorry I didn't come down last night."

"Oh, me too baby," Will wipes his eyes.

He didn't know what to think. He thought maybe she was falling out of love with him and didn't want to be around him. She wasn't avoiding him after all. Julia didn't want to be reminded of Avery, and now Avery's come between them permanently.

He could keep this to himself…Julia would never have to know! But he would know, and Julia would sense it… she knows him so well.

"I'll come up on Friday night. Maybe I can get out of work early," he murmurs, feeling sick inside, "Jules, I've gotta go. My stomach…"

"I love you, Will. Feel better."

He closes his eyes, holding onto her words.

"I will always love you, Julia."

He hangs up the phone and runs to the bathroom.

***

It's happening! Finals are next week and then she's done! Julia Grasso will be a college graduate! She can't wait to see Will tonight. Only two more weeks and they'll be together everyday, she smiles every time she thinks about it. She has three exams next week and she knows she'll ace them. The pressure is finally off.

Tonight, Julia has a special celebration planned for the two of them. She hasn't seen him in three weeks and her body craves his touch. A piece of her is missing when they're apart.

It's not just physical…they're connected on so many levels. She once read that love activates the same parts of the brain as any habit-forming addiction. It makes people feel like they can do anything, be anything, achieve anything. And once they taste it…they want more.

Yeah. That's how she feels. She's a love junkie. She's addicted to Will.

He's been so strange on the phone this week. He said he's not feeling well, but something else is going on, she feels it in her bones. Maybe he's upset with her for cancelling last weekend? She's been kicking herself for not going all week, but she senses it's more than that. She can't pinpoint it, but she knows something's wrong, she can hear it in his voice.

She'll know soon enough. He'll be walking through the door any minute…

He's late.

Julia's been sitting on the couch for hours, watching the minutes tick by at a snail's pace. She called him around eight, and when he didn't answer she figured he was on the road and hit traffic. Two hours later, the phone rings and the hairs on her arm stand on end. It has to be Will, and she's nervous.

On the fourth ring she picks up.

"I'm sorry Jules, I had to work late. I'm not going to make it tonight."

"Why didn't you call me hours ago? I could've taken the train down."

"I was really bogged down and lost track of time."

"Will, is everything okay?" Her stomach is in knots. She knows he's keeping something from her, something is very wrong.

The gut is never wrong.

"Yes, everything's fine."

He's lying, I feel it.

"Are you coming tomorrow?"

He takes a long pause before he answers.

"Uh huh. I'll call you in the morning."

"Okay…Will?"

"Yes?"

"I love you," she whispers.

"Always. I love you, Julia."

Julia stares at the phone after Will hangs up. He's avoiding her. *Why?* She lies in bed, tossing and turning all night, the hours slowly passing by. It's unbearable. *What's going on with him?* Her heart is pounding against her ribs. All week she's had the feeling something was going on with him, and their phone call earlier confirmed it.

Staring at the ceiling and listening to the sounds of her neighborhood settling in for the night, worst case scenario's fill her head.

He's met someone else.

He doesn't love me anymore.

He doesn't think I'm enough.

He doesn't want me to move in with him.

It could be anything, and whatever it is, it's bad. So bad, he can't bear to see her. *But he loves me!* The voice in her head repeats over and over again. *Doesn't he?*

By five o'clock in the morning she can't take anymore. She throws back her covers, tosses a change of clothes in her bag and takes the subway to Penn Station. She dozes on the train to DC but adrenaline is driving her forward.

Before she knows it, she's standing on the sidewalk looking up at Will's townhouse. She knows when she walks through that door something terrible is going to happen. Petrified to put her key in the lock, she sits on the front steps for a few minutes, her thoughts racing.

Then, with the dawn of sudden clarity, Julia gasps, tears filling her eyes. There's only one thing Will would feel so guilty about he'd avoid her completely…and that would be sleeping with Avery. She rests her head in her hands, wiping the tears away.

Please God, let me be wrong.

It's almost ten o'clock when she finally unlocks the front door and enters the foyer. She quietly investigates the first floor for evidence of Avery, but it looks the same as the last time she was here, no additions or modifications that she can see.

She drops her bag and climbs the stairs, the stale aroma of alcohol assaulting her as she climbs. The den is a mess, dirty plates and glasses, and several empty bottles of vodka litter the end table and floor.

When she opens the door to his room, she spots a few more empty bottles and his clothes are in piles everywhere. Will's still in bed, lying on his side, and she crawls into bed beside him, wrapping her arm around his waist and buries her face in his neck.

"Will?"

He grasps her hand tightly, bringing it to his lips. He pulls her close and she doesn't know what to do, so she holds onto him and goose bumps rise all over her body. Eventually he turns around but he won't look at her. She stares at his scruffy face, the dark circles under his eyes.

"Will, look at me."

He slowly raises his eyes to meet hers and sees pain and guilt reflected in them.

He did it. I was right.

Julia closes her eyes and shakes her head, her body trembling.

"No."

Will wraps his arms around her, tears running down his face and she allows him to hold her for a minute. Two minutes.

"Please say you didn't. No."

He's silent, but holds her tight. The silence is killing her. She grabs his t-shirt and shakes him.

"Tell me I'm wrong, Will, please."

"I'm so sorry, Julia....I..."

That's all she needed to hear. She covers her ears and rolls onto her back. She doesn't want to hear one more word, wants to block out his voice. She squeezes her eyes shut and prays when she opens them, she'll be back in her bed in Brooklyn, and this will have been a bad dream.

Eventually she opens her eyes and studies him. *Who is this person?* Will's eyes, normally so clear and full of love are cloudy and pained, wet with tears.

"I have to get out of here." She sits up abruptly, pushing him away.

"Julia...I'm so sorry. Please let me explain."

"No, I have to go."

Frantic, she sprints down the stairs, grabs her bag and flies out the door, running to the Metro station around the corner. She has to get back to New York, away from Will. She wants to get as far away from this place as possible. Waiting for the train to Union Station, Julia sits on a bench, her arms clutching her stomach and sobs.

Somehow she made it to New York, through a haze of tears, and was back in her apartment by three-thirty that afternoon. When her roommate Rhonda stopped home for a change of clothes an hour later, she found Julia disconsolate on the couch, surrounded by hundreds of used tissues.

"What happened, Jules?"

Julia shakes her head. She can't say it out loud.

"Is it Will?"

Just hearing his name brings on a fresh wave of tears.

"Oh Julia, I'm sorry honey. Come here."

Rhonda helps her to her bedroom and consoles her as best she can. Once Julia's tears subside, she shares her heartbreak, describing to Rhonda what happened with Will.

"Well, I'm gonna tell you what we're going to do," Rhonda sits up and makes her intentions known, leaving no room for argument. "You're going to take a nap, then a shower and tonight we're going to the party at Roberto's. You need distraction."

She'd forgotten about the party. It's their big send off and she was supposed to go with Will. Julia rolls onto her stomach and buries her face in her pillow.

"Oh, Rhonda, I don't feel like going to a party."

"I'm not giving you a choice. You're going. You have two weeks until graduation and you're not going to sit in this apartment feeling sorry for yourself." Rhonda stands up, "No, you're going out with a bang, not a whimper. Honey, this is your time!"

The party is loud and packed with the friends Julia's made over the past four years. This is their last hurrah before graduation and she'll miss seeing them every day. Many are staying in New York and Julia made one decision this afternoon.

She's accepting the position at The Cloisters. She's cancelling the interview for her dream job at the Smithsonian.

There's no way she's moving to Washington, DC. She could get her own place to live, but she'd be breathing the same air as Will…and Avery, and she can't bear the thought. It would be torture.

She managed to sleep for a couple of hours this afternoon, and Rhonda force-fed her a bagel before they left for Roberto's place.

Club music is blaring through the speakers throughout his apartment, and for once Julia doesn't mind, the heavy bass blocking out all thoughts of Will. A friend offers her a joint, but she declines that and a bevy of other mind-numbing narcotics in favor of alcohol. Rhonda, her self-appointed doctor, has been medicating Julia with endless drinks over the course of the night.

She is intoxicated enough to forget the pain for a little while, to laugh and dance. Drunk enough to say 'yes' to Brad when he asks for a slow dance and leads her into a bedroom. She doesn't protest when he kisses her and feels nothing as he slides her underwear to the floor. She closes her eyes and is numb while he takes her body for his own pleasure.

She doesn't feel a thing. The medicine worked. Julia slides to the floor, staring into the void and is empty inside.

This isn't really happening. None of this happened.

"Take me home please."

Brad helps her stand, adjusts their clothes and hails a cab to take them to Brooklyn.

***

A taxi pulls up in front of Julia's apartment building at two in the morning. Will's been waiting on the front steps for hours. After she left this morning he held the pillow that still smelled of her and stared at the ceiling. He stayed in bed until five o'clock then dragged himself downstairs, got into his car and started driving.

He didn't have a plan, he had no idea where he was going until he reached Pennsylvania. Then he knew. He has to see Julia, he has to explain what happened with Avery.

He can see Julia in the backseat of the cab but she's not alone. Will stands to get a better look and is stunned when Brad steps out of the taxi to help her, telling the driver to wait. Brad wraps her arm around Julia's waist, holding her up as they approach her building.

Will steps out of the shadows, his face pained. It takes a second, but Brad recognizes him, chuckles and hands Julia off to him. Without a word, he gets back into the taxi and is gone.

I'm in hell.

Julia's completely drunk and Will steadies her as she stumbles toward the door.

"Will?" Julia squints at him, confusion in her eyes, "Is that you?"

"Julia…" he whispers. "What did you do?"

She searches the street for Brad, then takes a step up, leans in inches from his face and sneers, "How does it feel?"

Turning away from him, she fumbles for the keys in her bag.

Will stands immobile, consumed with white-hot rage. *She slept with Brad?* His head's spinning and he can't think, only feel. Desperate to direct his anger at something, he punches his fist into the wall of her building, his hand exploding in pain, then sits on the step and hangs his head, blood dripping onto his shirt.

The pain in his hand is excruciating, but nothing compared to the pain in his heart. He did this to them. It's his fault Julia did *god knows what* with Brad.

"Will, just go back to Avery," Julia slurs, turning the key in the lock, then exclaims, "Jesus Christ! You're bleeding," she pauses and sighs, "Come upstairs."

He sits on the side of the tub while Julia kneels in front of him and washes and bandages his hand. The sight of his blood temporarily sobered her up. Neither of them speaks while she wraps his hand. What is there to say? He slept with Avery, and she turned to Brad for comfort, or revenge. Either way, it's his fault.

"You can stay on the couch tonight, but I want you gone in the morning."

Julia pulls herself up and stumbles toward her bed, then passes out fully clothed.

Will stands at the foot of her bed and fights the urge to climb in beside her. She'd never know. Instead he grabs a towel and a couple of washcloths, lathers them with soap and carries them into her bedroom.

His hand throbs with pain while he washes her face, her neck, her arms, her legs. He takes off her dress and rids her of Brad, washing her body clean. She hardly stirs. He pulls her nightgown over her head and tucks her in, then sits in the chair by her bed and watches her sleep.

God, I love her. He'd give anything to take back last Friday night. *Anything.*

Avery hasn't left him alone all week. She calls, she shows up at his house. He's ignored her so far. Yesterday her mother left a message on his answering machine. She said Avery's in a fragile state and to be careful, she doesn't want to pick up the pieces again. "Don't do this to her, Will. She's been through enough."

Guilt is eating him alive. He's never regretted anything more than opening his door to Avery that night.

He has no idea what he's going to say to Julia when she wakes up. He wants to apologize and beg her forgiveness. He loves her more than he thought possible. Julia doesn't love easily, he learned that during their 'friend' stage. Yes, she loves her friends and family, but the kind of love they share was hard won.

Julia's guarded. It took her so long to open her heart to him, but once she did, she opened it completely. Will knows how difficult that was for her and he tried to never take it for granted. This morning, he saw it in her eyes. *She'll never let me in again.* He will never feel the warmth of her love again.

***

The morning sun wakes Julia a few hours later and she finds Will asleep in the chair beside her bed. For a moment she forgets what happened the day before and her heart fills with love for him. *Why is he sitting in the chair? He should be in bed with me.*

The walls begin to close in on her as she remembers.

He slept with Avery. He isn't mine anymore.

The full magnitude of his betrayal hits her, a giant weight pressing upon her, forcing the air from her lungs.

Once she catches her breath, she quietly sits up, not wanting to wake him just yet. Her body is leaden, her heart aching in her chest. She wants to lie in his arms, wants him to make it all better. *But he can't.*

She was right after all. Love does make you weak, it can destroy you. *Well, I won't let him destroy me. I gave him my love, I can take it back.*

And as he stirs beside her, that's exactly what she does. Like a switch in her chest, she shuts off her feelings, and lets the numbness settle in.

With a start, Will sits up in the chair beside her. His shirt and pants are stained, dark brown splotches of dried blood covering him. *Before he goes he should change his bandage*, she thinks absently.

Will reaches for her hand and she pulls away, staring past him to the poster of *Romeo and Juliet* hanging on her wall. Romeo and Juliet…suckers, both of them. *This love that thou hast shown doth add more grief to too much of mine own…*Romeo got that right, love hurts.

"Julia. I'm so sorry."

She closes her eyes, recounting passages from the play, trying to block out Will's words by reciting Shakespeare in her head. *Dost thou love me? I know thou wilt say aye, and I will take thy word. Yet if thou swears, thou mayst prove false…*

Will sits beside her on the bed and touches her arm. Her body betrays her and she sways toward him, her head resting on his shoulder for a split second, before she scoots away and hugs her knees to her chest.

"Julia, please, I am so sorry."

"You've already said that."

"I don't know what happened. She showed up at my house last week and I was drunk. I don't remember anything but I woke up with her next to me."

"It doesn't matter," she covers her ears, can't bear to hear anymore. "I don't want the details."

She closes her eyes and imagines them in bed together, can see Avery's satisfied smile. She got what she wanted. Cloudy memories of last night's party fill her head. Dr. Rhonda and her medicinal cocktails…loud music…the bedroom.

Her stomach lurches. She remembers kissing, her body pressed against a wall, her legs wrapped around someone. *Who was it?* A familiar face flashes before her. *Brad? Oh God, what did I do?*

"Julia, I hate myself. I hate what I've done to you." Will brushes the hair from her face. "Is there any way we can get past this?"

"No." She turns to face him, "No, there isn't."

If ye should lead her into a fool's paradise, it were a very gross kind of behavior… They tried to build a world of their own, but they failed. They created a fool's paradise. She doesn't believe Will deliberately lead her into this illusory world. He wanted it to exist as much as she did.

She doesn't know why he succumbed to Avery, maybe it was inevitable. Avery's from his tribe, Julia's not. *Gram, you were so wrong.* Loving someone is not enough, the nincompoops do matter.

"Julia…we can go away, she'll never find us," Will pleads, desperation in his voice.

"Run away?" she laughs, "Do you hear yourself? Will, we can't run away from our lives. *The Averys* will always be there.

Our differences will always be there. No, I'm done. I told you, no one can make that promise."

"I never meant to hurt you. You have to know that, Julia." He reaches for her again.

"I know you didn't mean to, Will." She grasps his hand, "But you did and I won't let you do it again."

The pain in his eyes, the tears falling down his face, it's too much. She wavers for a moment, but it quickly passes. She's in control here. Julia's been here before...this feeling is familiar. All of these months, swirling in a whirlpool of love, she lost her power, she let her feelings control her.

Not anymore. Never again.

"I'll be right back," she says and returns a minute later with clean bandages and washcloths, and gently unwraps his bloody bandage, washes his swollen hand, and re-wraps it. She feels his eyes on her while she dresses his wound, can hear his ragged breathing. She's numb, completely removed from the scene being performed at this moment.

The finale.

"It's time to go," she stands and calmly meets his gaze. "Goodbye, Will."

He rises, holds her to him and whispers, "I'll always love you."

She nods and watches him walk away, gently closing the door behind him.

For never was there a story of more woe, than that of Juliet and her Romeo.

Chapter Thirteen

It should be a joyous occasion, her graduation, but it's not. Julia's a ball of anxiety but is trying valiantly to keep a smile on her face. Her father and stepmother are here, and her mother. This is the first time her parents have been in the same room together in years, the first time Julia has seen her dad and Sandra in almost a year.

The tension was thick when they met in the hotel lobby to pass out tickets to the ceremony. She would've told him to stay away, but he did pay for her education. She figures it's his right. Aunt Debra came with Uncle Larry, moral support for her mother.

Julia invited Ron, but Carol thought that would be awkward under the circumstances. And Gabby's here. She drove up with them the night before to celebrate, and to support Julia.

Her mother rented a two bedroom suite at the Hotel Pennsylvania, across from Penn Station and Julia and Gabby stayed up half the night talking. Julia's been calm since Will left. She misses him, but she hasn't cried. She hasn't felt much of anything.

Gabby asked a million questions, but Julia's brushed them all aside. It doesn't matter. All of Gabby's theories about 'love conquering all' were blown out of the water the minute Will had sex with Avery. Her friend can try to rationalize it any way she wants, it won't change her position.

Love isn't worth the heartache. *End of story.*

Rhonda was beside her during the ceremony and managed to lift Julia's spirits enough so that she was able to appreciate the significance of the moment. At the conclusion of the ceremony, Julia walked into the bright sunshine, feeling the warm breeze against her face and took a deep breath, then closed her eyes and smiled. *I'm a college graduate.* It does feel good.

Outside, she searches for her family and friends in the crowd but can't find them. Hundreds of people attended the ceremony, so she heads toward the meeting spot they selected near the auditorium and the first person she sees exiting the building is Will.

She freezes and her face falls, the sight of him sucking the air out of her lungs. The exhilaration of the past hour... gone.

"Congratulations Julia," Will says, walking toward her.

"Why are you here?" She holds her arm out, warding him off.

He looks awful with dark circles under his eyes, his face scruffy and pale. About as terrible as she's feeling at this moment. She's not prepared for this. She never thought she'd have to see him again, and in an instant he's thrown off the equilibrium she's managed to maintain since he left her apartment two weeks ago.

Tears fill her eyes and she blinks them back, scrambling to construct a façade of strength and determination. *I can't let him in again.*

"I promised you I'd come." Will lowers his head, fixing his gaze on the sidewalk.

"You promised a lot of things," she whispers, her wounded eyes meeting his. "I can't do this Will. Please don't do this to me today."

As her friend and family weave through the crowd, Julia and Will stand motionless, staring into each other's eyes. Gabby rushes to Julia's aid, stepping between them. "Congrats Jules!" Gabby holds her tight while the rest of her family circles around her.

"Help me," she whispers, clinging to Gabby. "This is too much. My dad, Will. It's just too much…" The façade is going to crumble if she doesn't get away from Will and that can't happen.

"Breathe Jules. I'll take care of this, okay?" Julia nods, discreetly wiping her eyes, and Gabby says, "I'll see you at Tavern on the Green at five o'clock."

***

This was a bad idea. He shouldn't have come today. When Will woke up this morning he tried to convince himself it was the right thing to do. After all, he promised he'd be here to celebrate her big day. And he was hopeful that maybe once she saw him, she might realize she misses him…she might even want him again.

But the look on her face…all he managed to do was strip her of whatever happiness she was feeling.

"Will! So good to see you." Gabby grabs his arm, "Come with me." She leads him away from the group. "Have you completely lost your mind? I can't believe you'd do this to her after all you've put her through."

He turns, hoping to see Julia again, but Gabby steers him around the corner.

"Will, you can't be here. This is Julia's day, not yours. You can't just show up like this!"

"I told her I'd be here."

"Yeah, when you two were together! You're not together anymore, or did you forget that along with the concept of fidelity?" she says, her eyes teeming with anger.

He feels faint and loses his footing, almost falling into the street, but Gabby pulls him from the curb and guides him to a bench.

"Do you have any idea what you've done to her? You ripped her heart out, Will. She'll never trust anyone again!"

Will recoils from her words, then with a surge of determination, or maybe desperation, he says firmly, "I want to talk to Julia."

"Well, that's not going to happen today. I'm the closest you're going to get to her, and right now I'd love to strangle you. I never thought you'd betray her like this. I've had your back for the past two years, and you turn around and cheat on her?"

"Gabby, you have no idea what happened that night." Will says forcefully and they stare each other down in silence. Eventually, Gabby sits beside him and sighs.

"Fine, Will, let's hear it. What happened with Avery? I'm all ears."

He explains the events leading up to Avery's visit, Julia cancelling, his drinking. How he thought Julia changed her mind when he heard the doorbell, and opened the door. Avery wouldn't leave, and then he woke up beside her.

"That's a pretty convenient story, Will," she says, her eyes boring into him, laser sharp.

"It's the truth. I hadn't spoken to Avery since January, and I haven't spoken to her since that night."

"You're telling me you have no memory of having sex with Avery? None?"

"No. None."

Gabby is silent for several minutes, studying the sidewalk in front of her. *What is she thinking? And can she help me with Julia?*

194

"Well, I believe you, Will," she sighs, looking up at the sky.

His heart jumps in his chest and he turns to her, hopeful.

"But that's not going to make any difference with Julia. She trusted you. Now she doesn't. There's no grey area here. If you think there is, then you don't know her at all. There's no way she's gonna give you another chance. Not after everything else that's happened."

His body sags, defeated, and he stares at his hands. The fist he punched into the brick wall still hurts. It's probably broken, but he hasn't been to the doctor.

He closes his eyes and the past two years flash before him, the good times and the bad. Yes, they hit a couple of bumpy spots, but the rest of their time together was beautiful, their relationship so strong.

"What about everything that was good?" he murmurs. "There was so much good."

"I know. That's what's so sad about this. You two had something very special. You two…fit. How many people ever meet their soulmate? I'm guessing not many…"

His mouth drops open, and he tries to compose himself. *Soulmates*…they're soulmates, and he destroyed them. His eyes brimming with tears, Will covers his face with his hands, and to his embarrassment, begins to cry.

He's spent his entire life masking his emotions to the outside world, but today, sitting on a bench in Washington Square with Julia's best friend, Will loses the ability to hide them any longer. He's inconsolable.

"What am I going to do?" he whispers through his tears. "I miss her so much. We were going to spend our lives together, have a family. This can't be happening…"

He's hardly slept or eaten in weeks. He's a hollow shell of the person he was just a month ago. The past is where he lives, it's all he has left of Julia. Memories. Living in the present is intolerable, his pain a constant reminder of his failure. Thinking about the future is another form of torture, his mind a whip, beating his insides raw with the possibility of what could have been, had he been a stronger person. All he sees are empty years stretching before him.

"I've gotta go," Gabby rubs his back sympathetically and rises. "Will. Here's my advice, for what it's worth. Give her space. If she wants to be with you, if she can find it within herself to forgive you, she'll reach out. I'll talk to her, but it's up to Julia now."

"Thanks Gabby." He wipes his face, and stands.

"I'll give it to you," she lightly punches his shoulder, "Showing up at her graduation took balls. I didn't think you had any."

<u>PART II</u>
FLAPPING

1994-1996

Chapter Fourteen

Julia hasn't had the luxury of feeling sorry for herself since her break up with Will. She had to scramble to find a place to live when the lease on her apartment in Brooklyn expired at the end of May.

She found a small studio in the city, started her new job at the museum in mid-June and has been working as much as possible since. In the bit of free time she does have, she hangs out with old friends, reads, goes to concerts or movies. She's trying to make a life for herself.

Activity is key. She keeps herself occupied so she doesn't have time to think about Will. Except at night. Julia dreams about him often and she has no control over that, though she's tried. She's tried sleeping pills, but the dreams became more vivid. She started drinking a glass of wine before bed, nothing worked. So she accepts them. *They can't last forever, can they?*

Before their break up, other than the night Gram said goodbye, she rarely remembered her dreams. Now, they haunt her. *Or taunt her.* Last night's dream lingered with her all day. She woke up and could smell his skin, hear his voice whispering in her ear, see his face so clearly. Her subconscious has turned against her, torturing her night and day.

Gabby came to stay with her over her birthday in September. Surprisingly, she's been Will's number one champion. Growing up, Gabby said she'd break the legs of anyone who hurt Julia. Well, Will hurt her, and then some. She didn't expect Gabby to go after him with an iron bar, but she thought her friend would do some verbal damage, a little Will-bashing peppered with fantasies of broken bones.

But no, she was wrong. Since Gabby spoke to Will at her graduation, she's been making a case for Julia to give Will another chance.

"Julia, what if you're wrong? What if he's completely innocent? Something doesn't feel right about this. Seriously Jules, I don't think he even had sex with her. He doesn't remember anything, and I believe him. You know I would've seen right through him. If Will was that drunk, he wouldn't have been able to get it up if he tried. If a guy has an orgasm, he's gonna remember it, right? I think Avery staged the whole thing. For her own warped purposes, Avery was in the right place at the right time. That night was like 'the perfect storm'."

"Does it even matter now?" She's only half-listening, having learned to tune her out. Every time Gabby brings up Will, it hurts. *Doesn't she see that?* "I'm finally getting my bearings, Gab. I've been in a fog for months and it's finally lifting. Please, leave it alone."

"Let me say this one thing, and then I'll shut up about it forever." Julia raises an eyebrow, skeptical, and Gabby throws up her hands. "Okay, for the rest of the weekend. I can't guarantee any longer than that."

"Fine." Julia sits up on her bed and crosses her legs, folding her arms over her chest, "Speak. But this is the last I want to hear about him for the duration of your visit."

"Okay, deal. I've given this a lot of thought, so bear with me. You and Will have all the ingredients for a wonderful relationship. All but two."

"I'm all ears, Buddha," she sighs. "Share your wisdom."

"Trust and courage," Gabby says, two fingers extended.

"Those are pretty big things, Gab."

"Will doesn't have the courage to fight for the life he wants on his own, but when he's with you, he does. You bring out the best in him. He was finding his way to a new life with you by his side."

"Maybe he needs to find the courage on his own." Julia feels tears prick the back of her eyes, "Isn't that what courage is about? Finding the strength within yourself?"

"Funny you should say that, Julia! Because you have the same issue. You need to find the strength within yourself to take a chance on love. You need to learn to trust. Will was helping you with that."

"Until he wasn't!" Julia scoffs. "You really believe his story? They were naked Gabby, what else could've happened?" Gabby raises an eyebrow and Julia sighs, "How could I ever trust him again?"

"Jules, your trust issues are so much more complex than what happened between you and Will. Yeah, I think you could trust him again. The problem is you don't trust yourself. Your parents did a number on you. You trusted them, and they hurt you. But that wasn't their goal, Julia. They're human, they fell prey to their own weaknesses. You're an innocent victim in their drama. Are you going to let their actions control the rest of your life?" Gabby scoots up on the bed and sits beside her, "Your fear is understandable."

"What fear is that?" Julia grabs a tissue and wipes her eyes.

"Abandonment," Gabby says and takes her hand. "You're afraid every person you love will leave you eventually. Not everyone leaves Julia. Barring death, some people stay for life. I'm afraid you're stuck with me forever."

Julia laughs through her tears and Gabby wraps an arm around her.

"There's no guarantee you won't get hurt again, but you can't shut everyone out because you're afraid they'll leave. Doing that guarantees you'll be alone forever, and I know that's not what you want. Think about it my friend, and I know you don't want to hear this… but think about calling Will and hearing him out. He really does love you, yours wasn't the only heart broken. He's heartbroken as well."

***

Will's been in a very dark place in the months since Julia left. He can't sleep and drinks too much while hibernating in his den and watching television all night. He has no social life. He has no life at all. A few weeks after her graduation, once he'd finished a half bottle of Jack Daniels, he picked up the phone and dialed her number.

He just wanted to hear her voice. Instead he got the operator's recording, *The number you have reached is not in service. Please dial again.* He carefully re-dialed her number and got the same message. Will slowly placed the phone on the receiver. She changed her number. Or left New York. He has no idea where she is.

When he visited Peter in August, Will drove by her apartment in Brooklyn, using his key to get into the building. He was about to knock on her door when her neighbor, Sarah, stopped in the hallway and told him Julia had moved out at the beginning of June. She didn't have any other information. Julia's gone.

His sister has been checking in with him a lot since their breakup, making sure he hasn't swallowed a bottle of pills. He's a mess.

Thanksgiving was his first visit to Rhode Island since July and Will met Ellie at the airport. His sister walked right past him, didn't even recognize him. When he called out after her, she turned around and her face said it all. Very few occasions have rendered Ellie speechless, this was one of them.

He didn't realize how much his days of drinking and staring blankly at a television screen had altered his appearance.

On the drive to their parents' house, his sister regained the power of speech.

"Will, you need to get a grip. I know you're heartbroken, but Jesus, you look awful! Have you looked in the mirror lately? You've lost so much weight and look at those dark circles under your eyes! You're scaring the shit out of me! What are you doing to yourself?"

"El, I'm fine. I'm just not hungry. Every time I eat, I want to throw up, so what am I supposed to do?"

"How about hooking you up to a fucking intravenous feeding tube?" she shouts, "Think that'll do the trick?"

"Don't be ridiculous. I'm not trying to starve myself to death. I'm sure my appetite will return...I don't want to feel like this, Ellie."

Doesn't she understand? He was sure his twin sister would instinctively get what he's going through, but Will was wrong. She doesn't get it, no one does.

I'm heartsick! What's the cure? Someone please tell me!

All weekend, his parents' faces have been pained with concern for him. During Thanksgiving dinner, he felt like a specimen under a magnifying glass, his entire family inspecting his eating habits, searching for signs of abnormalities.

He tried to put a smile on his face and eat what was in front of him. The last thing he wants to do is worry everyone, but apparently it's too late for that. They've been handling him with kid gloves, afraid he'll break if they're not careful.

After dinner, the family disbursed into the living room and Ellie was assigned the task of 'having a talk' with him. Sitting at the table, he has flashbacks of himself, waiting to be scolded for breaking a window, one of his many infractions growing up.

Except this time, it's Ellie instead of his father sitting in the grown up chair.

"Will, I don't think I need to spell this out for you. Clearly, everyone is worried sick about you. Mom and Dad are beside themselves with worry. She's wearing out her rosary beads praying for you. I know this has been a difficult time and you feel all alone, but you're not. We're here for you, Will, all of us. Please, tell me what we can do to help you."

"Can you turn back the clock? Hit rewind and make the past six months go away?"

"If I could, I would. But that's not possible. So, we need a Plan B. Time travel is not an option, so how can we help you get your life back on track?"

"Back on track? What track is that Ellie? The track that's been laid out for me? Or the track I want to take? Because the old track? Screw that. I don't want to go back down that path."

"No one is saying you have to go back to that life. We just want you to have a life. Period! Whatever kind of life you want. But live it, Will! Do something and live your life. Stop wasting it waiting for Julia to come back and make everything better. She's not coming back. It's up to you to make things better."

He rests his head on the table, her words striking a chord in his heart. *Julia's not coming back…* He feels so empty, but Ellie has a point. He needs to live his life and stop feeling sorry for himself.

He tried to fill the void Julia left behind with alcohol and television, but that's a dead end. He wasn't able to parlay the Red Sox's shitty season into a reason to live. No, he understands he needs to find something else to fill the spaces within him that Julia once occupied.

"Will, look at me. You have to try to move on. It's hard to find the light through the darkness, I get it. But if you aren't willing to keep looking for the light in the darkest of places, you never will. You'll get through this. I want you to promise me something," Ellie pleads, "Promise me you'll start taking better care of yourself."

"I don't know where to start." he sighs, sitting up and wiping his eyes.

"Pick one thing that makes you feel good. Something that'll get you out of the house."

"I haven't been to the gym in months."

"Great, start with that. Go two times next week, and three the next. Make it your goal to start running again by the New Year, once you've built up your strength. You've always loved running." He nods his head and she continues, "Find the light, Will. Don't make me go to DC and be your drill sergeant! You know I'll do it too! And for God's sake start eating, you're a scarecrow."

Chapter Fifteen

Julia wants to keep this visit home for Christmas brief. There are too many memories here, too much temptation. She would've stayed in New York and worked over the holiday if she could have, but her mother pleaded with her to come home.

This is the first year her mom isn't leaving for her annual vacation on Christmas Day. She and Ron postponed their trip by a couple of days, which Julia found odd at first, but now understands. Her mother is worried about her.

Since the divorce, she's spent this holiday with her father, until her presence was no longer desired. And over the past two years, Julia's spent it with Will's family. Her mother doesn't want her to be alone this year, which is nice, but unnecessary.

This morning, she received a surprise phone call from her father. He asked if she'd come by his house this afternoon for a talk. She hasn't seen him since graduation in May, a day she'd rather forget, but they still touch base with a brief call every six weeks or so.

She has no desire to see him, but agreed to go out of...*a sense of obligation? A subconscious desire for reconciliation?* She doesn't know why she said yes, but she did and is steeling herself for this meeting. *What does he want from me?*

A little before two in the afternoon, she pulls up to his house. Her father and his new family live in a raised ranch across town. The bushes out front are decorated with Christmas lights and a big wreath with a red bow hangs on the front door. They moved here when they got married six years ago.

They've installed a basketball hoop in the driveway for Sandra's son, Julia's stepbrother, Evan. He's a junior in high school and lives with them most of the time, staying with his father every other weekend.

Her jaw clenches, thinking about her stepbrother. She doesn't know him at all, has absolutely no opinion of the kid one way or the other. What she does know is her dad finally got the son he always wanted. *No wonder he found it so easy to cut me out of his life.*

She stares at the basketball hoop for a few minutes, remembering the hours she spent playing ball with her dad before he left, and almost puts the car in reverse. Before the divorce, she did everything with her father. They went to Red Sox, Celtics, and Patriots games with his friends and their sons, had Saturday morning breakfast together at Hope Diner, practiced pitching in the yard for hours, and shooting hoops in their driveway. Her father was the center of her universe.

Then he was gone. Just like that.

Finally, she takes a deep breath and climbs out of the car. Feet dragging, she walks up the front steps to ring the doorbell, and a moment later, her father opens it with a tight smile. *This is going to be painful,* she thinks, leaning in to give him a peck on the cheek.

"Hi Dad."

"Merry Christmas Julia. Come on in."

The last time she was here, they'd just moved in, her father telling her to think of this as her home as well. When he tried to hand her a key, Sandra practically sprinted across the room and asked to talk to her dad for a moment in private.

A few minutes later, he came out of their bedroom, his face red and his eyes downcast. He walked past Julia, and picked up the remote for the television. When she asked what was going on, her father changed the subject, as he always does when he's uncomfortable.

She could have left it at that, but she knew what had happened and she wanted to hear her father say it to her face. Julia asked for the house key he'd been in the process of handing her moments before, forcing him to tell her, his daughter, that she wouldn't need a key, because they'd always be there when she visits.

Her eyes narrowed into slits, her mouth drawn in a tight line.

"Dad, are you telling me I'm not allowed to be in your home, the home you just told me to think of as my own, without you here?"

Her father didn't know what to say, so he said nothing. She turned to Sandra and repeated her question. Her stepmother had no problem telling her she could only visit when they were home. Julia walked toward her father.

"You really are a gutless wonder."

Then she turned to Sandra, flipped her off, and left.

Trying to shake off that precious memory, Julia walks up the few steps to the main level of the house, making note of the changes they've made since she was last here. The living room has been refurnished and now has a brown leather sofa and love seat, and a matching recliner. *That has to be her dads*, she thinks absently, he loves recliners.

The walls are painted beige, and one is covered with family pictures. The Christmas tree is decorated with silver ornaments and colored lights, and the television is turned to ESPN, her father's favorite channel.

Sandra walks out of the kitchen, wiping her hands on a dishtowel, her face pinched.

"Hello, Julia. Nice to see you again."

Is she supposed to give her a hug? What's the proper protocol for a situation like this? Julia smiles and raises her hand in greeting and Sandra turns off the television, taking a seat on the couch beside her father.

"Please, sit, Julia."

She sits down as instructed, and hugs her coat to herself, itching to get out of here. She'd rather be almost anywhere than in this room, with her father and stepmother.

"So," she says after an awkward pause, "You wanted to talk to me?"

"Julia…" Sandra begins. "I want us to be a family. I know we've had our differences, but the stress of this ongoing feud between you and your dad is killing him. Literally, I'm afraid he's going to have a heart attack and die."

She stares at them blankly for a moment. Sandra has tears in her eyes, her father's face is drawn. *She wants us to be a family? Is she out of her goddamned mind?* It's a little too late for that!

Julia glances around the room, noticing pictures of Evan on almost every surface, one of her grandparents, another of Sandra's parents. Not one of Julia. Not even the one they forced her to pose for on graduation day.

"Have you been to the doctor, Dad?"

Sandra doesn't give him the opportunity to answer, "His blood pressure is through the roof. He needs peace in his life."

She raises an eyebrow and studies her father. He's aged quite a bit in the past few years.

"Sandra," she levels her eyes on her stepmother, "I'd like to have a word alone with my father."

Her stepmother doesn't look thrilled at the prospect.

"That's fine," her father says, "Sandy, why don't you take a trip to Almacs. You said you needed a few things for tomorrow's dinner."

Sandra nods and turns to Julia, "Remember his blood pressure."

Once her stepmother leaves, her father sits back on the couch and folds his arms over his chest, preparing for an attack. He hates conflict, despises confrontation. Julia knows the directives over the past few years have come directly from Sandra, not her dad.

But it was still wrong.

"Dad, I'm sorry you're having health issues. I don't want to contribute to them, but what do you want me to say? You tossed me out like a piece of garbage. I'm your daughter. Your only child! You told me to stay away, and now you expect me to just put it aside and pretend nothing ever happened?"

He closes his eyes, sits forward in his seat and rests his head in his hands. *Will does the same thing*, she thinks, her heart skipping a beat.

"Julia, I never wanted you to stay away, but Sandra was so uncomfortable around you after that argument. I didn't know what to do."

"You didn't know what to do? I'm your child! You tell her she's wrong! You grow some balls, Dad! You tell her that this is your home and therefore your daughter's home. You don't cut me out of your life! What kind of parent does that to their child?"

She's furious. This has been bottled up inside her for years and she finally has the chance to unload. Her father has turned grey, and Julia can hear Sandra's voice saying, *remember his blood pressure...*

"Look," she takes a deep breath, "I understand you have to live with her every day, and she's not easy. But you chose the path of least resistance. You didn't fight for me, Dad. Do you have any idea how much you hurt me?"

A tear rolls down her father's cheek. Then another, and another. Julia is stunned into silence. She's only seen him cry once before and it wasn't at either of his parents' funerals. The only other time was the day he told her about the divorce. She was blindsided, couldn't understand what was happening. She closed her eyes, covered her ears and screamed to block out his words and when she opened them, her father was crying on her bed.

She didn't know what to do then, and has no clue what to do now.

"Julia, I'm so sorry," he says, his shoulders shaking, "I was wrong, honey. What I did was wrong and I'm sorry I hurt you."

She stands up and paces around the room. *Do I forgive him?* She vowed she never would after he left home. When he chose to side with Sandra and cut her out of his life, he broke her heart. But, in spite of everything, she still loves her father.

She remembers what Gabby said in September. Her parents didn't mean to hurt her, they're human and made mistakes. If she can forgive her mother for her reckless behavior after the divorce, she should be able to forgive her father for his shortcomings.

Julia sits down beside her dad and touches his hand, not sure what she wants to say. Then her father does something completely unexpected, something he hasn't done in years. He wraps his arms around her and holds her, and her eyes fill with tears.

"I love you, sweetheart."

Julia squeezes him tightly and bursts into tears. She hasn't heard her father say those words to her in years and they're powerful. She knows deep down her father means what he's saying. *He loves me.*

"I love you too, Dad."

After she left her father's house, Julia took a long drive around town. She agreed to stop over for dessert the next day and even gave Sandra a hug before she left. They have a long way to go before they have anything resembling a relationship, but it's a step in the right direction.

A huge weight has been lifted, she didn't realize how much this rift with her father was dragging her down. Will helped fill the hole left by her dad, the depth of his love transcended the pain of her father's rejection. But since their breakup, she's felt the void more acutely than ever before. Her father's love means more to her than she thought it did.

When the sun begins to set, she knows it's time to go home and get ready for her aunt's Christmas Eve dinner. *This time last year I was in bed with Will.* They made love and laughed and talked. She wonders if she'll ever feel that way about anyone again. *Maybe you only get one great love?*

Her best friend has never stopped advocating for Will, not once in the past six months. Gabby believes Will is Julia's soulmate. She never believed in such things before she met Will, but their connection was definitely soulful, as if something bigger was drawing them together.

She's forgiven her father, maybe she can forgive Will?

She doesn't know what happened between Will and Avery that night, but has no doubt Avery pushed her way into his house at a vulnerable moment and took advantage of the situation.

Sitting at the stop sign on her way out of Colt Park, Julia fights the urge to drive to his parents' house. He has to be home for Christmas and they live less than two miles from this spot, she thinks, gripping the steering wheel tightly.

Turn right or left?

Right takes her to Will, left takes her home. Julia sits at the intersection for several minutes, the battle being waged between her heart and her head, until the cars behind her blare their horns.

Flustered, she turns left and spends the remainder of the evening at her aunt's house, watching the clock inching toward midnight. *I just want to see his face*, she tells herself, her heart beating hard against her chest. *I need to see him.*

At eleven-thirty she climbs into her car and drives to St. Margaret's for midnight mass. At church, she can see Will and not have to speak to him. Unless she wants to.

Julia shivers outside the church, waiting for the service to begin. When she hears the choir singing 'O Holy Night', she sneaks into the back of the church, finding a seat in the last row. It's a candlelight mass and the soft light illuminates the chamber, the pungent smell of incense permeating the air around her. The altar is decorated with dozens of poinsettia plants and Christmas trees with twinkling white lights adorn each side.

Everyone is standing during the priest's procession up the main aisle of the church, and Will is easy to spot near the front. He's taller than most of the congregation, his golden hair further setting him apart from the crowd. She can hardly breathe. She hasn't seen him in over six months and it's torture being in the same room.

Dear Lord, please tell me what to do, she kneels in the pew and prays, *I miss him so much.* A lapsed Catholic, Julia doesn't expect God to take notice of her now and no answers are forthcoming.

Throughout mass, she watches Will, but can only see the back of his head. After receiving communion, he returns to his seat and Julia catches a glimpse of his face for the first time. *His eyes are so sad...* She bows her head, trying to hold back the tears.

This was my choice, I turned him away.

Julia desperately wants to reach out and hold him, to take away his sadness and tell him she still loves him, but forces herself to stay put.

As mass ends, Will shakes hands with a few people sitting behind him, and his eyes scan the church. She remains seated, knowing if she doesn't leave now he'll see her...soon.

Her breath catches as their eyes meet, her heart swelling with emotion. Her reconciliation with her father has ripped a huge hole in her armor, and all she wants is to hold him. She doesn't care about the rest.

Will's eyes light up and he exits the pew quickly, trying to reach her, but gets caught up in the masses streaming into the aisle. She rises and their eyes lock as he squeezes through the crowds of people. She wants to talk to Will, needs to feel his arms around her, his mouth on hers.

She reaches down to pick up her bag and freezes, her face falling. Out of the corner of her eye, Julia spots Avery standing at the opposite side of the church, trying to exit through the side door.

Her stomach lurches and tears spring into her eyes. *Why is she here?* They can't be together, Avery's sitting clear across the church. Julia's chin trembles and Avery's voice echoes in her head, *Women like you don't end up with men like Will.*

Coming here was a mistake. Her heart's breaking all over again and she's desperate to get out of the church. Before Will can reach her, Julia slips out the back door, runs down the steps and disappears into the night, her face wet with tears.

Chapter Sixteen

Will began visiting a gym near his house after Thanksgiving, as he promised his sister he would. Most days, he heads there directly after work and exercises for over an hour, running on the treadmill and lifting weights. It has saved his sanity and helped him regain his appetite. He may look like himself again, but he doesn't feel like himself. At least not who he was with Julia. *Will I ever be happy again?*

Since May, his depression had only gotten worse, and who knows what would've happened if he hadn't made an oath to try and rebuild his life. His drinking was getting out of hand as he anesthetized himself, trying to dull the pain of losing Julia.

The first time Will saw Avery at his gym was the week after Christmas. He was finishing his workout when he spotted her on a treadmill across the room, and quickly left. Seeing Avery brought back the memory of that morning, waking up beside her, knowing he couldn't keep what happened from Julia, that it meant the end for them.

The sight of her made him sick inside. *What is she doing here? Is it a coincidence?*

The following day, he was running late and bumped into Avery in the lobby. Startled, he froze and felt the heat rising to his cheeks, anger lodging in his stomach. She smiled awkwardly and said, "Happy New Year, Will," then walked past him into the ladies locker room. If Avery's coming to this gym, maybe it's time for him to find another one.

If Will thought there was any chance of getting back together with Julia he would've switched gyms the second he saw Avery there. But now he knows there's absolutely no chance of that happening.

He tried desperately to reach her on Christmas Eve, but when he finally made it to the rear of the church, she was gone. He rushed into the cold night air, pulling his coat on, breathless with excitement and searched for her among the congregants gathered on the steps. But she had disappeared. Moments later, Ellie and Kevin met up with him outside.

"Will, what's gotten into you?"

"Ellie, Julia was here. She was sitting in the last row. I saw her."

"Honey, I think you're imagining things." Ellie and Kevin exchanged doubtful looks.

"No, I'm sure it was her." He grabbed his sisters hands, "We made eye contact. It was Julia."

"Will, she's gone," Ellie sighed. "If she wanted to talk to you she would've stayed."

His face fell and he stared out at the Town Common.

"Ellie, if she didn't want to see me…why would she come at all?"

"That, I don't know."

The next day, he drove to Julia's house and was surprised when her mother answered the door. She's usually away for Christmas.

"Hi Carol. Is Julia here?"

"Hello, Will. No, I'm afraid she's not home."

His face fell.

"I'd really like to talk to her…"

"I'm sorry, Will." Carol looked at the floor. "Julia asked that I not give you her contact information."

"What?" Her words hit him square in the chest. "When did she say that?"

"This morning. I really am sorry."

"Merry Christmas, Carol," he said with a sad smile and turned to leave.

"You too, Will," she said softly, closing the door.

He has to accept it's over with Julia. She doesn't want him in her life, and as painful as that is, he needs to come to terms with that fact. What choice does he have?

The third time he saw Avery, he realized it didn't matter whether she's a member of his gym or not. He hasn't made any real friends in the time he's been in Washington. He doesn't have a lot in common with his coworkers except maybe baseball. Whenever the Sox are in the area, he and a couple of guys from his office, both native New Englanders, attend games. That's the extent of Will's social life.

Everyone in DC wants to move up some invisible ladder, make connections with powerful people, and be seen at the right places. It reminds him a lot of the world he grew up in, except here, it doesn't matter as much the family you were born into, what's important is who you know, and how ambitious you are. Will has no political aspirations, and isn't power hungry. He couldn't care less about climbing a single rung of the Washington ladder.

What's become painfully obvious to him is the depth of his loneliness. He's never been this alone in his life. After the initial shock wore off, it felt good to see a friendly face. So, when Avery happened to be on the treadmill next to his the following week and started making small talk, he was a willing participant. It was innocent enough, she chatted about the weather, then they talked about how they spent their holidays. The hour went by quickly, and he left the gym with the slightest smile that night, his first in months.

Last week after his workout, Will stopped at the coffee shop he frequently visits and Avery was already in line. She wasn't at the gym that day, and he was a bit disappointed. They waited in line together, discussing her art classes, and he could've walked out when the barista handed him his drink, but he didn't. The shop was crowded, and Avery found a table, so he asked if he could join her.

The truth is he didn't want to be alone. He was tired of his own company. And Avery was there, and familiar. He didn't have to get to know her, he already did. Over the past two weeks, they've been getting coffee together most days after the gym. Will doesn't have to make an effort at conversation with her, she has lots of stories to share, and he just sits back, listens, and answers the occasional question.

"Will, I hate to bring this up, but it's like the elephant in the room and I'd like to clear the air. What happened between you and Julia?"

He looks down at his coffee for a moment, his jaw clenched, then directly into Avery's eyes, wanting to gauge her response.

"I told her what happened between us and she ended it."

"I'm so sorry for interfering with your relationship." A tear rolls down her cheek, and she wipes it away, "I don't know what I was thinking. I was so lonely down here, and I missed seeing you. I've been seeing a wonderful therapist. I told her what happened between us, when we were kids, and last spring, and she's helped me put a lot of things into perspective." Avery rests her hand on top of his, "I want you to know I deeply regret what happened between us in May. I am so sorry and I hope you can forgive me."

He sits back in his chair and stares out the window. He can't believe he's sitting with Avery, talking about his breakup with Julia. *How did I get here?* He's lonely and as warped as it seems, even to him, Avery is the closest thing he has to a friend.

"There's nothing to forgive, Avery. I'm just as much to blame."

RING! RING!

Will sits up in bed with a start and squints in the early morning light filtering through the frost-coated windows. *One day I'm going to remember to pull down those shades*, he thinks, groaning. He grabs his alarm clock, wondering who'd be calling him at six o'clock on a Saturday morning? Reaching for the phone, he remembers… it's January 30th.

Today is his twenty-fifth birthday.

It has to be his mother, no one else would call him this early. He picks up the phone and smiles sleepily, flopping back against his pillows.

"Happy birthday sweetheart," his mother says, sniffling, "I hate to wake you so early but I have something to tell you."

"What's wrong, Mom?"

"Will, Daddy's sick."

He sits up in bed, rubbing the sleep from his eyes, instantly wide-awake.

"What do you mean *sick*? Where is he?"

"He hasn't been feeling well and the doctor did some tests. Daddy has cancer, Will, and it doesn't look good. Please, pray for him."

"Mom, I'm coming home." He jumps out of bed and pulls on the nearest pair of pants, "I'll see you this afternoon."

For the first time in years, Will does the rosary on the flight home later that morning. Peter meets him at the airport and they wait another hour for Ellie's flight from Chicago to arrive in Providence.

They spend the week with their parents, meeting with doctors and discussing various options. The cancer is in his pancreas, and has spread to some of his lymph nodes. They're going to treat the disease aggressively, and his father starts chemotherapy this coming week.

The day Will's due to return to Washington, he takes a seat in the armchair beside his father, who's resting on the couch in the den.

"Dad, I think I should take a leave of absence from work. Stay home and help you and mom."

"Don't be ridiculous, Will. I won't have you neglect your responsibilities at work because of me. I'll be fine. I have your mother and nurses will come by every day to help."

"I want to be here."

"I want you to go live your life," his father says, sternly, "Come visit when you can. I'm going to be fine."

Will studies him for a moment, filled with sadness and fear. Then, his father's eyes soften and he squeezes Will's hand, reassuringly. In that moment, he understands just how much his father needs things to remain as normal as possible. He needs it to give him hope.

"I understand," Will nods his head. "I'll see you soon."

"That's my boy!"

On the flight back to Washington, all he wants to do is call Julia, tell her what's happening. He wants to crawl into bed with her and feel her arms around him, calming his fears. But he can't. Will's profoundly alone and has no one to turn to. Avery's all he has, his only friend in the world.

When he returns home, he calls her and later that night they meet for a drink. In a dimly lit bar a few blocks from his house, Will tells Avery about his father's illness and his grim prognosis. She holds his hand while he voices his fears and comforts him when he needs it. Her presence is soothing, and it feels so good to have someone care about him again.

He invites her back to his house and once inside the foyer, Will's consumed with the desperate need to feel something, anything but the emptiness that's been gnawing at his insides for close to a year. He wants to forget his father's cancer, forget about Julia. It's been so long since he's touched anyone.

He's sinking and Avery is his lifeboat, something to hold onto before he drowns in sorrow. Impatiently, Will sheds his clothes as they climb the stairs to his room, and silently, he prays for a miracle, that somehow he can transcend his pain and loneliness in her arms.

Afterwards, Avery curls up beside him, her arm around his waist, and a smile on her lips. His head is pounding. *What did I do?* He stares at the ceiling, his stomach knotted with dread and regret. He consciously chose to have sex with Avery, he can't blame alcohol for this one.

For him, sex was an escape, his pain fleetingly alleviated in the height of passion, only to come crashing down again moments later. But to Avery…this wasn't about sex, he can see it in her eyes. This was a promise, a commitment.

He closes his eyes, his heart sinking with understanding. There's no turning back now, having sex with Avery has sealed his fate. His future is mapped out, engraved in stone, and it's nothing like the one he'd envisioned with Julia.

But he's come full circle and has to accept the consequences of his actions. The woman beside him once carried his child and by inviting her back into his life, he's accepted responsibility for her.

Avery's here to stay.

Every single day Will tries to make peace with his choices. What if people are only allotted a certain amount of happiness in their lives? Maybe he used up his allotment of 'happy' with

Julia. He has to make it work with Avery, and continually seeks common ground, some way to connect with her on an emotional level, but he's coming up empty.

In the beginning, he thought maybe sex would be enough to draw them closer. Avery initiates sex as often as possible, and during those first few weeks it was a relief to lose himself in the moment, but now he sees their behavior for what it is.

A diversionary tactic.

If they're having sex, they don't have to talk about anything of substance. Small talk was fine while they were friends, but now? It's not enough.

One weekend in early March, a freak storm hit DC, burying the city in four feet of snow. Will and Avery were trapped inside his townhouse for three days. The first day wasn't so bad. They spent the day in bed, having sex, sleeping and eating.

By noon on the second day, they needed to find other ways to spend their time. After two painful hours of listening to Avery babble about nothing in particular, Will suggested they retreat to the den and watch a movie marathon on television.

On the third day, Avery stayed in the kitchen, talking for hours with friends on the telephone, while Will sat in the library, pretending to read a book, and wondering what the hell he was going to do next. *I can't spend my life like this!*

Maybe this storm was a blessing in disguise. Maybe Avery will realize their relationship has no foundation, and she'll decide to end things. It has to come from her. Will can't be the one to break it off.

There's nothing about their relationship that comes close to the level of intimacy, friendship and passion he shared with Julia. Will hasn't dated a lot of women, but he knows what they had was special. Gabby called them soulmates, and he believes they are, if such a thing exists. And if that's the case, he lost his soulmate and will never feel that way about anyone again. So, what he has with Avery, Will figures, is as good as it's going to get for him.

Avery didn't end their relationship after their snowbound weekend and they never spoke of it again. But since then, she's made sure they always have somewhere to go or something to do. Aided and abetted by his good friend Vodka, Will follows Avery's lead. Over the past few months she's reconnected him with old friends, people he wrote off years ago, and they travel to parties and go to the yacht club when they're in Rhode Island.

Will has his old life back. It's not the life he would have chosen for himself, but he's determined to make the best of things. Enough is enough. It's time to stop wallowing in self-pity over what he can never have. He may not be in love with Avery, but he's never alone. That's got to count for something.

He keeps in close touch with his father, calling him daily and visiting every other weekend. His dad was always a strong, vibrant man and watching him shrivel and shrink, and become dependent on his mother's care has deeply affected Will. He wants to make his father proud, now more than ever. He needs to prove he's grown into a responsible, respectable adult, just as his father hoped. He may not have much time left to do that.

Avery's with him on this latest trip to Rhode Island. She's joined him a few times over the past four months, foregoing parties and other social events of importance to her, in order to support Will through this tough time. Whenever he's down about his father, she's there with a hug, a kiss, a little something to show she cares. In this regard, Avery's been of some comfort to him.

Compassion seems to be Avery's strength. She sits with his father for hours doing crossword puzzles, relieves his mother of cooking duties so she can rest, and runs errands for the family if needed. These small kindnesses mean a lot to him.

He knows he's grasping at straws, but whenever she drags him to parties, or thinks about how little they actually have in common, he remembers the compassionate side of Avery, and it sustains him for the moment. Long enough for him to dispel any notion of running away.

Today, after sitting with his dad for an hour, Will and Avery took a walk down to the water. His father has a few more sessions of chemotherapy before they start radiation and he tires easily. Will hardly recognizes him anymore.

His mother has been amazing through all this. She's quietly run their home and family since the early days of his parents' marriage, but his father was the dominant personality. Not anymore. She's a force to be reckoned with. She refuses to lose faith, conferring with the doctors about his treatments, doing her own research on the disease and alternative therapies.

She keeps his father on a schedule, deals with the nurses, makes sure he's fed, bathed, and medicated. His mother is fully in charge, and Will has to admit, he's impressed. He honestly didn't know she had it in her.

"He doesn't seem to be getting any better," Avery says, massaging his back. "Your father wants to see you settled down, Will. Married, with children. I think that'd make all the difference to him, whether his health improves or god forbid, doesn't."

Will sits on a rock and covers his eyes. He understands what Avery's saying, has thought of that himself. *But marry Avery?* He can't imagine standing before God and his family, pledging his life to her. He knows it's the next step, but his stomach turns at the thought.

What would life be like if he married Avery? Well…it'd be exactly like this, the same life he's known for all but two years of his life. *The happiest two years.* It isn't awful. They have 'friends' in common, and have a good time when they go out. What Will doesn't understand is how he can still feel lonely when he's constantly surrounded by people? He never felt lonely with Julia.

Maybe this is my penance? He betrayed the woman he loves, now he must suffer. *Ten Hail Marys and Our Fathers aren't enough to wash away my sins.* From the corner of his eye, he studies Avery sitting on the rock beside him, and tries to assess his feelings for her.

Grateful is the word that comes to mind. He's grateful for the compassion she's shown him and his parents these past few months. He's grateful to her for getting him out of the house again and back into the world. And what better way to make things right with Avery, to make amends for what he did to her so many years ago, than to marry her and give her a child?

Chapter Seventeen

Will proposes to Avery a few days before Independence Day. The irony is not lost on him. He took her out on his father's boat, bought champagne and flowers, and knelt down and asked her to marry him in the moonlight.

His proposal was thoroughly unoriginal, but Avery didn't seem to mind. She had tears in her eyes when she said yes, but when she looked down at the ring he bought, he could tell she wasn't thrilled. Quickly, before she even had the chance to touch it, he snapped the lid shut and lied. He said it was a family heirloom, a placeholder for the one she could pick out for herself the next day.

Lying alone in his bed later that night Will took the ring out of its black leather box and studied it. He was drawn to it the moment he saw it. Set in an antique platinum setting, it's about one carat in size with delicate flowers etched onto the sides. Holding it up to the light, his heart sinks as he realizes...*I didn't buy this ring for Avery, I bought it for Julia.* He bought an engagement ring for a woman he can't have.

Will fell asleep with the ring in his hand, and dreamt he was back at Mount Vernon with Julia. They were lying on a blanket by a pond and she wore the white sundress she had on the night they met. The cherry trees were in full bloom and the sun warmed them as they lay together, watching the clouds float by.

He slid the ring onto her finger, knowing in his heart they're meant to be together. It felt so right. Julia's face broke into a radiant smile, and with a gasp…Will woke up in a cold sweat, his breathing labored and squeezed his eyes shut, willing himself back to sleep.

Julia… Julia… don't go.

He wants to be back at Mount Vernon with Julia. It was so real, he could smell her, feel her…. But it was just a dream. Clasping the ring tightly in his hand, Will rolls over and cries into his pillow, finally understanding what he's sacrificing marrying Avery. *Joy. Love. Hope.*

But if I can't have Julia, what difference does it make who I marry?

Will can't make eye contact with Ellie. He and Avery have just announced their engagement at the family party the night before the Fourth of July, and his sister's mouth dropped open in shock or horror. Probably both. Ellie grabbed Kevin's arm and for a moment Will thought she was going to faint. He never should've made this announcement before sharing the news with Ellie. The moment the words came out of his mouth he regretted his oversight.

He knows what she's going to say, and he doesn't want to hear it. Ellie's made her disapproval known the second she found out about them dating back in February. After a screaming match over the telephone, during which Ellie did ninety percent of the yelling, his sister refused speak to him for over a month, and even now will only talk to him if Avery isn't around. Ellie hates his bride-to-be, and he wishes she'd leave the past where it belongs. That's what he's trying to do.

Hoping to avoid a confrontation in front of his relatives, Will makes a plan. He figures as long as he remains by Avery's side, he's safe. Ellie won't say anything in front of Avery, so that's what he's going to do. Stick to his fiancé like glue for the rest of the evening.

"Will! Avery! Wow! I don't know what to say!" Ellie declares, as she and Kevin descend upon them.

Ellie's eyes are fixed on Will, her feelings a neon sign flashing across her forehead, and embarrassed, Will feels the heat rising from his neck to his face. *She can't do it, can she?* Ellie can't wish them well and save the lecture for later.

Kevin is the polar opposite of his sister, the yin to her yang. Will knows Kevin doesn't like Avery either, but he'd never show it. Ever the diplomat, he shakes Will's hand and kisses Avery on the cheek, congratulating them. Will wants to shout, *See Ellie! It can be done! Watch and learn from your fiancé!*

"Wow!" Ellie laughs. "Just…wow!"

Avery's eyes open wide and she clutches his hand, while Will clenches his jaw, praying she'll stop. People are starting to stare. Their engagement is a joke in her mind, and Ellie does what she does best and makes a scene, laughing uncontrollably. Kevin tries to pull her away, but her fingers are a vice gripping Will's arm, and she won't let go.

"Excuse us, Avery."

He grabs his sister's arm and steers her around the corner, to the side garden, which is blessedly free of relatives. His parents decided to throw their annual party, despite his father's health, and Will thought it would be the perfect setting to announce their engagement.

What the hell was I thinking? He wasn't, that's the problem. This discussion should have happened pre-party so Ellie could get her ranting out of the way.

"Am I dreaming, Will?" Ellie laughs, "Did someone slip me acid? Am I hallucinating? Jesus H. Christ! Please, someone tell me *what the fuck* is going on here!" she yells, her voice laced with hysteria.

"I can't believe you're doing this to me, El. To Mom and Dad! You're embarrassing everyone and making a spectacle of yourself."

"This cannot be happening. Will, you can't marry Avery! How can you even stand to be in the same room with that bitch after what she did to you and Julia? Are you fucking high?"

"I'm a grown man. I make my own decisions. You need to butt out of this."

"I'm sorry, have we met? My name is Eleanor Kennedy, and you are...?" Ellie's eyes grow sad, "You know I can't butt out of this. I won't keep my mouth shut when my twin brother is about to walk off a cliff!"

He takes a seat on one of the stone benches in the garden, resting his head in his hands. He knows there's nothing he can say to make this situation palatable to his sister, but he's made up his mind.

Kevin rounds the corner and joins them, rubbing Ellie's shoulders. They've been engaged since Christmas and are getting married next month. Last year, Ellie sat their parents down and explained how much Kevin means to her and when she mentioned his race, she said they stared at her blankly for a moment, and then their father said, "Ellie, I didn't raise my children to judge people by the color of their skin. If you love him, if he's good to you and treats you the way you deserve...well, that's all we could ask for."

He'd never discussed race with his parents, Bristol being the whitest town in America. Will wasn't sure how they'd react to Kevin and was relieved when they welcomed him into the family. There's been some talk in society circles, but his parents say if anyone has a problem with Kevin they can stay away, that other people's ignorance isn't their concern. Sometimes his parents really do surprise him.

Ellie sits beside Will and takes his hand in hers.

"Will, what are you doing? You don't love her."

"Ellie you don't know what I feel," he says.

"We shared a womb, remember? I know you're not in love with Avery. I've seen you in love, and this ain't it."

"Why would you do that?" He turns to her angrily, "I can't have the woman I love, she's gone! Don't you get it? I'll never have that again."

"I'm sorry, Will, I didn't mean to pick the scab." She strokes his arm, "Listen to me. You may not have Julia, but you could fall in love with someone else. I want that for you. Why would you settle for anything less?"

He shakes his head and stares at their father, sitting in his wheelchair beneath a tree. He doesn't expect Ellie to understand.

"Don't do this for Dad, Will." He turns sharply, looking into Ellie's eyes. "Marrying her won't save him. Dad's fate is in God's hands, not yours."

"Be happy for me, Ellie, please."

***

There's nothing like Bristol, Rhode Island on the Fourth of July. Julia's hometown proudly hosts the oldest Independence Day parade in the country and it's a big deal to pretty much everyone in town. Living there, it's impossible to avoid getting swept up in the spirit of the holiday, unless you hibernate for the two weeks surrounding it.

Every year she sits through three hours of marching bands and elaborate floats in weather ranging from blistering heat and oppressive humidity to freezing rain, and she wouldn't dream of missing it.

The Fourth of July Committee selects a Grand Marshall to preside over the festivities and hosts a contest to name the most patriotic house. People all over town decorate their homes with flags, red, white and blue bunting, and patriotic floral arrangements.

A local pageant is held annually to select Miss Fourth of July and her Court, which seems strange to Julia, considering the reason for celebrating this holiday...independence from King George, freedom from the monarchy.

In the ten days leading up to the parade, the town sponsors a different concert every night in front of Colt School, with music ranging from country music, polka, to classic rock, and folk. A little something for everyone. The Boston Pops play at Independence Park the night before the parade, with a grand fireworks display following the concert.

The parade itself is televised and marching bands from all over the country participate. The street divider along the parade route is painted red, white and blue instead of yellow or white, and people who live along the four-mile route sit outside in lawn chairs nightly to watch thousands of people streaming into town for the festivities. To say it's an experience would be an understatement.

This is Julia's first visit home since Christmas. She's been in Bristol for two days and plans on staying the week. She's been casually dating a musician from New York for a month or so. Ted's tall and thin with long light brown hair, blue eyes, and a scruffy chin.

He plays guitar in an alternative rock band that's starting to get some traction, and takes his music very seriously. He seems to be moderately intelligent, but she honestly doesn't care if he is or isn't, she's not dating him for his mind.

Since Christmas, despite Gabby's protests, Julia's had a few purely sexual involvements. She's done with emotional entanglements. Will cured her of that. She's not interested in getting to know these men, they're for pleasure only. As soon as she senses they want more from her, she breaks it off.

Julia made the mistake of telling Ted about Bristol's 'famous' parade. They were out with a group of mutual friends and someone asked what she was doing over the holiday. She described how unbelievably patriotic her hometown is and Ted said he had to see it for himself. He grew up in Queens and has never been to a Fourth of July parade. Every year his family has a cookout and sets off their own fireworks, that's the extent of the celebration.

Before she left for college, Julia assumed everyone celebrated Independence Day with as much fervor as her townspeople, but that's definitely not the case. Over the years, many of her friends from New York have come to stay with her over the holiday and they've never been disappointed.

Ted borrowed a friend's car and drove in early this morning. Honestly, she's surprised he showed up at all. He had a gig last night in New York City and apparently drove straight to Rhode Island after the show. She heard the knock on her mom's door around five this morning and they got a couple hours sleep before they left for the parade.

He's only here for the day. His band has another show later tonight back in the city, and that's plenty for her. Before today, their interactions were limited to sex, music, and dancing. Conversation? Not so much.

Walking along the parade route, Ted's amazed by the size of the crowds, the red, white and blue everything and, in his words, "over-the-top patriotism." They've never discussed politics before, but she's not surprised that he's an anti-establishment, revolutionary kind of guy. She said if he's a rebel, he should read up on John Adams, Thomas Jefferson, and Benjamin Franklin.

"They could've been hung for spreading sedition against the Crown. They're the ultimate revolutionaries."

"You're such a dork," he laughs.

"Thank you, Ted," she rolls her eyes, "I'm proud of my dorkiness."

Arm in arm they walk down the road, Julia scanning the crowd as they make their way down Hope Street and into the downtown district. The weather is closely watched in the days leading up to the parade, and today they've been blessed with the 'perfect day,' sunny, not too hot, low humidity.

She's wearing cut off jean shorts with a white ribbed tank top and Birkenstock sandals, her hair piled on top of her head in a loose bun. Ted looks like the rocker he is, in a faded black Pink Floyd t-shirt and tan cargo shorts, his hair pulled back in a ponytail.

She's surrounded by familiar faces, and friends from high school run up to her on the street and hug, making promises to stay in touch she knows they'll never keep. She waves to scores more.

"What are you? A local celebrity?" Ted asks.

"Nah. This is small town America. Everyone knows everybody here."

When they reach Linden Place the crowd thins out a little. She always loved the mansion and the gardens surrounding it, even if it was built with blood money. It's an impressive dwelling and Ted points to it as they approach.

"Who lives there?"

"No one anymore." She stops and walks up to the wrought iron gate. "It was built by the DeWolf family and the Colt's lived here for years, but now it's a museum and event space. People have weddings and parties here."

There are dozens of people socializing on the lawn.

"What's going on now?" Ted asks.

"Every year people with too much money pay a small fortune to attend a party here on the Fourth." She rolls her eyes, "They watch the parade behind their private iron gate, away from we plebes."

Julia steps up onto the stonewall and looks through the bars of the gate and her breath catches in her throat.

Will is on the lawn of the mansion. *With Avery.*

Her eyes open wide in horror and she loses her balance, almost falling onto the crowded sidewalk. Ted steadies her and she quickly steps down. Will is at the parade with Avery. She's nauseous, her stomach churning. *I have to get out of here.*

"Come on, let's go," she grabs hold of Ted's hand.

"Julia!" Will quickly walks to the gate separating them.

She's a caged animal, trapped by the people surrounding her. A marching band is playing in front of them and the revelers have stopped to listen, boxing her in. Her throat is closing and her survival instincts have taken over rational thought.

Escape! She needs to run, but can't move. Julia turns away from the sound of his voice, hoping the band with block it out and tries to catch her breath.

"Jules," Ted elbows her, "Someone's calling you. The dude with the bowtie."

If I turn to look at him, will I turn into a pillar of salt?

Julia plasters a smile on her face and slowly turns. Will's standing three feet away from her, but they're light years apart.

He's with his tribe, she's with hers.

She takes a moment to take in his outfit. He's wearing navy blue pants, a white short-sleeve button down shirt and, sure enough, a patriotic bowtie. *Who picked out this costume?* Avery, of course.

Will reaches through the iron bars surrounding the grounds of the mansion and Julia stares at his hand for a moment, the fingers that know every inch of her so well, and instinctively places her hand in his.

The electricity is still there.

She hasn't felt it with any of the lovers she's taken over the past year. She blinks and forgets where she is, that Avery is somewhere on the lawn, ready to stake her claim. The sound of her heart beating and the blood rushing to her head drowns out the noises around her. Their eyes lock for what feels like minutes, but couldn't have been more than a few seconds. For this brief moment, they're alone, just the two of them.

"Hi," she says.

"Hi," Will smiles.

"Hello, Julia. What a surprise." Avery joins them at the fence, her face pinched, and Julia quickly releases Will's hand, and remembers she's not alone.

"I'm sorry. This is Ted. Ted, this is Will and…" she blinks, her mind a blank. *What is her name?*

Ted gives Julia a strange look, then raises his hand in greeting. Will's gaze is fixed on her face, and doesn't acknowledge Ted, just continues to stare at her in silence.

"Hello, Ted. I'm Avery, Will's fiancé." Avery holds up her hand and flashes an enormous diamond solitaire engagement ring.

Julia's heart stops and her mouth drops open. There is absolutely no way she can hide her dismay. She turns to Will in confusion, not bothering to hide her pain.

You're marrying her? Her eyes fill with tears and Will looks down, rubbing his hand across his brow.

"Congratulations," she murmurs, then turns to Avery, "Good work."

Avery's eyes narrow and she smiles, gratification and smugness oozing from her pores.

"Goodbye, Will."

Julia swallows hard and grabs hold of Ted's hand, pushing her way through the crowds. They weave through the marching band, across Hope Street and down the nearest side street to the water.

As soon as the crowds part, she breaks into a run and finds herself at Rockwell Park, on the same dock she sat with Will the night they met, and buries her face in her hands.

They're getting married! Will and Avery are getting married! How could he marry the woman who tore us apart? This isn't happening, she cries into her hands, *he can't do this!*

"What happened there, Julia?" Ted asks, catching up to her.

"I'm sorry Ted. I just need a minute." She can't stop crying and is desperate to be alone.

"I'll be over there if you need me." Ted points to the swings, and squeezes her shoulder before he walks away.

She's in agony, trying desperately to make sense of this. Will is marrying Avery. *He's marrying her!* The words reverberate, a relentless ringing in her head. Julia covers her ears, praying for the words to fade away. *Please stop!* She can't bear the thought.

If you frustrate love, you get an ocean made out of lovers' tears. What else is love? It's a wise form of madness. A form of madness... Shakespeare nailed it again.

This news is madness and she cries an ocean of tears, sitting in the spot Will first showed her the constellations in the night sky.

When she's regained control of her emotions, she sits on the swing beside Ted, thankful he gave her the space she needed.

"He's my ex-boyfriend. I've had a tough time getting over him. His engagement... threw me. I'm sorry." She makes an effort to smile, but fails.

"It's okay, Jules." He wraps his arm around her, "I have an ex too. She broke my heart. It gets easier with time."

"Thanks, Ted." She smiles weakly, leaning into him for comfort.

"For what it's worth, that guy's still in love with you."

"It doesn't matter." She shakes her head, "He's getting married."

Julia's done a lot of soul searching since July and it's time to let go of Will and move on with her life. After the parade, Ted drove back to New York and Julia took to her bed for the remainder of her vacation. Gabby came over every day, trying to snap her out of her depression, but it was her mother who finally helped her rise above her pain.

"Sweetheart, it's killing me to see you like this."

"You were right all along, Mom. Love makes you weak. I'll never let another man do this to me again. Never..." she cries, and curls into a ball under her comforter, her eyes red and swollen.

"Julia, I never said that! When did I ever say that?"

Didn't she? She's sure her mother must've said those exact words a thousand times. Her mom suffered for years after her father left, she saw it with her own eyes!

"Julia, listen to me. I don't regret marrying your father. He gave me you. And I'm not sorry he left. Of course it was painful, but it made me strong. I never dreamed I'd be put in the position of having to take care of myself. That just wasn't done in my day. Women graduated high school, maybe went to college, then got married and had babies. I never questioned that."

"When your father left I was upset, but mostly, I was paralyzed by fear. I didn't think I could do it Julia, for years I doubted myself. But I was wrong. I can take care of myself, and I feel good in a way I never did before my divorce. You know better than anyone how long it took me to get here, but I did it."

"Didn't you love Dad?" She sits up in bed, her brow furrowed. She's never heard her mother talk about her father or her life like this before.

"That's a tricky one, Julia. I loved him, but I don't think I was ever 'in love' with him. At least, not enough to marry him. But I was twenty-one, and that's what was expected of me. I was old enough to get married, so I did. I just happened to be dating your father. That sounds callous, but like I said, it was a different time."

Her mother strokes her hair and smiles.

"But you, Julia? You're an independent, strong, intelligent young woman. No one is telling you what to do with your life. You can make it whatever you want, and whatever you chose, I'll know it's because it's what you want, what you love. I couldn't ask for more. Honey, don't be afraid to love. It's a beautiful thing, whether it lasts a day or a lifetime. Love can only make your life richer."

"It hurts so much. Why won't it stop hurting?" Julia cries into her hands.

"It will stop eventually, sweetheart. One day, you'll look back on this period in your life and realize you've learned something about yourself, that you've grown in some way. Don't let the pain harden you, baby. Let it remind you that you're capable of loving deeply, and you will love again, Julia."

The world didn't end when she broke up with Will, and it's still rotating now that he's engaged to Avery. Gram said it wasn't often you meet someone who fills your heart and feeds your soul, but she didn't say there was *only one*.

Julia has to believe there are other people in this great big world who are able to light her heart and soul with love and possibility, and it's time to meet those people. She's always wanted to travel and explore Europe and can think of no better time to start.

She's young, she's single, she's childless. Julia's free to do as she pleases.

Italy will be her home base. She's flying into Rome in late October, her first destination on a very long list of places to explore. She's kept track of all the cities she wants to visit on a world map hanging in her bedroom at her mom's house. Red pins for places she wants to go, green for those she's visited. There are a lot of red pins on her map, but that's about to change.

She's flying out of Boston so she can spend a few days visiting with friends and family in Rhode Island before her journey. She has no idea how long she'll be gone but has enough in personal savings to last several months if she's frugal. It'll be the trip of a lifetime.

A few days before she's due to leave for Europe, her mother takes her out for a farewell dinner at the Capital Grill in Providence and over dessert, she hands Julia an envelope.

"What's this?"

"Open it." Her mother smiles, "Go ahead! A little surprise."

She lifts the flap on the envelope and opens it to find a cashier's check in the amount of twenty-thousand dollars in her name. She's dumbfounded. Her mother doesn't have this kind of money to give away!

"Mom, where did you get this?"

"That, my dear girl, is the money I've been saving for your wedding since the day you were born. I thought you'd make better use of it exploring the world than throwing a fancy party one day."

"Mom..." she stares at the check, her eyes wide. "How big did you think my wedding was going to be?" Julia laughs.

"Well, we have a big family!"

She can't believe it. With this money she can travel for well over a year, easily.

"Thank you, Mom."

"You're more than welcome, baby." Carol squeezes her daughter, "You're an adventurer, go see the world! Have the time of your life. And remember to call me at least once a week!"

"I promise." She closes her eyes and hugs her mom tight.

Before she leaves for the airport, Julia stops to say goodbye to her father, then drives to the cemetery to visit Gram's grave. She can't believe her grandmother's been gone for over two years. She thinks Gram would approve of her impending adventure.

Julia sits cross-legged on the ground beside her gravestone. *Mary Bianco Grasso. 1907-1993. Beloved wife, mother and grandmother.*

She believed Will was her Romeo. *Gram, help me move on from Will.* She rests her hand on the side of the cool marble stone. *Please Gram...*

A bird perches itself on top of her grandmother's gravestone, a robin. Gram used to point out different species of birds and explain their symbolism to her when she was small. What does a robin represent? She stares at the bird and the answer comes to her.

Robin, the sign of Spring, rebirth, new beginnings.

She smiles, that's exactly what she's hoping for, a new beginning. *Thank you, Gram.* The bird flies away and Julia watches as it disappears into the sky.

Chapter Eighteen

Romeo, Romeo, where for art thou Romeo? Julia has spent the past three glorious weeks wandering about Italy. She began her journey in Rome, then moved on to Venice, Florence, and Genoa. Now, she's on the train east travelling toward Verona, Italy's own 'City of Love'.

She's always felt a special connection to this city, the setting of Shakespeare's *Romeo and Juliet*. She thinks of Gram as the train moves closer to her destination, can hear her voice asking, *Julietta, where's your Romeo?* Julia smiles. *Ah, Gram, that remains to be seen!*

Her vocabulary was limited to the few curse words and terms of endearment she learned from her grandparents, but she has an ear for languages and learns a few new phrases every day. She belongs here, the home of her ancestors, she feels it in her bones.

Every day she takes a step toward her future, and away from her past. She's filling her journal and her heart with the people and places she's encountered on her travels.

For at least the next four nights she'll be sleeping in Juliet's guesthouse. She splurged and rented a room in *Il Sogno de Giulietta*, literally translated, *Juliet's Dream*. The room is luxurious, much nicer than any she's stayed in thus far. She wants to stretch this trip as long as possible, so most nights she sleeps in cheap youth hostels.

Julia has something she wants to do in Verona and needs a comfortable bed and a private bath for the next few days.

A wooden four-poster bed fills most of her room. Rich tapestries adorn the walls and the bed linens and Italian sheets are of the highest quality. Julia sighs as she reclines on the bed. *This is a little bit of heaven.* There's also a small sitting area and a balcony overlooking the courtyard opposite the real Juliet's house.

Most people don't realize the story of *Romeo and Juliet* is based on actual events between two warring clans from Verona, the Capuleti and Montecchi families. She was disappointed to learn the famous balcony affixed to Juliet's house was added in the twentieth century. Mr. Shakespeare used a little creative license.

Another reason for her stop in Verona has to do with an interesting article she read years ago. For more than two centuries, people from all over the world have written letters to 'Juliet' asking for advice and support in all matters of the heart.

Many people send mail directly to the city, their envelopes addressed simply *Juliet, Verona, Italy.* Thousands of others make the pilgrimage to leave their letters of heartbreak and unrequited love on the wall outside Juliet's house.

Every day Juliet's 'secretaries', as they're called, gather the love letters from the wall and bring them back to headquarters, where a team of romantics dedicate their time to answering every single letter they receive, by hand. A personal, thoughtful response, not a form letter.

Julia's writing her letter today. She isn't looking for advice, she's seeking closure. Today, Julia's writing to say goodbye to Will, and even now, a year and a half after they parted ways, the thought is painful.

Her face is tense as she walks across the courtyard, while dozens of tourists snap photographs of Juliet's balcony. She carries her satchel close, among its contents a fountain pen and stationary purchased specifically for this occasion.

Her stride is purposeful as she passes under the stone arch and walks across via Cappello to the Piazza delle Erbe. Once a Roman marketplace, there are several cafes and dozens of stalls selling fruit, vegetables, herbs, and souvenirs.

It's late afternoon and the air is turning crisp. She searches for the most secluded area in the square, and pulling her suede jacket close for warmth, she selects a table outside the Tosca Café Nuova and reaches into her bag for her pen and a sheet of thick ivory paper as a handsome, young waiter approaches her table.

"*Buon pomeriggio bella signorina.* May I take your order?"

"*La bicchiere de vino rosa, per favore.*" She repeats one of the many handy phrases she's picked up over the past week.

"Yes, miss."

"*Grazie,*" she says. *Mille grazie!* Julia looks to the sky and once her red wine arrives, she raises her glass.

To me. To new beginnings.

She swallows the contents of her wineglass in three sips and stares at the paper. She knows what she wants to say and begins to write.

Dear Juliet…

An hour later, she sits back in her chair, seals the envelope containing her letter and is filled with relief. *It's done. I said goodbye.* Julia doesn't expect to magically forget Will's existence, but she feels freed from the overwhelming sadness that has gripped her heart since she learned of his engagement to Avery.

Julia walks back to Casa de Giulietta where she finds about a dozen men and women sitting on the cobblestones, pouring their hearts out on paper. More than a few of them are crying. A woman about her age is sitting on a bench, scribbling away, her face intense. *What's brought her here? Who broke her heart?* Julia wonders.

A statue of Juliet stands next to a wall covered with dozens of letters, and a young man is posing for a photograph with his hand on the statue's bronze breast. The gentleman standing beside her must have noticed her confusion and explains, in a hushed voice, that people touch her breast for luck in love.

Really? Luck in love?

She lingers in front of the statue, debating whether to touch the bronze breast of good fortune, unsure if she's ready for love just yet. Reluctantly, she places her hand on the statue, then quickly turns and approaches the repository wall, resting her hand against it. This wall has been the recipient of so much heartache. She can only imagine the tales it would tell if it could talk, though the smooth, worn bricks speak volumes.

A woman carrying a large straw basket enters the courtyard and begins to remove the letters from the wall. *She's one of Juliet's secretaries!* Julia wants to ask her a million questions, but this place has a church-like quality.

When the secretary reaches her, Julia holds out her letter. The woman is young, maybe thirty? Her face is gentle and kind. She must have read and replied to hundreds of these letters. Now, she takes Julia's letter in one hand and places her other hand on her arm, a light supportive squeeze. The secretary solemnly nods and finishes removing the evidence of hundreds of broken hearts.

When Julia returns to her hotel room, she draws a warm bubble bath, pours herself another glass of wine and soaks for almost an hour. She's exhausted though it's only seven in the evening. Saying goodbye was as draining as she expected it would be. Tonight she's grateful for her cozy bed with the soft sheets and down comforter, and falls into a deep, dreamless sleep.

Before the clock strikes noon the following morning, Julia takes a seat near the fountain in the piazza and orders espresso, because that's what you do in Italy. She never drank it back home but the taste is growing on her.

Chewing on her pen, she mulls over todays possibilities. She'll be in Verona for several days and has plenty of time for sightseeing, so she decides this afternoon, her only plan is to relax. She bought some postcards from a vendor in the piazza and wants to write home to family and friends, and maybe wander about and see what the day brings.

Julia opens her journal, her constant companion, and begins to write. She doesn't want to forget anything about her journey and carefully records the details on its pages several times each day. Absorbing the sounds and smells around her, she closes her eyes and smiles.

The sun feels good against her skin. It's warm for mid-November, in the low sixties, and she's wearing a long-sleeved white cotton shirt, her favorite soft ivory cable-knitted cardigan sweater, and faded jeans.

A few moments later she opens her eyes, and someone is standing still a few feet in front of her, but the sun is blinding and the person is in silhouette.

"*Si?*" she asks and reaches for her sunglasses, shading her eyes with her hand. *It can't be!* she gasps, sitting straight up in her chair. Confused, her eyes wander the piazza. *Where am I? Am I hallucinating?* She blinks again.

No, it's Will. All six feet, two inches of him, wearing khakis and a light blue, long sleeve polo shirt, a sweater thrown over his shoulders. His piercing blue eyes search her face and neither of them utters a word.

Her body turns cold, a knot forming in her stomach as she pulls her sweater close and tries to catch her breath. She wants to escape, to run as far away from him as possible, but she's paralyzed. All she can do is stare, her lips parted, tears filling her eyes.

Seriously Juliet? Is this some sick cosmic joke?

She came to Europe to start over and make new memories. To get Will out of her heart forever. The journal sitting open in front of her is full of new and beautiful experiences. Now, the words are swimming around, mocking her.

Goddammit, I wrote the letter! I said goodbye.

Julia shakes her head in denial and closes her eyes.

No. He can't be here.

***

Lowering himself into the empty chair beside Julia, his legs are shaking and he has to steady himself. He's wanted to talk to her so many times over the past year and a half, but never thought he'd have the opportunity to be alone with her again. He has to be careful with his words, she's in flight mode, he can see it on her face. He doesn't want to scare her away, but is well aware he has no right to ask her to stay.

He's been in Italy for the past five days. Avery is spending the semester in Florence taking art classes at the university, and he's halfway through his trip. He's just going through the motions with this engagement. No matter how long and hard he prays he can't find peace within himself.

But he can't break off his engagement, he wouldn't do that after everything he's already put Avery through. And he wouldn't do that to his parents. It would be a major embarrassment. The announcement was published in the newspaper, and his parents threw an engagement party for them in September before Avery left for Italy.

The wedding is set for June and her mother's planning everything. Will and Avery just have to show up.

His train arrived in Verona about an hour ago. Avery has an all-day seminar and later tonight they're supposed to go to a party. "Signore Medici throws the best parties," she said. It seems to him all Avery does in Florence is go to parties and visit art museums and galleries. They haven't had an evening alone since his arrival, and that hasn't bothered him at all...which can't be a good sign.

The first night he was jet lagged and she went out without him, but over the past three nights they've attended various parties and she's introduced him to dozens of people. Will understands his role perfectly. It's taken him a while to get it, but it couldn't be clearer.

He's a prop on Avery's arm.

No one expects him to participate in their conversations, all he has to do is smile and tune out while she and her international group of friends discuss art and travel all night long. After three nights of this, he's just about partied out.

Today presented Will with the opportunity to escape and visit Verona. Avery will be busy with school all day, so he's free to roam wherever he pleases.

"Why would you want to go there?" she asked, "There's so much to see in Florence."

"Shakespeare set several of his plays there. I've always wanted to go," he said, casually, flipping through the tour book of Italy he brought with him.

"I didn't realize you were such a fan," Avery laughed.

Will shrugged. He's really not a huge Shakespeare fan, but the story of *Romeo and Juliet* means a lot to him. His Juliet read the play to him one snowy afternoon a lifetime ago.

His motives for going to Verona were not pure. A week before Will left for Italy, he bumped into Gabby and she told him Julia's in Europe, that she flew into Rome a few weeks ago. He asked if she knew exactly where she was, and after some consideration, Gabby said she called earlier in the week from Venice and was heading toward Florence, then Verona. He knows it's a long shot, but...*it's possible.*

Knowing Julia's in Italy has made him hyper-aware every time he sees a woman with long, dark, curly hair. After five days here, he's resigned to the fact that there are a lot of women in Italy with long, dark, curly hair, and Julia won't be so easy to spot. Over the past few days he's stopped in his tracks dozens of times, thinking, *maybe this time it's her.*

This morning, he took the hour and a half train ride from Florence, and was on his way to visit Juliet's house, walking through the piazza, when he stopped near the fountain in the middle of the square, the *Fontana di Madonna*, according to his map.

He didn't have high hopes when he saw the woman with long, dark, curly hair sitting at the café, not far from where he was standing, but something made him look again. Just then she smiled at the waiter and threw her head back laughing, causing Will's heart to stop beating in his chest. *He would know Julia's laugh anywhere.* That's when he knew she was really here, just a dozen feet away from him.

I can't believe I found her...

His instinct was to run up to her and beg her forgiveness, but he was sure that'd send her running. Instead, he sat at a table, hiding behind a menu, and watched her drink espresso, writing in her journal.

His chances of finding Julia in Italy were basically zero. *But I did find her.* And now that he has, what's his plan? He never got that far in his thinking. The fact is, nothing has changed. He's still getting married.

For a moment he considered walking away, his heart sinking. *Nothing has changed.* What is he doing here? This can only end badly for both of them. He tried, but he couldn't walk away. He flew halfway around the world with the hope of seeing her again. Praying he'd have the opportunity to talk with her…to apologize…to explain.

He'll never forget the pain on Julia's face when Avery told her they were engaged. It was a reflection of his own and it tore him apart. She was sucker punched, stunned and hurt. She couldn't hide those feelings, and there was nothing he could do. He spent the rest of that day in a daze, constantly searching the crowds on the street, hoping to see her again.

"What are you doing here?" she whispers, looking down at her journal.

"I flew over a few days ago." He can't bring himself to say Avery's name. "She's taking a course this semester in Florence." Julia's eyes roam the square, frantically scanning the crowd.

"She's not here, Jules. She's at a seminar. I've wanted to come here since…" his voice trails off. Her cheeks have turned pink, letting him know she remembers exactly when they made their plan to visit Verona. They were naked, her limbs wrapped around him, pulling him deeper inside of her.

He closes his eyes, filled with longing, then clears his throat and says, "I'm here for the day. Taking the train back later tonight."

She shakes her head and brings her hands to her face, wiping the tears from her eyes. They sit in silence for several minutes, then he moves his chair closer and leans forward.

"Julia," he rests one hand lightly on her arm, but she won't look at him. He tucks a stray curl behind her ear. "I've missed you so much," he whispers.

***

"I have to go," she mumbles and rises. She can't think or see straight, not with Will so close. Gathering her belongings, she shoves everything into her bag, "I'm not feeling very well."

This is a nightmare. She needs to get away from him, but Will reaches out to stop her, clasping her arms and preventing her from moving. A tear escapes, rolling down her cheek. If she doesn't get away from him soon she's going to dissolve in a puddle of tears.

"Please. Let me go."

Will shakes his head, and pulls her down onto his lap, wrapping his arms around her tightly. Her body sighs into his, and she buries her face into the crook of his neck, her arms winding around him. He strokes her back, running his fingers through her hair, and she knows with every fiber of her being...*I'm home.*

It's a broken home, but it's where her heart lives.

Eventually she opens her eyes and takes a deep breath, her shoulders sagging in defeat. *I give up.* Fate has brought them together again. She loves him. She'll always love him, but in her heart she knows they have this one day together. He'll go back to Avery, she doesn't doubt it for a moment.

It's not rational, his feelings of obligation and guilt, his fear of disappointing his parents, but she knows there's nothing she can say to change him. *How do you make a blind man, see?* Only Will can do that, and he's not ready to open his eyes. He may never be ready.

Today, however, there are bigger forces working to bring them together and she doesn't have the strength to fight it anymore. She sees this twist of fate for what it is.

A gift.

She won't deny herself the pleasure of this day with Will. For all she knows it's the last one she'll ever spend with him. *Carpe diem, Julia.* Seize the day.

***

Together, they walked around the city for hours, climbing the Lamberti Tower, then crossing the river to visit the ancient Roman Theater. He told Julia about his father's illness, how his health is miraculously improving, and about Ellie and Kevin's wedding this past summer.

They explored the old Roman Gates of Porta Bra and Porta Borsari and toured the Archeological Museum. Julia told him about her life since graduation, her work at the Cloisters, her apartment in the city, how she and her father have patched things up. She shared stories about her travels over the past few weeks, her excitement contagious.

They discussed everything except Avery. Julia never asked him about their relationship and he had no desire to spoil their perfect day.

By late afternoon they're starving and stop at a market to pick up supplies for a picnic. They fill their basket with bread and cheese, some prosciutto, tomatoes, fresh basil and a bottle of red wine.

They've been walking about Verona for over five hours without so much as holding hands, but as they leave the market, Will takes both of Julia's hands in his and searches her face. He knows it's wrong, but he wants to touch her, to hold her in his arms again.

Julia brushes her fingertips over his lips, and his entire body's electrified by her touch. She smiles and holds her hand out to him, leading him to her hotel room. He doesn't care if he goes straight to hell. It can't be worse than living without her.

For Will, hell is right here on earth, and marrying Avery, he's walking directly into the inferno.

Spending tonight with Julia, feeling fully alive and in love for one more night, is worth eternal damnation.

He misses the last train back to Florence, at least that's what he tells Avery. When they enter Julia's room, Will drops their groceries on a chair and takes the phone into the bathroom. He wants to get this over with so he can fully concentrate on the sin he's about to commit. *I'm not married yet,* he rationalizes, but he knows it's basically the same thing.

Avery answers on the third ring.

"I'm sorry. I'll be back by the time you're out of class tomorrow."

"You're going to miss the party tonight!"

"I'm sure there'll be others." He rolls his eyes, says goodbye and doesn't give her another thought.

Will walks into the bedroom and there are no more words, only feelings. Julia is waiting for him, that's all that matters right now.

They stand at the foot of the bed and look into each other's eyes, their breathing already labored. Will removes his sweater, then his shirt. Julia pulls off her shirt and unhooks her bra. His heart is pounding in his chest as he steps forward and unbuttons her pants, then his own, his hands roaming her body as he removes her jeans, pulling them over her hips, down to the floor, quickly shedding his own.

Julia smiles and they climb onto the bed, kneeling, facing one another but not touching. He can feel the heat radiating from her body.

She closes her eyes and he kisses her forehead, her cheeks, the tip of her nose, her collarbone. He's dizzy with desire as his hands re-discover her body. He touches her breasts, gently squeezing them, and she moans as his mouth finds the hard peaks.

She's kept her arms by her side the entire time, hasn't touched him at all. He wants to feel her hands on him, his body is yearning for her touch.

He removes his boxers and Julia's lips part when she sees the evidence of his desire, then bites her bottom lip and looks into his eyes. He can see her longing, her eyelids are heavy, her cheeks flushed.

"Please," he whispers, touching her face.

She doesn't say a word, just reaches down to slide off her panties, then takes him in her hand. He's throbbing and with her touch he groans, his head tilting back.

"Look at me," Julia whispers. His eyes meet hers again, and she shakes her head. "No eyes closed. You need to look at me."

He nods, understanding...she wants him to know who he's with. *As if there could be any doubt.* He waits for Julia to put her lips on his again and within seconds she does. His mouth comes down hard on hers, his tongue exploring, devouring her, and Julia returns his kiss with equal passion.

Will pulls Julia onto his lap, her legs on either side of him, and she raises herself onto her knees. He can feel her heart beating against his chest as she lowers her body, taking him in so slowly, but he needs her now.

A moment later he grabs her hips and they both gasp as he pulls her down, thrusting deep inside of her. Julia wraps her legs around him and they move together, rhythmically, slowing down, taking their time, neither wanting this moment to end. Every nerve ending is alive, sensitized.

Their bodies slick with sweat, he can feel her beginning to lose control as they look deeply into each other's eyes. Her breath starts to quicken, her back arching and he holds her tightly against him. *Oh, how he's missed her.* He runs his hand along her ribcage, cupping her breasts, caresses every curve.

He knows her body, understands her sounds. And she knows his.

They move together in perfect unison… she closes her eyes and a moment later, he feels her tightening around him and he knows it's time, he doesn't have to wait any longer.

"Oh god, Julia. Yes," he whispers, his body trembling, riding a wave of ecstasy.

She holds him close and cries out his name. They are one heart. One body.

Their breathing slowly returns to normal, their arms clasped tightly around one another and Julia buries her head in his chest. He sees a tear land on his thigh.

"Julia, look at me." She takes a deep breath and slowly raises her watery eyes to meet his. He wipes away her tears and smiles, mouthing the words, *I love you.* Julia sighs, her face breaking into a smile, then kisses him and whispers in his ear, "Always."

The night won't last forever but neither wants it to end. They savor each other's bodies until the sun rises and finally give into exhaustion, falling asleep, their limbs entwined.

The sun is shining bright through the windows when Will eventually opens his eyes. He's disoriented for a moment, and then remembers… Julia. His heart races, afraid last night didn't really happen, and reaches out for her… and she's there, lying beside him.

With a sigh of relief, he wraps his arms around her, breathing her in and holds her close as she nestles into his arms. *Nothing has ever felt so good… so right.* Will leans over and kisses her lips, his fingers running along her hairline, down her face, along her neck, over her breasts until his hand comes to rest on her hip.

He can't think about leaving her, though he knows he has no choice. But how? How can he possibly walk away? How can he live the rest of his days without her? *God, please help me!*

Will didn't say goodbye to Julia. They stayed in bed, making love and holding each other until it was time for him to leave. She said she didn't want goodbyes, so he held her close and waited until he was certain she was asleep.

He watched her sleeping while he quietly got dressed, then leaned down and breathed her in one last time, kissed her lightly on her forehead, then whispered in her ear, "Always, Julia. I will love you always." Then, forcing himself to turn away, he gently closed the door behind him.

It's the hardest thing he's ever done.

He left part of himself in that room with Julia. The best part. His hope, his love, his joy.

The pain is excruciating, unbearable…and no less than he deserves. The self-flagellation began the moment he closed the door. He's a sinner. A selfish man. Pathetic. He walked away from the woman he loves, too weak to handle the complications of staying, afraid of disappointing everyone but Julia. She's the sacrificial lamb.

During the train ride back to Florence, Will brings his emotions into check, steeling himself for his 'reunion' with his fiancé. He doesn't want to give Avery any reason to question his activities during his absence, if she's even curious.

He stares absently out the window of the train into the darkness. His body is tense, and his jaw aches from clenching it tightly over the past few hours. He'll crumble if he allows himself the luxury of feeling anything at all.

By the time the train approaches the station in Florence, what's left of his mangled heart is as hard as stone.

Chapter Nineteen

It's a blur, the six months since his return from Italy, a time of huge life changes, and a whirlwind of meaningless activity. He intentionally keeps his mind occupied with tasks, big and small, or it'll break into a million small pieces.

When he returned to the States in November, Will made the decision to move back to Rhode Island. He wants to be near his family and now that his father's health is improving, he has no objection to Will moving back home.

Julia's always on his mind. No matter where he is or what he's doing, she haunts his every waking breath. Lying in bed at night he replays every moment of their two days in Verona in his head, over and over again. He's become a masochist, torturing himself with memories of their time together, caught somewhere in the gap between pleasure and pain, and it has to stop!

Something snapped in him on the train back to Florence and he hasn't been the same since. Will's angry with God, and himself, and fate. He's in an impossible situation. He can't win, no matter what.

If he follows his heart, he destroys Avery again, and embarrasses his parents. If he stays with her, he forfeits his happiness, but everyone else is satisfied. *Except Julia.* By forfeiting his happiness, does he take away hers? That thought plagues him.

While Avery was still in Europe, Will called to inform her of his plan to relocate. He hoped she'd refuse to move and break off their engagement, indignant that he'd made a life-altering decision without her.

But she didn't care. She thought it was a wonderful idea, and plans to finish her associate's degree at RISD, and help her mother with the final details for their wedding upon her return from Florence.

By December, Will had the townhouse on the market and began applying for jobs in the Providence-Boston metro area, and in February he accepted a new job at a private equity firm in Providence and bought a house on Poppasquash, a few streets over from his parents.

The house is on the water, and cost more than he wanted to spend, but his new base salary is more than double what he was making working for the government. He wants to be on the water, it soothes him.

Avery loves the new house. Or will love it, she said, once they finish remodeling. Will is living there alone until the wedding. He's doing some of the work on the place himself and has insisted Avery wait until after the wedding to move in, out of respect for his parents. She thinks he's being ridiculous, but he's not budging an inch on this one.

He needs this time to himself. Just a few months to wrap his head around the next stage of his life.

He had another dream about Julia last night and in it they were married, and she was having his baby. These dreams tear him apart. While he's dreaming he feels such happiness, he wants to stay asleep so he can be with Julia, but the disappointment he feels when he opens his eyes is too much.

In two weeks he's marrying Avery. What's going to happen when he wakes up next to his wife, having spent the night dreaming of another woman? *My wife...* he can't begin to think of Avery as his wife! *It's wrong, all of this...just wrong.*

Every time he dreams of Julia it takes him half the morning to snap out of his fog of sadness. And once he does, he gets angry. Will doesn't want to be around anyone, especially his sister.

Ellie's made her feelings clear about his impending marriage. *He's making a huge mistake.*

He's made his feelings clear to her. *Stay the fuck out of it.*

He doesn't know what to do with these feeling of rage. There's no one to point a finger at, no one to blame for his current circumstances. He did this to himself. All of his sins have caught up to him and he is paying the price.

This morning he tried to fall back asleep, wanted desperately to believe he was married to Julia...*but they're not.* It's just a fantasy. *She will never be my wife.*

He jumped out of bed and splashed cold water on his face, then he ran for miles, hoping to outrun his memories. When that didn't work, he came down into the basement, turned up the music and picked up a hammer, pounding it into two pieces of wood, over and over, smashing them until the boards splinter.

Throwing the hammer down to the ground, he slides to the floor, his back against the washing machine, and covers his eyes, his shoulders shaking, trying desperately to hold back the tears. *Why? Why can't I forget her? Why can't I have her?*

"Will."

He lifts his head, and quickly wipes his face as Ellie walks toward him. *How long has she been standing there?* She sits on the basement floor beside him, wraps her arm around him and he clings to her, six months worth of tears spilling onto her shoulder.

He's tried to be strong, especially in front of Ellie, but she knows him too well. She and Kevin are moving back to town, and under different circumstances, he'd be happy his sister will be living close by again, but not now. He'll be living under the microscope of Ellie's watchful, judgmental eye.

"Start from the beginning," she says opening the bottle of vodka she brought with her and hands it to him. He takes a big swig from the bottle, passes it back to her and she does the same. Will rests his head against the washer and sighs.

"I saw Julia in Italy…"

He tells Ellie about their chance meeting, spending the day and night with her, and Julia's acceptance of his situation.

"She didn't seem bitter or hurt. She never once asked me about Avery." He takes another drink, "I don't know El, she seemed… happy." He rubs his fingers over his eyes and turns to his sister, "She said our time together was a gift."

"How did you leave things with her?" Ellie asks, wiping away her tears.

"Julia asked me to hold her till she fell asleep and slip out so she wouldn't have to say goodbye." He swallows hard and closes his eyes. "So I did."

He'll never get that image out of his head…Julia sleeping in a white cloud of sheets and blankets. And he'll never forget the sound of the door locking behind him as he walked away from her.

"You left her there sleeping?" Ellie blows her nose with her shirt and he nods his head. She takes a huge gulp of vodka and passes the bottle to him.

"Will…what are you going to do?"

Here it comes.

He takes a swig from the bottle, steeling himself for the ensuing argument. He knows how she feels, and he can't change that.

"Will, please listen to me." She grabs his hand, squeezing it between hers, "You can't marry Avery. I beg you to reconsider this. God brought you and Julia together in a foreign land for fuck's sake! That wasn't a chance meeting, Will. That was fate!"

"It's too late, El." He shakes his head, "I'm getting married in two weeks."

"So what!" She kneels in front of him, "People cancel weddings all the time!"

"I can't do that to Avery."

"Avery! What about you?" Ellie shouts. "What about your happiness? Why are you willing to sacrifice your life for that woman? It doesn't make any sense! Please tell me why?"

Her eyes are pleading with him to explain, but Will can't do this again. *I can't have this argument with Ellie again.* His face hardens with determination, an icy mask forming a barrier between them.

"The reasons I do things, Ellie, are my own. I won't discuss them."

She recoils from his words and rises, her body trembling with anger.

"Will. You are my brother, and I love you dearly. But I'm telling you now, you'll live to regret this decision. God sent you a miraculous sign from above, a precious gift and you're throwing it back in His face. Shame on you. I won't watch you ruin your life. I will not go to that sham of a wedding."

He meets his sister's gaze with a steely glint in his eyes, his resolve firmly back in place.

"Then don't come."

Ellie opens her mouth to speak, then closes it, nods her head and leaves.

***

Julia never regretted the night she spent with Will in Verona. When she woke from her nap later that evening, he was gone as she expected he would be. Her heart ached but she couldn't muster up a single tear.

She wants to be with him more than anything, but he has to come to her with an open heart and a guilt-free conscience or what they have, no matter how beautiful and special, will never work. It's out of her hands.

She has a better understanding of their relationship now. They may never be together, but they'll always share something special, even if Will never knows it. She can't change that. She loves him, but she's experienced a love more meaningful in the wake of their night together.

They created something so precious…a constant reminder of their soulful connection. A bit of beauty in the midst of darkness, an unexpected gift when she needed it most.

His name is Liam, and from the moment he was born, he's become the light and love of her life.

Living out of her backpack, travelling from city to city, and country to country, she simply didn't notice she'd skipped two cycles. The grand discovery was made when Julia was about twelve weeks along.

She never had any morning sickness, but her breasts were tender and her bras were getting tight. One night in early March, she was lying in her bed at a youth hostel in Paris, thinking about Will, about their last night together, and it clicked. *Sore and swollen breasts. No period. I'm pregnant.*

She was numb for about five minutes, then holding her hands over her bloated stomach, she was overcome with emotion. *Will's here with me.* The words floated through her head all evening, comforting her.

The following day she took three tests and confirmed her suspicion, and when the plus signs appeared in the window on all three pregnancy tests she could hardly breathe. The feeling of peace she experienced the night before, when her pregnancy was just a possibility, quickly disappeared and was replaced with fear.

She wandered along the banks of the Seine and took a few days to consider her options, unwilling to make this decision without careful consideration, but in the end she understood this baby was meant to be.

Something bigger than them brought Julia and Will together in Verona, and this baby is the physical evidence of their love for one another. She can't have Will, but she can have his child to love. *That has to be enough.*

Once she made the decision to keep their baby, Julia embraced her situation. She had no doubt there'd be many challenges along the way. The life of a single mother isn't easy, but she was ready for the responsibility. Well...as ready as anyone could be under those circumstances.

This isn't the life path she thought she'd follow. She was going to run a museum, that was her plan. Leaving the Cloisters wasn't the end of her career, it was the beginning. Throughout her journey, she's been investigating opportunities at various museums. *Florence? Rome? Venice? Paris? London? Prague?* Which city would she call home?

The possibilities were endless...until she peed on that stick.

Now? The lens of life's camera has zoomed in, narrowing her choices to what she can see through the little viewfinder, her focus fixed on making a home for her child and being able to support him or her.

Julia flew back home shortly after she found out about her pregnancy to tell her parents in person, before she was too far along to fly. She had no idea how they'd take the news and part of her wanted to keep it to herself. She wasn't due back in the States until well after she had the baby. She could show up one day with a six month old in her arms. Surprise! But that didn't seem like the right thing to do.

Her mother was thrilled for Julia, once she had a glass of wine and got over the initial shock. Her father wanted to know if the baby's father was ready to marry her. Julia couldn't help but laugh. She explained he's someone she loves dearly, but isn't part of the picture anymore.

His Catholic sensibilities came bubbling to the surface and it was Sandra who calmed him down and helped him understand that Julia was perfectly capable of raising a child herself and didn't need a man to do it. She was shocked and grateful. She never imagined Sandra would be the person to smooth things over with him.

Eventually, he resigned himself to the idea of his daughter bearing an illegitimate child, and fell in love with his grandson the moment he held him.

Her parents made a strong argument for Julia to remain in Rhode Island. They want to help her raise their grandchild, but Julia was vehemently against it. She had no desire to return to America, at least not yet. She wanted to be in Verona when she had the baby, where he was conceived, and that's where she returned after her week in the States.

She took a crash course in Italian, found a part-time job curating the letters received at Casa di Giulietta, rented a small apartment off the piazza, and became one of Juliet's secretaries, answering the letters written in English.

The other secretaries took her under their wing, mothering her throughout her pregnancy, issuing advice on parenting. They became her family, her support system in Italy. Most of the women are married, some are mothers, and a couple are grandmothers. Mariana, the woman Julia met in the courtyard collecting letters outside Juliet's house, became her closest friend and confidant.

Julia wanted to call Will so many times to share the news, but something stopped her. She prayed every day for months that he'd come to his senses, break off his engagement, and find her. But he never did.

It was Gabby who called to tell her she saw his wedding announcement in the newspaper about six weeks before her due date. Julia was silent and hung up the phone, and then lay in her bed and cried.

Her prayers hadn't been answered. They'll never be a family. He'll never know his child and their baby will never know him. That was more upsetting to her than anything. But she didn't wallow in these thoughts for too long. She had his baby to prepare for, and she couldn't wait to meet him.

Her mother was by her side during the delivery. She'd flown to Italy two weeks before Julia's due date, and stayed for two weeks after his birth. When the nurse placed Liam on her chest, he grasped her pinky and looked into her eyes. It was the most beautiful moment of her life. Every ounce of pain she'd ever endured was worth it to experience the joy of holding her son.

Oh Will, I wish you were here to see him. He's perfect.

Julia believes Will would leave Avery if he knew about his son, but that's not enough for her anymore. She doesn't want him to hand over his life to them as a sacrifice, carrying his heavy cross of guilt and self-loathing, a black cloud over them all.

No! Liam is better off without his father under those circumstances. She'll do anything to protect her son from Will's toxic relationship with Avery. Until he makes peace with himself and is completely free from Avery's tangled web, Will can't be part of their lives. *We deserve more.*

Julia's had a constant stream of visitors since the baby was born and she's exhausted. No one expects her to take them sightseeing, but meeting the demands of a newborn and interacting with grown ups day and night has taken its toll.

She's a zombie and tries to rest when the baby sleeps, but finds it almost impossible. Before he was born, Julia could sleep soundly through a thunderstorm, now she wakes up every time Liam makes the slightest sound.

No one ever told her how difficult the transition into motherhood would be. It's a well kept secret with good reason. Nobody would volunteer for this job if they knew how hard it was going to be in advance.

Julia adores her son, but sometimes she fights back the urge to run away from her life. For someone who's incredibly good at being alone, bearing sole responsibility for the health and wellbeing of another human is overwhelming.

Three weeks after Liam was born, Gabby flew to Italy for a visit. Julia was lying in bed, and trying to get some much needed rest while Gabby rocked the baby.

"Are you going to tell him?" Gabby asks, placing the pacifier in Liam's mouth.

"Hmm?" Julia murmurs half asleep, "Tell who, what?"

"Will." Gabby smiles and coos at Liam, "Are you going to tell Will he's a father?"

Julia never told anyone Will is Liam's father, not even Gabby. When she asked, Julia changed the subject. She's sure her mother and best friend figured it out before his birth, but she couldn't bring herself to say the words out loud.

Turns out, she didn't need to, the resemblance is so strong. One look at Liam, and it's clear to anyone who knows Will, he's the father of her child. He's a beautiful baby with Will's sea blue eyes and blond hair, and her soft curls and olive complexion. There's no point denying it.

She sits up in bed, then turns to Gabby and shakes her head.

"Do you think that's fair to him?" she asks.

"No."

"Then why?" Gabby scowls.

"Well," she sighs. "The obvious reason is he's married. But far worse than that is who he's married to. Would you expose your child to that woman? Suppose he found out and chose to stay with Avery? Fought me for joint custody? No, Gabby! She'll never get near my baby."

"I understand your concern, Julia. But one day, Liam's going to want to know about his father. He'll see Will's name on his birth certificate and he'll find him. How do you think Will's going to react when he discovers you kept his son from him?" Gabby asks.

"Neither of them will ever know," Julia says, folding her arms across her chest.

"Of course they will! It's on his birth certificate!"

"No, it's not…I put 'father unknown.'"

"You did not!"

The baby cries and Julia reaches for Liam. She looks down at her son and smiles.

"For him? Yes I did."

PART III
GLIDING

2001

Chapter Twenty

Tonight, Will and Avery are celebrating their fifth wedding anniversary. His wife has organized a party and no less than two hundred people will be attending. A huge tent is set up in his yard and caterers and other workers have been in and out of the house all day. This blessed celebration has a hefty price tag, but it's still only a fraction of the amount Avery's mother spent on their wedding extravaganza.

Will had left all of the wedding arrangements to Avery and her mother and had no idea what was in store for him. He tried not to think about their nuptials in the weeks leading up to the big day. He knew they were getting married at St. Margaret's in Bristol, and the reception was being held at her mother's house in Newport. She lives in a mini mansion off Bellevue Avenue with a rolling lawn extending to the Atlantic.

He wasn't at all prepared for the five hundred guests in attendance, over half of whom he'd never met. His wedding day was over the top and completely overwhelming, just like Avery. He would have preferred a small wedding with just close family and friends, but no one asked what he wanted.

After the obligatory first dance with his bride, the champagne toasts and the cutting of the cake, Will took a walk alone by the water, desperate to escape the circus meant to celebrate their true love. He thought of Julia across the ocean and wondered where she was that day.

Paris? Stockholm? London? Is she thinking about me?

She said she'd be in Europe for over a year and had at least five months before she returned to the States. He wanted to call her so many times, but had no way of reaching her. And what would he say if he could?

Ellie was true to her word. She did not attend their wedding. Kevin did, and when people asked where she was, he said she had food poisoning, but Will knew the truth. Ellie hardly spoke to him for close to a year, and she steers clear of Avery entirely. She said she'll never understand how both he and Peter ended up with elitist snobs for wives.

Ellie and Kevin bought a house around the corner from his place and over time, their relationship has gradually improved, especially since the birth of her children. Will adores his niece and nephews and spends as much time with them as possible, but he isn't nearly as close to his twin as he was before his marriage. He doesn't think they'll ever be that close again.

He'd rather spend a quiet evening at home with his dog, Max, than attend this anniversary soiree, but he's used to these events by now. This is par for the course. Avery expects the best of everything, loves throwing parties and is high-maintenance in every aspect, *but one.*

Emotionally, Avery demands nothing of him. For this one thing, he is thankful.

In exchange for his emotional detachment, he will gladly work eighty-hour weeks to support her lifestyle.

They now own two homes, the house in Bristol and another on the island of Nantucket, off the coast of Cape Cod. At first he balked when she suggested they buy a second home, but then he found an old whaling captain's house on the island during one of his solo morning walks. He called the real estate agent and went to see it the same day. It was a fixer-upper but he fell in love with it and made an offer, without consulting his wife.

They rarely argue, but this was one of the few occasions they fought. She thinks is old and drafty and would have preferred one of the newer homes built near the beach. Avery couldn't understand how he could make such a purchase without her consent, and in the end Will conceded she had a point.

But he kept the house.

She dislikes it so much she stays with friends on the island, refusing to step foot in the house. Will prefers it this way. His little captain's house on Orange Street is his oasis, where he recharges and can relax free from Avery's social demands.

It needed tons of work when he bought it and he's been doing all the work himself. It's exactly what he needed, a huge project to distract himself. Most weekends he brings Max with him and works through his frustration laying brick, sanding floors, hanging sheetrock, refinishing the woodwork, and replacing shingles.

Other than the time he spends with his niece and nephews, working on his house on Nantucket is when he feels closest to happy.

His wife travels extensively. He joins Avery and his family in Aspen after Christmas every year, and splits his weekends between Nantucket and Bristol, but other than that he doesn't travel much.

She's been to Europe several times since they married, but he refuses to go with her. He associates Europe with Julia and doesn't want to go back. Avery doesn't seem to mind, she has plenty of friends to accompany her on her voyages. In the past five years he figures they've spent as much time apart as they have together.

He's been told time and time again that he and Avery are the perfect couple, with a fairytale life. *People are blind.* If anyone bothered to scratch a fraction of an inch below the surface, it'd be painfully obvious how hollow their lives really are. *Not that I want anyone to scratch!* Ellie and Kevin know, he's sure, but keeping everyone in the dark has become an art form.

His life is an endless round of parties, dinners, galas, and yachting events. All he has to do is remember to smile and nod and no one seems to notice his unhappiness.

Avery, on the other hand, is perfectly satisfied with their life together, just the way it is. She says she wouldn't change a thing, that they are 'blessed'. He doesn't know which is worse, that she truly believes they're happy in this shell of a marriage, or the possibility that she's aware it's a hollow partnership and simply doesn't care.

He has one real friend, Tommy, the owner of the Hope Diner. Will has season tickets to the Red Sox and he and Tommy go to Fenway often. They've never discussed Julia, it's an unspoken understanding between them, though he's sure Tommy has seen her over the years, and Julia's father goes into the diner all the time. Will's seen him there on several occasions, but has never introduced himself. What would be the point?

Will wants to have children of his own, at least then he'd have someone to love, but so far they haven't had any luck. They already know she can get pregnant, but something's going on and he wants answers. Whenever he suggests they go to a fertility specialist, Avery makes an excuse.

It's been five years, clearly there's a problem.

He takes note of when she gets her period and counts the days on a calendar to figure out when she'll be most fertile. If she's in town, he makes sure they have sex at least twice during that three day period. It's pretty much the only time they do have sex now, and for Will, it's just a means to an end.

***

Julia and Liam moved back to the United States in May. Her father's had a few health issues this past year and she's been gone long enough. She loved every minute she spent in Europe over the past six years, but she misses home, and she wants her son to be closer to his grandparents.

They've visited her family every year since Liam was born, staying with her mother and stepfather, Ron, for the month of August so her parents can celebrate Liam's birthday. It means a lot to them. Her baby has helped heal the rifts between her parents, and between herself and Sandra. They adore their grandson and are putty in his little hands.

Liam's turning five this summer, and will be starting kindergarten in September. She can't believe how quickly the time has flown. *My baby is growing up!*

Spending so much time in Rhode Island every summer has been tricky. Gabby found out Will moved back to Bristol before he got married when she bumped into him at the grocery store shortly after Liam was born. They spoke briefly, Will asked about Julia and Gabby let him know she decided to stay in Europe indefinitely. She said Will nodded his head, his face forlorn and walked away.

Julia's paranoid she'll bump into one of the Kennedys, so she avoids public places and visits friends at their houses. No restaurants, no parades, no parks on the East Bay. If she does have to run out she leaves Liam with someone and drives two towns over to decrease the possibility of bumping into anyone. So far, she's been lucky.

Gabby thinks she's being ridiculous, believes Julia should live her life openly and let the cards fall where they may. She's hoping the cards fall directly into Will's lap, that he'll have an epiphany and leave his wife for Julia, miraculously guilt-free. Gabby doesn't know Will very well at all. It would be a disaster of epic proportions. Will's world would completely unravel and who would be there to pick up the pieces? *Not me!*

She's renting a small cottage on the East Side of Providence, near Wayland Square and the location is ideal for their purposes. They're walking distance to pretty much everything they need in the city. There's a Whole Foods a couple of blocks away, a farmer's market a short walk up Blackstone Boulevard, bookstores and restaurants, a Starbucks, and a small gated park next to their house where Liam can run free with other children from the neighborhood.

They are creating a life for themselves in Providence. She loves the East Side, and it's far enough from Bristol, she's decreased the probability of bumping into anyone from Will's family considerably.

Julia accepted a part time position at a private school nearby, teaching history three mornings a week and starts in September. The main reason she applied for the position is the faculty discount. Liam will be attending kindergarten there and she receives a fifty percent tuition reduction, well worth the twenty hours a week she'll spend teaching and planning lessons.

She also writes freelance articles occasionally for various academic journals and works part-time for the Rhode Island Historical Society. Her life is busy, and she's content.

On Friday nights, Liam sleeps at either her mom or dad's house, freeing her up to go out with or without friends, or simply relax with a glass of wine and watch a movie, knowing she won't be interrupted by the pitter patter of little feet.

Saturday mornings she takes yoga at the YMCA, runs errands, and gets in a little reading or writing. It's been wonderful having her family so close by.

This week, her mother and Ron dropped Liam off at four in the afternoon. They've been married for four years now and Julia's so happy her mother met such a kind man. Ron's wonderful with Liam and her son loves his 'Bampy.'

Julia waves as they drive away and gathers Liam into her arms, kissing his forehead. *God, I miss him when he's gone!* At the same time she's grateful for the alone time. It's the paradox of motherhood.

When she was in Italy, her friend Mariana babysat Liam while she worked, and the other secretaries gladly watched him when she needed additional childcare. She's fortunate to have so many wonderful people in her life.

She knew she'd come back home eventually, that she'd reach a point and know it was time. Her father having two surgeries in one year was that point. Her parents aren't going to be around forever and as much as she misses Italy, she's glad to be back home.

"Mama, I want to go to the park."

"You got it little man." She grabs her water bottle and his juice box and they walk up the street together.

As soon as Julia swings open the heavy wrought iron gate, Liam runs across the park and up the hill to join a group of children gathered there. Julia doesn't recognize a few of them, but the rest are from the neighborhood.

Taking a sip of water, she sits on a bench in the shade and watches him play. The park is loaded with donated toys and Liam's got his hands on a yellow plastic dump truck. He's pushing the truck up the hill, filling it with rocks, then rolling it back down to the sandbox. This should keep him occupied for another hour, she figures. She closes her eyes and smiles to herself.

When someone sits beside her on the bench a moment later, Julia opens her eyes to say hello, expecting to find one of the neighborhood moms. Instead, her mouth opens, her voice catching in her throat.

"Ellie! Oh my god!" Her heart races as she scans the park for Liam, and locates him on top of the hill. *This can't be happening.*

"I can't believe it's you!" Ellie wraps her arms around her, "It's so good to see you, Jules! When did you get back?"

"From Europe?" Her hands have turned to ice, "Last month. I'd heard you and Kevin moved to Bristol. What're you doing here in Providence?"

"I'm here with the kids," Ellie waves her hand toward the hill. "We had a play date at a friend's house. She lives a few streets over and we decided to stop here on our way home. I love this park."

What are the chances? There are dozens of these little parks scattered around town, and Ellie comes to this one. She knew this day would come, despite her precautions. It was inevitable living in such a small state, but she never considered what she would say.

Liam is playing with Ellie's kids right now. *His cousins.* She never thought about Liam having cousins, but he does... three of them. Ellie's children are beautiful, with light brown skin, and soft brown curly hair.

"Mama, can I have my juice?" Liam runs up and flings his arms around her. She can't breathe, just nods her head and fishes the juice box out of her bag.

"Here you go, baby. Go play."

They sit in absolute silence for a few minutes, Julia wishing the earth would open up and swallow her whole. Finally, Ellie speaks.

"Julia," she whispers. "What's his name?" Julia's quiet, can feel the blood draining from her face. Ellie grabs her hand, squeezing it firmly, "What's my nephew's name?"

"Liam," Julia wipes a tear from the corner of her eye, and turns to Ellie, her face distressed, "His name is Liam."

Ellie wraps her arms around Julia and they hold each other tight.

Their children are playing together in the sandbox a few feet in front of them, fast friends.

"I can't believe this. I have a nephew. Will told me about your time in Verona. That's when it happened?"

"Yes. I didn't know I was pregnant for a few months."

"Why didn't you call Will? Tell him you were having his baby?"

"What would be the point?" She looks down at her hands, her face sad.

"The point? Julia! He has a child! Doesn't he have the right to know that?" Ellie asks, her voice incredulous, "How can you even ask that?"

"Ellie, I prayed every night he'd make peace with his demons, leave Avery and find me. And then I found out he married her. I knew he'd never leave her. He thinks he owes her something."

"What are his demons, Jules? Why does he feel like he owes Avery anything?"

Julia bites her lip. She shouldn't have said that. If Will wanted Ellie to know, he would have told her.

"Please tell me Julia, I've been banging my head against a wall for the past six years trying to figure out why my brother would marry someone he doesn't love. Please."

Oh, to hell with it! She's tired of being the keeper of Will's secret. Maybe Ellie can help him in some way with this information. Who knows? She hesitates for another minute.

"He got Avery pregnant in college."

"What?" Ellie gasps.

"She had an abortion and apparently had a nervous breakdown shortly after. Will blames himself."

Ellie sits back on the bench, running her fingers through her hair.

"Why didn't he ever tell me? I've been trying to figure out what hold Avery has on him for years…Now I know…" she pauses, shaking her head. "Avery's playing my brother. He's being manipulated by that bitch."

"Shhh…" Julia pats her hand, "The kids!"

Ellie slaps her hand over her mouth and turns to her.

"Jules, I've known Avery since we were kids. She's a lying, manipulative, piece of shit," Ellie pauses, gritting her teeth. "The things I used to hear about my lovely sister-in-law in high school! The girl couldn't keep her legs together, and her partying was out of control. What possessed my brother to ever date her I'll never know! If she went off the deep end it had nothing to do with Will, nothing to do with an abortion. Shit! I've heard through the grapevine she's had more than one!"

This isn't exactly news to Julia. Avery's been manipulating Will since the moment she came back into his life. It was clear to everyone but Will.

"He needs to know about Liam, Julia," Ellie sighs. "He's missing out on his son's life."

"No!" she sits up, grabbing Ellie's hands. "He can't know."

"Why, Jules?" Ellie shakes her head, "I don't understand why you would keep Liam from his father!"

"Not while Avery's a part of his life. I don't want her anywhere near my son, Ellie. She's poisonous!"

Ellie stares ahead at the kids playing together.

"I can't blame you for not wanting to expose Liam to Avery. She's a bitch…but my brother! He wants a child so desperately…"

"Ellie, look at me. If he finds out, I'll disappear. I'll take my son back to Europe to keep him away from that woman."

Ellie nods, rubbing her hands over her eyes. Liam, Aidan, Ryan, and Caitlin run toward them.

"We're hungry!"

"I can order pizza," Julia offers. "We live just down the road."

She wants to make sure Ellie understands that she's serious. She would disappear before she'd let Avery get anywhere near Liam.

Later that evening, after the kids devoured their pizza, Julia sets them up in the living room to watch *The Lion King*.

She pours the grownups a glass of wine while Ellie carries the plates into the kitchen, then sits across from her at the dining room table.

"Will's not the same person anymore."

"What do you mean?" Julia frowns and Ellie takes a sip of wine.

"After he left you in Verona, he became a different person. It's like something died in him. He's cold, aloof. He won't get close to anyone, even me." Ellie shakes her head, "He shut me out, Jules. My twin brother hardly talks to me anymore."

"But you were so close…" Julia says, her eyes wide.

"He's a very unhappy person," Ellie drinks her wine, her eyes brimming with tears.

"I am so sorry to hear that." She leans forward and takes Ellie's hand, "I love him Ellie, I'll always love him. It pains me to hear that, truly. He's given me so much joy." She looks at Liam and smiles, "I hope Will realizes he deserves happiness. He's such a good man."

Ellie wipes her eyes and nods, "Me too."

They both sit back and watch the children. Caitlin and Ryan are asleep on the couch, and Liam and Aidan are lying on cushions on the floor together.

"I won't tell Will about Liam, though it breaks my heart to think of him missing out on his son's life. Promise me you won't keep him away from me, or his cousins."

"I promise, and Ellie…thank you." She closes her eyes and takes a deep breath, hugging Will's sister to her, "You're welcome here anytime."

Ellie has stopped by with and without the kids several times over the past few weeks. At first, Julia thought it'd be awkward spending time with his sister, but that's not the case. They were friends outside of her relationship with Will, and they are again. Last Friday, they enjoyed a child-free girls night out, laughing and talking into the early hours of morning.

There hasn't been time to make friends in the area, she's only been back in the States for three months and is just getting settled in. She's made acquaintances with the neighborhood moms at the park, and it's nice to spend time with someone who understands her past and her present.

Gabby lives in Mystic, Connecticut with her husband and has a thriving private practice. She's always busy and Julia's only seen her three times since her return, though they talk on the phone at least once a week.

Earlier today, Ellie stopped by on her way to the zoo, hoping Julia and Liam could join them on their latest adventure. Julia was frazzled, unsuccessfully trying to entertain Liam while doing research for an article. Her son wanted to be outside, playing with other children and she would have loved to oblige, but she couldn't!

He was driving her insane with his whining, before Ellie arrived on her doorstep like Mary Poppins, and magically made it all better. Ellie offered to take Liam so she could work without interruption for a few hours and Julia almost cried with relief.

A couple of hours later, in need of her mid-afternoon caffeine pick me up, she walked to the neighborhood Starbucks, research packet in hand, and found a table tucked away in the corner where she could drink her coffee and begin to write her article.

Thankfully, it was a short walk, it's brutally hot outside today. *She can't imagine the kids will last much longer at the zoo in this heat*, she thinks, picking up her phone to check in with Ellie. Before she dials, she catches a glimpse of a familiar face across the crowded room and freezes in her chair, her heart leaping in her chest.

Sitting in one of the leather chairs by the fake fireplace, just a few yards away, is Will, reading the newspaper. Something so ordinary, something she's seen him do hundreds of times in the past. But she's never seen him read the paper wearing a ring.

The glint of light reflecting off his wedding band hypnotizes her for several minutes.

The last time she saw him, they were in bed in Verona. She closes her eyes, flooded with memories of their last night together, the night they made Liam...and the years she's spent raising their child alone.

Fueled with emotions ranging from love to anger, regret, shame, joy and concern, Julia rises from her chair, a woman possessed, and squeezes through the crowded coffee shop, until she's standing beside him, her hand resting on his shoulder.

Will looks up from the paper and almost chokes on his coffee, their eyes meeting for the first time in almost six years. She can't look away, no matter how hard her heart pounds against her ribcage, she's in some sort of trance. *I'm dreaming right now,* she thinks. *If I close my eyes he'll disappear.*

"Hi," she says, softly.

Will rises and takes both of her hands in his, and her knees almost buckle beneath her.

They return to her table and sit across from one another in awkward silence while Julia collects her papers, trying to think of something appropriate to say. *I had your baby, Will. He just turned five. I've missed you so much. Why didn't you come find me?*

She can't say what she's thinking, and although she knows the answer to this question, she asks, "How's your father, Will? The last time we spoke his health was improving."

"You remember that?"

"Of course I do." *Do I remember that? Doesn't he know how much he meant to me? Still means to me?* "Will, I remember everything about our time together."

"Yeah. Me too."

Will stares absently out the window and Julia studies him. He's aged considerably and looks older than his thirty-two years. Unhappiness is a heavy cloak weighing him down. She can see why Ellie is so concerned about him.

"Will, are you all right?"

"No, Jules…I'm not. I haven't been for a long time."

Is this somehow my fault? she wonders. *Could I have helped him in some way?* She wants to take away his sadness, wants him to be happy. But what can she do?

"Come with me." Julia rises and holds out her hand to him, "Come on. I'm driving your car."

For the next hour, they lay on the dock at India Point Park. She discovered this spot last week while on a walk with Liam. Julia eases naturally into the crook of Will's arm and rests her arm around his waist, her head against his chest and listens to his heartbeat.

His arms encircle her and she's transported to a simpler time, when they were carefree kids lying on the dock at Rockwell Park.

But time has passed and they aren't the same people they were nine years ago. She can't forget that, no matter how good…how right it feels to be in his arms again.

"You have to look for the joy in life, Will," she says against his chest. "Sometimes it's the little things that get me through the day."

Just as she's about to drift off, comfortable and safe in his arms, wrapped in a fantasy about the road not taken, her cell phone beeps, jolting her back to the present.

I'm a mother. Will is married to another woman.

She sits up, and reads the text message from Ellie: *We're back. Where r u?* Grateful for this dose of reality, Julia types: *Be there in 10.*

"I have to get going, Will."

He pulls her to her feet and tucks a curl behind her ear, just the way he used to, his fingers lingering against her cheek, sending shivers down her spine. She wants to kiss him. *God how I want him!*

Their eyes connect for a long moment but she can't do this. She can't be the other woman. It takes all the strength she has to say no, slowly shaking her head. Will nods and they return to his car, tightly gripping each other's hands.

She doesn't want to leave him, but she has to. His son is waiting for her at home. As he pulls into the parking lot at the coffee shop, she swallows hard and tries to sound cheerful.

"No goodbyes." She leans in and kisses his cheek, "I'll see you."

It's a five-minute walk home, and she fights to keep her emotions in check, but as soon as Julia sees Ellie, she bursts into tears. *I didn't want to leave him. I never want to leave him.*

Worried, Liam wraps his arms around her waist and tries to soothe her, which only makes her feel worse. *What kind of mother am I?* She tries to collect herself and kneels down to comfort him, but as soon as she looks into her son's eyes she crumbles. *He looks just like Will*, she thinks, sobbing.

Ellie grabs Julia's keys and herds the kids into the playroom, then lifts Julia off the sidewalk and practically carries her into the house. She cries into a pillow on the couch and when she finally calms down, Ellie sits beside her, handing Julia a glass of wine.

"What happened, sweetie?" Ellie asks.

Her voice hoarse and chin trembling, Julia explains where she was and who she was with. Ellie's mouth drops open, and her eyes light up with excitement. She wants to know every detail about Julia's interaction with Will.

"Did he open up at all?" Ellie asks.

Julia nods, her eyes sad, "He's so unhappy, Ellie. What happened to him?" She shakes her head thinking about the wrinkles around his eyes, and the creases on his forehead, "I couldn't believe how old he looked when I first saw him. I didn't want to leave him, El. I had to tear myself away. He's my home, Ellie! When I'm with him, I'm home. How can I still feel like this after all of these years?"

"You feel like this because you still love him. You two are meant to be together and that bitch stole your husband! It isn't right. You know, since you told me about the abortion I have some understanding as to why my brother made this colossal mistake. What I don't understand is what Avery gets out of it? A date on New Year's Eve? Money? She buys whatever she wants, goes wherever she wants. But she has her own money so it doesn't make any sense."

Julia lies back on the couch, exhausted.

"Maybe she really loves him, Ellie. I loathe the woman, but I got the impression she cared about him in a warped way. Like she thought she'd be saving him from a life of banality by taking him away from me."

"Okay, one, that's fucking twisted. Two, fuck her! I don't give a shit if she loves my brother, Avery can suck it. My brother loves you, he wants you, and he deserves to be happy with you and Liam. Would you ever consider…?" Ellie sighs, squeezing her hand.

"You really do have the filthiest mouth, El. Are you asking me if I'd have an affair with Will? If you hadn't sent me that text message when you did, I would've brought him back here and made him forget all of his worries. But Ellie, I can't be his mistress. As much as I want him, I have to keep Avery and their noxious relationship as far from me and Liam as possible.

Why do you think I stayed in Europe all of those years? I missed home. I missed my family. And I missed Will... every day."

"I'm sorry. I wasn't trying to pimp you out. I just want you two lovebirds to be together."

"If Avery were out of the picture I wouldn't hesitate."

"Then we're going to get her out of the fucking picture." Ellie grins, a devilish gleam in her eye.

Julia laughs for the first time today, "What do you suggest? Hit man? My Uncle Vinny on Federal Hill will do it for nothing!"

"I wish!" Ellie giggles, "No, something's got to give. She's no saint. I'm going digging, and I'm going to find something."

Chapter Twenty-One

Liam has caught an awful cold and it's only the second week of school. He's staying in Bristol with her mother while Julia teaches this morning, then she has to go home and tweak her article.

She's proud of the piece she's been working on for weeks, but between teaching and writing, she's strung out. She has to get her article in by Friday and her parents agreed to keep Liam for the entire week so she can focus and get it done.

Julia loves teaching and is grateful for the discount on tuition, but she'd love to take this week off. She doesn't think that would make a very good impression with the Head of School.

On this beautiful September morning, the sun is shining bright, while Julia's in the middle of her first class, comparing the elements of American culture to foreign cultures. Some of her students have travelled extensively and they're having a lively discussion when the middle school director walks into her room and pulls her aside.

"I don't want to alarm the students, but a plane crashed into the World Trade Center in New York. We think the plane may have flown out of Boston and we aren't sure if anyone's parents are involved."

"Oh my god." Her eyes grow wide with horror.

"Let's keep it business as usual until we know more," he whispers.

"Where were we?" She turns to her students and forces a smile.

Julia tries to focus on their discussion, but her thoughts are with the people in the World Trade Center and the plane passengers. Why would a pilot be flying that close to the city skyscrapers? Was it a commuter plane? Is it foggy in New York today? *God, what a nightmare!*

A few minutes before class is dismissed, the director comes back into her room. His face is pale, his eyes watery and the hairs on her arms stand on end.

"Another plane crashed into the South Tower. Both towers are on fire."

She raises her hand to her mouth, and shivers. *We've been attacked.* One plane, a horrible accident. Two planes? This was planned.

She lived in New York when a car bomb went off in the basement of the North Tower in 1993. Six people died and hundreds more were injured. That was deeply unsettling. This is a catastrophe.

"We are contacting parents to pick up their children and cancelling classes for the rest of the day. Perhaps for the week. Check your email tonight."

Julia's in shock. All students are directed to go to their homerooms and wait for further instructions, but since she works part-time and doesn't have a homeroom, she's free to leave.

She walks out of the building, and looks up at the bright blue sky, not a cloud in sight. It's a beautiful day, cool, dry, and sunny. Fall is around the corner, she can feel it in the air.

And two hundred miles away her beloved New York is under attack. *How many people will die before this day is over?* She needs information and climbs into her car, tuning the radio to NPR.

She checks her watch. It's nine-thirty. Should she head home? Go to Bristol and be with her family? She's in a daze, but feels the need to be around other people, and tries to remember what's open at this time of day that would have a television. Bars are closed…

The deli on South Main has a television! She pulls out of her assigned parking space, and picks up her cell phone to check on Liam.

She wasn't the first person to think of the deli. Dozens of people have stopped in to watch developing news, mostly businessmen and women who work downtown. It's crowded, so she leans against the counter, her eyes mesmerized by the events unfolding on television.

The reporter is interrupted, "Apparently a plane has crashed into the Pentagon. There are reports of a fire on The National Mall and we're being told that the Capital building and White House are being evacuated." Everyone in the deli gasps. *This is insanity!* Julia scans the room, noting the fear etched on every face.

And then she sees him.

Will is sitting at a table close to the television and she closes her eyes and sighs, filled with relief. *He's here. I need him and he's here.* He's been in her thoughts day and night since she last saw him, three weeks ago at Starbucks.

She's been tormented with guilt, questioning herself and her choices. Has she done the right thing keeping Liam from Will all these years? Every time she looks at her son, she sees Will. Of course she's always seen the resemblance, but over time the details of Will's face had faded, and Liam has become separate from Will in her mind.

Not anymore. Their resemblance is uncanny.

She's meant to see him today. This isn't a coincidence. Julia doesn't hesitate for a moment, and weaves through the crowded deli, until she's by his side, her hand on his shoulder. Will's eyes meet hers and he stands, gathering her into his arms, and she holds onto him tightly, breathes him in and sighs. Reluctantly, they release their embrace and Julia sits beside him.

A few minutes later they watch in shock as the South Tower of the World Trade Center collapses. It disappeared in a matter of seconds, one hundred and ten stories, gone. The television screen turns black as the entire city is covered in a cloud of soot and ash, the bodies of the dead disintegrating. Her eyes are wide with fear and she buries her face in Will's chest.

How does a skyscraper collapse from fire in less than an hour? That's not supposed to happen!

Moments later there's another newsflash. All planes have been grounded, but there are reports that a plane has crashed into a field in Pennsylvania. Reporters speculate that the intended target was the US Capital building.

The world has turned upside down in the space of two hours.

At ten-thirty Julia and Will watch as the North Tower collapses. *How many people died in those buildings?* Thousands of innocent lives lost in a senseless act of terror. She shakes her head, leaning into Will.

"All of those people woke up this morning, maybe took a shower, ate some breakfast, got dressed and went to work. Like any other day. And now they're just…gone." She pauses, "Let's get out of here. I can't take anymore."

Death is all around them, she's suffocating in the crowded deli. She needs fresh air, wants to feel alive.

Will follows her outside and they walk along the Providence River. At the end of the river walk, Julia hops up and sits on the stone wall, Will standing beside her, his arms folded, looking at the sky.

"What are you thinking about?" She touches his arm. He turns to face her, and she can tell he wants to say something, can see the emotions flicker across his face.

"Nothing," he says a moment later, shaking his head and turning away from her.

She could leave it at that, but she has something she wants to say to him. In light of today's events it seems foolish to keep it to herself. *Who does it serve?*

"Now that's a lie. I'll start."

Julia takes Will's left hand in hers, touches his wedding band, and tugs it off his finger. His eyes grow wide but he doesn't stop her. She holds it in her hand for a moment, feeling the weight of the platinum band that legally binds him to another woman.

"I'd love to throw this in the river right now." She carefully slides it into the pocket of his pants, and gazes into his eyes. "I love you, Will. I know I shouldn't say that. I understand your situation, but after today," her eyes fill with tears and she shakes her head in disbelief, "I just want you to know that you're loved. You're never alone, because you're always in my heart."

Will closes his eyes, his face transforming before her. He smiles, takes a deep breath and pulls her close to him, covering her mouth with his. They kiss with such passion and longing... When they come up for air, his hands are tangled in her hair and his eyes are searching her face. She's flushed, breathless, her body burning with desire.

"I've always loved you, Julia," he kisses her again, gently now.

"Will… come home with me."

He nods, lifting her off the stone wall and into his embrace, then follows her home and sits in her driveway to make a phone call. Julia doesn't care who he's calling, as long as he walks through that door when he's done.

She sweeps through the living room, picking up as many toys as she can and shoves them into the playroom, closing the door behind her. There's no way she can hide the fact that she has a child, there are photographs of Liam everywhere, drawings framed on the wall and hanging on the refrigerator.

She isn't sure what she'll tell him, but right now she doesn't care. As the awful events of today have proven, life is too short. Julia wants Will here with her.

She opens the front door, pulling him into the house and removes his suit jacket, loosens his tie and begins to unbutton his shirt. She needs to feel his skin against hers. Quickly, Will unbuttons her blouse, and unzips her skirt, the fabric falling to her feet.

Julia leads him upstairs to her bedroom in her bra and panties. *Does he see the stretch marks? The subtle roundness of my stomach?* She's close to thirty, not the twenty-one year old girl he first made love to. She sits on her bed and unbuckles his belt, removing his pants and he kneels down, wrapping his arms around her, his head pressed against her chest.

"Will?" Julia pauses, running her fingers through his hair, "We don't have to do this."

"I want to." He turns his face to her, "I've never stopped loving you Julia. Not for one second of one day. I don't know how everything got so screwed up, but I want to be here with you. There's no place I'd rather be."

"I don't have any expectations." She leans down and kisses him, "I just want to love you."

If there was ever any doubt in Julia's mind they were made for one another, they're gone forever. Their bodies fit together perfectly, two pieces of a puzzle, and bring each other such intense pleasure. She's never experienced anything close to this with any other man. Only Will.

"Jules, you've brought me back to life."

"Baby, you were alive, just not living. I'm so sorry you've been unhappy all of these years." She wraps her arms around him and kisses his neck.

"What about you?" Will reaches for a pillow, propping himself up in her bed, "You haven't told me anything about your life."

She rests her head on his chest and stares at a picture of Liam on her dresser. *What should I tell him?*

"It's been busy..."

Will is waiting for her to elaborate, but she doesn't know what to say. She won't tell him Liam is his son, not unless he leaves Avery.

"That's it? Busy?"

She sits up and reaches for the framed photograph on her nightstand. The light in the room is dim, it's after six-thirty and the sun will be setting soon.

"Will, I have something to tell you," she whispers, and pauses, "I have a son."

Will blinks several times, not comprehending, and with a start his eyes open wide.

"What?" his voice is hoarse, "Are you married?"

"No, I've never been married."

She hands him the photograph and Will holds it inches from his face. This picture was taken of them when Liam was two. They're both in profile and she doesn't think he'll see the resemblance.

"What's his name? How old is he?" Will turns to her, astonished.

She wants to tell him Liam is his, but she just can't, so she does something she swore she would never do. She lies to Will.

"His name is Liam. He's four years old."

Will nods, running his finger over the photograph, staring at it intently.

"Who's his father?"

"Someone I met in Italy." Julia swallows hard and looks down at her hands, "He's never been part of the picture."

"Where is Liam tonight?"

"He's staying with my parents this week." She takes a deep breath and sighs. *He doesn't seem to suspect Liam is his son.* "Tonight he's at my moms. I'm supposed to be working on an assignment, but I don't think deadlines apply anymore."

"What's he like? Liam?"

"He is the light of my life," she smiles. "He's a precocious little boy, smart, sweet. A cuddlebug. He loves trains and baseball." She turns toward Will and he's smiling. "When I taught at the American School I'd take him out to the playground during lunch and we would watch the kids playing baseball. He was fascinated and has been obsessed since. I'm going to take him to Cooperstown sometime this year."

"I've always wanted to go there. The Baseball Hall of Fame. Is he a Sox fan?"

"Of course!" she smiles.

"I'd love to meet him."

"You will." Julia touches his cheek. He's in conflict right now, she can see it on his face. "Hey," she whispers. "What's the matter?"

"I wish I could go back in time." His eyes are sad, his face serious, "I wouldn't make the same mistakes again."

Tears fill her eyes. There are so many things she wishes she could change. She set these events in motion by not trusting him. She should have had faith in him.

"We both made mistakes, this isn't all you're doing. I shouldn't have turned you away. We wouldn't be where we are now if I had just believed in us." She kisses his lips and he holds her to him, "For that, I am so sorry." She runs her hand down his chest, "While you're here, you're mine. I don't care about the rest. If this is all we can have, a night here and there, I'll take it. It's better than not being with you at all."

"Jules, I just want to be with you. I can't live like that anymore. I don't feel guilty being here. We belong together."

His hand caresses her face, and he runs his fingers down her body, his hand coming to rest on her stomach.

"You had a baby in there." Will shakes his head. "I had a dream you were pregnant once...a few months after I last saw you...you looked so beautiful..."

Julia's heart stops. *He dreamt I was pregnant when I was carrying Liam?* Will moves his hand in a circular motion around her abdomen.

"Julia...I feel another sin coming on."

"Another one?" She raises an eyebrow. Will nods and rolls on top of her, kissing her deeply. "Ah... this is why they invented confession, I get it now."

Will smiles and she wraps her legs around him.

"Jules, we're going to keep those priests busy."

Close to eight o'clock, Julia runs downstairs for food and water. This whole day has been surreal. Will is in her bed, after all these years, and her country is under attack. She wonders what's going on in New York, Washington, DC and *god only knows where else*, but she doesn't want to break the blissful spell they're under by turning on the television. She knows she's in denial, trying to keep reality at bay. It's just too awful...so many innocent lives snuffed out.

She wants to check on Liam before he's asleep for the night, but suspects that window is closed. Julia picks up her cell phone to call her mother and sees she's missed three calls and has two voicemails from Ellie.

What's going on? She listens to the first message.

"Jules, it's Ellie. Is Will there with you? I've been trying to reach him all afternoon but his phone is off. He called me earlier this morning and asked me to watch his dog for the next few days...He wouldn't tell me who he's with so I'm taking a chance here. If he's with you, please have him call me."

Her brow furrows and she presses the button to listen to the next message. Ellie wouldn't call here looking for Will unless something was very wrong.

"Jules, it's me again. It's an emergency. We haven't heard from Peter all day. We can't get through to his cell, and he hasn't called anyone in the family. If Will is there, and dear Lord I hope he is, please have him call me."

Julia looks at the time the last message was received. Ellie called an hour ago. She runs up the stairs.

"Will, where's your phone?"

"In the car, why?"

"Ellie left two messages on my phone. She's been trying to reach you all day." He's visibly confused. "It's about Peter."

***

Will's heart stops. *Peter?* He didn't call Peter this morning because his brother is on vacation this week, and then he saw Julia and... *My brother is supposed to be on Martha's Vineyard with Sloane. What's going on?* Surely someone has been in touch with Sloane. He pulls on his pants and undershirt and runs to his car, grabbing his cell phone.

Julia is waiting for him downstairs on the couch and his hand shakes as he presses the power button and turns his phone on. When he called Ellie earlier to ask her to watch Max, she was her inquisitive self, wanting to know who he was with, but he evaded her questions, turned off his phone and left it in his car, not wanting anyone to disturb his time with Julia.

Oh my god. He's missed thirteen calls, most from his sister, a few from his parents.

Not one from my brother.

He calls Ellie immediately and she picks up on the first ring.

"Where the fuck have you been? Will, no one has heard from Peter today. He hasn't called anyone." His sister's voice is panicked, her breathing rushed.

"Ellie, take a deep breath." He runs his hand through his hair, "Pete's on vacation this week. Has anyone heard from Sloane?"

"Yes, she's on the Vineyard. She's been in touch with Mom and Dad all day. She's freaking out. He flew back to New York last night. He had to go back to the city for an early meeting this morning, and was supposed to fly back to the island this afternoon."

Will closes his eyes, his heart sinking. No. There has to be a reasonable explanation why his brother hasn't called. Where could he be?

"Has anyone tried his office?"

"Of course, we couldn't get through."

"The phone lines are jammed in New York." He rubs his hand over his eyes, "He might not be able to get through to anyone today. There's nothing we can do tonight, Ellie. If we haven't heard from Peter by noon tomorrow then we need to make a plan. I'll drive to New York and find him myself."

"Okay. Keep your phone on. And tell Jules I said hello." Ellie hangs up and he stares at his phone.

What the hell?

"Ellie said to say hello...?" He turns to Julia, confused, "How could she possibly know I'm here? We haven't talked about you in years."

"Will, what's going on with Peter?" Her eyes are filled with concern.

"I don't know what to think." He leans back on the couch, "He doesn't work downtown. They said on the radio earlier that so many people have been trying to reach family and friends in the city and can't get through. Something about the cell towers not being able to handle the volume of traffic."

"That makes sense. He should be able to reach you tomorrow."

"Yes…" he pauses. "Julia, how could Ellie possibly know I'm here?"

"I bumped into Ellie a couple of months ago. She's been here a few times with the kids since then. She took Liam to the zoo the day I saw you at Starbucks and I told her we had coffee together. I guess she put two and two together?"

He nods his head. He's not surprised Ellie didn't tell him she saw Julia. They don't tell each other much anymore.

"You know, she misses you, Will. She said things haven't been good between you two in years, but she never told me why."

"I miss her too," he sighs. "It's a very long story. Another time, okay?"

"Of course."

Peter is missing? Manhattan must be chaos today, but wouldn't he be able to reach someone…somehow? *Email? Text message?* He doesn't have a good feeling about this. He's trying to stay calm, but he's scared. He's absolutely terrified something horrible has happened to his brother.

"Let's see what's going on now," Julia says, turning on the television, then grabs the blanket from the back of the couch and throws it over them.

Will turns to her, so thankful they found their way back to one another.

"I love you, Julia," He holds her face in his hands and can see his love reflected in her eyes. Nothing feels better than loving someone with your whole heart, and knowing they feel the same for you. His heart is swelling with emotion, his eyes brimming with tears.

"Always," she smiles, then reaches out and touches his face. "Will, if you go to New York tomorrow, I'm going with you. I want to help."

"Thank you, Jules. Let's hope it doesn't come to that."

They are quiet while the President addresses the nation. "Today, our fellow citizens, our way of life, our very freedom came under attack in a series of deliberate and deadly terrorist acts. The victims were in airplanes or in their offices. Secretaries, businessmen and women, military and federal workers. Moms and dads. Friends and neighbors. Thousands of lives were suddenly ended by evil, despicable acts of terror."

He pulls Julia close to him, his eyes fixed on the television. "This is a day when all Americans from every walk of life unite in our resolve for justice and peace. America has stood down enemies before, and we will do so this time. None of us will ever forget this day, yet we go forward to defend freedom and all that is good and just in our world."

"Will, we live in a nation at war." Julia wipes her eyes. "How do we fight a war against terror? Who are we fighting exactly? Some fundamentalist group scattered around the globe?"

He shakes his head. It does seem hopeless.

"An eye for an eye makes the whole world blind...my Gram used to say that. No one wins when revenge is the goal. Yet something has to be done..."

Will holds onto her tightly. *His country is at war, his brother might be a casualty, and he's sitting beside the love of his life.* He's not alone anymore. He can never go back to the life he was living before today.

They stayed up well past midnight. He asked to see more pictures of Liam and Julia pulled out a couple of photo albums. Together, they went through the photographs and he studied each one intently, memorizing each picture, imagining he was there with them while Julia shared stories about their lives in Italy.

"Liam is a well-travelled little man. Been all over Europe and speaks two languages."

"He speaks two languages?" he asks, amazed.

"Kids are sponges. They pick up languages so much faster than adults when they're immersed in the culture. It took me at least six months to learn Italian, and I wasn't fluent by any means. Now I am."

"Where was he born?"

"Verona."

"You stayed in Verona?"

"I went back there when I was pregnant. I wanted to be there for so many reasons," she looks into his eyes, "I thought about you all of the time, Will. You were with me throughout my pregnancy, on the day he was born, and every day since. You are a part of me."

"I've tried so hard to forget you Julia, to accept my life as it is, but not a single day has passed that you haven't crossed my mind. My wedding day was one of the worst days of my life. I felt like a fraud. Pretending to be happy, to be in love. I remember walking to the water and wondering where you were. What you were thinking about, if you ever thought about me."

"Now you know." Julia clasps his hand, "I thought of you every single day."

"Ellie didn't go to the wedding." He lies back on her bed, "That's what happened between us. She said she couldn't watch me ruin my life. She was right. I made a huge mistake."

"Will, I've always known you didn't marry her for love. You married her to pay for your sin." Julia places a finger under his chin, turning his face toward her, "I think you're paid in full. It's time to stop punishing yourself."

"I agree. Now I have to get out of this mess."

Chapter Twenty-Two

Something's different. Julia begins to stir, her eyes slowly opening. She's not alone in her bed. She feels Will's arms around her and she runs her hand along his chest. She isn't dreaming, he's really here. She grins ear to ear and looks into his eyes.

"Good morning, beautiful." Will leans down to kiss her.

"Good morning…How long have you been up?

"I don't think I ever slept. I didn't want to close my eyes and wake up to find you gone. That being with you was a figment of my imagination."

"I'm not going anywhere," she smiles, then remembers he's waiting for a phone call. "Any word from Peter?"

"Nothing yet." Will puts his phone down on the nightstand, "Come here."

She rests her head against his chest, and listens to his heartbeat in the warmth of his embrace. *It doesn't get much better than this*, she thinks, then cringes. Peter could be dead and all she can think about is how good it feels to be in Will's arms again.

"Try his number," she whispers. "See if you can get through."

"It's ringing!" he says and they both sit up. *One. Two. Three. Four. Five.* Will's face falls. "Voicemail." He dials Peter's apartment, then shakes his head, "No answer."

"That doesn't mean anything. For all you know he's helping with the rescue efforts. He could be anywhere."

"Then why hasn't he called? He has to know we're worried sick about him. Julia, I have a very bad feeling about this…I think he's gone…"

"We don't know what he's gone through in the past…" she checks the clock on her nightstand, "twenty-one hours, Will. Don't give up hope."

"I can't wait around anymore, I need to do something."

"Then let's go." She climbs out of bed, "Let's head to New York now. Why wait six more hours?"

"I need to stop at my house and change, grab a few supplies. See my parents."

"I'm going to stop and see the baby before we go. I'll take my car and meet you at Ellie's."

"I'd like to meet Liam…if that's okay."

She figures if Will hasn't noticed the resemblance after seeing two hundred pictures of Liam, then he's not likely to make the connection in person, though how he can miss the resemblance is beyond her. Maybe he's in denial and doesn't want to believe he's missed so much of his son's life. *Or maybe he just believes me*, she thinks, her heart sinking.

They pull up to her mother's house around eight-thirty and Julia's sure Liam's been up for a couple of hours by now.

"Mom? Liam?" She walks into the kitchen, "Where are you two?"

"We're back here honey!" her mother calls from the patio.

"It's hardly changed," Will says, looking around the kitchen.

"Not much does around here."

Liam runs into the kitchen, wearing his Batman pajamas, and flings himself at her legs.

"Mama!"

"Hey sweetie pie." She leans down and scoops him up, "You're feeling better I see!"

"Yes, but Gran said I don't have to go to school today."

She kisses his cheek, suddenly very nervous. *What was I thinking bringing Will here?* Will's staring at Liam, his mouth half open, his eyes glazed over.

Her mother walks into the kitchen and freezes in her tracks.

"Will."

He snaps out of his daze and turns toward her mother.

"Hi Carol," he kisses her on the cheek. "It's good to see you again."

"You too, Will," she says robotically, "Julia?"

"Liam, this is my very good friend Will."

"Nice to meet you." Liam raises his eyes, a little shy, and holds out his hand.

Will smiles and bends down, shaking his son's hand and continues to stare at Liam.

"Nice to meet you too. Your mom tells me you like baseball."

"Want to see my baseball cards?" Liam's face lights up, and Will nods, smiling. He grabs Will's hand and pulls him down the hall to Julia's old room, which is now his room.

"Julia, what the hell is going on?" Her mother whispers, pulling her into the dining room.

"Mom, I don't know where to begin. I haven't told him so don't say anything."

"Jules, do you think he doesn't know?" Her mother is in shock. "Did you see the look on his face?"

"Mom, he saw hundreds of pictures of him at my place and never registered an ounce of recognition." Carol raises an eyebrow and shakes her head. "We're going to New York City. His brother is missing."

"You're going where? Out of the question, Julia! It's dangerous. You're a mother. You have forfeited the right to do foolish things."

"Mom, it was my home for years, and it's probably the safest place in the country right now, other than DC."

"Julia, what are you doing with him? Sweetheart, I know how much he means to you but he's a married man!"

"I'm going to tell him about Liam once he files for divorce," she meets her mother's gaze defiantly, hands on hips. Julia doesn't want to think of herself as someone who would have an affair with a married man. *But this is Will! He's the father of my child!* She's not breaking up a happy marriage.

"He said he's getting a divorce?"

"Not in those exact words."

"Julia, please," Carol throws her hands up in the air. "Be sensible."

Indignant, she walks away from her mother, down the hall to Liam's bedroom. They're facing each other, looking at this year's Red Sox team. Seeing Will and his son sitting on the floor together, so alike, her breath catches in her throat.

She never thought this moment would come. She never believed Will would meet his son. The sight of them together, doing something they might've done, had he always been a part of their lives, paralyzes her in the doorway.

"He's my favorite." Liam points out Pedro Martinez, and Will picks up the card.

"Hey, mine too!" Will gives him a high five.

"I like Trot Nixon, too. Mama doesn't like his last name. She said that's the name of a crook." Will laughs and ruffles his hair, and Julia forcibly snaps herself out of her trance.

"Well, it is!" she says and enters the room, kneeling on the floor beside him. "Sweetheart, I'll see you in a few days, okay? I have a lot of work to do, but Gran will take good care of you, and I'll call you every day. Promise."

"Okay, I love you Mama." He wraps his arms around her neck and squeezes tight.

"I love you too." She kisses his cheek.

Liam turns to Will, "Want to watch a Red Sox game with me?"

"You bet." Will looks into Liam's eyes, "Have you ever been to Fenway?"

"No! But my mom has. Have you?" Liam's face lights up with curiosity.

"I go all the time. Maybe you and your mom can come with me sometime."

"Please, oh please?" Liam turns to her, his eyes pleading.

"That would be wonderful."

Julia's quiet on the drive to Ellie and Kevin's house and wrings her hands, feeling torn. She feels so guilty about lying to Will. She wants to tell him the truth, but she has to wait until she knows he's really leaving Avery. Once the papers are filed she'll tell him. She keeps repeating that to herself like a mantra, *once the papers are filed, once the papers are filed…*

"Are you okay?" Will asks, squeezing her knee.

"I just miss him, that's all."

"He's a great kid, Jules. I'm glad I got to meet him. Thank you."

"He really liked you too," she smiles weakly, staring out the window, then turns to study Will's profile.

Seeing them together was unsettling, more than she imagined it'd be. They were so comfortable with one another, so…happy. The magnitude of the lie she's told is a weight pressing on her heart.

Dear Lord, what have I done?

Ellie's eyes are swollen and puffy when she opens the door, but her face lights up when she finds Julia standing beside Will.

"Two of my favorite people, together again." She pulls them inside the house and wraps her arms around her brother. "I am so happy to see you two, you have no idea! I've waited years for this moment."

Ellie hugs Julia to her, and whispers in her ear, "Does he know?" Julia shakes her head and mouths, *no.*

"Have you heard anything from Peter yet?" Ellie asks Will and he shakes his head. Her chin trembles, "What if something happened to him, Will?"

"I don't know Ellie." Will hugs her again, "One day at a time, right? I'll find him, no matter what." Ellie nods and wipes her eyes.

"Where's Kevin?" Julia asks. She's sitting with Will on the couch, going through pictures of Peter.

"He finally found a rental car and has been driving all night from Cleveland." Ellie sighs, "He should be home in an hour or so."

"How about this one?" Will holds out a photo. It's a close up shot and Peter's smiling. Ellie takes it from him and nods.

"That's a good one," she says, her voice thick with emotion.

"Do you have a scanner and printer here?" Julia asks.

"In the study."

"I'm going to run home and change." Will rises, "I'll be back soon."

"Show me where everything is," Julia says. "I need a marker, paper, tape."

"How did this happen?" Ellie walks her into the study, "I'm over the moon excited for you both. Tell me!"

"Fate." Julia grabs the sharpie and starts writing, "I bumped into him at the deli yesterday after the attacks. Life's too short, Ellie. I told him I've always loved him." She shrugs, "I'll be the mistress if I have to, I don't care! I just want to be with him. Does that make me a home wrecker?"

"Ha!" Ellie snorts, "There's no home to destroy. The bitch wrecked your home years ago."

"Will met Liam this morning."

"What?!" Ellie's eyes bulge from their sockets.

"Yes, we stopped at my mom's on the way here." She turns to Ellie, "It was crazy. I feel so guilty, Ellie. They're two peas in a pod, totally enamored of one another. They talked baseball." Julia's eyes fill with tears.

"And he didn't realize…?" Ellie asks, stunned.

"Nope," Julia shakes her head.

"How is that possible?" Ellie's brow furrows, "Liam is the spitting image of him…"

"I think people see what they want to see." Julia holds Ellie's hands in hers, "I hate lying to him, it's tearing me up inside. When he asked me about Liam's father, I almost choked. I'll tell him the truth, Ellie. I will. But what if he hates me? What if he can't forgive me?"

"Julia, stop. What's done is done. You have to believe he loves you enough to forgive you. You did it to protect your son. His son!" Ellie cries. "When are you going to tell him?"

"When he files for divorce," Julia looks her in the eye, "And not one second sooner."

"Jules, my brother is back," Ellie smiles. "I see the fire in eyes again. He's not a zombie anymore."

"He said I brought him back to life."

"You did. Now let's find my other brother in the same condition."

Julia places the poster on the scanner and prints two hundred copies of the "Missing" sign she created. She picks up the stack of paper and hugs Ellie to her.

"I pray we don't need to use these, El."

***

Will and Ellie walk to their parents' house and their mother greets them in her housecoat, her eyes bloodshot and swollen. She's aged overnight. A pillar of strength throughout their father's illness, the idea of losing one of her children is too much for her to bear.

Their father is sitting on his favorite leather chair in the den, a blanket wrapped around his legs. The television is on low, the screen filled with images from the rescue efforts currently underway at what is being called *Ground Zero*.

Ellie kisses her father on top of his head and sits on the couch while their mother paces around the room with her rosary beads.

"They pulled someone out of the rubble alive a little while ago," his father says, eyes glued to the television screen. "There's still hope for others."

"Dad, I'm heading to the city to find Peter." Will pulls the ottoman next to his father's chair, and takes his hand. "We haven't been able to reach him by phone and it's been more than twenty-four hours."

His mother sits beside Ellie on the couch and weeps into her hands.

"Mom, we don't know if Peter was downtown. He could be anywhere. I'll find him. Has Sloane been able to get off the Vineyard?"

"Yes. She called a little while ago. She'll be here a little after noon. I'm so worried about her and the baby."

Will sits up, startled. *The baby?*

"She's pregnant again?" Ellie asks, her eyes wide.

"She's only eleven weeks along and they didn't want to tell anyone yet."

Sloane's had three miscarriages in the past five years, all in the first trimester. Each loss has devastated both Peter and

Sloane. He rubs his hands over his eyes, tears springing up at the possibility of his brother never seeing his child. *Jesus Christ.*

"Before you go, let's all say a prayer." His mother rises, shaky on her feet, and begins, "Hail Mary, full of grace…"

There aren't many cars on the road as Will and Julia make their way toward New York, until they reach the Connecticut-New York border. There isn't any train service into the city and the bridges and tunnels into Manhattan are still closed.

They've been listening to the radio and their best bet is to take a ferry into the city from New Jersey. That's been the only way on and off the island over the past twenty-eight hours. Over five hundred thousand people were ferried off Manhattan yesterday in less than nine hours, as boats from all over answered the Coast Guard's call for help.

"It's mind-boggling." Julia shakes her head. "It took nine days to evacuate three hundred and thirty thousand soldiers from Dunkirk during World War II."

Julia studies the map while he weaves in and out of traffic, her eyes squinting in concentration, turning the map around to get a better look.

"We should take the Tappan Zee Bridge off the Interstate to New Jersey and try to get on the Palisades Parkway. There's a ferry terminal in Edgewater that can take us to mid-town."

He takes her left hand in his and holds it to his lips and Julia smiles, her eyes filled with warmth. He's so thankful she's here with him, that she's part of his life again. It's a miracle. And now that she's here, there's no turning back for him.

During the drive he's been thinking about his situation. He's going to file for divorce. He'll talk to Avery as soon as she's back from California. Avery isn't going to go without a fight, but if he has to give her every penny to his name, he'll do it.

As long as he has Julia, he has everything he needs. And Liam. Her son's never had a father and he wants that privilege. When he sat with Liam this morning, he was filled with love for her child. He's part of Julia, how could he not?

His parents are going to be disappointed. There's never been a divorce in his family. He's not looking forward to that conversation either, but he doesn't care if they approve anymore.

Will finally understands. He doesn't owe his parents anything except his love, but he does owe it to himself to be happy. It's taken him thirty-two years, and a national tragedy to finally get it. *This is my life and I'm not going to waste another day of it.*

***

It's warm out today, close to eighty degrees. The ferry terminal in Edgewater is filled with hundreds of people who've gathered to make the journey into the city in search of missing loved ones, and there's a hush over the crowd. No one wants to say the unspeakable, that their search is probably in vain.

Julia holds onto Will's arm, studying the faces of the people around her. Parents, spouses, siblings, friends, of all races and creeds. Everyone at the terminal is united by one thing, *hope*. Hope that the person they love is somewhere on the other side of the Hudson River. *Alive.*

She stares at the list of New York City hospitals she wrote down a few minutes ago. If Peter isn't at his apartment, the hospitals are their next stop. Thousands of people are being treated in area hospitals, though very few are survivors from inside the World Trade Center.

As Will parked the car, they heard over the radio that a man was rescued from the depths of the debris just a little while ago. He survived for twenty-seven hours, perhaps there are more?

Will looks nervous, but determined. Who knows what they're going to find when they reach the island, but he's handling this difficult situation with strength. This morning he shared his fear that Peter is gone. If his brother was alive he would've found some way to make contact with the family.

It would be absolutely devastating if he turns out to be right, but she doesn't believe he'll fall apart like he would've in the past. Will told her about Sloane's pregnancy, and her history of miscarriages. This has to be extraordinarily stressful for her, and as much as Julia disliked Sloane, she wouldn't wish this on anyone.

As the ferry makes its way down river toward the Manhattan terminal at 39th Street, the city skyline comes into view, the smoke still billowing over lower Manhattan. Her breath catches at her first sight of it, her hand flying to her mouth in shock.

Despite seeing them fall to the ground live on television yesterday morning, she didn't really believe the Towers were gone. But they are, just as surely as the people who were in those buildings are gone. There's a gaping hole in the skyline... and in the lives of the victims' families.

The Twin Towers were Julia's point of reference in her early days living in the city. She could always navigate using them as her guide. *Those monsters.* She's filled with fury at the people responsible for this devastation.

What did the terrorists think they'd accomplish by killing all of those innocent people? She's shaking with anger, and if she's honest with herself, fear. If they're willing to do this, what else are they capable of?

Will wraps his arm around her shoulders and pulls her into his embrace. She takes a deep breath, holding him close. Feeling the warmth of his body against hers, she feels…safe.

They docked in mid-town and even here the evidence of the destruction is apparent. The city is covered in soot, a white powdery substance. The streets are eerily silent and virtually deserted, a movie set of post-apocalyptic New York.

The ferry travelers disburse in different directions, each with a purposeful stride. Will and Julia walk over to Lexington Avenue and take the green line uptown to 77th Street. Subway service resumed this morning to points north, but the trains are nearly empty. The entire city has been transformed.

They reach Peter and Sloane's apartment building on 78th and Park by three o'clock and Will explains the situation to the doorman, who solemnly nods and lets them into the apartment.

Peter isn't here, that's clear. They didn't expect he would be, but they're hoping to find some sort of clue as to where he went yesterday. Sloane didn't know where his meeting was being held.

Will picks up a picture of his family as they enter the living room. It was taken on a ski trip when they were young and he turns to Julia and smiles. Will and Peter have their arms around each other's shoulders and big grins on their faces.

She wraps her arms around his waist. "You okay?" Will nods, takes a deep breath and places the photo back on the table.

Peter left the English muffins out on the counter yesterday, the coffee pot is half full and his dirty mug is sitting in the sink. In his bedroom, they find Peter's brown leather duffle bag with a change of clothes and a bag of toiletries. He was planning to fly back to the Vineyard after his meeting yesterday and had already packed.

"Oh Julia…" Will sighs, and sits on his brother's bed, his head in his hands. She sits beside him for a moment, then goes in search of clues.

Where were you yesterday morning, Peter?

Rummaging through the papers on the desk in the study, she finds invitations to a wedding and baby shower, and underneath an opened bill, an appointment book. The book is black leather and her heart stops when she notices Peter's initials embossed on the cover.

She flips through the pages until she reaches September 11, 2001. Peter had scribbled on the calendar, *Cantor Fitzgerald, 8:30am.*

"Will! Come here!" Julia shouts and he rushes into the study. "Look." She points to the page.

He grabs the book from her and his face turns ghostly white, then drops it, his body swaying.

"Will…where's Cantor Fitzgerald?" she asks, but knows the answer just by the look on his face.

"The World Trade Center," he whispers.

"Oh my god… Oh, no…" she murmurs.

Will cries out in anger and wipes the desk clear, the papers flying around the room. He kneels down and the tears begin to fall, a steady stream down his face. Julia helps him to the guest bedroom and they lay together, Will's head on her chest. She holds him close and strokes his back, trying to soothe him.

"How do I tell my parents? Sloane? Ellie?"

Julia doesn't want to give him false hope, but thinks they should check the hospitals before they say anything to the family.

"We should exhaust every possibility, check the hospitals, hang up the signs. Maybe someone has seen him…"

Outside of Grand Central Station she saw hundreds of missing person posters on lampposts, the sides of buildings, and inside the station. What if someone saw Peter at a hospital and he's unconscious? She knows it's unlikely, but they can't be one hundred percent certain he's dead. They both saw the television footage of people fleeing the Towers.

While Will's in the bathroom, she turns on the computer in Peter's study, and does a search for Cantor Fitzgerald. The company's headquarters are located in the North Tower of the World Trade Center. She scrolls down a little further. The company occupies five floors... the 101st through 105th floors.

She closes her eyes, her stomach churning. She heard the plane struck the skyscraper between the 93rd and 99th floors. People above the strike zone were trapped and had no chance of survival.

She switches to CNN's website and a photograph of a man falling head first from the North Tower makes her gasp in horror. *Oh my god.* People were jumping!

Those poor souls had to make one of three horrible choices, die in an inferno, suffocate from the intense smoke, or take control of their last moments on earth and jump, ending their suffering.

Will walks up behind her and she hears him groan. Quickly, she turns off the monitor and finds him clutching his stomach, his face contorted with grief, the image too painful.

"I'm so sorry, Will."

They make the rounds of the hospitals Wednesday evening, but they're just going through the motions. Mt. Sinai, Bellevue, New York Presbyterian, Lenox Hill. They've shown Peter's picture to hundreds, if not thousands of people, and hung posters up all over the city.

Later that evening they attend mass at St. Patrick's Cathedral with hundreds of other mourners, Will finding comfort in the rituals.

He knows there's no way his brother survived the attack. If Peter was on the 101st floor at eight-thirty that Tuesday morning, and it's now clear that he was, he couldn't have escaped the firestorm. *Peter never had a chance.*

Will called his parents and said he didn't have any luck today, but didn't share the information they found in the appointment book. He wants to do that in person.

They spend the night at Peter and Sloane's apartment, but neither of them can sleep. Will holds onto her all night, and she comforts him as best she can during these dark hours.

On Thursday morning, Will wants to go to Ground Zero, to see for himself where his brother died. They take a bus as far downtown as they can get, then walk toward Vesey Street. Security is tight, but they get close enough to see the fires still raging, the firefighters and rescue workers carefully removing the debris in search of more survivors, one bucket at a time.

Will kneels in the street, his clothes covered in the soot that coats the city and prays, saying goodbye to his brother while Julia stands beside him, horrified by the destruction surrounding them.

They leave the city that afternoon, returning to New Jersey by ferry and drive home so Will can share the devastating news with his family, and Peter's pregnant wife.

Chapter Twenty-Three

Peter was one of eight Rhode Islanders to die on September 11th. His picture has been all over the local news and Will's been receiving condolence messages at home and work from people he hasn't heard from in years. The outpouring of support from the community has been overwhelming, not just for him, but his whole family. They're private people, and need this time alone to grieve.

He deeply mourns the loss of his brother, and is enraged by the senseless act of violence that caused his death, but he finds solace with Julia and Liam. The loss of his brother is always with him, but Julia's home is his sanctuary, her arms a refuge from darkness.

Her presence calms him and spending time with her son fills him with joy. He lives completely in the moment with Liam and when the three of them are together, he feels a surge of love unlike anything he's ever known. They're the family he thought he'd never have.

Every night, Will has the same nightmare. He's in the North Tower with Peter, suffocating from the smoke, his skin blistering from the heat of the flames. He's coughing, choking and crawls toward his brother.

Peter stands on the ledge of the window, his face calm and free from worry. He tells Will to join him, to come get some fresh air. Will leans over the windowsill and looks down at the street...so far below and shakes his head in fear. He tells his brother to get off, to come down from the ledge but Peter looks up at the sky, unconcerned.

"Pete, please be careful. What if you fall?"

"Will..." his brother turns to him, "What if I fly?"

Peter smiles and jumps into the fresh air, his arms open wide, and soars above the buildings, disappearing from sight.

Will wakes up soaked in sweat, his heart pounding hard inside his chest and reaches for Julia. His brother jumped to his death, he's sure of it. There's some comfort knowing Peter took control of his own fate and didn't suffer in those final moments. What keeps him up half the night is the thought his brother was forced to choose how he died. No one should ever have to make that decision, yet hundreds of people did that day.

They've been home from New York for just over a week. Mid-morning Will drives to Bristol and pulls up in front of his house. He needs to walk Max and pick up a change of clothes before he heads back to Julia's. He can't sleep if he's not beside her.

Shifting his car into park, Will stares at the house he's lived in for the past six years. He bought it for the water views and its proximity to his parents, not because he liked the house itself. It's modern and sleek, not at all his style.

The interior is cold and impersonal. Avery decorated it with *Architectural Digest* in mind, not comfort. But the view is incredible. The wall facing the water is floor to ceiling windows and he's spent many nights alone in the living room, sitting in the dark, listening to the water lapping onto shore, and watching the moonlight dance on the harbor.

This has never been a home to him, just somewhere to sleep. Now he understands, *home isn't a place, it's a feeling.* His home is with Julia and Liam, no matter where they live.

Avery's car is in the driveway and he's dreading seeing her. He's avoided her for the most part, telling her his parents need him now. It hasn't been easy. When she came home from her trip last weekend, she attempted to comfort him in the only way she knows how. Sex.

The night she arrived, he stopped by to walk the dog and found her in a silky negligee, with candles lit and a bottle of wine on the table. He stared at her, dumbfounded. *My brother was murdered. Did she really think a romantic evening would make me feel better?* He grabbed Max's leash, walked him to his sister's house and drove to Julia's, sickened by the sight of Avery.

This morning, he finds Avery sitting by the picture window, staring out the window, and drinking a glass of wine. He's never seen her drink before noon.

"Where were you last night?" she asks, her voice flat. He can tell she's had a couple of drinks already.

"I slept on the boat." He walks into the kitchen and pours himself a glass of water.

"Why didn't you come home?"

"Because I wanted to sleep on the boat."

He fastens the leash around Max, walks out the door, and takes a deep breath. He has to tell her it's over. There's never a 'right time' for this kind of conversation.

He wanted to wait until after Peter's memorial service this coming week, for his parents' sake. He doesn't want to add to their sorrow, but it has to happen sooner. They need to be prepared in case she shows up at their door in a state of…who knows what state Avery will be in! She could be relieved, or she could fly into a rage.

He has no idea how she'll react, but his parents have had enough stress. They just lost their son in one of the most horrific ways possible, but that won't stop Avery from dragging them into their business.

His parents and Sloane are in deep mourning. Earlier today, he stopped by his parents' house and found his father in the den, staring at the news. He's been wearing the same bathrobe and watching CNN around the clock since the tragedy.

His heart heavy, Will headed upstairs to check on his mother. She's hardly gotten out of bed in the past week and a half and spends her days in prayer, doing the rosary over and over again.

Sloane was lying in Peter's bed, staring at the ceiling, totally unresponsive. Everyone's very concerned about her health. The whole family desperately wants her to carry this baby to term, so part of Peter will live on. He doesn't know how to reach her. No one does.

His sister has been incredibly strong over the past week. When he and Julia returned from New York they stopped there first and shared what they discovered about Peter's whereabouts the morning of the attack with Ellie and Kevin. His sister held onto him and sobbed while Julia took the kids outside to play. "It's just the two of us now."

They walked to their parents' house together and shared the news with the family. His mother burst into tears and ran from the room, his father stared at Will, in shock, and then followed his mother to their bedroom.

Sloane sat in the armchair motionless. The only sign of distress on her face the tears rolling down her cheeks. Ellie kneeled beside her and asked if there was anything she could do. Sloane slowly turned her head toward Ellie, a dazed expression on her face, "I'm going to bed." She stood and placed her hand over her stomach, "The baby needs to rest."

From his house, he walks Max to his sister's. "Hello? Ellie?" He enters her house with the dog and there are toys strewn everywhere, piles of laundry folded on the coffee table, and

Sesame Street on the television. He can hear his niece and nephews tearing it up in the next room.

"Hey there." She walks into the living room, wiping her hands on a dishtowel, and kisses his cheek, "I was just making lunch. Do you want to stay? I'm creating a culinary masterpiece with two boxes of macaroni and cheese and a head of broccoli."

"I'll pass, thank you," he laughs. Ellie is not known for her cooking abilities. "It's Julia's birthday and I'm heading up to Providence. Can you watch Max?"

"Of course." She nods her head, smiling.

He follows his sister into the kitchen and sits on a stool at the counter, pensive.

"Ellie. I'm going to tell Avery I'm filing for divorce this week."

Her face lights up and a smile spreads across her face. Ellie flings her arms around him, tears in her eyes.

"Hallelujah! That is music to my ears!" His sister is glowing with joy. "You'll be rid of the albatross at last!"

"I think Avery's getting suspicious. She was drinking when I stopped home and asked me where I was last night. Thankfully, Dad told me she was there looking for me earlier." Ellie raises an eyebrow. "I said I slept on the boat."

"Fuck her!" Ellie grits her teeth, sticking both of her middle fingers in the air, "I fucking hate her!"

A comment like that would have pissed him off a month ago. Not anymore.

"I'm nervous how she'll react. I don't care if she unleashes on me, but I don't want her to involve Mom and Dad."

"They may be upset, but after losing Peter...I don't think they'll be overly distraught. Do you want me to be there?"

"No. I'm a big boy. I can do this on my own."

Ellie takes the pot of macaroni off the stove and walks to the sink.

"Have you told Jules?"

"No, I'm going to tell her tonight…"

"And?" Ellie turns and raises an eyebrow. "I hear an 'and' in your voice."

"And…I'm going to ask her to marry me."

Ellie's mouth opens, her eyes growing wide. She drops the pot of pasta in the sink and jumps up and down, then throws her arms around him.

"Oh my god! Something good has come out of this nightmare. Peter is your guardian angel, Will. He's been guiding you toward happiness."

Will can't disagree. He and Julia were reunited almost moments after his brother's death. They both see Peter's hand in this.

"When are you asking her? Ahhhh, I'm so excited!"

"Calm down, not tonight. I want to plan something special."

"Do you want me to help you pick out a ring?"

He shakes his head and smiles.

"I bought her a ring years ago."

While Julia is grocery shopping, Will is with Liam at the park. It's late Sunday morning and a beautiful fall day. The trees have begun to turn brilliant autumn colors, but it's still warm enough they don't need to wear coats. He's smiling as he pushes Liam on the swing, thinking how his entire life has turned around in the best possible ways since that awful day.

Two weeks ago he was miserable, in a loveless marriage, and feeling trapped. He never imagined he'd see Julia again, let alone be with her. In the past he would have been overcome with guilt for being happy in this time of grief, but not now. He feels Peter's presence every day and his brother has given him the courage to live the life he wants. His brother would want him to be happy. Will closes his eyes in gratitude.

Thank you, Peter.

"Higher! Higher!" Liam calls out and Will obliges.

"Your son looks just like you." The woman pushing her daughter on the next swing over smiles and says, "How old is he?"

He likes the sound of that. *My son.*

"He's four."

"I'm five!" Liam shouts.

Will frowns. He's sure Julia told him Liam is four. The woman beside him raises an eyebrow.

"He's not my son," he explains.

"Oh!" She seems confused. "You're not his father? Are you his uncle? He's the spitting image of you. Really! His eyes, his nose… everything!"

My spitting image… he's five…

"Yes," he slowly nods his head. "We're related."

"I thought so. He's adorable." She smiles and joins her daughter at the jungle gym.

Will stops pushing the swing and stares at Liam. *Is it possible…?*

"Hey!" Liam cries out and pumps his legs to get some extra height. "Don't stop!"

"Liam…" Will moves to the side of the swing. "When's your birthday?"

"August 3rd."

Doing the calculations in his head, he asks "You turned five in August?"

"Uh huh, I had a big birthday party at Nana and Papas. There was a bouncy house and everything!"

Will takes a deep breath in, slowly exhales and closes his eyes.

I'm an idiot.

Liam's in kindergarten, he's bigger than his nephews. *He looks exactly like me. How could I not know?*

"You're a big boy now." He lifts Liam off the swing and hugs him.

"Tell Mama. She still thinks I'm a baby." Liam wiggles out of his embrace, and runs to the sandbox.

Will studies Liam from the bench. *He has my eyes, my nose, my mouth, even my hands. Why didn't Julia tell me? Why would she keep my son from me?*

His eyes well up as he thinks about the five years of Liam's life he's missed... the five years he's been married to Avery. He was already married when Liam was born. Was she punishing him for leaving her alone in Verona?

He didn't fight for Julia, he just let her go. Worse than that...*I walked away.*

What would he have done had he known about Liam years ago? He would have wanted to be part of Liam's life, surely. But would he have been ready to make the changes he's willing to make now? Would he have had the strength to leave Avery? He's not sure. God only knows what Avery would have done! She would have made their lives hell.

Julia understood this, she must have. Why else would she keep his son away from him? She was protecting Liam. By all rights he should be furious with her, but he's not. She was right to protect their son from the drama. He wouldn't have been able to give all of himself to either of them and that wouldn't have been fair to *anyone.*

Everything is different now, he's not the same person he was even a month ago. September 11th changed everything. This is his life, and letting go of his past has freed him. He won't miss another day of Liam's life, not one second.

"Will? When can we go to Fenway?" Liam climbs onto the bench and sits on his lap. He closes his eyes and breathes him in, his heart full of love. *My son.* He can't believe it.

"Do you want to go next week?"

"Yes!" Liam's face lights up, and he wraps his little arms around his neck, his soft cheek against his.

"I'll talk to Mom and see what she says."

Liam rests against him, his back pressed against his chest. *I'm filing for divorce tomorrow, I'm not waiting one day longer.* He wants his family together, under one roof.

Will's on his way to Bristol to tell his parents about divorcing Avery. It's a horrible time to have this discussion, but he has to do this now. *I have a son!* He's still wrapping his head around this.

When Julia joined them at the park a little while ago, he was going to tell her he finally figured it out, it must be eating away at her, but he wants to show her the divorce papers. He wants her to know this is real.

Turning the corner onto his parents' street, he watches Avery running to her car and hears the squeal of her tires as she pulls away from their house. His heart sinks. *What was she doing here? Checking up on me again?*

He pulls into the driveway and runs into the house. Something doesn't feel right. In a panic, he runs up the stairs and stops outside of Peter's room when he overhears Sloane talking to Ellie...

"The baby was Joe Butler's," Sloane is saying. "Avery had a fling with him and he dumped her. She wanted to get back together with Will, but your brother wasn't interested. He got very drunk at a party and they fooled around, but Avery was already pregnant. She found out the week before your brother came home from school."

What is she talking about? His heart is racing. *Is she saying that Avery was pregnant with Joe's child...not mine? That I've felt guilty and responsible for Avery all of these years for nothing?*

"Sloane, you don't have to talk about this now," Ellie says.

"I want to. I regret my part in all of this. I helped her break them up, Will and Julia. He never cheated on her. He passed out after Avery forced her way in."

Will slides to the floor in the hallway, his head in his hands. *I never cheated on Julia...*Deep down he knew he didn't... couldn't...but she was naked...he was naked. *Avery said we had sex!* What the hell was she thinking? Why would she do that?

"I don't understand." Ellie says, "How did you help her?"

"I kept her in the loop about Will's love life for years. I told her where he was living and about his relationship with Julia. At the time I thought it was best for Will...and he was so easily swayed."

Sloane helped Avery destroy my relationship with Julia? He and Julia were the victims of a sick woman's lies, and everyone paid for it, including his son. He feels rage building and spreading from his stomach into his chest.

"Why, Sloane? Why would you help Avery do something so awful?" Ellie asks.

"I can't even remember." Sloane pauses, "Avery was one of my best friends and I wanted to help her. I'm so sorry, Ellie. Your brother never knew... he would've hated me. It upset him to see Will so miserable. I know you've never liked me Ellie, and I deserved it, but I love Peter. Now I'll never see him again." Sloane begins to cry.

"I know you love Peter, and he loved you." Ellie says once Sloane's quieted down, "Thank you for telling me the truth about Avery. Peter will protect you and the baby Sloane, you have to believe that."

"Do you think so?" Sloane asks.

"I know so," Ellie says.

Will rouses himself and walks down the stairs, his heart heavy, and sits at the table in the kitchen, staring blankly out the window. He was deceived, right from the beginning. *All of these years…wasted.*

Why would Avery do this to me? To herself! Why would she want to be with someone who doesn't love her, who's never loved her?

His hatred for his wife is a vice gripping his heart. He knows if he drives to his house and confronts her right now, he won't be able to control himself, he could actually strangle her the way he's feeling, but she's not worth spending the rest of his life in prison. No, he just wants her out of his life so he can enjoy the rest of his days with Julia and Liam.

"Will!" Ellie enters the kitchen and rushes to his side, "I need to talk to you."

He looks up at his sister.

"I heard… the baby wasn't mine. I never cheated on Julia."

"I'm so sorry, Will. I can't believe anyone would do something so sick and twisted." Ellie takes his hand in hers and squeezes it. "Avery's fucking evil. I knew something was wrong with that woman! Will, listen…she knows about you and Julia."

"What? How do you know this?" Will sits up in his chair, his heart racing.

"I overheard Avery asking for Sloane's help. She followed you to Julia's last night, and saw you together. She knows you slept there and she wanted Sloane's help to come up with a plan to break you two up."

Will leans forward in his chair, gripping his sister's hands. *This is insane!*

"You should've heard Sloane, Will! She screamed at Avery. Told her to get out. She said she couldn't care less about Avery's farce of a marriage."

"Ellie, I have to go. She knows about us…I have to go to Julia's. Who knows what Avery's capable of right now."

By the time Will flies around the corner onto Julia's street, his heart is in his throat. He hasn't been able to contact her by phone in the twenty minutes it took him to reach her house. He can't count the number of traffic violations he committed to get here, and is thankful he wasn't pulled over by the police.

There are several cars parked along the street and Will spots Avery's Audi in front of Julia's house. Fear lodges in his stomach. If she touches one hair on either of them he'll kill her himself.

He pulls into the driveway, runs toward the front door, then notices Avery sitting in the car, staring at him. He pauses for a moment, rooted to the spot and glares at his wife, hatred spilling from his eyes.

Using his key, he unlocks the front door and twists the deadbolt behind him. He wants to make sure they're safe. "Jules? Liam?" He runs from room to room but no one's home. *Thank god.* He sits on the couch with his head in his hands and takes a deep breath.

What does Avery hope to accomplish here? She has to know Ellie's told him everything by now. He wanted to talk to his parents first, but now is the time. He's getting this confrontation over and done with, hopefully before Julia and Liam come home.

He opens the door and approaches Avery, who's now leaning against her convertible, her arms folded across her chest with a smile plastered across her face.

"Well, hello darling. Fancy meeting you here."

"What are you doing Avery?" He stops a few feet away from her, grim and determined.

"Well, I've hardly seen you since my return sweetheart." Avery holds her left hand in front of her, staring at her two-carat solitaire and wedding band, her thumb playing with the rings, twisting the diamond back and forth on her finger. "I thought I'd come visit you and your whore."

"After everything you've done…" He takes a step toward her, his anger rising to the surface, "You stay away from us. Do you hear me? You've done enough harm. I won't let you hurt either of us again."

"Ha!" she snorts, "I've hurt her? She's sleeping with my husband!"

"I'm your husband in name only. You lied to me, Avery. Our entire relationship has been based on your lies. Joe Butler? Really? And don't get me started about the night you pushed your way back into my life. Literally!"

"Lies? Will, I've always loved you. That wasn't a lie. I was there for you when no one else was. That wasn't a lie. All of these years…you never complained, you never said you were unhappy with our life. Don't you think we owe it to ourselves to give this relationship a real chance?"

Her eyes are wide open, and sincere. *She's good*, he'll give her that, *the consummate liar.*

"See, I have a few problems with that Avery…One, I don't believe a word you say. Two, you were there for me because you made damned sure Julia wasn't. And three? I've never loved you, and you know it. You know what this is? This is pathetic. I've been miserable since before we were married, and you never even noticed, never bothered to ask! I'm done. This is over, Avery. I'm filing for divorce tomorrow."

"Divorce! You would do that to your parents, now? In their time of grief and suffering? I'm shocked Will. Truly shocked that you'd deliberately hurt them more than they've already been. You're so incredibly selfish. This would be the nail in their coffins."

"I don't answer to my parents." He takes a deep breath, praying he doesn't do something he'll regret. "I make my own decisions. But I'm sure they want me to be happy, something I haven't been since the day you came back into my life."

"I will take you for all you're worth, Will. Everything. Every. Single. Penny." She jabs her finger into his chest with each word, "You'll have nothing when I'm through with you."

He stares at her for a moment then bursts out laughing.

"I'm serious, Will." Avery's face falls, the smirk dissolving. "I'll take everything. And then you'll continue to pay me alimony till the day you die."

"You really don't know me at all. Go ahead, try and take it all. If you succeed, good for you. But I wouldn't count on it."

"Everything, Will!" she screams, her eyes bulging from their sockets.

"Do it," he says, perfectly composed. She has nothing to hold over him. How could he have married this woman? She's a stranger to him.

"Liam! No!" Will turns towards the sound of Julia's voice and watches Liam stop in his tracks just a few feet away from them. Julia reaches him in seconds and scoops him into her arms, her eyes wide with fear.

"Julia, take Liam into the house."

Will stands as a shield between them. He didn't want Avery to know about his son. But it's too late. As soon as Avery rests her gaze on Liam, her mouth opens with the shock of recognition. She stares after them as Julia runs up the front steps, shutting the door behind them.

"Oh, how clever! Liam. William. She named her bastard child after my husband as well. You hypocritical asshole! You talk about secrets and deception? You had a child with that woman! You have a whole other family!" Avery punches him in the chest.

"*Other* family?" He grabs her wrists, and says with contempt, "Are you fucking kidding me? They are my *only* family."

336

She wrenches her wrists from his grasp and drops her purse, the contents spilling at their feet. Avery bends down to pick up her belongings and Will catches sight of a round plastic disc near the tire of her car. Julia used to have something like this. He picks it up and opens the lid.

Birth control pills.

He smirks and shakes his head, then starts laughing. He should have known. When Avery rises, he hands the pills to her and she snatches the case from his hand.

"Thank you for that. Really, Avery...thank you. Now I have absolutely no reason to see you again." Her face turns red and she backs away from him. He continues, "You need to leave right now. And Avery, don't ever come near my family again."

Avery stumbles against her car. "Are you threatening me, Will?" she asks, steadying herself, her eyes narrowing into slits.

"Yeah," he nods, "You'd better fucking believe I am."

***

"Mama, what's the matter?" Julia sits on the couch, holding Liam to her. *What am I going to do now?* "Who is that lady?"

She's lost the power of speech, her thoughts swimming in her head. Avery knows Liam is Will's son. *Please God, don't let her be the one to tell him!* She opens the curtains, watching as Avery climbs into her car and drives away, then unlocks the door to let Will inside. She's shaking as he wraps his arms around her.

"It's okay, baby. It's done." Will takes a deep breath, "I told her I'm filing tomorrow."

She pulls him closer, doesn't ever want to let him go. *Avery didn't tell him about Liam? Why?* She's certain Avery figured it out.

"Is the scary lady gone?" Liam pulls on Will's shirt.

"Yup, and she's never coming back." Will lifts Liam into his arms.

"Pinky promise?" Liam's eyes are wide.

"Pinky promise," Will smiles, holding out his finger.

Liam watches a movie while she makes dinner, and Will fills her in on what he overheard earlier and about his exchange with Avery. She's riveted by the story Sloane shared with Ellie.

Their lives would have been so different if Avery hadn't set her sights on Will. Then again, she might not have Liam if anything had been different. That doesn't excuse Avery's lies and deceit, but maybe...*just maybe, everything unfolded as it was meant to.*

She has to tell Will about Liam tonight and she's petrified. Her hands have been trembling since she saw Avery standing in front of her house. The fact is she's been lying to Will for the past two weeks. *Hell, for the past six years!*

She remembers how upset she was when she found out he kept Avery's visits a secret from her, and all they did was decorate his house! That was Will's big lie of omission. Julia had a child. His child. And she kept it from him for over five years!

That's more than a lie of omission... *is there even a word for what I've done?*

Earlier today, when Julia and Liam took a walk to the bookstore after his nap, Liam asked her about Will.

"Mama, is Will going to be my daddy now?" he asked.

She's dated a few men over the years, but never introduced Liam to any of them. This is a new experience for her son.

"We'll have to wait and see. Do you like him baby?"

"Yeah. He'd be a good daddy."

"Yes he would." She stopped walking and hugged him to her. Has Liam felt the absence of a father figure? He's never asked about having a father before now. She always believed the depth of her love made up for Will's absence.

That night, after they put Liam to bed, Julia takes Will's hand in hers and says she needs to speak with him. Her hands have turned to ice, and she's shaking when she asks Will to sit beside her on her bed.

Then, closing her eyes, she steels herself for the worst possible outcome. He could storm out of here and never want to see her again. She knows he'll stay in Liam's life, but he might not want Julia in his.

"Will, I don't know how to say this," she pauses, tears filling her eyes, and looks down at her hands. "It's about Liam…"

"Julia, I already know."

"You do?" she whispers. *What does he think he knows?* Will nods, and kisses her hand.

"Liam's my son."

Her eyes grow wide and her mouth drops. *How long has he known?* Lightheaded and nauseous, she clutches her stomach and lies back on the bed. *He knows and he's still here!* A tidal wave of relief surges through her body. Will lies beside her, their fingers intertwined.

"Was it Ellie?" she asks in a hushed voice.

"No," he shakes his head. "It was Liam."

"What?" Confusion spreads across her face. *Liam doesn't know Will's his father!*

"Jules, Liam's five. A woman at the park asked me his age. I said four and Liam corrected me. He turned five in August."

She searches his face. *No anger. Nothing but love.*

"You don't hate me?" she asks, her voice soft.

"No, Jules. I love you. I love Liam. I feel like an idiot. How could I not see it?"

"I'm so sorry I lied to you." Tears roll down her face. "That I didn't tell you sooner…I didn't want you to feel obligated to us. I wanted to make sure Avery was out of the picture. I know that doesn't make it right, Will. I am so, so sorry. I thought I was doing the right thing at the time...you had just gotten married..."

"Shhh. Jules, I understand." He wraps his arms around her, "Listen to me Julia. I really do understand why you didn't tell me. Of course I'm upset, but I don't blame you. I was a mess back then, a disaster. If I had known before I married Avery...I probably wouldn't have gone through with it, but I would've been so guilt ridden..." he pauses, shaking his head.

"If I had found out after the wedding? That scenario is even worse. I don't think our relationship would have survived under either of those circumstances. You would've grown to hate me. Everything is different now, baby. I'm sorry I wasn't there for you, for either of you. And Julia, I am so sorry I left you alone in Verona. I'm sorry I didn't fight for you, for us. I'm so thankful to have you and Liam in my life. You two mean everything to me."

The following morning, Liam runs into their bedroom in his baseball pajamas, and dives under the covers, snuggling up to Will and Julia. When they're fully awake, they tell Liam the truth, together.

"Sweetie, do you remember when you asked me if Will was going to be your daddy?" Liam nods and smiles. "I know this might be confusing, but Will is your daddy sweetheart. He always has been."

"You've always been my daddy?" He turns to Will, his face scrunched up, confused. Will's too choked up to speak, and just nods. Liam looks down at his hands, his face sad, "How come you never came to see me before?"

Will turns to her, tears in his eyes, then lifts Liam onto his lap.

"It's a long story big guy. I didn't know where you were. But now I do, and I'll always be here with you."

"Promise?" Liam places his little hand on Will's cheek.

"Promise." Will wraps his arms around him, his voice ragged. A moment later Liam pulls away and smiles at Will.

"Will...can I call you Daddy?" Liam asks, tentatively.

That sends Will over the edge, and the tears spill onto his cheek.

"I'd really like that."

Chapter Twenty-Four

"Mom? Dad?" Will calls out as he enters their house. Peter's memorial is being held tomorrow morning and he hopes they're strong enough to make it through the service. They've been in deep mourning since Will returned from New York, but today, he finds his mother in the kitchen, making a cup of tea and kisses her cheek. She's showered and dressed, which is more than she's done in the past two weeks, and her face has some color, it's not ghostly white.

"Where's Dad?"

"He's sitting on the patio." She points outside.

What a relief. His father's obsessed with the search for the terrorists responsible for the attacks. This is the first time his father's been out of the house to Will's knowledge.

"Mom, I need to talk to you and Dad." She turns to him, fear in her eyes. "Mom, everyone is fine." She exhales and lifts her cup of tea.

"Let's join your father outside. It's a beautiful day."

His father is on the lounge chair, his eyes closed.

"Dad?"

"Hello, Will. The sun feels good, don't you think?"

He loves his parents. They've been through so much and he'd do just about anything to save them from more heartache. Anything...*but stay married to Avery.*

"Mom, Dad..." He takes a deep breath, "I have something to tell you."

His father nods, and indicates for him to take a seat. His mother stands beside him, her hand resting on his father's shoulder.

Will clasps his hands together, takes a deep breath, and decides to rip the bandage off the wound. "I'm getting a divorce."

His mother's eyes grow wide and his father sighs, leans forward and takes Will's hand between his own.

"I'm surprised you've stayed with her this long."

Will's completely taken aback. *They've been expecting this? But…Kennedys don't get divorced!* That's been drilled into his head since he was a kid. Once you're married, you stay married. Marry in haste, repent at leisure, the list of clichés goes on and on. He gapes at his father, then turns to his mother.

"Will, we're not blind. We know how unhappy you've been these past few years. You two aren't suited, that's very clear to us. Maybe we should have said something to you sooner, we've been so worried about you, but we figured you'd talk to us when you were ready."

"Sweetheart, you're a grown man." His mother takes a seat beside him, her eyes filling with tears. "You have to do what makes you happy. Life is so short…"

"I thought I'd disappoint you if I left her." He whispers, trying to hold back his tears.

"Marriage is difficult, Will," his father sighs. "I've made mistakes along the way, but I've always loved your mother. That's what keeps us together. Not our children, not the money. We have a foundation built on mutual love and respect. That's what we want for you. That's what we've always wanted for our children."

Will wipes away his tears and stands, looking out at the harbor. *How could I have been so wrong about my parents?* He didn't give them enough credit. Of course they want their children to be happy. That's what he wants for his own son.

His father rises and places his hand on Will's shoulder.

"I know I've been hard on you in the past. Maybe pushed you too hard when it came to your career and for that I'm so sorry. We've always been proud of you, son. Your happiness is all that matters to us. You have to live your life on your own terms. Don't waste it trying to be someone you're not."

"Thank you, Dad," he embraces his father, accepting the absolution he's always sought, but realizes he no longer needs. Still, he's filled with gratitude and relief.

The worst is over. Now, he has to tell them about Liam and Julia.

"I have something else to tell you." They all take a seat around the table. "Do you remember Julia Grasso?"

"Of course," his father says.

"Oh, she was a delightful girl," his mother smiles. "Whatever happened to her?"

"Well…"

Will explains what happened between them, how Avery deceived them both, breaking them up in the process.

"I saw Julia in Italy… and…" He blushes and looks down at his hands with a shy grin.

"We get the picture Will." His father chuckles, "Why are you telling us this?"

"Julia had a baby." He takes a deep breath and sits upright in his chair, "I have a son."

His mother gasps, holding her hands to her chest.

"How long have you known?" His father sits back, his eyes narrowing.

"I found out a few days ago."

His father's brows draw together, his eyes sad.

"Mom, Dad, do you believe in fate?" They both nod their heads. "I've loved Julia since the day I met her. Not a single day has passed that I haven't thought of her. We've had some major roadblocks, but something always brings us back together. Time, distance, none of that matters when it comes to Julia. When I saw her again on September 11th…" He shakes his head and shrugs his shoulders. "I just knew. Nothing else mattered. We're meant to be together. I'm never letting her go again. And I'm not missing another day of my son's life."

His mother's eyes fill with tears. "I have another grandson! When can I meet him?"

They knew there'd be a lot of people at Peter's memorial service, but because of the national spotlight shining on the circumstances of his death, it's turned into something of a media circus. The press isn't allowed in the church, but several news crews are set up outside.

Will surveys the scene as he escorts his parents and Sloane up the steps of the church. Vans with satellite dishes are parked along High Street, reporters speaking into microphones, some interviewing people, others talking directly into the lens of the camera. Photographers are everywhere, their flashes blinding them as they make their way into the church.

The press didn't attempt to interview family, even they knew that would be crossing the line, but their every move was captured on film, from the moment they exited the car until the church doors closed behind them.

Julia was right not to come to the service. Avery is here, sitting in the pew behind the family. He can't stop her from attending this memorial, but if she says one word to his parents or Sloane, he'll throw her out himself, in front of the television cameras.

Will and Kevin are both gripping Ellie's hands, physically restraining her. When she first saw Avery sitting in the church, he thought his sister was going to leap over the pew and attack her.

He told her to ignore Avery, but Ellie's been shooting her the fiercest looks throughout the service, and when it was time to shake hands in peace with the people surrounding them, his family embraced each other, ignoring Avery.

Not Ellie, though.

He held his breath when she turned, grasped Avery's hand and whispered, "I hope you rot in hell." His sister's not messing around. Avery wisely remained silent and left the church as soon as mass ended.

Throughout the service, Sloane is composed, even peaceful. Ellie brought her to the obstetrician yesterday and she's officially in her second trimester, the furthest she's ever carried a child. The doctor appointment put her mind at ease, and she feels Peter is with her, protecting their child.

After the service, his parents invited family members to join them at home. Once the majority of mourners have gone, Julia arrives with Liam and his niece and nephews. Ellie's kids tear through the house, but Julia and Liam linger in the entryway.

Will catches her eye and crosses the room to greet them, lifting Liam into his arms, and wrapping his arm around Julia. She's nervous about seeing his parents. She's afraid they'll be upset with her for keeping Liam from him. He's told her that's not the case, but he can tell she's still fearful.

He kisses her cheek and smiles reassuringly as he leads them to the backyard where his parents are waiting.

His father stands, his eyes growing wide as they approach the table. His mother is seated and her mouth drops when her eyes alight on Liam's face.

"Liam, these are my parents, your Grandma and Grandpa." Liam's head is down and he looks at them through his long eyelashes.

"Nice to meet you," Liam says, holding out his little hand.

"I'm so happy to meet you Liam." His father's face breaks into a big grin as he shakes his grandson's hand.

His mother slowly rises, her eyes fixed on Liam, and walks toward them. She places her hands on his son's face and Liam smiles.

"Hello Liam, can I have a hug?" she asks, and he nods, wrapping his arms around her. "Oh my goodness. You look just like your daddy when he was a boy!" She kisses him and squeezes Will's hand.

Ryan, Aidan and Caitlin join them on the patio.

"Come on Liam, let's go!" Ryan says, pulling at his cousin's shirt.

"Can I go play?" Liam asks.

"Of course you can." Will ruffles his hair.

The children run to the swing set installed for them a couple of years ago. His parents embrace Julia and they all take a seat around the table.

"Julia. It's so wonderful to see you again! I feel like I just stepped back in time...Liam looks just like Will!" his mother exclaims.

"I've always thought so," Julia says and looks down, tightly grasping his hand.

"Will explained the circumstances to us," his father says. "Of course we wish things had been different, but...we understand you were in a difficult situation, and we want you to know how happy we are to welcome you and Liam into our family."

"Julia," his mother smiles, "I haven't seen my son happy in many years, and despite the loss of our Peter, we're thrilled to meet our grandson, and couldn't be more delighted about you two finding each other again."

Julia closes her eyes and sighs, her face breaking into a smile.

Chapter Twenty-Five

The house lights rise as the curtain falls on Act Two of Trinity Repertory's production of *Romeo and Juliet*. Every morning, Julia wakes up filled with gratitude for all of life's blessings. And they are blessed. As Gabby once said, how many people ever meet their soulmate? Not many.

They're two of the lucky few, and what makes it even more special, is they realize how fortunate they are, and appreciate each other that much more. It took them almost ten years to get here, but every ounce of pain seems worth it now that they're together.

"*My true love is grown to such excess I cannot sum up sum of half my wealth*," Julia sighs and smiles. This has always been her favorite play, and she knows most of it by heart.

"This is good stuff." Will squeezes her hand, and looking into her eyes paraphrases the Friar's words, "You shall not stay alone till we are made one."

"That could very well be the most romantic thing you've ever said to me." She smiles and leans in for a kiss.

Will pulls her to her feet and they join the crowd in the lobby. They don't go out often, preferring to stay home with Liam, or spend time with family during these chilly fall evenings, but tonight is a special treat, a gift from Will.

"If you will excuse me, kind sir, I will be back anon."

"Are you going to be speaking old English for the rest of the evening?" Will raises an eyebrow.

"Thou desirest me to stop?" She flutters her eyelashes, a smile on her lips.

"Ah, no, fair gentlewoman. Tis like softest music to my attending ears."

"Spoken like the Bard himself!" she laughs.

Will wraps his arms around her, holding her close.

"I love you fair Juliet."

"I love you, my Romeo. Wow! That was so corny!"

"Yeah, it was, wasn't it?" He kisses the tip of her nose and smiles.

"I'll be right back, I don't think I can take too much more of this mushy stuff," she laughs and winks, making her way to the ladies room. "Oh, a gimlet for me please!"

Why is the line for the ladies room always ten times longer than the men's? Julia wonders. The temptation to sneak into the men's room is strong, but she doesn't, and sighs with relief when she finally reaches a stall. The bell signifying the end of intermission is ringing when the door opens and Julia hears a familiar voice...and a familiar name.

"Avery, what's going on? What is Will doing here kissing my son's teacher?" the woman asks in a hushed voice.

Really? In the bathroom? Don't these women ever check to see if anyone else is present before they start talking about other people? She peeks through the crack in the stall and finds Lacey Bennett, a volunteer parent at her school, standing by the mirror with Avery, her eyes filled with concern.

Avery is pale and Julia wonders how she plans to get out of this one. Obviously Avery hasn't told anyone that she and Will are getting a divorce.

She's been surprisingly quiet over the past couple of months. Avery's stalling over the paperwork, but hasn't bothered them at all. All communication has been through their lawyers, and Will has been more than fair with the terms.

The house on Poppasquash and everything in it is Avery's, though Julia suspects she'll sell. She's not from Bristol originally, why would she want to live near Will's family? And the house on Nantucket goes to Will. There's not much else to negotiate. She gets half of all Will's assets, but she can't touch his trust fund, and they are selling the boat and splitting the proceeds.

The last thing on the table is alimony. Will wants this done and is ready to hand over whatever Avery wants, but his lawyer told Will to let him do the negotiating. If all goes well, the divorce should be final by April.

"She's Dex's teacher?" Avery asks, her voice strained.

"Yes! She teaches history at The Academy. What's going on between you and Will? You don't seem very surprised to see him with another woman. Did you know about his affair?"

"I've had my suspicions. They were involved before we were married and…" Avery shakes her head, then begins to cry and Lacey comforts her on the loveseat in the ladies lounge.

Julia rolls her eyes at the absurdity of this situation. *What should I do? I'm trapped!* She may have to wait it out, but Will is undoubtedly on the other side of the door waiting for her, drink in hand. It could get ugly if Avery walks out of the bathroom before she does.

On the other hand, Julia doesn't want to confront Avery here, now! Especially not in front of Mrs. Bennett, a mother of one of her students for Christ's sake! No matter what happens, this will be all over school by first bell Monday morning.

Good god! Lacey Bennett of all people! She's not known for discretion. Julia's spent a bit of time with her this year, organizing classroom events and field trips, and despite her penchant for gossip, they work well together. She's a board member and one of a small group of parents actively involved in the PTO.

It all hinges on what Avery says next, because if she crosses the line, the gloves are coming off.

"We've been having some…difficulties lately. Peter's death has been so hard on the whole family, Will in particular. And…we recently received more bad news." Avery lowers her voice to a whisper, "Will is sterile."

Julia almost bursts out laughing. *Really, Avery? Sterile?*

"Oh, honey, I'm so sorry to hear that. That's awful! No wonder he's acting out. Men are big babies when it comes to their virility. They become cavemen, beating their chests to prove how manly they are. He'll come around."

"I just can't believe he'd bring his mistress out in public! I could take the humiliation in private, but for him to flaunt his indiscretion…I don't know what to do!" Avery sighs dramatically, the tears continuing to flow.

Did Avery think she could pretend to be married to Will indefinitely? Lacey shakes her head, squeezing Avery's hand.

"Just goes to show, you never know some people. I've spent a lot of time at school with Julia Grasso and I never took her for a home wrecker. She seems so nice!"

"Nice!" Avery snorts, "She's been chasing my husband since the day we got married."

Julia grits her teeth, her fists clenched tight.

That bitch.

Well, the line has definitely been crossed! She flushes the toilet, opens the door to the bathroom stall and steps out, facing the two women. The scene greeting her on this side of the door is so different from the one Julia faced all those years ago at the infamous wedding.

Back then the women were snide and superior and she felt humiliated. Now Julia sees two nervous women sitting on the couch, and she's holding all of the cards.

"Mrs. Bennett! So nice to see you! Isn't the show wonderful?" Lacey's eyes are wide, her mouth slack. "How's Dexter? Don't forget, his project is due this week."

Avery rises and Julia can see the fear in her eyes. *My, how the tables have turned!*

"Avery. Well, this is a surprise. You never learn, do you? Why don't you tell your friend the truth about Will, or are you incapable of honesty?"

Avery's eyes narrow into slits, but she remains silent.

"No? You don't want to tell her?" Julia turns to Lacey, "Avery and Will are getting a divorce, Mrs. Bennett. They've been separated for months. And Will isn't sterile." Julia stares pointedly into Avery's eyes, "We know that, don't we, *Ave?*"

"Julia…Don't…" Avery takes a step forward, panic in her eyes.

"Don't? Don't what?" Julia raises an eyebrow, her arms folded across her chest. She's enjoying this way too much. "Oh, don't worry, *Ave*, I won't spill your dirty little secrets, that's not my style. But don't you dare spread lies about me and Will. Your friends may not believe *me*, but they'll believe *Will*. And they'll believe Sloane and Ellie. Their collective voice will be loud enough to destroy your precious reputation. So you might want to reconsider your approach to this situation, because I'm done with your bullshit."

Her face red with embarrassment, Avery walks toward the door, but Julia blocks her, shaking her head, "Oh, and do you remember that day, long before you were married, when you told me there was no way I'd end up with Will?" Julia raises an eyebrow and smirks, "I guess you were wrong."

Avery's face falls, and Julia steps aside to allow her to make her escape. When the door closes, she leans back against the counter, rubbing her fingers over her temples, her head pounding, then remembers Lacey is still in the bathroom. She's still standing beside the couch, staring at Julia, apparently in shock.

"I'm sorry you had to see that, Mrs. Bennett. I hope you enjoy the rest of the show."

Over Christmas break Will and Julia plan a trip to Nantucket for a long weekend. He's considering selling this house, but wants her to see it before he makes a decision. When Will first mentioned the trip, she was hesitant to stay at his place, not wanting to spend time in a home he shared with Avery, but he explained that Avery preferred to stay with friends when she was on the island. Will doesn't associate Nantucket with Avery at all.

Two days after Christmas, they take the ferry from Hyannis to Nantucket. Liam is staying with Will's parents while they're away. Whenever Will talks about this house, his face lights up. He's proud of the work he's done and she can't wait to see it.

He once said every ounce of frustration and anger he's felt over the past two years has been worked out there, his oasis in the desert of his loveless marriage. Nantucket is the only place Will has felt some semblance of peace and he hopes she loves the island.

Julia's very excited, she's never been to Nantucket before, but ever the proud history geek, she's been reading up on it. The island has a rich history, and she's eager to explore. The Athenaeum and Maria Mitchell's Observatory are high on her list of places to visit, as well as the village of Siasconset, which will be deserted this time of year.

They brought the car with them so when the ferry docks two and a half hours later, they drive the short distance from the terminal to his house on Orange Street. Main Street is paved with cobblestones from the eighteenth century and it's a bumpy ride through town.

Today is sunny, brisk, but beautiful. Downtown Nantucket is decorated for the holiday season with dozens of Christmas trees lining the sidewalks in front of the shops, galleries and restaurants along Main Street, all but the pharmacy are closed for the winter.

Will pulls into the driveway of his house. It's typical of the area with weathered grey shingles, white trim, two chimneys, flowerboxes in each window, and boxwoods around the perimeter of the property.

When he opens the heavy red wooden front door, she enters the foyer and smiles. Behind the weathered façade is a sunny, cheerful space. Will preserved period details such as the worn wood beams crisscrossing the ceiling, wide plank wood floors, original crown molding and chair rails, and the classic six-over-six windows. A beautifully restored staircase leads upstairs.

"Oh Will, it's gorgeous."

He drops their bags and scoops her into his arms, carrying her up the stairs to the second floor.

"Aren't you going to show me the rest of the house first?" she laughs.

"No way. I love Liam to death, but I want to hear you cry out in ecstasy. I miss that sound."

"Do you?" she smiles seductively. "You like to hear me call out your name?"

"I love to hear you come."

Will carries her to the bedroom where they impatiently shed their clothes, and are as loud as they want for several child-free, uninterrupted hours of bliss.

Later that evening, Will stokes the fire in his t-shirt and pajama bottoms, while Julia's sitting in bed, enjoying their picnic of bread, cheese and fruit, wearing Will's flannel pajama top.

"I have something for you…" he says turning toward her.

"You do?" she smiles, popping a grape into her mouth.

"Uh huh. A surprise."

Will reaches into his coat pocket and pulls out a little black box and an envelope. Her heart stops beating for a moment and she brings her hands to her mouth.

"Which one do you want first?" he sets them in front of her and climbs onto the bed. Liam's handwriting is on the envelope. She bites her lip, then picks it up and looks into Will's smiling eyes.

"Go ahead, open it."

Julia slowly opens the letter and reads her son's message aloud.

"*Deer Mommy. Daddy askd me for permishon to marry you.*" Her eyes fill with tears and she looks up at Will. He's grinning ear to ear. She continues, "*I sed yes. I love you mommy and daddy. From, Liam.*"

"I've waited a long, long time to ask you this." Will takes her hand in his, "Julia, I love you with everything I am. Will you marry me?" He opens the black box, but she can't see anything through her tears. He could have made a ring out of a paperclip, she wouldn't care. Her answer would be the same.

"Yes." Julia nods, her face glowing with happiness, "Yes, I'll marry you."

She laughs as he slips the antique ring onto her finger and she catches her first glimpse of it. It's absolutely gorgeous. Julia softly kisses his lips and climbs onto Will's lap, wrapping her arms and legs around him, holding him close.

"I love you," she whispers in his ear.

"Always."

LANDING

2004

Epilogue

Will and Liam are sitting at a café in the Piazza delle Erbe, waiting for Julia. They've been in Verona for the past five months and are enjoying a quiet afternoon together. Liam's finishing second grade at the American School and Will's kept himself busy fixing up their new place. A little while ago, they went shopping for groceries for dinner and are relaxing before they head back to the house.

"Dad, is this the table you sat at with Mom before I was born?"

"No, this is where I was sitting when I watched her writing in her journal over there." He points to a table several feet away.

"I always mix them up."

Will takes a sip of his espresso and his mouth puckers. He still hasn't developed a taste for it. He grabs the empty coffee cup he requested, pours the espresso in and stirs some milk into the porcelain mug.

"Dad," Liam looks up from his book and laughs, "You know if you add milk it's not espresso anymore. It's a latte."

"Shhh…" He raises his finger to his lips, "Our secret."

"Wimp." Liam shakes his head, and buries his nose back in his book.

Will has immersed himself in renovating their new home. They purchased a farmhouse just outside of Verona four months ago and he's restoring it with the help of Liam and a few local tradesmen. It needed a lot of work, but he loves doing it.

When he restored the house in Nantucket, he did it to save his sanity. At the time he didn't have a family to make a home for, and didn't believe he'd ever have one of his own. This experience has been so different. Their home in Italy is a labor of love.

They came upon the farmhouse on one of their mystery rides through the countryside a month into their travels abroad. Julia spotted the 'for sale' sign near the stonewall that surrounds the property and out of curiosity they drove up the long winding driveway to see the house.

It was love at first sight.

The two-storied stone house is located on a hill and is surrounded by olive groves, wheat fields and cypress trees. They wandered the grounds and Liam couldn't contain his excitement when he saw the in-ground pool located a short distance from the house. Off the pool area is a small guesthouse, and another stone outbuilding, beautiful gardens and a covered terrace for outdoor dining.

It wasn't the first house they looked at, but it would be the last. Julia called the real estate agent that night and they were given the tour the following day. By the end of the month, the farmhouse was theirs.

The original structure was built in the fifteenth century and has been remodeled by different owners over the years. The ground floor was originally the stables and storage area, but has been renovated into an oversized living room with a stone fireplace, a dining room, and a connecting kitchen with another large fireplace.

A stone staircase leads to the family quarters which includes another living area with stunning views of the countryside and the city just beyond, a master bedroom with an en-suite bathroom, three smaller bedrooms, and two additional bathrooms, which Will is in the process of remodeling.

He's highly motivated to finish the renovations and should be done with the majority of the work before the arrival of the newest addition to their family. *He or she will be here soon!*

***

Julia enters the Piazza, her back aching from leaning over and writing letters for the past four hours. She resumed her duties as one of Juliet's secretaries a few months ago. Today, she's exhausted, but smiles as she walks toward Will and Liam, who have taken up residence at their 'regular' table near the fountain. She finds them here most days after her shift.

Volunteering to answer the questions of the lovelorn masses is one of the most satisfying things she's ever done. She loved doing this work before she returned to the United States, but now she feels truly qualified to offer advice on the topic of love.

Will's eyes light up as she makes her slow approach. She was so relieved when he quit his job at the equity firm after September 11th. He hated the work he'd been doing since college.

Before they came to Italy, Will was buying and restoring old houses, selling them once he'd finished. He really didn't care if he made much money off the sales, he loves doing the work, and she's thrilled he found something he's passionate about. She's never seen him happier.

Once he finishes their home here, he wants to continue growing his business, whether here or in the States, they don't know. Will was building a solid reputation for himself back home for the quality of his craftsmanship and preserving the historic integrity of the few homes he's renovated.

"Hello sweetheart." Will stands to greet her, kissing her lips and pulling out a chair.

"What are you two up to today?" She ruffles Liam's hair and leans over to kiss his head.

"We've been up to no good, right Dad?"

"No good at all." Will shakes his head, his face serious.

She smiles and leans back against the metal chair, wincing in pain.

"Are you feeling all right?" Will asks, his eyes filling with concern.

She nods and smiles, her exhaustion evident.

Will rests his palm on her stomach and rubs it in a circle. An elbow or shoulder or knee moves under his hand and she smiles watching Will's eyes grow bright as the baby shifts inside her body, her stomach changing shape in the process.

"It's a miracle, Jules. We've made another baby." He shakes his head in awe, then takes her hand and looks into her eyes. "I think it may be time for you to stop channeling Juliet for a little bit. You're due in twelve days, babe."

She shifts in her seat, trying to get comfortable, but it's hopeless.

"I know. I told Mariana it's time to take a break. I need a little rest before this package arrives."

When Julia found out they were having another baby, she wanted to be in Verona for sentimental reasons, and Will agreed. Her love affair with Italy is far from over and she wants her children to have dual citizenship.

Once the baby is born they'll split their time between Italy and the United States. They haven't figured out the details yet, wanting to wait and see what works best for them as a family, then take it from there. They still own the house on Nantucket, and can stay with family when they're in Rhode Island. Maybe they'll buy a house there too? Who knows what the future holds? It's ripe with possibilities.

Over the past two weeks she's found it increasingly difficult to do much of anything. She feels like a giant water balloon ready to explode. Her hands and feet are swollen, her back aches, she has to pee every five minutes, and her patience is non-existent.

She doesn't remember it being this difficult with Liam, but she was twenty-four then, not almost thirty-two. The last month of pregnancy is for the birds in her opinion.

She was on the phone with Sloane the other day, sharing that very sentiment, and her sister-in-law couldn't agree more. They've made peace with Sloane. She's a different person since Peter died, and Julia and Ellie have grown close to her over the past few years.

Little Peter is just over two years old now, and before he was born, Sloane sold their apartment in New York and decided to stay in Rhode Island to be near Peter's family. They live in Bristol and spend a lot of time with his grandparents. Their baby grandson is the apple of their loving eyes.

Will stands up and holds out his hands to help her to her feet and hugs her to him, rubbing her back.

"I feel for you sweetie. We are having a baby, but you have to do all of the work."

"Yeah, yeah, spare me. If men had to go through this, the human race would be extinct," she teases him.

He's been so good, trying to ease her load in whatever way he can. They've always been a good team, sharing household chores, but he insisted that he and Liam take over all home-related responsibilities over the past few months, cooking, cleaning, doing the laundry, tending the garden, washing and drying the dishes. They've been a huge help.

Liam's totally engrossed in his book and Will taps him on the shoulder.

"Hey big guy, let's pack up and take Mom home."

After dinner, Julia soaks in the big claw foot bathtub. Their neighbor Angela, a seventy-five year old widow who reminds them of Gram, has been very kind, delivering meals two or three times a week, sometimes joining them to dine, and giving Will cooking and Italian lessons while she's working.

Tonight, Will made a delicious chicken soup from scratch and served it with crusty Italian bread. He's getting quite good under Angela's tutelage. Julia hasn't had much of an appetite this week, so tonight's light meal was perfect.

This is her favorite time of day. She can hear Will and Liam in the kitchen cleaning up after dinner, and smiles as she lathers up the washcloth and rubs it over her body. In the water, she's almost buoyant, the pressure of their growing baby temporarily alleviated.

She's ready to have this baby and reclaim her body. Julia hasn't said anything to Will, but she started having mild contractions this morning. They're more than fifteen minutes apart, but she's having this baby in the next day or two. She knows the minute she tells him, he'll become a mother hen, clucking over her, and jumping every time she winces.

Will's excitement over the baby is heartwarming. He missed this with Liam and doesn't want to miss anything this time around. She still feels guilty for keeping Liam from him all of those years, no matter how understanding he's been. They both feel it was the right thing for her to do under the circumstances, but still…

After Julia confronted Avery at the play, Will's ex-wife left town and moved to northern California, telling her lawyer to quickly settle the divorce, waiving her right to alimony. Maybe

Avery thought Julia would spread rumors about her, and this was her way of shutting her up? She wouldn't have done that, no matter how much she'd love to tear that woman's reputation to shreds. She's just grateful Avery's out of their lives for good.

Will enters the bathroom and sits on the stool next to the tub. He's accompanied Julia to all of her doctor appointments, gets teary-eyed every time he hears the baby's heartbeat, and stared in wonder while they did the ultrasound. He's smitten.

They chose not to find out the sex of the baby before the delivery, but she has a feeling it's a girl. This pregnancy has been so different.

Her husband holds her hand, gazes at her body, and grins.

"You're staring." She looks at him, eyebrow raised.

"Yes I am," he laughs.

"Stop! You're making me self-conscious!"

Will kneels on the ground, takes the washcloth from her and runs it along her swollen breasts and stomach.

"You have nothing to be self-conscious about. You've never been more beautiful." He kisses her neck then her lips.

"I am an elephant." Will takes her hand and places it on him. He's totally aroused. Her eyes open wide, "You can't be serious."

He nods his head and helps her out of the bathtub, wraps a towel around her and gently dries her body, his eyes never leaving hers. They've made love regularly throughout her pregnancy. Will said knowing she's carrying his child has only made her sexier in his eyes.

"Mrs. Kennedy, right this way." He leads her to their bed and turns the lock on their door.

***

Will wakes to the sound of moaning. It's dark outside, the middle of the night and he reaches for Julia but she's not in bed. With a start, he sits up and turns on the lamp to find Julia sitting in the rocking chair, her eyes closed, clearly in pain.

Oh my god, this is it! He runs over to her.

"Babe. Tell me what's happening."

She breathes through the pain for a few more seconds, then looks down at the watch in her hand.

"It's time. The contractions are less than six minutes apart."

He's never been more nervous or excited in his life. He kisses her and pulls on jeans and a t-shirt, slips on his shoes and runs next door to Angela's house. They asked her to stay with Liam if Julia went into labor before her mother arrives from the States. Carol and Ron are flying in tomorrow.

Will impatiently knocks on their neighbor's door. It's three in the morning, but Angela answers a moment later, fully clothed. She nods and closes the door and he gives her a quizzical look.

"How did you know?" he asks.

"*La luna.*" She points to the sky, "It's full. I've been waiting."

It's a fifteen-minute drive to the hospital and they're the only car on the road. Julia's water broke two minutes into the ride, her contractions dramatically increasing in speed and intensity. She squeezes his hand with each contraction and he's trying hard to keep his eyes focused on the road.

I have to get her to the hospital! She's writhing in agony, howling in pain so horribly, he almost pulled over, but she swatted his leg, "Just keep driving! I'll make it...Ahhhh!" She lets out another primal scream.

When they arrive at the University Hospital of Verona, Julia's contractions are coming one on top of the other, and he catches a glimpse of his reflection in a mirror near the door. His face is ghostly white. *What on earth did I do to her?* He's never heard a human being make those sounds. He holds Julia's hand as she's wheeled into an examination room and the doctor on duty checks her cervix then sends the nurse from the room.

"*Tua sposa è dieci centimetri dilatata.*"

Will shakes his head, uncomprehending. Unlike his son, he doesn't have an ear for languages, despite Angela's patient instruction. He has no idea what the doctor is saying. Julia lets out another scream.

"What? *Cosa? Parlare inglese?*"

"You wife," The doctor sighs, holds up ten fingers and slowly says, "*Dieci centemetri.*"

Ten centimeters? Already? Will swallows hard and nods, then leans over Julia, wiping the sweat-soaked hair from her forehead and kisses her.

"Jules, it's time to meet our baby." Her eyes are glazed over with pain, but she touches his face and smiles.

Will holds Julia's hand for over an hour as she pushes, until at last, he hears their baby's cry.

"*Signore, si dispone di una bellissima bambina.*" Will's eyes are wide and brimming with tears. *A girl.* Julia's collapses against the bed, completely exhausted but smiling. He kisses his wife, wiping the damp hair from her brow.

"Jules, we have a daughter." Her eyes fill and she nods, reaching out for him.

"You hold now?" The nurse asks Will in broken English. He turns to Julia and she smiles and nods her head.

"I was the first to hold Liam," she says, wiping away a tear, "You should be the first to hold our daughter."

He sits beside Julia in bed and holds his arms out, his heart swelling with emotion as the nurse places his baby daughter into his arms. *I can't believe she's here!*

"She's perfect," he whispers, kissing her tiny forehead. She has wispy dark hair on her head, big brown eyes, and a beautiful round face. He didn't think his heart could contain more love, but it can. The love he feels for his wife, son and baby daughter, *his family*, is infinite.

"What will we call her?" he asks. They haven't selected any names. Julia said they'd know when they see the baby in person.

"I'd like to call her Mary Grace, after my grandmothers." Julia leans back on the bed, her eyes closed, "Mae was Gram's nickname."

"Mary Grace Kennedy." Will squeezes her shoulder and she smiles lovingly into his eyes, "Welcome to the world sweet Mae."

"I wish Gram was here. I want to tell her I found my Romeo, and we have a family. That our daughter has her name…"

"She is, my Juliet." Will sits beside her, kissing her softly, "She'll always be with us."

About the Author

What if I Fly? is Jayne Conway's debut novel. Jayne has written dozens of short stories, poems, song lyrics, and other meandering thoughts, for her own amusement. One day, she decided to share the stories dancing in her head with others. What started off as a daydream, something to tick off her bucket list, has turned into a passion. She lives in Rhode Island with her three beautiful children and is currently writing her second novel.